FOOTBALL'S *Best*
SHORT STORIES

Edited by Paul D. Staudohar

CHICAGO
REVIEW
PRESS

Library of Congress Cataloging-in-Publication Data

Football's best short stories / edited by Paul D. Staudohar.
    p.   cm.
   ISBN 1-55652-330-0 (cloth)
   ISBN 1-55652-365-3 (paper)
   1. Football stories. 2. Short stories, American. I. Staudohar,
   Paul D.
   PS648.F65F66   1998
   813'.0108355–dc21   98-22350
                                CIP

©1998 by Paul D. Staudohar
All rights reserved
Published by Chicago Review Press, Incorporated
814 North Franklin Street
Chicago, Illinois 60610
ISBN 1-55652-330-0

Printed in the United States of America   5 4 3 2 1

ACKNOWLEDGMENTS

It is impossible to put together a collection of stories without input from several capable people. I was fortunate enough to have worked with the editors at Chicago Review Press on previous books, and it was their preliminary interest that got me going. Many thanks to Linda Matthews and Cynthia Sherry for this. The next step was to talk to writers and editors about football stories. Here, valuable advice was provided by professor Ron Carlson of Arizona State University; Pat Harmon, former sports editor of the *Cincinnati Post*; C. Michael Curtis, senior editor, and Lucie Prinz, staff editor, at *Atlantic Monthly*; Alice K. Turner, senior editor at *Playboy*; Robert Scheffler, researcher at *Esquire,* and writer W. C. Heinz. Then, there was a group of outstanding archivists and librarians who knew about bibliographical sources and helped me access them. These persons include Lynne LeFleur at California State University, Hayward; Kent Stephens at the College Football Hall of Fame; Tricia Trilli at the Pro Football Hall of Fame; Michael Salmon from the Amateur Athletic Foundation, and Erin Overby at the *New Yorker.* Florence Bongard of Cal State, Hayward was secretary for the project, in association with Linda Wickwire. Finally, thanks to my colleagues who offered support and counsel: Drew Hamrick, Harry Koplan, Nick McIntosh, and Professor Richard Zock.

–Paul D. Staudohar

CONTENTS

INTRODUCTION

Storytelling is one of the oldest of human pleasures. Long before formal literature, people told stories to enlighten, recall the past, and amuse themselves. The modern short story preserves this tradition and is a rich literary source. Although the main purpose of the short story is to entertain the reader, it can also stimulate understanding and inspire imagination.

Sports is the theme of some of the best American short stories, about organized games as well as simply play for body and spirit. Regarding ball games, writer George Plimpton tells us that the larger the ball the less creative writing there is about the sport. Thus, there are many worthy tales of golf and baseball, but hardly any on basketball and none on beachball. So where does football fit in?

There are fewer short stories on football than on baseball or golf. But the best football stories are comparable to those of the other sports. There are a number of famous authors who have penned excellent football stories, such as John Updike, Ellery Queen, Damon Runyon, and Howard Nemerov. My objective as editor of this book was to unearth and select the best short stories on football. When all was said and done, the quantity of material was somewhat less than for my earlier books, *Baseball's Best Short Stories* (1995) and *Golf's Best Short Stories* (1997). But the quality is every bit as good.

Football provides much to attract writers and readers. The idea of the game is straightforward: to score by moving the ball past eleven determined opponents. Implicit in this objective is breaking away from personal obstacles in order to achieve liberation by crossing the goal. Any freedom-loving man or woman can relate to this. Football also furnishes a colorful ambiance in which games are played, with its green fields, turning leaves, tailgating, uniformed bands, and ebullient cheerleaders. The pageantry unfolds with a display of controlled violence, revealing an athleticism of precision, speed, and power that is almost superhuman. And, for all its glamour, football is still just a staged show, lending itself to critique as well as romanticism.

Football's origins stem from antiquity. The ancient Spartans played a game similar to rugby, called *harpaston*. The earliest written documentation on a game resembling football comes from England in 1175, and it is said that this game was a widely disparaged and often outlawed sport of the lower classes. Modern rugby got started in England around 1840 as an elite sport for gentlemen.

American football, derived from rugby, began on a bleak November day in 1869 when Princeton took the field against Rutgers. The Ivy League schools not only pioneered the game but also fielded the best teams until about the 1920s. Much of football's tradition stems from this period. Famous coaches like Walter Camp, Amos Alonzo Stagg, Pop Warner, and Lou Little came from Ivy League schools. Noted players include John Heisman and John Outland, after whom prized trophies are named.

While the Ivy League dominated the early years, the best-known college player was Harold "Red" Grange, halfback from the University of Illinois. Nicknamed the "Galloping Ghost," the swift and elusive Grange played in one of the greatest games in college football history. In 1924 against the University of Michigan, Grange took the opening kickoff 95 yards for a score. He added three more touchdown runs of 67, 56, and 45 yards, all in the first twelve minutes of the game. Altogether, Grange had 402 rushing and return yards, scored five touchdowns, and completed six passes, one for a touchdown, as Illinois won 39–14. This performance was so spectacular that sportswriter Grantland Rice called Grange

A streak of fire, a breath of flame,
Eluding all who reach and clutch;
A gray ghost thrown into the game
That rival hands may rarely touch.

Grange not only sparked the boom in college football in the 1920s, but also helped ignite the fledgling professional game. Professional football had been played since the 1890s in industrial towns in Ohio and Pennsylvania, but was overshadowed by the college game. The first major professional league was formed in 1920, with famous college player Jim Thorpe as president. By 1925 this league, which had changed its name to the National Football League, attracted attention when Red Grange signed with the Chicago Bears. Large crowds watched the pro game for the first time. Pro football had difficulty sustaining fan support, however, and it wasn't until the 1960s that it really took off. With national television agreements arranged under the leadership of NFL Commissioner Pete Rozelle, pro football would become the most popular spectator sport in America. Of the top ten most-watched shows ever to be televised, eight have been Super Bowls.

The stories in the book are fictional. They reflect virtually all aspects of the game at all levels: kids, high school, college, and professional. Themes are quite varied. There are the inevitable tales of competition. Who will win the big game? Can adversity be overcome? The reader will also find many stories that reveal human character, that are more about people and life than football itself.

As with the earlier collections on baseball and golf, care was taken to ensure that only the very highest quality material is included. One gauge of this is the sources of materials. Another is the authors. Most of the stories are from the most popular modern magazines, like *The New Yorker, Esquire, Sports Illustrated, Playboy,* and *Atlantic Monthly,* with others from old standards like *Collier's* and *Saturday Evening Post.* Besides great authors from the past, like Queen and Runyon, there is ample representation from contemporary writers who are in the front rank: T. Coraghessan Boyle, Don DeLillo, Frank Deford, Irwin Shaw, Michael Chabon, and others.

The game has changed a lot over the years. Therefore, the reader may encounter some unfamiliar names for positions and different player roles and formations from what we are accustomed to. Terms like "wide receiver" and "free safety" didn't exist in the past. This is illustrated by a trivia question: Who was the first NFL player to intercept four passes in a game, a record that has since been equaled by many? The answer is quarterback Sammy Baugh of the Washington Redskins, against Detroit on November 14, 1943. In those days quarterbacks played defense too. This doesn't happen today, except in rare circumstances, because both the college and pro games are more specialized.

Despite the fact that football has evolved into a specialized high-tech game of aerial fireworks, it's still about teamwork and competition, blocking and tackling, strength and skill, affection of fans for their teams, and getting together with friends. In recent years the spectacle and business sides of the game, both college and pro, have given rise to charges of corruption, greed, hypocrisy, and callousness towards the fans. The game, however, has always had these elements, even though they seem more pronounced today.

The classic ballad and twenty-one stories in the book provide enlightened entertainment on the great game of football. These fictional accounts bring to life the emotions and deeper meanings of the sport in the way that only great writers can. They add an important dimension to fans' appreciation of this exciting game. So let's tee up the old pigskin and kick off!

–Paul D. Staudohar

Grantland Rice (1880–1954) was America's best known and most beloved sportswriter. He was born in Tennessee and educated at Vanderbilt University, where he played varsity football. Rice covered all of the major sports and was the confidant of players from the "Golden Age," like Ty Cobb (about whom he wrote his first story), Babe Ruth, Jack Dempsey, Walter Hagen, Bobby Jones, and footballers Red Grange, Jim Thorpe, Knute Rockne, and Pop Warner. His most remembered story was in the New York Herald-Tribune in 1924, about the Notre Dame–Army football game. The opening lines of the story brought immortality to the Fighting Irish backfield: "Outlined against a blue-gray October sky, the Four Horsemen rode again. In dramatic lore they are known as Famine, Pestilence, Destruction, and Death. These are only aliases. Their real names are Stuhldreher, Miller, Crowley, and Layden." Most of all, Rice loved poetry, and his most famous poem is presented below. Like baseball's "Casey at the Bat," it tells a great story.

Grantland Rice

ALUMNUS FOOTBALL (1923)

BILL JONES HAD BEEN THE shining star upon his college team.
His tackling was ferocious and his bucking was a dream.
When husky William took the ball beneath his brawny arm
They had two extra men to ring the ambulance alarm.

Bill hit the line and ran the ends like some mad bull amuck.
The other team would shiver when they saw him start to buck.
And when some rival tackler tried to block his dashing pace,
On waking up, he'd ask, "Who drove that truck across my face?"

Bill had the speed—Bill had the weight—Bill never bucked in vain;
From goal to goal he whizzed along while fragments strewed the plain,
And there had been a standing bet, which no one tried to call,
That he could make his distance through a ten-foot granite wall.

When he wound up his college course each student's heart was sore.
They wept to think bull-throated Bill would sock the line no more.
Not so with William—in his dreams he saw the Field of Fame,
Where he would buck to glory in the swirl of Life's big game.

Sweet are the dreams of college life, before our faith is nicked—
The world is but a cherry tree that's waiting to be picked;
The world is but an open road—until we find, one day,
How far away the goal posts are that called us to the play.

So, with the sheepskin tucked beneath his arm in football style,
Bill put on steam and dashed into the thickest of the pile;
With eyes ablaze he sprinted where the laureled highway led—
When Bill woke up his scalp hung loose and knots adorned his head.

He tried to run the ends of life, but with rib-crashing toss
A rent collector tackled him and threw him for a loss.
And when he switched his course again and dashed into the line
The massive Guard named Failure did a toddle on his spine.

Bill tried to punt out of the rut, but ere he turned the trick
Right Tackle Competition scuttled through and blocked the kick.
And when he tackled at Success in one long, vicious prod
The Fullback Disappointment steered his features in the sod.

Bill was no quitter, so he tried a buck in higher gear,
But Left Guard Envy broke it up and stood him on his ear.
Whereat he aimed a forward pass, but in two vicious bounds
Big Center Greed slipped through a hole and rammed him out of bounds.

But one day, when across the Field of Fame the goal seemed dim,
The wise old coach, Experience, came up and spoke to him.
"Old Boy," he said, "the main point now before you win your bout
Is keep on bucking Failure till you've worn that piker out!

"And, kid, cut out this fancy stuff—go in there, low and hard;
Just keep your eye upon the ball and plug on, yard by yard,
And more than all, when you are thrown or tumbled with a crack,
Don't sit there whining—hustle up and keep on coming back;

"Keep coming back with all you've got, without an alibi,
If Competition trips you up or lands upon your eye,
Until at last above the din you hear this sentence spilled:
'We might as well let this bird through before we all get killed.'

"You'll find the road is long and rough, with soft spots far apart,
Where only those can make the grade who have the Uphill Heart.
And when they stop you with a thud or halt you with a crack,
Let Courage call the signals as you keep on coming back.

"Keep coming back, and though the world may romp across your spine,
Let every game's end find you still upon the battling line;
For when the One Great Scorer comes to mark against your name,
He writes—not that you won or lost—but how you played the Game."

T. Coraghessan Boyle

56–0 (1994)

IT WASN'T THE CAST that bothered him—the thing was like rock, like a weapon, and that was just how he would use it—and it wasn't the hyperextended knee or the hip pointer or the yellowing contusions seeping into his thighs and hams and lower back or even the gouged eye that was swollen shut and drooling a thin pale liquid the color of dishwater; no, it was the humiliation. Fifty-six to nothing. That was no mere defeat; it was a drubbing, an ass-kicking, a rape, the kind of thing the statisticians and sports nerds would snigger over as long as there were records to keep. He'd always felt bigger than life in his pads and helmet, a hero, a titan, but you couldn't muster much heroism lying facedown in the mud at fifty-six to nothing and with the other team's third string in there. No, the cast didn't bother him, not really, though it itched like hell and his hand was a big stippled piece of meat sticking out of the end of it, or the eye either, though it was ugly, pure ugly. The trainer had sent him to the eye doctor and the doctor had put some kind of blue fluid in the eye and peered into it with a little conical flashlight and said there was no lasting damage, but still it was swollen shut and he couldn't study for his Physical Communications exam.

It was Sunday, the day after the game, and Ray Arthur Larry-Pete Fontinot, right guard for the Caledonia College Shuckers, slept till two, wrapped in his own private misery—and even then he couldn't get out of bed. Every fiber of his body, all six feet, four inches and two hundred sixty-eight pounds of it, shrieked with pain. He was twenty-two years old, a senior, his whole life ahead of him, and he felt like he was ready for the nursing home. There was a ringing in his ears, his eyelashes were welded together, his lower back throbbed and both his knees felt as if ice picks had been driven into them. He hobbled, splayfooted and naked, to the bathroom at the end of the hall, and there was blood in the toilet bowl when he was done.

All his life he'd been a slow fat pasty kid, beleaguered and tormented by his quick-footed classmates, until he found his niche on the football field, where his bulk, stubborn and immovable, had proved an advantage—or so he'd thought. He'd drunk the protein drink, pumped the iron, lumbered around the track like some geriatric buffalo, and what had it gotten him? Caledonia had gone 0–43 during his four years on the varsity squad, never coming closer than two touchdowns even to a tie—and the forty-third loss had been the hardest. Fifty-six to nothing. He'd donned a football helmet to feel good about himself, to develop pride and poise, to taste the sweet nectar of glory, but somehow he didn't feel all that glorious lying there flat on his back and squinting one-eyed at Puckett and Poplar's *Principles of Physical Communications: A Text*, until the lines shifted before him like the ranks of X's and O's in the Coach's eternal diagrams. He dozed. Woke again to see the evening shadows closing over the room. By nightfall, he felt good enough to get up and puke.

In the morning, a full forty hours after the game had ended, he felt even worse, if that was possible. He sat up, goaded by the first tumultuous stirrings of his gut, and winced as he pulled the sweats over each bruised and puckered calf. His right knee locked up on him as he angled his feet into the laceless high-tops (it had been three years at least since he'd last been able to bend down and tie his shoes), something cried out in his left shoulder as he pulled the Caledonia sweatshirt over his head, and then suddenly he was on his feet and ambulatory. He staggered down the hall like something out of *Night of the Living Dead*, registering a familiar face here and there, but the faces were a blur mostly, and he avoided the eyes attached to them. Someone was playing Killer Pussy at seismic volume, and someone else—some half-witted dweeb he'd gladly have murdered if only his back didn't hurt so much—had left a skateboard outside the door and Ray Arthur Larry-Pete damn near crushed it to powder and pitched right on through the concrete-block wall in the bargain, but if nothing else, he still had his reflexes. As he crossed the courtyard to the cafeteria in a lively blistering wind, he noted absently that he'd progressed from a hobble to a limp.

There was no sign of Suzie in the cafeteria, and he had a vague recollection of her calling to cancel their study date the previous evening, but as he loaded up his tray with desiccated bacon strips, mucilaginous eggs and waffles that looked, felt and tasted like roofing material, he spotted Kitwany, Moss and DuBoy skulking over their plates at one of the long tables in the back of the room. It would have been hard to miss them. Cut from the same exaggerated mold as he, his fellow linemen loomed over the general run of the student body like representatives of another species. Their heads were like prize pumpkins set on the pedestals of their neckless shoulders, their fingers were the size of the average person's forearm, their jaws were entities unto themselves and they sprouted casts like weird growths all over their bodies.

Ray Arthur Larry-Pete made the long limp across the room to join them, setting his tray down gingerly and using both his hands to brace himself as he lowered his bruised backside to the unforgiving hardwood slats of the bench. Then, still employing his hands, he lifted first one and then the other deadened leg over the bench and into the well beneath the table. He grunted, winced, cursed, broke wind. Then he nodded to his teammates, worked his spine into the swallowing position and addressed himself to his food.

After a moment, DuBoy spoke. He was wearing a neck brace in the place where his head was joined to his shoulders, and it squeezed the excess flesh of his jowls up into his face so that he looked like an enormous rodent. "How you feeling?"

You didn't speak of pain. You toughed it out—that was the code. Coach Tundra had been in the army in Vietnam at some place Ray Arthur Larry-Pete could never remember or pronounce, and he didn't tolerate whiners and slackers. *Pain?* he would yelp incredulously at the first hint that a player was even thinking of staying down. *Tell it to the 101st Airborne, to the boys taking a mortar round in the Ia Drang Valley or the grunts in the field watching their buddies get blown away and then crawling six miles through a swamp so thick it would choke a snake with both their ears bleeding down their neck and their leg gone at the knee. Get up, soldier. Get out there and fight!* And if that didn't work, he'd roll up his pantleg to show off the prosthesis.

Ray Arthur Larry-Pete glanced up at DuBoy. "I'll live. How about you?"

DuBoy tried to shrug as if to say it was nothing, but even the faintest lift of a shoulder made him gasp and slap a hand to the neck brace as if a hornet had stung him. "No . . . big thing," he croaked finally.

There was no sound then but for the onomatopoeia of the alimentary process—food going in, jaws seizing it, throats closing on the load and opening again for the next—and the light trilling mealtime chatter of their fellow students, the ones unencumbered by casts and groin pulls and bloody toilets. Ray Arthur Larry-Pete was depressed. Over the loss, sure—but it went deeper than that. He was brooding about his college career, his job prospects, life after football. There was a whole winter, spring and summer coming up in which, for the first time in as long as he could re-member, he wouldn't have to worry about training for football season, and he couldn't imagine what that would be like. No locker room, no sweat, no pads, no stink of shower drains or the mentholated reek of oint-ment, no jock itch or aching muscles, no training table, no trainer—no chance, however slim, for glory. . . .

And more immediately, he was fretting about his coursework. There was the Phys. Comm. exam he hadn't been able to study for, and the quiz the professor would almost certainly spring in Phys. Ed., and there were the three-paragraph papers required for both Phys. Training and Phys. Phys., and he was starting to get a little paranoid about Suzie, one of the quintessentially desirable girls on campus, with all her assets on public view, and what did he have to offer her but the glamour of foot-ball? Why had she backed out on their date? Did this mean their en-gagement was off, that she wanted a winner, that this was the beginning of the end?

He was so absorbed in his thoughts he didn't register what Moss was saying when he dropped his bomb into the little silence at the table. Moss was wearing a knee brace and his left arm was in a sling. He was us-ing his right to alternately take a bite of his own food and to lift a heap-ing forkful from Kitwany's plate to Kitwany's waiting lips. Kitwany was in a full-shoulder harness, both arms frozen in front of him as if he were a sleepwalker cast in plaster of Paris. Ray Arthur Larry-Pete saw Moss's mouth working, but the words flew right by him. "What did you say, Moss?" he murmured, looking up from his food.

"I said Coach says we're probably going to have to forfeit to State."

Ray Arthur Larry-Pete was struck dumb. "Forfeit?" he finally gasped, and the blood was thundering in his temples. "What the hell do you mean, forfeit?"

A swirl of snow flurries scoured his unprotected ears as he limped grimly across the quad to the Phys. Ed. building, muttering under his breath. What was the Coach thinking? Didn't he realize this was the seniors' last game, their last and only chance to assuage the sting of 56–0, the final time they'd ever pull on their cleats against State, Caledonia's bitterest rival, a team they hadn't beaten in modern historical times? Was he crazy?

It was cold, wintry, the last week in November, and Ray Arthur Larry-Pete Fontinot had to reach up with his good hand to pull his collar tight against his throat as he mounted the big concrete steps brushed with snow. The shooting hot-wire pains that accompanied this simple gesture were nothing, nothing at all, and he barely grimaced, reaching down automatically for the push-bar on the big heavy eight-foot-tall double doors. He nodded at a pair of wrestlers running the stairs in gym shorts, made his way past the woefully barren trophy case (*Caledonia College, Third Place Divisional Finish, 1938* read the inscription on the lone trophy, which featured a bronzed figurine in antiquated leather headgear atop a pedestal engraved with the scores of that lustrous long-ago 6-and-5 season, the only winning season Caledonia could boast of in any of its athletic divisions, except for women's field hockey and who counted that?), tested his knees on the third grueling flight of stairs, and approached the Coach's office by the side door. Coach Tundra almost never inhabited his official office on the main corridor, a place of tidy desks, secretaries and seasonal decorations; of telephones, copiers and the new lone fax machine he could use to instantaneously trade X's and O's with his colleagues at other colleges, if he so chose. No, he preferred the back room, a tiny unheated poorly lit cubicle cluttered with the detritus of nineteen unprofitable seasons. Ray Arthur Larry-Pete peered through the open doorway to find the Coach slumped over his desk, face buried in his hands. "Coach?" he said softly.

No reaction.

"Coach?"

From the nest of his hands, the Coach's rucked and gouged face gradually emerged and the glittering wicked raptor's eyes that had struck such bowel-wringing terror into red-shirt freshman and senior alike stared up blankly. There was nothing in those eyes now but a worn and defeated look, and it was a shock. So too the wrinkles in the shirt that was always pressed and pleated with military precision, the scuffed shoes and suddenly vulnerable-looking hands—even the Coach's brush cut, ordinarily as stiff and imperturbable as a falcon's crest, seemed to lie limp against his scalp. "Fontinot?" the Coach said finally, and his voice was dead.

"I, uh, just wanted to check—I mean, practice is at the regular time, right?"

Coach Tundra said nothing. He looked shrunken, lost, older in that moment than the oldest man in the oldest village in the mountains of Tibet. "There won't be any practice today," he said, rubbing his temple over the spot where the military surgeons had inserted the steel plate.

"No practice? But Coach, shouldn't we—I mean, don't we have to—"

"We can't field a team, Fontinot. I count sixteen guys out of forty-two that can go out there on the field and maybe come out of their comas for four consecutive quarters—and I'm counting you among them. And you're so banged up you can barely stand, let alone block." He heaved a sigh, plucked a torn battered shoe from the pile of relics on the floor and turned it over meditatively in his hands. "We're done, Fontinot. Finished. It's all she wrote. Like at Saigon when the gooks overran the place—it's time to cut our losses and run."

Ray Arthur Larry-Pete was stunned. He'd given his life for this, he'd sweated and fought and struggled, filled the bloated vessel of himself with the dregs of defeat, week after week, year after year. He was flunking all four of his Phys. Ed. courses, Suzie thought he was a clown, his mother was dying of uterine cancer and his father—the man who'd named him after the three greatest offensive linemen in college-football history—was driving in from Cincinnati for the game, his last game, the ultimate and final contest that stood between him and the world of pay stubs and mortgages. "You don't mean," he stammered, "you don't mean we're going to *forfeit,* do you?"

For a long moment the Coach held him with his eyes. Faint sounds echoed in the corridors—the slap of sneakers, a door heaving closed, the far-off piping of the basketball coach's whistle. Coach Tundra made an unconscious gesture toward his pant leg and for a moment Ray Arthur

Larry-Pete thought he was going to expose the prosthesis again. "What do you want me to do," he said finally, "go out there and play myself?"

Back in his room, Ray Arthur Larry-Pete brooded over the perfidy of it all. A few hours ago he'd been sick to death of the game—what had it gotten him but obloquy and bruises?—but now he wanted to go out there and play so badly he could kill for it. His roommate—Malmo Malmstein, the team's kicker—was still in the hospital, and he had the room to himself through the long morning and the interminable afternoon that followed it. He lay there prostrate on the bed like something shot out in the open that had crawled back to its cave to die, skipping classes, blowing off tests and steeping himself in misery. At three he called Suzie—he had to talk to someone, anyone, or he'd go crazy—but one of her sorority sisters told him she was having her nails done and wasn't expected back before six. Her *nails*. Christ, that rubbed him raw: where was she when he needed her? A sick sinking feeling settled into his stomach—she was cutting him loose, he knew it.

And then, just as it was getting dark, at the very nadir of his despair, something snapped in him. What was wrong with him? Was he a quitter? A whiner and slacker? The kind of guy that gives up before he puts his cleats on? No way. Not Ray Arthur Larry-Pete Fontinot. He came up off the bed like some sort of volcanic eruption and lurched across the room to the phone. Sweating, ponderous, his very heart, lungs and liver trembling with emotion, he forced all his concentration on the big pale block of his index finger as he dialed Gary Gedney, the chicken-neck who handled the equipment and kept the Gatorade bucket full. "Phone up all the guys," he roared into the receiver.

Gedney's voice came back at him in the thin whistling whine of a balloon sputtering round a room: "Who is this?"

"It's Fontinot. I want you to phone up all the guys."

"What for?" Gedney whined.

"We're calling a team meeting."

"Who is?"

Ray Arthur Larry-Pete considered the question a moment, and when finally he spoke it was with a conviction and authority he never thought he could command: "I am."

At seven that night, twenty-six members of the Caledonia Shuckers varsity football squad showed up in the lounge at Bloethal Hall. They filled the place with their presence, their sheer protoplasmic mass, and the chairs and couches groaned under the weight of them. They wore Band-Aids, gauze and tape—miles of it—and the lamplight caught the livid craters of their scars and glanced off the railway stitches running up and down their arms. There were casts, crutches, braces, slings. And there was the smell of them, a familiar, communal, lingering smell—the smell of a team.

Ray Arthur Larry-Pete Fontinot was ready for them, pacing back and forth in front of the sliding glass doors like a bear at the zoo, waiting patiently until each of them had gimped into the room and found a seat. Moss, DuBoy and Kitwany were there with him for emotional support, as was the fifth interior lineman, center Brian McCornish. When they were all gathered, Ray Arthur Larry-Pete lifted his eyes and scanned the familiar faces of his teammates. "I don't know if any of you happened to notice," he said, "but here it is Monday night and we didn't have practice this afternoon."

"Amen," someone said, and a couple of the guys started hooting.

But Ray Arthur Larry-Pete Fontinot wasn't having any of it. He was a rock. His face hardened. He clenched his fists. "It's no joke," he bellowed, and the thunder of his voice set up sympathetic vibrations in the pole lamps with their stained and battered shades. "We've got five days to the biggest game of our lives, and I'm not just talking about us seniors, but everybody, and I want to know what we're going to do about it."

"Forfeit, that's what." It was Diderot, the third-string quarterback and the only one at that vital position who could stand without the aid of crutches. He was lounging against the wall in the back of the room, and all heads now turned to him. "I talked to Coach, and that's what he said."

In that moment, Ray Arthur Larry-Pete lost control of himself. "Forfeit, my ass!" he roared, slamming his forearm, cast and all, down on the nearest coffee table, which fell to splinters under the force of the blow. "Get up, guys," he hissed in an intense aside to his fellow linemen, and Moss, DuBoy, Kitwany and McCornish rose beside him in a human wall. "We're willing to play sixty minutes of football," he boomed, and he had the attention of the room now, that was for sure. "Burt, Reggie, Steve, Brian and me, and we'll play both ways, offense *and* defense, to fill in for guys with broken legs and concussions and whatnot—"

A murmur went up. This was crazy, insane, practically sacrificial. State gave out scholarships—and under-the-table payoffs too—and they got the really topflight players, the true behemoths and crackerjacks, the ones who attracted pro scouts and big money. To go up against them in their present condition would be like replaying the Gulf War, with Caledonia cast in the role of the Iraqis.

"What are you, a bunch of pussies?" Ray Arthur Larry-Pete cried. "Afraid to get your uniforms dirty? Afraid of a little contact? What do you want—to have to live with fifty-six-to-nothing for the rest of your life? Huh? I don't hear you!"

But they heard him. He pleaded, threatened, blustered, cajoled, took them aside one by one, jabbered into the phone half the night till his voice was hoarse and his ear felt like a piece of rubber grafted to the side of his head. In the end, they turned out for practice the following day—twenty-three of them, even Kitwany, who could barely move from the waist up and couldn't get a jersey on over his cast—and Ray Arthur Larry-Pete Fontinot ascended the three flights to the Coach's office and handed Coach Tundra the brand-new silver-plated whistle they'd chipped in to buy him. "Coach," he said, as the startled man looked up at him from the crucible of his memories, "we're ready to go out there and kick some butt."

The day of the game dawned cold and forbidding, with close skies, a biting wind and the threat of snow on the air. Ray Arthur Larry-Pete had lain awake half the night, his brain tumbling through all the permutations of victory and disaster like a slot machine gone amok. Would he shine? Would he rise to the occasion and fight off the devastating pass rush of State's gargantuan front four? And what about the defense? He hadn't played defense since junior high, and now, because they were short-handed and because he'd opened his big mouth, he'd have to go both ways. Would he have the stamina? Or would he stagger round the field on rubber legs, thrust aside by State's steroid-swollen evolutionary freaks like the poor pathetic bumbling fat man he was destined to become? But no. Enough of that. If you thought like a loser—if you doubted for even a minute—then you were doomed, and you deserved 56–0 and worse.

At quarter to seven he got out of bed and stood in the center of the room in his undershorts, cutting the air savagely with the battering ram of his cast, pumping himself up. He felt unconquerable suddenly, felt blessed, felt as if he could do anything. The bruises, the swollen eye, the hip pointer and rickety knees were nothing but fading memories now. By Tuesday he'd been able to lift both his arms to shoulder level without pain, and by Wednesday he was trotting round the field on a pair of legs that felt like bridge abutments. Thursday's scrimmage left him wanting more, and he flew like a sprinter through yesterday's light workout. He was as ready as he'd ever be.

At seven-fifteen he strode through the weather to the dining hall to load up on carbohydrates, and by eight he was standing like a colossus in the foyer of Suzie's sorority house. The whole campus had heard about his speech in the Bloethal lounge, and by Wednesday night Suzie had come back round again. They spent the night in his room—his private room, for the duration of Malmstein's stay at the Sisters of Mercy Hospital—and Suzie had traced his bruises with her lips and hugged the tractor tire of flesh he wore round his midsection to her own slim and naked self. Now she greeted him with wet hair and a face bereft of makeup. "Wish me luck, Suze," he said, and she clung to him briefly before going off to transform herself for the game.

Coach Tundra gathered his team in the locker room at twelve-thirty and spoke to them from his heart, employing the military conceits that always seemed to confuse the players as much as inspire them, and then they were thundering out onto the field like some crazed herd of hoofed and horned things with the scent of blood in their nostrils. The crowd roared. Caledonia's colors, chartreuse and orange, flew in the breeze. The band played. Warming up, Ray Arthur Larry-Pete could see Suzie sitting in the stands with her sorority sisters, her hair the color of vanilla ice cream, her mouth fallen open in a cry of savagery and bloodlust. And there, just to the rear of her—no, it couldn't be, it couldn't—but it was: his mom. Sitting there beside the hulking mass of his father, wrapped up in her windbreaker like a leaf pressed in an album, her scalp glinting bald through the dyed pouf of her hair, there she was, holding a feeble fist aloft. His *mom*! She'd been too sick to attend any of his games this year, but this was his last one, his last game ever, and she'd fought down her pain and all the unimaginable stress and suffering of the oncology ward just to see him play. He felt the tears come to his eyes as he raised his fist in harmony: this game was for her.

Unfortunately, within fifteen seconds of the kickoff, Caledonia was already in the hole, 7–0, and Ray Arthur Larry-Pete hadn't even got out onto the field yet. State's return man had fielded the kick at his own thirty after Malmstein's replacement, Hassan Farouk, had shanked the ball off the tee, and then he'd dodged past the entire special teams unit and on into the end zone as if the Caledonia players were molded of wax. On the ensuing kickoff, Bobby Bibby, a jittery, butterfingered guy Ray Arthur Larry-Pete had never liked, fumbled the ball, and State picked it up and ran it in for the score. They were less than a minute into the game, and already it was 14–0.

Ray Arthur Larry-Pete felt his heart sink, but he leapt up off the bench with a roar and butted heads so hard with Moss and DuBoy he almost knocked himself unconscious. "Come on, guys," he bellowed, "it's only fourteen points, it's nothing, bear down!" And then Bibby held on to the ball and Ray Arthur Larry-Pete was out on the field, going down in his three-point stance across from a guy who looked like a walking mountain. The guy had a handlebar mustache, little black eyes like hornets pinned to his head and a long wicked annealed scar that plunged into his right eye socket and back out again. He looked to be about thirty, and he wore Number 95 stretched tight across the expanse of his chest. "You sorry sack of shit," he growled over Diderot's erratic snap-count. "I'm going to lay you flat out on your ass."

And that's exactly what he did. McCornish snapped the ball, Ray Arthur Larry-Pete felt something like a tactical nuclear explosion in the region of his sternum, and Number 95 was all over Diderot while Ray Arthur Larry-Pete stared up into the sky. In the next moment the trainer was out there, along with the Coach—already starting in on his Ia Drang Valley speech—and Ray Arthur Larry-Pete felt the first few snowflakes drift down into the whites of his wide-open and staring eyes. "Get up and walk it off," the trainer barked, and then half a dozen hands were pulling him to his feet, and Ray Arthur Larry-Pete Fontinot was back in his crouch, directly across from Number 95. And even then, though he hated to admit it to himself, though he was playing for Suzie and his mother and his own rapidly dissolving identity, he knew it was going to be a very long afternoon indeed.

It was 35–0 at the half, and Coach Tundra already had his pant leg rolled up by the time the team hobbled into the locker room. Frozen, pulverized, every cord, ligament, muscle and fiber stretched to the breaking point, they listened numbly as the Coach went on about ordnance, landing zones and fields of fire, while the trainer and his assistant scurried round plying tape, bandages and the ever-present aerosol cans of Numzit. Kitwany's replacement, a huge amorphous red-faced freshman, sat in the corner, quietly weeping, and Bobby Bibby, who'd fumbled twice more in the second quarter, tore off his uniform, pulled on his street clothes without showering and walked on out the door. As for Ray Arthur Larry-Pete Fontinot, he lay supine on the cold hard tiles of the floor, every twinge, pull, ache and contusion from the previous week's game reactivated, and a host of new ones cropping up to overload his nervous system. Along with Moss and DuBoy, he'd done double duty through the first thirty minutes—playing offense and defense both—and his legs were paralyzed. When the Coach blew his whistle and shouted, "On the attack, men!" Ray Arthur Larry-Pete had to be helped up off the floor.

The third quarter was a delirium of blowing snow, shouts, curses and cries in the wilderness. Shadowy forms clashed and fell to the crunch of helmet and the clatter of shoulder pads. Ray Arthur Larry-Pete staggered around the field as if gutshot, so disoriented he was never quite certain which way his team was driving—or rather, being driven. But mercifully, the weather conditions slowed down the big blue barreling machine of State's offense, and by the time the gun sounded, they'd only been able to score once more.

And so the fourth quarter began, and while the stands emptied and even the most fanatical supporters sank glumly into their parkas, Caledonia limped out onto the field with their heads down and their jaws set in grim determination. They were no longer playing for pride, for the memories, for team spirit or their alma mater or to impress their girl-friends; they were playing for one thing only: to avoid at all cost the humiliation of 56–0. And they held on, grudging State every inch of the field, Ray Arthur Larry-Pete coming to life in sporadic flashes during which he was nearly lucid and more often than not moving in the right direction, Moss, DuBoy and McCornish picking themselves up off the ground at regular intervals and the Coach hollering obscure instructions from the sidelines. With just under a minute left to play, they'd managed (with the help of what would turn out to be the worst blizzard to hit the area in twenty years) to hold State to only one touchdown more, making it 49–0 with the ball in their possession and the clock running down.

The snow blew in their teeth. State dug in. A feeble distant cheer went up from the invisible stands. And then, with Number 95 falling on him like an avalanche, Diderot fumbled, and State recovered. Two plays later, and with eight seconds left on the clock, they took the ball into the end zone to make it 55–0, and only the point-after attempt stood between Caledonia and the unforgivable, unutterable debasement of a second straight 56–0 drubbing. Ray Arthur Larry-Pete Fontinot extricated himself from the snowbank where Number 95 had left him and crept stiff-legged back to the line of scrimmage, where he would now assume the defensive role.

There was one hope, and one hope only, in that blasted naked dead cinder of a world that Ray Arthur Larry-Pete Fontinot and his hapless teammates unwillingly inhabited, and that was for one man among them to reach deep down inside himself and distill all his essence—all his wits, all his heart and the full power of his honed young musculature—into a single last-ditch attempt to block that kick. Ray Arthur Larry-Pete Fontinot looked into the frightened faces of his teammates as they heaved for breath in the defensive huddle and knew he was that man. "I'm going to block the kick," he said, and his voice sounded strange in his own ears. "I'm coming in from the right side and I'm going to block the kick." Moss's eyes were glazed. DuBoy was on the sidelines, vomiting in his helmet. No one said a word.

State lined up. Ray Arthur Larry-Pete took a deep breath. The ball was snapped, the lines crashed with a grunt and moan, and Ray Arthur Larry-Pete Fontinot launched himself at the kicker like the space shuttle coming in for a landing, and suddenly—miracle of miracles!—he felt the hard cold pellet of the ball glancing off the bandaged nubs of his fingers. A shout went up, and as he fell, as he slammed rib-first into the frozen ground, he watched the ball squirt up in the air and fall back into the arms of the kicker as if it were attached to a string, and then, unbelieving, he watched the kicker tuck the ball and sprint unmolested across the goal line for the two-point conversion.

If it weren't for Moss, they might never have found him. Ray Arthur Larry-Pete Fontinot just lay there where he'd fallen, the snow drifting silently round him, and he lay there long after the teams had left the field and the stands stood empty under a canopy of snow. There, in the dirt, the steady drift of snow gleaming against the exposed skin of his calves and slowly obliterating the number on the back of his jersey, he had a vision of the future. He saw himself working at some tedious, spirit-crushing job for which his Phys. Ed. training could never have prepared him, saw himself sunk in fat like his father, a pale plain wife and two grublike children at his side, no eighty-yard runs or blocked points to look back on through a false scrim of nostalgia, no glory and no defeat.

No defeat. It was a concept that seemed all at once to congeal in his tired brain, and as Moss called out his name and the snow beat down, he tried hard, with all his concentration, to hold it there.

Bill McGrane has had a long career in football. He was a reporter for the Des Moines Register *and the* Minneapolis Tribune, *and has contributed regularly to* Pro *and* GameDay *football magazines. He is Director of Administration for the Chicago Bears, and has also been an executive with the Minnesota Vikings and the National Football League. McGrane's book on football coach Bud Grant is called* Bud: The Other Side of The Glacier *(1986). Pro football training camps are where rookies are hazed, harassed, and humiliated in order to weed them out or toughen them up for the coming season. As a sportswriter and pro football executive, McGrane has been to many training camps. His unique experience provides interesting behind-the-scenes material for this story.*

Bill McGrane

ROOKIES (1985)

July

I**T IS YOUR STANDARD SMALL** town. The divided highway says good-bye at the off-ramp in front of the Holiday Inn. You bump across the railroad tracks on Front Street, then go over the bridge and past three downtown streets.

The residential streets are old, which means they also are wide, quiet, and made of brick, although marred here and there by blacktop resurfacing. There's elm and oak, old enough and tall enough to form a shady cathedral nave over the old, red bricks.

You go south, a block past the Presbyterian church, left to the bookstore, then you take a right at the fork and up the hill.

The hill road winds up and around with the box elder growing almost out to the curbings. You come out of the last curve abruptly, onto the top, surprised at the sudden absence of trees and shade; however, trees and shade come in second when a hilltop gets bulldozed to build a college campus.

It is July, and just past one in the afternoon and the streets are deserted because the first summer session is over. It's also deserted because afternoon practice is still two hours off.

At the east end of the campus, past the library and the administration building and the fieldhouse, the twin-towered dorm shimmers in the heat. Fire doors are propped open in violation of codes and in search of a breeze. Windows are open on the three floors where the players live and an occasional curtain—institutional green—flaps half-heartedly.

On the uppermost of the player floors, a rookie running back lies on his bunk and attempts to look comfortable, which he isn't. He is wearing red shorts, a Grossinger's T-shirt, blue tennis shoes, and a forced smile. The latter is attributable to the verbal brickbats being left at his doorsill by every passerby.

A national television crew is filming the rookie for a segment to run in a preseason telecast. They've laid enough cable that the floor of his room looks as if it's covered with spaghetti. The lights have raised the temperature 10 degrees. The director, out from New York, is wearing a new safari jacket, jeans with clever stitching at the pockets, desert boots, and a beard.

"Hey, Eddie . . . tell 'em about that five-flat forty you run yestiddy mornin'."

The forced grin stretches as he hollers at his antogonist: "But it was rainin'!"

"Rained on ole Murphy, too, 'n' he done four-seven!" comes the retort.

The director mops his brow and the back of his neck with a new red farmer handkerchief.

"Just relax, guy . . . won't be a minute, here." The director turns to a member of the crew and rages in a controlled whisper: "Let's get the damned thing running! Can you do that?"

The camera purrs agreeably, and lights are refocused to correct for movement.

"We're rolling. Now, the first question will be, are you still disappointed that you weren't a number-one draft choice?"

There is loud cackle in the hallway, and the rookie shakes his head.

"Aw . . . hey, do you know what's goin' on here? I mean, I'm tryin' to make this football team! Man, the draft was a long time ago . . . and this is now! I'm hangin' by my fingernails, 'n' you come on with worrying about where I got drafted!"

The director's beard is the color of dirty straw. The grin parts it.

"Not what we were going for, but I like it . . . you like it, Ralphie?"

Ralphie is the size of somebody's kid brother, but identifiable as corporate because of his sweat-dampened corduroy suit, dusty Guccis, and wire-trimmed glasses. Ralphie stabs his Cross pen through a script line on a blue flimsy and nods:

"I like it."

They wrap it up just before two o'clock and the rookie walks down three flights, out through the fire door and into an ambush of 11-year-olds brandishing ballpoints and autograph books. He keeps walking as he signs, the key to survival.

By three o'clock it's leveled off at 90 and the sun is an unblinking adversary. Three guys faint during practice and the rookie survives a similar fate only by biting his lip until it bleeds.

After 90 minutes of practice he gets extra grass drills—a hideous blend of running in place, flopping onto belly or back, then back on your feet. He gets extra grass drills a couple times a week because he had a big reputation in college and doesn't mind standing up to veterans. He has to fight hard during grass drills to keep from throwing up.

After practice he wades back into the autograph guerrillas, sings his school song three times at the evening meal, and fights the drowsies during meeting.

He goes down the hill with two other rookies after meetings for beer at Bruiser's. Back at the dorm, he has 20 minutes before lights out.

His handwriting is tight and disciplined, childlike, on the ruled tablet. He is not a letter writer, but his mother is alone now, living over the restaurant in the Bronx, and he knows she worries:

"Dear Ma: Things are okay here but pretty different from college. It's hard, here. It's hot, like home, during the day, but there's generally a breeze at night. . . ."

A defensive back wearing bib overalls and no shirt surveys the prospects while balancing his tray on one hand and scratching his chest with the other. He approaches a table where two rookies are staring into their roast beef with the same total involvement microbiologists might give to their slide plates.

There is a smile behind the defensive back's moustache, and his voice is so soft as to be almost inaudible against the background noises of the dining hall:

"Good evening. I wonder if one of you gentlemen might be good enough to give us a song?"

The farther rookie shifts his X-ray gaze from the roast beef to the mashed potatoes, but has the good sense not to look up.

The near rookie—a lean end from the Dakotas with red hair and a sun-burn—is less fortunate. He looks up . . . and says, "Pardon me?"

Before the defensive back can repeat his question, a veteran tackle, who grew up in the Texas Panhandle, comes up behind the rookie. The Texas tackle has a voice like a rockslide:

"SING, Rook!"

The Dakota rookie scrambles up to stand on his chair in less time than it took the Texas tackle to make his request. Due to the abruptness of the journey, there is now a large splotch of roast beef *jus* on the rookie's shirt front.

The rookie begins his school song in a reedy tenor:

"Oh. . . ."

"Rook!"

The call is from a bespectacled flanker, peering over the afternoon newspaper. His face shows no emotion . . . unless viewed from an angle that catches the gleam in the eyes behind the thick lenses.

The rookie turns, teetering, toward his questioner:

"Yes, sir?"

"Rookie . . . do you have a heart?"

"Yessir," the boy answers, clapping his right hand up high against his chest.

Now the flanker is standing, hands on hips: "Do you know where it is, rookie? You have your hand on your Adam's apple!"

The boy shifts his hand and begins anew:

"Oh. . . ."

A running back in the chow line shouts:

"Louder! I can't hear you!"

Louder: "Oh. . . ."

A guard, seated near the wretch, looks up, his face rich with indignation:

"Sing . . . don't shout! You're ruining my dinner."

The bespectacled flanker has moved from his table to the coffee urns. He fills a cup and turns to stare at the rookie:

"You have a dreadful voice," he says. "This is a bad camp for singing and you are the worst of a bad lot."

The defensive back in bib overalls—the one who started it all—stands in front of the stricken singer. His hands are crossed on his chest and his head is bent as if in meditation.

Shakily, now: "Ooooh. . . ."

Suddenly, the defensive back holds up a hand.

"Wait! I think I've got it!"

The smile behind the moustache is equal parts tolerance and comradeship. Probably, it is not unlike the smile the wolf reserves for the deer it has run to ground.

"You're not singing with emotion!"

The defensive back turns toward a vast defensive end seated nearby:

"John . . . do you think this man is singing with emotion?"

The defensive end's brow puckers in concentration before he answers:

"No . . . no way. Karl, I think that man is a very unemotional singer."

The defensive back looks up at the rookie.

"You're from the Dakotas, aren't you?"

"Yessir."

The defensive back turns toward the vast defensive end:

"He's from the Dakotas, Moose."

The vast defensive end smiles and shakes his head in pleasant reflection.

"The Dakotas are beautiful, Karl," he replies. "The Dakotas have rolling wheat fields . . . those monuments carved on the mountain . . . the Black Hills."

The defensive back nods in agreement. Through it all, the rookie singer has the look of a man in need of one of those tidy little bags labeled "For Motion Discomfort" by the airlines.

The defensive back shouts to the rear of the room, where the bespectacled flanker is finishing his coffee and kidding a defensive coach.

"Flakey, do you think this man should sing with more emotion?"

"I think it is wrong for him to sing about such a beautiful area . . . an area with such proud traditions . . . in such a horrible voice. I think we are doing a disservice to the Dakotas."

The bespectacled flanker studies the rookie for a long moment. "Sing, 'Jingle Bells' instead," he says.

The rookie does . . . poorly and haltingly, because by now he can not remember his middle name, to say nothing of "Jingle Bells."

The bespectacled flanker regards him for a long moment.

"Merry Christmas," he says with a smile.

The Dakota rookie has fair hands and he'll block but he doesn't have even good speed, let alone big speed. So he won't make it.

But this fall, in a Dakota beer joint, he will be in great conversational demand, envied for his insights into the personalities that make up one of the pro teams all of them watch so faithfully on television.

He will chuckle and shake his head in pleasant reflection and he will say:

"Listen, that's a great bunch of guys."

A lady catching the prop-job back to Billings stopped to stare.

She was sixtyish and small, but she clamped her son-in-law's arm in a no-nonsense grip. She peered over her spectacles with a proper scowl.

What on earth, she wondered, were all of those big fellows doing, loafing at that unposted gate? She sniffed in mild reproof and yanked the son-in-law back into the stream of concourse traffic.

A veteran running back entered the waiting area. The rookies had been bused up from camp and now the veterans straggled in. Some brought wives and children.

The veteran running back had dressed only to a level that might be classified as "standard" cool . . . no sense going too heavy on a preseason trip. He wore a machine-faded denim jacket-and-pants outfit; a figured shirt with enough collar and cuff showing to let you know it was a designer original; lizard boots that should have cost $300 but didn't; and a cream-colored rancher's straw hat, sized just a shade too small, so as to fit properly.

The veteran running back's luggage was at sharp odds with his outfit. He carried only a slim, cowhide briefcase.

He click-clacked across the marble waiting area and planted a dutiful kiss on the cheek of a linebacker's wife just arrived from "down home." Then he slumped into a chair to await the boarding call. In the process of tilting the rancher's straw down even further over his eyes, the running back glanced at a rawboned rookie flanker from Huron.

The training camp sun had left the rookie flanker's nose and neck the same deep and angry shade of red once popular in roofing shingles. The rookie flanker wore his hair short enough so it wouldn't show under his helmet. He also wore a heavy plaid suit, a patterned tie, and a white shirt with a stiff collar. And, under the veteran's steady gaze, he wore an expression of vague discomfort.

The running back thumped up his rancher's straw in a manner previously unique to Marshall Dillon . . . the more remarkable, because never in his life had the running back lived south or west of Royal Oak, Michigan. He stared at the rookie flanker and whistled softly:

"My God . . . is that a real suitcase?"

The rookie flanker fluttered briefly in his chair and jammed his plaid knees together . . . as if that could hide the elderly two-suiter. The suit-case was the color of coffee with not enough cream. It had a dent on one side and a travel sticker from St. Louis on the other.

The running back glanced down at his own sleek attaché case and shook his head in wonder.

"Rook . . . are we goin' on the same trip? I thought this was overnight . . . not a month!" The running back inserted a gentle nudge into a large section of ribs in the next chair. The ribs belonged to a vast defensive tackle who appeared to be sleeping.

"Growler," asked the running back, "you own a suitcase . . . a honest-to-God suitcase?"

The vast defensive tackle did not move, nor did he open his eyes, but his voice rumbled up from some depth; a similar sound announces new oil wells.

"Mah daddy had one once. . . . when Ah was in high school. That was when Daddy was travelin'."

The rookie flanker swallowed against his stiff collar and stared at the toes of his brown shoes.

Now the huge defensive tackle's eyes were open. His face wrinkled as he studied the rookie and the suitcase. He looked as if he suddenly had become aware of an unpleasant odor.

"Rook. . . ." He sounded like the front end of a summer thunderstorm in Kansas. "You fixin' to brang that?"

That rookie now stared through the toes of his brown shoes and into the marble floor. Silently, he asked God to make either himself or the suitcase vanish. God refused.

"Damned shame," growled the defensive tackle, "for a man to mar a fine trip like this with a ugly old suitcase."

The running back stroked his chin in reflection.

"What's in it?"

"Just clothes and my playbook." The rookie recognized the voice as his own . . . barely.

The running back returned to stroking his chin. The defensive tackle went back to dozing.

"Growler," said the running back, "how much Coors you figure that old suitcase could hold?" The running back's eyes gleamed softly.

The defensive tackle belched spectacularly; mine shafts have collapsed with less provocation.

"Best part of two cases, Ah'd reckon."

The running back nodded his assent: " 'Bout a case apiece," he mused.

The rookie flanker stared through his brown shoes and through the marble floor and into that nether region reserved for the damned . . . and the rookies.

The defensive tackled opened his eyes again and impaled the rookie flanker on a steely smile . . . quite a bit of it terrifying.

"Why," he croaked, "don't I bring some back in my suitcase?"

This is a great yarn about a beleaguered football coach who is trying to sal-
vage a bad season by winning a big game. Author Mary Robison, born in 1949
in Washington, D. C., currently lives in Texas. She is an accomplished writer of
novels, short stories, and screenplays. For many years Robison has been a reg-
ular contributor to The New Yorker. *She has taught at Harvard and the Uni-*
versity of Houston. Among her books are Oh! *(1981),* Believe Them *(1988),*
and Subtraction *(1991). "Coach," originally published in* The New Yorker,
was selected for The Best American Short Stories 1982. *The story also ap-*
pears in Robison's book, An Amateur's Guide to the Night *(1983).*

Mary Robison

COACH (1981)

THE AUGUST TWO-A-DAY practice sessions were just sixty-seven
days away, Coach calculated. He was drying breakfast dishes. He
swabbed a coffee cup and made himself listen to his wife, Sherry, who
was across the kitchen, sponging the stove's burner coils.

"I know I'm no Renoir, but I have so much damn fun trying, and this
little studio, that one room, we can afford," Sherry said. "I could get out
of your way by going there, and get you and Daphne out of my way. No
offense."

"I'm thinking," Coach said.

Sherry coasted from appliance to appliance. She swiped the face of the oven clock with her sponge. "You're thinking too slow," she said. "Your reporter's coming at nine, and it's way after eight. Should I give them a deposit on the studio, or not? Yes or no?"

Coach was staring at the sink, at a thread of water that came from one of the taps. He thought of a lake place where they used to go, in Pennsylvania. He saw green water being thickly sliced by a power boat—the boat towing Sherry, who was blond and laughing on her skis, her back rounded and strong, her suit shining red.

"Of course, of course. Give them the money," he said.

Their daughter, Daphne, wandered into the kitchen. She was a dark-haired girl, lazy-looking, fifteen; her eyes lost behind her bangs. She drew open the enormous refrigerator door.

"Don't lean on that," her mother said.

"And what are you after?" Coach asked.

"Food, mainly," Daphne said.

Coach's wife went away, to the little sun patio off the kitchen. He pushed the glass door after her, and it smacked shut.

"Eat and run," he said to Daphne. "I've got a reporter coming in short order. Get dressed." He spoke firmly, but in the smaller voice he always used for his child.

"Yes, sir," Daphne said. She opened the freezer compartment and ducked to let its gate pass over her head. "Looks bad. Nothing in here but Eggos," she said.

"Have Eggos. I did. Just hustle up," Coach said.

"Can't I be here for this guy?" Daphne said.

"Who guy? The reporter? Uh-uh. He's just from the college, Daph. Coming to see if the new freshmen coach has two heads or none."

"Hey, lookit," Daphne said. She blew a breath in front of the freezer compartment and it made a short jet of mist.

Coach remembered a fall night, a Friday game night long ago, when he had put Daphne on the playing field. It was during the pre-game ceremonies before his unbeaten squad had taken on Ignatius South High. Parents' Night. He had laced shoulder pads on Daphne, and draped the trainer's gag jersey—No. 1/2—over her, and placed Tim . . . Tim Somebody's enormous helmet over her eight-year-old head. She was lost in the getup—a small pile of equipment out on the fifty, from which warm wisps of air trailed now and then.

She had applauded when the loudspeaker announced her name, and the P.A. voice, garbled by amplification and echo, rang out, "Daughter of our coach Harry Noonan and his lovely wife: Number One-Half—Daphne Noonan!"

She had stood transfixed in the bath of floodlights as the players and their folks walked by when they were introduced—the players grim in their war gear, the parents looking tiny and apologetic in everyday clothes. The co-captain of the team, awesome in his pads and cleats and steaming from warm-up running, had playfully palmed Daphne's big helmet and twisted it sideways.

From behind, Coach had heard a great "Haaa!" from the home stands as Daphne turned in circles, trying to right the helmet. Her left eye had twinkled out through one earhole, Coach remembered. "God, that's funny," the crowd said. And "Coach's kid."

On the sun porch now, his wife was doing a set of tennis exercises. Framed by the glass doors, she twisted her torso from one side to the other between Coach and the morning sunlight. Through the loose weave of her caftan, he could make out the white image left by her swimsuit.

"I knew you wouldn't let me," Daphne said. She had poured a glass of chocolate milk. She pulled open a chilled banana. "I bet Mom gets to be here."

"Daph, this isn't a big deal. We've been through it all before," Coach said.

"Not for a college paper," Daphne said. "Wait a minute, I'll be right back." She left the kitchen.

"I'll hold my breath and count the heartbeats," Coach said.

They were new to the little town, new to Ohio. Coach was assuming charge of the freshmen squad; it was a league where freshmen weren't eligible for the varsity. He had taken the job not sure if it was a step up for him or a risky career move. The money was so-so. But he wanted the college setting for his family—especially for Daphne. She had seemed to begin to lose interest in the small celebrity they achieved in high-school towns. She looked bored at the Noonans' Sunday spaghetti dinners for standout players. She had stopped fetching plates of food for the boys, some of whom were still game-sore. She had even stopped wearing the charm bracelet her parents had put together for her—a silver bracelet with a tiny megaphone, the numerals 68 (a league-championship year), and, of course, a miniature football.

Coach took a seat at the kitchen table. He ate grapes from a bowl. He spilled bottled wheat germ into his palm. On the table were four chunky ring binders, their black Leatherette covers printed with the college seal, which still looked strange to him. They were his playbooks, and he was having trouble getting the tactics of the new system into his head. "Will you turn off the radio?" he yelled.

The bleat from Daphne's upstairs bedroom ceased. A minute later, she was back down in the kitchen. She had a cardboard folder and some textbooks with her. "Later on, would you look at this stuff and help me?" she asked Coach. "Can you do these?"

He glanced over one of her papers. It was pencilled with algebra equations, smutty with erasures and scribbled-out parts. "I'd have to see the book, but no anyway. Not now, not later. I don't want to and I don't have time."

"Just great," Daphne said. "And Mrs. Math Genius told me 'Do it yourself.' Well, I can't."

"Your mother and I got our algebra homework done already, Daph. We turned ours in. That was in 1956. She got an A and I got a C."

"Mom!" Daphne called, pushing aside the glass door.

"Forget it, if it's the homework you want," Sherry said.

"Don't give in to her," Coach said. "I know you. The last time, you did everything but go there and take the tests for her, and she still flunked. This is summer school, and she's on her own."

"But I can't do it," Daphne said.

"Besides, I've got my own homework," Coach said, and frowned at his playbooks.

Toby, the boy sent from *The Rooter* to interview Coach, was unshaven and bleary-eyed. He wore a rumpled cerise polo shirt and faded jeans. He asked his questions wearily, dragging his words. Twice, he yawned during Coach's answers. He took no notes.

"You getting this, now?" Coach said at last.

"Oh, yeah, it's writing itself. I'm a pro," Toby said, and Coach was not certain if the boy was kidding. "So you've been here just a little while then. Lucky you," Toby said. "Less than a month."

"Is that like a question? It *seems* less than a month—less than a week. Seems like a day and a half," Coach said. For the interview, he had put on white sports slacks and a maroon pullover with a gold collar—the school's colors. He had bought the pullover at Campus World. The clothes had a snug fit that flattered Coach and showed off his straight stomach and heavy shoulders. He and Toby were on either end of the sofa, in the living room.

"And you bought this house—right?" Toby said. He stood up. "Well, believe it or not, I've got enough for a couple sticks," he said. "That's two columns, among us press men. If you're going to be home tomorrow, there's a girl who'll come and take your picture. Marcia. She's a drag, I warn you."

"One thing about this town, there aren't any damn sidewalks and the cars don't give you much room if you're jogging," Coach said, getting up, too.

"When I'm hitching, I wear a safety orange poncho and carry a red flag and paint a big 'X' on my back," Toby said. "Of course, I realize I'm just making a better target for the speeders."

"I run down at the track now. It's a great facility, comparable to a Big Ten's. I like the layout," Coach said.

"O.K., but the interview's over," Toby said.

"Well, I came from high schools, remember. In Indiana and Pennsylvania—good schools with good budgets, but high schools nonetheless."

"Yeah, I got where you're coming from," Toby said.

"Did you need to know what courses I'll be handling? Fall quarter, they've got me lined up for two. 'The Atlantic World' and 'Colloquium on European Industrial Development,' I think it is. Before, I always taught world history. P.O.D. once or twice."

"That 381 you're going to teach is a gut course. It always has been, in case no one's informed you. It's what we call 'lunch,' " Toby said.

"It's in the nature of a refresher course," Coach said.

Daphne suddenly came into the room from the long hall. Her dark hair was brushed and lifting with static. Her eyes seemed larger than usual to Coach, and a little sooty around the lashes.

"You're just leaving, aren't you, Buster?" Coach said to her.

"Retrieving a pencil," Daphne said.

"Is your name really Buster?" Toby asked.

"Get your pencil and scoot. This is Toby, here. Toby, this is Daphne," Coach said.

"Nice to meet you," Daphne said. She slid into a deep chair at the far corner of the living room.

"Can she hear us over in that county?" Toby said. "Do you read me?" he shouted.

Daphne smiled. Coach saw bangs and her very white teeth. "Come on, Daph, hit the trail," he said.

"I've got a joke for her first," Toby said. "What's green and moves very fast?"

"Frog in a blender," Daphne said. "Dad? Some friends asked me to go swimming with them at the Natatorium. May I?"

"You must see the Nat. It's the best thing," Toby said.

"What about your class, though? She's in makeup school here, Toby, catching up on some algebra that didn't take the first time around."

Toby wrinkled his nose at Daphne. "Algebra? Blah! At first, I thought you meant makeup school. Like lipstick and rouge."

"I wish," Daphne said. She slipped her left foot from her leather sandal and casually stroked the toes.

"She's a nut for swimming," Coach said.

"You'll be so bored here," Toby said to her. "Most nights, your options are ordering a pizza or slashing your wrists. Those are the choices of what there is to do."

"Yes, sure," she said, disbelievingly.

"Take it from Toby," he said, waving goodbye.

Coach let Toby out through the front door and watched until he was down the street.

"He was nice," Daphne said.

"Aw, Daph. That's what you say about everybody. There's a lot better things you could say—more on-the-beam things."

"I guess you're mad," she said.

Coach went to the kitchen, back to his playbooks.

Daphne came after him. "Aren't you?" she said.

"I guess you thought he was cute," Coach said. He flipped through some mimeographed pages, turning them on the notebook's silver rings. "I don't mean to shock you about it, but you'd be wasting your time there. You'd be trying to start a fire with a limp wet match."

Daphne stared at her father. "That's sick!" she said.

"I'm not criticizing him for it. I'm just telling you," Coach said.

"This is completely wrong," Coach said sadly. He read further. "Oh, no," he said. He drowned the newspaper in his bathwater and flung the wet pages over into a corner.

His wife handed him a dry copy, one of the ten or twelve *Rooters* Daphne had brought home. Sherry was sitting parallel to Coach on the edge of the tub, with her back braced against the tiled wall. "Oh, cheer up," she said. "Probably nobody reads a free newspaper."

Coach folded the dry new *Rooter* into a oblong around Toby's article. "O.K., I wasn't head coach at Elmgrove, and I sure wasn't Phi Beta Kappa. Ugly, ugly picture," Coach said.

"Your head looks huge."

"You were never at Mount Holyoke. Where did he get that one? I didn't bitch about the sidewalks this much."

"You didn't? That's almost too bad. I thought it was the best part of the article," Sherry said.

Coach slipped deeper into the warm water, until it came up to his chin. He kept the newspaper aloft. "Oh, come on, give me some credit here!" he cried. "Don't they have any supervision over in Journalism? I don't see how he could get away with this. It's an unbelievably sloppy job."

"It's just a dinky article in a handout paper, Coach," Sherry said. "What do you care? It wouldn't matter if he said we were a bright-orange family with scales."

"He didn't think of that or he would have. This breaks my heart," Coach said.

"Daph liked it," Sherry said.

Coach wearily chopped at the bathwater with the side of his hand. "They read this in the football office. I'll spend my first year here explaining how none of it's true."

"Lie," his wife advised him. "Who'll know?"

"And sure Daphne liked it. She was called 'pretty' or whatever. The pretty Noonan daughter who'll be attending Flippo High School in the fall," Coach said.

" 'Petite,' actually. 'The petite brunette,' " Sherry corrected.

"Daphne's not that small," Coach said.

"I just think the person who's going to come out of this looking bad is that reporter, finally," Sherry said.

"I could kill him," Coach said. "Then he'd look bad."

Now Coach had a little more than a month before the start of the two-a-days. He was seated awkwardly on an iron stool at a white table on the patio of the Dairy Frost. Daphne was beside him, fighting the early-evening heat for her mocha-fudge ice-cream cone. She tilted her head at the cone, lapping at it.

"You aren't saying anything," Coach said.

"Wait," Daphne said. She worked on the cone.

"I've been waiting."

"If you two want to separate, it's none of my business," she said.

Out in the parking lot, a new powder-blue Pontiac turned off the high-way, glided easily onto the gravel, and took the parking slot by the door. The boy in the driver's seat looked familiar to Coach. Good-looking shoulders. The couple in the back–the boy's parents, Coach thought–were both talking at once.

"Have I been wasting my breath for nothing?" Coach said. "*Not* a separation. Not anything like it."

"All right, *not*," Daphne said. She stopped her attack on the cone long enough to watch the Pontiac boy step out. A blob of ice cream streamed between her knuckles and down the inside of her wrist.

"You're losing it, Champ," Coach said.

Daphne dabbed around the cone and her hand, making repairs.

"Hell, real trouble–your father wouldn't tell you about at a Dairy Frost," Coach said. "This apartment your mom found is like an office or something. A place for her to go and get away every now and then. That kid's in my backfield. What the *hell's* his name?"

They watched as the young man took orders from his parents, then came into the Dairy Frost. He looked both wider and taller than the other patrons–out of their scale. His rump and haunches were thick with muscle.

"Bobby Stark!" Coach said, and smiled very quickly at the Pontiac. He turned back to his daughter.

"She wants to get away from us," Daphne said.

"Definitely not. She gave me a list, is how this started. She's got things she wants to do, and you with your school problems and me with the team, we're too much for her. She could spend her whole day on us, if you think about it, and never have a second for herself. If you think about it fairly, you'll see."

"That guy looks dumb. One of the truly dumb," Daphne said.

"My halfback? He's not. He was his class salutatorian," Coach said.

"He doesn't know *you*."

"Just embarrassed. Can't we stick to the point, Daphne?"

She gave a sigh and marched over to a trash can to deposit her slumping cone. She washed up after at a child's drinking fountain. When she came back to the table, Coach had finished his Brown Cow, but he kept the plastic spoon in his mouth.

"What was on this list of Mom's?" Daphne asked.

"Adult stuff, Daphne."

"Just give me one example," she said.

Coach removed the spoon and cracked it in half.

"Dad!" Daphne said.

"I always do that. Your mother's list is for five years. In that time, she wants to be living differently. She wants to be speaking French, regularly. She wants to follow up on her printmaking, and we both know she's got talent there, with her lithographs and all."

"This is adult stuff?" Daphne said.

Coach raised a hand to Bobby Stark. Stark had three malt cups in a cardboard carrier and he was moving toward his car. "Hey, those all for you?" Coach said cheerfully.

"I still got a month to get fat, Coach. Then you'll have five months to beat it off me."

Some of the people at the tables around Coach's lit up with smiles at the conversation. Stark's parents were grinning.

"Every hit of that junk takes a second off your time in the forty," Coach said.

Stark pretended to hide the malteds behind his arm. He was blushing.

"Duh," Daphne said in a hoarse voice. "Which way to duh door, Coach?"

"He can hear you," Coach said.

"Duh, kin I have a candy bar, Coach?" she said. "Kin I? Kin I?"

They watched Stark get into the Pontiac. He slammed the door and threw Daphne a wink so dazzling that she went silent.

Coach was in the basement laundry room, with both his arms hugging a bundle of jogging clothes. He was waiting for Sherry to unload her clothes from the washer.

"The Dallas Cowboys are soaking their players in a sense-deprivation tub of warm salt water," she said.

"We know," Coach said.

"If Dallas is doing it, I just thought you might like to consider it."

"We have. Hustle up a little with your stuff," Coach said.

"It's like my apartment," Sherry said. "A place apart."

Coach cut her off. "Don't go on about how much you love your apartment."

"I wasn't," Sherry said. She slung her wet slacks and blouses into the dryer.

Coach had two weeks before the start of the heavy practices. His team would have him then, he knew, almost straight through to the Christmas holidays. "You already spend all your time there," he said.

A little later, Coach and his wife were on the side patio together, sharing a Tab. They could hear the hum and tick of the dryer indoors.

"You know what's odd? Daphne's popularity here," Sherry said. "I don't mean it's *odd*." She was taking sun on her back, adding to her tan.

"No, that isn't new. She's always done terrific with people," Coach said.

"Your people, though. These are hers," Sherry said. "The phone hardly ever stops."

"Well, she's out of math trouble, I guess," Coach said. "And you have your apartment hideout, and you're adjusted here. Now, if only I can have the season I want."

"I love it with her and that reporter," Sherry said.

Daphne had become tight friends with Toby after she telephoned her gratitude for what he had written about her in *The Rooter*.

"Yeah, they're like sisters," Coach said.

"You're still bitter?"

"I'm really not," Coach said. "I live one careful day at a time now. No looking back for a second. Fear motivates me."

"You're fearful," Sherry said.

"Shaking with it," Coach said.

It was eight days before the two-a-day practice sessions would begin. The sky was colorless and glazed, like milk glass. When Coach flicked a glance at the sun, his eyes ached as if he were seeing molten steel. He had run some wind sprints on the stadium field, and now he was doing an easy lap on the track. A stopwatch on a noose of ribbon swung against his chest. He cut through the goalposts and trotted for the sidelines, where he had dumped his clipboard and a towel.

Bobby Stark came out from under the stands. His football shoes were laced together and draped around his neck. He was in cutoff shorts and a midriff-cut T-shirt. He walked gingerly in white wool socks. "Did everybody go, or am I the first one here?" he called to Coach.

" 'Bout a half hour," Coach said, heaving.

Stark sat down to untangle his shoes, and Coach, sweating, stood over him. Coach spat. He folded his arms in a way that pushed out his muscles. He sniffed to clear his lungs, twisting his whole nose and mouth to one side. "You know, Stark, I heard you were salutatorian for your class," he said.

"High school," the boy said. He grinned up at Coach, an eye pinched against the glare.

"That counts, believe me. Maybe we can use you to help some of our slower players along—some of the linemen."

"What do you mean—tutor?" Stark said.

"Naw. Teach them to eat without biting off their fingers. How to tie a necktie. Teach them some of your style," Coach said, and Stark bobbed his head.

Stark settled the fit of his right shoe. He said, "But there aren't really any dumb ones on the squad, because they just flunk out here. Recruiters won't touch them in this league."

Coach planted his feet on either side of a furrow of lime-eaten grass. Above the open end of the stadium, the enormous library building was shimmering and uncertain behind sheets of heat that rose from the empty parking area.

Stark got up and watched his shoes as he jogged in place. He danced twenty yards down the field, loped back. Other players were arriving for the informal session. Coach meant to time them in the mile and in some dashes.

Stark looked jittery. He walked in semicircles, crowding Coach.

"You worried about something?" Coach asked him. "Girl problems? You pull a muscle already?"

Stark glanced quickly around them. He said, "I've lived all my life two doors down from Coach Burton's house. My mom and Burton's wife are the best of friends, so I always know what's really going on. You probably know about it already anyway. Do you?"

"What the hell are you talking about, Stark?"

"Oh, so you don't. Typical. Burton's leaving, see, like the end of this year. His wife wants him out real bad, and the alumni want him out, because they're tired of losing seasons. They're tired of finishing third in the league, at best. Everybody says he should go to Athletic Director, instead. So what I heard was that you were brought in because of it, and if we do well this season—because people think you're a winner and pretty young—like, *you'll* be our varsity coach next year."

"That's conjecture," Coach said. But his voice sounded strange to him.

"We could go through four years together. I respect Coach Burton, but I don't see why in four years *we'd* ever have to lose a single game," Stark said. He took a stance, his body pushing forward.

"Ho!" Coach barked, and Stark lunged out.

"See me after this practice!" Coach called to him.

It was three o'clock, still hot. Coach was going along a sidewalk with Stark, who was balanced on a racing bike, moving just enough to keep the machine upright.

"Three things," Coach said. "I've seen all the game films from last year, and I came here personally and witnessed the Tech game. No one lost because of the coaching. A coach can work miracles with a good team, but he's helpless if his folks don't want it bad enough. That's the worst thing about running a team—you can't climb down into your people's hearts and change them."

Some college girls in a large car passed and shrieked and whistled at Bobby Stark. "Lifeguards at the pool," he explained.

"I don't know if Burton's leaving or not, but if his wife wants him to, he'll probably go," Coach said. "If you're ever thinking about a career in coaching someday, Bob, think about that. Your family's either with you or you've had it. You drag them all over hell—one town to another—and bury them, and whether you stay anywhere or not depends on a bunch of *kids*, really. I swear, I'd give up a leg for a chance to get in a game myself—just one play, with what I now know."

"I wish you could," Stark said. He swerved his bike's front tire and let it plunk off the curb into a crosswalk. He stood on the pedals for the jolt of the rear tire.

"The last thing is, don't mention the varsity-coach thing to anybody, and I mean anybody. Do you read me?" Coach said.

Stark nodded. They went on a block, and he said, "I turn here. You going to tell your beautiful daughter about it?"

"My daughter. You want a kitten? Because when I tell her, she's going to have kittens," Coach said.

No one was home. A plastic-ladybug magnet held a note to the face of the refrigerator. The note read, "Noonan, I'm at my place. Daph's with Toby K. somewhere, fooling around. Be good now. Sherry Baby."

"Dope," Coach said, smiling. He felt very good.

He took a beer upstairs and drank it while he showered. He cinched on a pair of sweat pants and went back down and fetched another beer. He watched some of a baseball game on cable television. He thought over the things he had told Bobby Stark.

"Boy, is that true!" Coach said, and then wasn't sure why he had said it.

He frowned, remembering that in his second year of college, the only year he had been on the varsity team, he had proved an indifferent player. "Not now," he whispered. He squeezed his beer can out of shape and stood it on top of the TV.

There was a thump over his head. The ceiling creaked. Someone had come home while he was in the shower. He took the stairs in three leaps and strode into the bedroom, saying, "Sherry?"

The dark figure in the room surprised him. "Hey!" he yelled.

Daphne was dancing in front of the full-length mirror on Sherry's closet door. She had improvised a look—sweeping her hair over her right ear and stretching the neck of her shirt until her right shoulder was bared. A fast Commodores song thumped from her transister radio.

"Nothing," she said.

"You're not home. Aren't you with Whoosis? You're supposed to be out. You are *beet* red," Coach said.

Daphne lowered her head and squared her shirt, which bagged around her small torso. "O.K., Dad," she said.

"No, but how did your audience like the show? I bet they loved it," Coach said. He smiled at himself in the mirror. "I'm just kidding you. You looked great."

"Come *on*, Dad," Daphne said, and tried to pass.

He chimed in with the radio song. He shuffled his feet. "Hey, Daph. You know what time it is?"

"Let me out, please," she said.

"It's Monkey time!" Coach did a jerky turn, keeping in the way of the exit door. "Do the Shing-a-Ling. Do the Daphne." He rolled his shoulder vampishly. He kissed his own hand. He sang along.

"Thanks a lot," Daphne said. She gave up trying to get around him. She leaned over and snapped off the radio. "You've got to use a mirror, so you don't look stupid on the dance floor. Everybody does," she said.

"I really was kidding you. Seriously. I know dancing is important," Coach said.

"May I go now? I've got algebra," Daphne said. She brought her hair from behind her ear, which was burning pink.

"Before that, you have to hear the news," Coach said. "Here's a news bulletin, flash extra."

"You're drunk. You and Mom are going to live in different cities. Somebody shot somebody," Daphne said.

"No, this is good news. There's a chance I'll be head coach here, of the varsity. The varsity coach. Me." Coach pointed to his chest.

"Let me out, please," Daphne said.

Coach let her pass. He followed her down the thin hallway to her bedroom. "More money. I'll even be on TV. I'll have my own local show on

Sundays. And I'll get written up in the press all the time, by real reporters. Daphne?"

She closed her door, and, from the sound, Coach thought she must have leaned against it.

"What's going on? Tell me, why am I standing here yelling at wood?" he said.

By dusk, Coach was drunk at the kitchen table. He was enjoying the largeness of the room, and he was making out a roster for his dream team. He had put the best kids from his fifteen years of coaching in the positions they had played for him. He was puzzling over the tight-end spot. "Jim Wyckoff or Jerry Kinney? Kinney got that tryout with the Broncos later," he said out loud. He penciled "Kinney" onto his diagram.

He heard Daphne on the stairs, and it occurred to him to clear the beer cans from the table. Instead, he snapped open a fresh can. "Daphne?" he said.

"Wait a second. What?" she said from the living room.

"Just wondered who else was alive besides me. I know your mom's still out."

Daphne entered the kitchen.

"You're sorry you were rude before?" Coach said. "That's O.K., Daph, just forget it."

Daphne made the slightest nod. "You *drank* all those?" she said.

"Hold still. What've you got on?" Coach asked. He hauled his whole chair about so he could see Daphne, who had gone behind him.

"Two, four, five," Daphne said, counting the cans. She wore one of the fan shirts that Coach had seen on a few summer coeds. On the front of the shirt, against a maroon field, were the golden letters "GO." Across the back was "GRIFFINS!"

"Now you're talking," Coach said.

"It was free. This guy I met—well, these two guys, really, who work at Campus World gave it to me. But, I don't know, I thought I'd wear it. I wanted you to see that I care if you get that big job. I do care. I want to stay here. Do you think we can? Do your people look any good for this year?"

"Winners," Coach said.

"Yeah, but you always say that," Daphne said.

Coach skidded his chair forward. "Have a beer. Sit down and let me show you on paper the material they've given me to work with."

Daphne took the can Coach offered, sipped at it, shook her head, and said, "Ooh, it burns. No wonder people burp."

"These guys are fast and big, for once. I'm not overestimating them, either. I've seen what I've seen," Coach said.

A car swept into the drive, and then its engine noise filled the garage. Coach and Daphne were quiet until Sherry bustled down the short hall that connected the garage with the kitchen.

"Really late, sorry, sorry," she said.

"It's a party, I warn you," Coach said to her.

"So I noticed." Sherry was carrying a grocery sack, not very full. There were bright streaks of paint on her brown arms. Daphne got up and plucked a bag of Oreo cookies from the groceries.

"Shoot me one of those," Coach said.

"Any beer left for me?" Sherry said. "I want to drown my disappointment. I can't paint."

"You can paint," Coach said.

"Ugh. My ocean today looked like wavy cement. My rocks looked like big dirty marshmallows." She put her sack down on the kitchen counter.

"Tell Dad he's got to do well so we can stay here," Daphne said to her mother.

Coach said, "Man, Daphne! I hope somebody finds your 'off' switch." He told his wife, "Plant your behind in that chair, Picasso. Let me tell you how we're moving up in the world."

"Every August," Sherry said, "Coach wants us to get packed up for a trip to the moon."

"The Eighty-Yard Run" is probably the most revered football short story of all time. It has appeared in many short story and sports anthologies over the years since its original publication in Esquire. *The story is timeless stuff, by one of America's best writers, Irwin Shaw. After graduating from Brooklyn College, where he played varsity football, Shaw served in World War II. This experience led to his highly acclaimed first novel,* The Young Lions *(1948), which was made into a movie featuring Marlon Brando in one of his greatest roles. This was followed by many other novels, plays, short stories, and screenplays. Among his books are* Lucy Crown *(1956),* Evening in Byzantium *(1973), and* Bread Upon the Waters *(1981). In 1961 Shaw was honored by having his* Selected Short Stories *published by the Modern Library of the World's Best Books.*

Irwin Shaw

THE EIGHTY-YARD RUN (1941)

THE PASS WAS HIGH AND wide and he jumped for it, feeling it slap flatly against his hands, as he shook his hips to throw off the halfback who was diving at him. The center floated by, his hands desperately brushing Darling's knee as Darling picked his feet up high and delicately ran over a blocker and an opposing lineman in a jumble on the ground near the scrimmage line. He had ten yards in the clear and picked up speed, breathing easily, feeling his thigh pads rising and falling against his legs, listening to the sound of cleats behind him, pulling away from them, watching the other backs heading him off toward the sideline, the whole picture, the men closing in on him, the blockers fighting for position, the ground he had to cross, all suddenly clear in his head, for the first time in his life not a meaningless confusion of men, sounds, speed. He smiled a little to himself as he ran, holding the ball lightly in front of him with his two hands, his knees pumping high, his hips twisting in the almost-girlish run of a back in a broken field. The first halfback came at him and he fed him his leg, then swung at the last moment, took the shock of the man's shoulder without breaking stride, ran right through him, his cleats biting securely into the turf. There was only the safety man now, coming warily at him, his arms crooked, hands spread. Darling tucked the ball in, spurted at him, driving hard, hurling himself along, his legs pounding, knees high, all two hundred pounds bunched into controlled attack. He was sure he was going to get past the safety man. Without thought, his arms and legs working beautifully together, he headed right for the safety man, stiff-armed him, feeling blood spurt instantaneously from the man's nose onto his hand, seeing his face go awry, head turned, mouth pulled to one side. He pivoted away, keeping the arm locked, dropping the safety man as he ran easily toward the goal line, with the drumming of cleats diminishing behind him.

How long ago? It was autumn then and the ground was getting hard because the nights were cold and leaves from the maples around the stadium blew across the practice fields in gusts of wind and the girls were beginning to put polo coats over their sweaters when they came to watch practice in the afternoons . . . Fifteen years. Darling walked slowly over the same ground in the spring twilight, in his neat shoes, a man of thirty-five dressed in a double-breasted suit, ten pounds heavier in the fifteen years, but not fat, with the years between 1925 and 1940 showing in his face.

The coach was smiling quietly to himself and the assistant coaches were looking at each other with pleasure the way they always did when one of the second stringers suddenly did something fine, bringing credit to them, making their $2,000 a year a tiny bit more secure.

Darling trotted back, smiling, breathing deeply but easily, feeling wonderful, not tired, though this was the tail end of practice and he'd run eighty yards. The sweat poured off his face and soaked his jersey and he liked the feeling, the warm moistness lubricating his skin like oil. Off in a corner of the field some players were punting and the smack of leather against the ball came pleasantly through the afternoon air. The freshmen were running signals on the next field and the quarterback's sharp voice, the pound of the eleven pairs of cleats, the "Dig, now, *dig!*" of the coaches, the laughter of the players, all somehow made him feel happy as he trotted back to midfield, listening to the applause and shouts of the students along the sidelines, knowing that after that run the coach would have to start him Saturday against Illinois.

Fifteen years, Darling thought, remembering the shower after the workout, the hot water steaming off his skin and the deep soapsuds and all the young voices singing with the water streaming down and towels going and managers running in and out and the sharp sweet smell of oil of wintergreen and everybody clapping him on the back as he dressed and Packard, the captain, who took being captain very seriously, coming over to him and shaking his hand and saying, "Darling, you're going to go places in the next two years."

The assistant manager fussed over him, wiping a cut on his leg with alcohol and iodine, the little sting making him realize suddenly how fresh and whole and solid his body felt. The manager slapped a piece of adhesive tape over the cut and Darling noticed the sharp clean white of the tape against the ruddiness of the skin, fresh from the shower.

He dressed slowly, the softness of his shirt and the soft warmth of his wool socks and his flannel trousers a reward against his skin after the harsh pressure of the shoulder harness and thigh and hip pads. He drank three glasses of cold water, the liquid reaching down coldly inside of him, soothing the harsh dry places in his throat and belly left by the sweat and running and shouting of practice.

Fifteen years.

The sun had gone down and the sky was green behind the stadium and he laughed quietly to himself as he looked at the stadium, rearing above the trees, and knew that on Saturday when the 70,000 voices roared as the team came running out onto the field, part of that enormous salute would be for him. He walked slowly, listening to the gravel crunch satisfactorily under his shoes in the still twilight, feeling his clothes swing lightly against his skin, breathing the thin evening air, feeling the wind move softly in his damp hair, wonderfully cool behind his ears and at the nape of his neck.

Louise was waiting for him at the road, in her car. The top was down and he noticed all over again, as he always did when he saw her, how pretty she was, the rough blonde hair and the large, inquiring eyes and the bright mouth, smiling now.

She threw the door open. "Were you good today?" she asked.

"Pretty good," he said. He climbed in, sank luxuriously into the soft leather, stretched his legs far out. He smiled, thinking of the eighty yards. "Pretty damn good."

She looked at him seriously for a moment, then scrambled around, like a little girl, kneeling on the seat next to him, grabbed him, her hands along his ears, and kissed him as he sprawled, head back, on the seat cushion. She let go of him, but kept her head close to his, over his. Darling reached up slowly and rubbed the back of his hand against her cheek, lit softly by a street-lamp a hundred feet away. They looked at each other, smiling.

Louise drove down to the lake and they sat there silently, watching the moon rise behind the hills on the other side. Finally he reached over, pulled her gently to him, kissed her. Her lips grew soft, her body sank into his, tears formed slowly in her eyes. He knew, for the first time, that he could do whatever he wanted with her.

"Tonight," he said. "I'll call for you at seven-thirty. Can you get out?"

She looked at him. She was smiling, but the tears were still full in her eyes. "All right," she said. "I'll get out. How about you? Won't the coach raise hell?"

Darling grinned. "I got the coach in the palm of my hand," he said. "Can you wait till seven-thirty?"

She grinned back at him. "No," she said.

They kissed and she started the car and they went back to town for dinner. He sang on the way home.

Christian Darling, thirty-five years old, sat on the frail spring grass, greener now than it ever would be again on the practice field, looked thoughtfully up at the stadium, a deserted ruin in the twilight. He had started on the first team that Saturday and every Saturday after that for the next two years, but it had never been as satisfactory as it should have been. He never had broken away, the longest run he'd ever made was thirty-five yards, and that in a game that was already won, and then that kid had come up from the third team, Diederich, a blank-faced German kid from Wisconsin, who ran like a bull, ripping lines to pieces Saturday after Saturday, plowing through, never getting hurt, never changing his expression, scoring more points, gaining more ground than all the rest of the team put together, making everybody's All-American, carrying the ball three times out of four, keeping everybody else out of the headlines. Darling was a good blocker and he spent his Saturday afternoons working on the big Swedes and Polacks who played tackle and end for Michigan, Illinois, Purdue, hurling into huge pile-ups, bobbing his head wildly to elude the great raw hands swinging like meat-cleavers at him as he went charging in to open up holes for Diederich coming through like a locomotive behind him. Still, it wasn't so bad. Everybody liked him and he did his job and he was pointed out on the campus and boys always felt important when they introduced their girls to him at their proms, and Louise loved him and watched him faithfully in the games, even in the mud, when your own mother wouldn't know you, and drove him around in her car keeping the top down because she was proud of him and wanted to show everybody that she was Christian Darling's girl. She bought him crazy presents because her father was rich, watches, pipes, humidors, an icebox for beer for his room, curtains, wallets, a fifty-dollar dictionary.

"You'll spend every cent your old man owns," Darling protested once when she showed up at his rooms with seven different packages in her arms and tossed them onto the couch.

"Kiss me," Louise said, "and shut up."

"Do you want to break your poor old man?"

"I don't mind. I want to buy you presents."

"Why?"

"It makes me feel good. Kiss me. I don't know why. Did you know that you're an important figure?"

"Yes," Darling said gravely.

"When I was waiting for you at the library yesterday two girls saw you coming and one of them said to the other, 'That's Christian Darling. He's an important figure.' "

"You're a liar."

"I'm in love with an important figure."

"Still, why the hell did you have to give me a forty-pound dictionary?"

"I wanted to make sure," Louise said, "that you had a token of my esteem. I want to smother you in tokens of my esteem."

Fifteen years ago.

They'd married when they got out of college. There'd been other women for him, but all casual and secret, more for curiosity's sake, and vanity, women who'd thrown themselves at him and flattered him, a pretty mother at a summer camp for boys, an old girl from his home town who'd suddenly blossomed into a coquette, a friend of Louise's who had dogged him grimly for six months and had taken advantage of the two weeks when Louise went home when her mother died. Perhaps Louise had known, but she'd kept quiet, loving him completely, filling his rooms with presents, religiously watching him battling with the big Swedes and Polacks on the line of scrimmage on Saturday afternoons, making plans for marrying him and living with him in New York and going with him there to the nightclubs, the theatres, the good restaurants, being proud of him in advance, tall, white-teethed, smiling, large, yet moving lightly, with an athlete's grace, dressed in evening clothes, approvingly eyed by magnificently dressed and famous women in theatre lobbies, with Louise adoringly at his side.

Her father, who manufactured inks, set up a New York office for Darling to manage and presented him with three hundred accounts and they lived on Beekman Place with a view of the river with fifteen thousand dollars a year between them, because everybody was buying everything in those days, including ink. They saw all the shows and went to all the speakeasies and spent their fifteen thousand dollars a year and in the afternoons Louise went to the art galleries and the matinees of the more serious plays that Darling didn't like to sit through and Darling slept with a girl who danced in the chorus of *Rosalie* and with the wife of a man who owned three copper mines. Darling played squash three times a week and remained as solid as a stone barn and Louise never took her eyes off him when they were in the same room together, watching him with a secret, miser's smile, with a trick of coming over to him in the middle of a crowded room and saying gravely, in a low voice, "You're the handsomest man I've ever seen in my whole life. Want a drink?"

Nineteen twenty-nine came to Darling and to his wife and father-in-law, the maker of inks, just as it came to everyone else. The father-in-law waited until 1933 and then blew his brains out and when Darling went to Chicago to see what the books of the firm looked like he found out all that was left were debts and three or four gallons of unbought ink.

"Please, Christian," Louise said, sitting in their neat Beekman Place apartment, with a view of the river and prints of paintings by Dufy and Braque and Picasso on the wall, "please, why do you want to start drinking at two o'clock in the afternoon?"

"I have nothing else to do," Darling said, putting down his glass, emptied of its fourth drink. "Please pass the whiskey."

Louise filled his glass. "Come take a walk with me," she said. "We'll walk along the river."

"I don't want to walk along the river," Darling said, squinting intensely at the prints of paintings by Dufy, Braque and Picasso.

"We'll walk along Fifth Avenue."

"I don't want to walk along Fifth Avenue."

"Maybe," Louise said gently, "you'd like to come with me to some art galleries. There's an exhibition by a man named Klee—"

"I don't want to go to any art galleries. I want to sit here and drink Scotch whiskey," Darling said. "Who the hell hung those goddam pictures up on the wall?"

"I did," Louise said.

"I hate them."

"I'll take them down," Louise said.

"Leave them there. It gives me something to do in the afternoon. I can hate them." Darling took a long swallow. "Is that the way people paint these days?"

"Yes, Christian. Please don't drink any more."

"Do you like painting like that?"

"Yes, dear."

"Really?"

"Really."

Darling looked carefully at the prints once more. "Little Louise Tucker. The middle-western beauty. I like pictures with horses in them. Why should you like pictures like that?"

"I just happen to have gone to a lot of galleries in the last few years . . ."

"Is that what you do in the afternoon?"

"That's what I do in the afternoon," Louise said.

"I drink in the afternoon."

Louise kissed him lightly on the top of his head as he sat there squinting at the pictures on the wall, the glass of whiskey held firmly in his hand. She put on her coat and went out without saying another word. When she came back in the early evening, she had a job on a woman's fashion magazine.

They moved downtown and Louise went out to work every morning and Darling sat home and drank and Louise paid the bills as they came up. She made believe she was going to quit work as soon as Darling found a job, even though she was taking over more responsibility day by day at the magazine, interviewing authors, picking painters for the illustrations and covers, getting actresses to pose for pictures, going out for drinks with the right people, making a thousand new friends whom she loyally introduced to Darling.

"I don't like your hat," Darling said, once, when she came in in the evening and kissed him, her breath rich with Martinis.

"What's the matter with my hat, Baby?" she asked, running her fingers through his hair. "Everybody says it's very smart."

"It's too damned smart," he said. "It's not for you. It's for a rich, sophisticated woman of thirty-five with admirers."

Louise laughed. "I'm practicing to be a rich, sophisticated woman of thirty-five with admirers," she said. He stared soberly at her. "Now, don't look so grim, Baby. It's still the same simple little wife under the hat." She took the hat off, threw it into a corner, sat on his lap. "See? Homebody Number One."

"Your breath could run a train," Darling said, not wanting to be mean, but talking out of boredom, and sudden shock at seeing his wife curiously a stranger in a new hat, with a new expression in her eyes under the little brim, secret, confident, knowing.

Louise tucked her head under his chin so he couldn't smell her breath. "I had to take an author out for cocktails," she said. "He's a boy from the Ozark mountains and he drinks like a fish. He's a Communist."

"What the hell is a Communist from the Ozarks doing writing for a woman's fashion magazine?"

Louise chuckled. "The magazine business is getting all mixed up these days. The publishers want to have a foot in every camp. And anyway, you can't find an author under seventy these days who isn't a Communist."

"I don't think I like you to associate with all those people, Louise," Darling said. "Drinking with them."

"He's a very nice, gentle boy," Louise said. "He reads Ernest Dobson."

"Who's Ernest Dobson?"

Louise patted his arm, stood up, fixed her hair. "He's an English poet."

Darling felt that somehow he had disappointed her. "Am I supposed to know who Ernest Dobson is?"

"No, dear. I'd better go in and take a bath."

After she had gone, Darling went over to the corner where the hat was lying and picked it up. It was nothing, a scrap of straw, a red flower, a veil, meaningless on his big hand, but on his wife's head a signal of something . . . big city, smart and knowing women drinking and dining with men other than their husbands, conversation about things a normal man wouldn't know much about, Frenchmen who painted as though they used their elbows instead of brushes, composers who wrote whole symphonies without a single melody in them, writers who knew all about politics and women who knew all about writers, the movement of the proletariat, Marx, somehow mixed up with five-dollar dinners and the best looking women in America and fairies who made them laugh and half-sentences immediately understood and secretly hilarious and wives who called their husbands, "Baby." He put the hat down, a scrap of straw and a red flower, and a little veil. He drank some whiskey straight and went into the bathroom where his wife was lying deep in her bath, singing to herself and smiling from time to time like a little girl, paddling the water gently with her hands, sending up a slight spicy fragrance from the bath-salts she used.

He stood over her, looking down at her. She smiled up at him, her eyes half closed, her body pink and shimmering in the warm, scented water. All over again, with all the old suddenness, he was hit deep inside him with the knowledge of how beautiful she was, how much he needed her.

"I came in here," he said, "to tell you I wish you wouldn't call me 'Baby.'"

She looked up at him from the bath, her eyes quickly full of sorrow, half-understanding what he meant. He knelt and put his arms around her, his sleeves plunged heedlessly in the water, his shirt and jacket soaking wet as he clutched her wordlessly, holding her crazily tight, crushing her breath from her, kissing her desperately, searchingly, regretfully.

He got jobs after that, selling real estate and automobiles, but somehow, although he had a desk with his name on a wooden wedge on it, and he went to the office religiously at nine each morning, he never managed to sell anything and he never made any money.

Louise was made assistant editor and the house was always full of strange men and women who talked fast and got angry on abstract subjects like mural paintings, novelists, labor unions. Negro short-story writers drank Louise's liquor, and a lot of Jews, and big solemn men with scarred faces and knotted hands who talked slowly but clearly about picket lines and battles with guns and leadpipe at mine-shaft-heads and in front of factory gates. And Louise moved among them all, confidently, knowing what they were talking about, with opinions that they listened to and argued about just as though she were a man. She knew everybody, condescended to no one, devoured books that Darling had never heard of, walked along the streets of the city, excited, at home, soaking in all the million tides of New York without fear, with constant wonder.

Her friends liked Darling and sometimes he found a man who wanted to get off in the corner and talk about the new boy who played fullback for Princeton, and the decline of the double wingback, or even the state of the stock market, but for the most part he sat on the edge of things, solid and quiet in the high storm of words. "The dialectics of the situation . . . and the theatre has been given over to expert jugglers . . . Picasso? What man has a right to paint old bones and collect ten thousand dollars for them? . . . I stand firmly behind Trotsky . . . Poe was the last American critic. When he died they put lilies on the grave of American criticism. I don't say this because they panned my last book, but . . ."

Once in a while he caught Louise looking soberly and consideringly at him through the cigarette smoke and the noise and he avoided her eyes and found an excuse to get up and go into the kitchen for more ice or to open another bottle.

"Come on," Cathal Flaherty was saying, standing at the door with a girl, "you've got to come down and see this. It's down on Fourteenth Street, in the old Civic Repertory, and you can only see it on Sunday nights and I guarantee you'll come out of the theatre singing." Flaherty was a big young Irishman with a broken nose who was the lawyer for a longshoreman's union, and he had been hanging around the house for six months on and off, roaring and shutting everybody else up when he got in an argument. "It's a new play, *Waiting for Lefty,* it's about taxi-drivers."

"Odets," the girl with Flaherty said. "It's by a guy named Odets."

"I never heard of him," Darling said.

"He's a new one," the girl said.

"It's like watching a bombardment," Flaherty said. "I saw it last Sunday night. You've got to see it."

"Come on, Baby," Louise said to Darling, excitement in her eyes already. "We've been sitting in the Sunday *Times* all day, this'll be a great change."

"I see enough taxi-drivers every day," Darling said, not because he meant that, but because he didn't like to be around Flaherty, who said things that made Louise laugh a lot and whose judgment she accepted on almost every subject. "Let's go to the movies."

"You've never seen anything like this before," Flaherty said. "He wrote this play with a baseball bat."

"Come on," Louise coaxed, "I bet it's wonderful."

"He has long hair," the girl with Flaherty said. "Odets. I met him at a party. He's an actor. He didn't say a goddam thing all night."

"I don't feel like going down to Fourteenth Street," Darling said, wishing Flaherty and his girl would get out. "It's gloomy."

"Oh, hell!" Louise said loudly. She looked coolly at Darling, as though she'd just been introduced to him and was making up her mind about him, and not very favorably. He saw her looking at him, knowing there was something new and dangerous in her face and he wanted to say something, but Flaherty was there and his damned girl, and anyway, he didn't know what to say.

"I'm going," Louise said, getting her coat. "I don't think Fourteenth Street is gloomy."

"I'm telling you," Flaherty was saying, helping her on with her coat, "it's the Battle of Gettysburg, in Brooklynese."

"Nobody could get a word out of him," Flaherty's girl was saying as they went through the door. "He just sat there all night."

The door closed. Louise hadn't said good-night to him. Darling walked around the room four times, then sprawled out on the sofa, on top of the Sunday *Times*. He lay there for five minutes looking at the ceiling, thinking of Flaherty walking down the street talking in that booming voice, between the girls, holding their arms.

Louise had looked wonderful. She'd washed her hair in the afternoon and it had been very soft and light and clung close to her head as she stood there angrily putting her coat on. Louise was getting prettier every year, partly because she knew by now how pretty she was, and made the most of it.

"Nuts," Darling said, standing up. "Oh, nuts."

He put on his coat and went down to the nearest bar and had five drinks off by himself in a corner before his money ran out.

The years since then had been foggy and downhill. Louise had been nice to him, and in a way, loving and kind, and they'd fought only once, when he said he was going to vote for Landon. ("Oh, Christ," she'd said, "doesn't *anything* happen inside your head? Don't you read the papers? The penniless Republican!") She'd been sorry later and apologized for hurting him, but apologized as she might to a child. He'd tried hard, had gone grimly to the art galleries, the concert halls, the bookshops, trying to gain on the trail of his wife, but it was no use. He was bored, and none of what he saw or heard or dutifully read made much sense to him and finally he gave it up. He had thought, many nights as he ate dinner alone, knowing that Louise would come home late and drop silently into bed without explanation, of getting a divorce, but he knew the loneliness, the hopelessness, of not seeing her again would be too much to take. So he was good, completely devoted, ready at all times to go anyplace with her, do anything she wanted. He even got a small job, in a broker's office and paid his own way, bought his own liquor.

Then he'd been offered the job of going from college to college as a tailor's representative. "We want a man," Mr. Rosenberg had said, "who as soon as you look at him, you say 'There's a university man.' " Rosenberg had looked approvingly at Darling's broad shoulders and well-kept waist, at his carefully brushed hair and his honest, wrinkle-less face. "Frankly, Mr. Darling, I am willing to make you a proposition. I have inquired about you, you are favorably known on your old campus, I understand you were in the backfield with Alfred Diederich."

Darling nodded. "Whatever happened to him?"

"He is walking around in a cast for seven years now. An iron brace. He played professional football and they broke his neck for him."

Darling smiled. That, at least, had turned out well.

"Our suits are an easy product to sell, Mr. Darling," Rosenberg said. "We have a handsome, custom-made garment. What has Brooks Brothers got that we haven't got? A name. No more."

"I can make fifty, sixty dollars a week," Darling said to Louise that night. "And expenses. I can save some money and then come back to New York and really get started here."

"Yes, Baby," Louise said.

"As it is," Darling said carefully, "I can make it back here once a month, and holidays and the summer. We can see each other often."

"Yes, Baby." He looked at her face, lovelier now at thirty-five than it had ever been before, but fogged over now as it had been for five years with a kind of patient, kindly, remote boredom.

"What do you say?" he asked. "Should I take it?" Deep within him he hoped fiercely, longingly, for her to say, "No, Baby, you stay right here," but she said, as he knew she'd say, "I think you'd better take it."

He nodded. He had to get up and stand with his back to her, looking out the window, because there were things plain on his face that she had never seen in the fifteen years she'd known him. "Fifty dollars is a lot of money," he said. "I never thought I'd ever see fifty dollars again." He laughed. Louise laughed, too.

Christian Darling sat on the frail green grass of the practice field. The shadow of the stadium had reached out and covered him. In the distance the lights of the university shone a little mistily in the light haze of evening. Fifteen years. Flaherty even now was calling for his wife, buying her a drink, filling whatever bar they were in with that voice of his and that easy laugh. Darling half-closed his eyes, almost saw the boy fifteen years ago reach for the pass, slip the halfback, go skittering lightly down the field, his knees high and fast and graceful, smiling to himself because he knew he was going to get past the safety man. That was the high point, Darling thought, fifteen years ago, on an autumn afternoon, twenty years old and far from death, with the air coming easily into his lungs, and a deep feeling inside him that he could do anything, knock over anybody, outrun whatever had to be outrun. And the shower after and the three glasses of water and the cool night air on his damp head and Louise sitting hatless in the open car with a smile and the first kiss she ever really meant. The high point, an eighty-yard run in the practice, and a girl's kiss and everything after that a decline. Darling laughed. He had practiced the wrong thing, perhaps. He hadn't practiced for 1929 and New York City and a girl who would turn into a woman. Somewhere, he thought, there must have been a point where she moved up to me, was even with me for a moment, when I could have held her hand, if I'd known, held tight, gone with her. Well, he'd never known. Here he was on a playing field that was fifteen years away and his wife was in another city having dinner with another and better man, speaking with him a different, new language, a language nobody had ever taught him.

Darling stood up, smiled a little, because if he didn't smile he knew the tears would come. He looked around him. This was the spot. O'Connor's pass had come sliding out just to here . . . the high point. Darling put up his hands, felt all over again the flat slap of the ball. He shook his hips to throw off the halfback, cut back inside the center, picked his knees high as he ran gracefully over two men jumbled on the ground at the line of scrimmage, ran easily, gaining speed, for ten yards, holding the ball lightly in his two hands, swung away from the halfback diving at him, ran, swinging his hips in the almost girlish manner of a back in a broken field, tore into the safety man, his shoes drumming heavily on the turf, stiff-armed, elbow locked, pivoted, raced lightly and exultantly for the goal line.

It was only after he had sped over the goal-line and slowed to a trot that he saw the boy and girl sitting together on the turf, looking at him wonderingly.

He stopped short, dropping his arms. "I . . ." he said, gasping a little though his condition was fine and the run hadn't winded him, "I . . . Once I played here."

The boy and the girl said nothing. Darling laughed embarrassedly, looked hard at them sitting there, close to each other, shrugged, turned and went toward his hotel, the sweat breaking out on his face and running down into his collar.

Damon Runyon (1880–1946) had newspapers in his blood, since both his grandfather and father were printers and he grew up around the presses. Born in Kansas, his family migrated to Colorado and young Damon got his first by-line for the Pueblo Evening Post. *Runyon began his fiction writing with humorous short stories on sports, but evolved into a star reporter for the Hearst newspapers covering big news events of the day. From his base in New York, he was the most prominent newspaper writer in the nation for a long time. When he returned to fiction writing he took up more universal themes, featuring tough-guy heroes and bums. Runyon wrote about gamblers, murderers, bookies, thieves, rumrunners, hijackers, dope smugglers, and an assortment of other disreputable characters. He placed them into stories about war, the wild West, and especially Broadway guys and dolls who spoke "Brooklynese." Runyon's stories appeared in* Harper's, Cosmopolitan, Saturday Evening Post, *and* Collier's.

Damon Runyon

HOLD 'EM YALE (1931)

WHAT I AM DOING IN New Haven on the day of a very large football game between the Harvards and the Yales is something which calls for quite a little explanation, because I am not such a guy as you will expect to find in New Haven at any time, and especially on the day of a large football game.

But there I am, and the reason I am there goes back to a Friday night when I am sitting in Mindy's restaurant on Broadway thinking of very little except how I can get hold of a few potatoes to take care of the old overhead. And while I am sitting there, who comes in but Sam the

Gonoph, who is a ticket speculator by trade, and who seems to be looking all around and about.

Well, Sam the Gonoph gets to talking to me, and it turns out that he is looking for a guy by the name of Gigolo Georgie, who is called Gigolo Georgie because he is always hanging around night clubs wearing a little mustache and white spats, and dancing with old dolls. In fact, Gigolo Georgie is nothing but a gentleman bum, and I am surprised that Sam the Gonoph is looking for him.

But it seems that the reason Sam the Gonoph wishes to find Gigolo Georgie is to give him a good punch in the snoot, because it seems that Gigolo Georgie promotes Sam for several duckets to the large football game between the Harvards and the Yales to sell on commission, and never kicks back anything whatever to Sam. Naturally Sam considers Gigolo Georgie nothing but a rascal for doing such a thing to him, and Sam says he will find Gigolo Georgie and give him a going-over if it is the last act of his life.

Well, then Sam explains to me that he has quite a few nice duckets for the large football game between the Harvards and the Yales and that he is taking a crew of guys with him to New Haven the next day to hustle these duckets, and what about me going along and helping to hustle these duckets and making a few bobs for myself, which is an invitation that sounds very pleasant to me, indeed.

Every college guy is entitled to duckets to a large football game with which his college is connected, and it is really surprising how many college guys do not care to see large football games even after they get their duckets, especially if a ticket spec such as Sam the Gonoph comes along offering them a few bobs more than the duckets are worth.

Anyway, many college guys are always willing to listen to reason when Sam the Gonoph comes around offering to buy their duckets, and then Sam takes these duckets and sells them to customers for maybe ten times the price the duckets call for, so Sam does very good for himself.

I know Sam the Gonoph for maybe twenty years, and always he is speculating in duckets of one kind and another. Sometimes it is duckets for the world's series, and sometimes for big fights, and sometimes it is duckets for nothing but lawn-tennis games.

But in all those years I see Sam dodging around under the feet of the crowds at these large events, or running through the special trains offering to buy or sell duckets. I never hear of Sam personally attending any of these events except maybe a baseball game, or a fight, for Sam has practically no interest in anything but a little profit on his duckets.

He is a short, chunky, black-looking guy with a big beezer, and he is always sweating even on a cold day, and he comes from down around Essex Street, on the lower East Side. Moreover, Sam the Gonoph's crew generally comes from the lower East Side, too, for as Sam goes along he makes plenty of potatoes for himself and branches out quite some, and has a lot of assistants hustling duckets around these different events.

When Sam is younger, the cops consider him hard to get along with, and in fact his monicker, the Gonoph, comes from his young days down on the lower East Side, and I hear it is Yiddish for thief, but of course as Sam gets older and starts gathering plenty of potatoes, he will not think of stealing anything. At least not anything that is nailed down.

For such a game as this, Sam has all his best pedlars, including such as Gyp Louie, Nubbsy Taylor, Benny Southstreet and old Liverlips, and to look at these parties you will never suspect that they are top-notch ducket hustlers. The best you will figure them is a lot of guys who are not to be met up with in a dark alley very late at night.

Now while we are hustling these duckets out around the main gates of the Yale Bowl I notice a very beautiful little doll of maybe sixteen or seventeen standing around watching the crowd, and I can see she is waiting for somebody, as many dolls often do at football games. But I can also see that this little doll is very much worried as the crowd keeps going in, and it is getting on toward game time. In fact, by and by I can see this little doll has tears in her eyes and if there is anything I hate to see it is tears in a doll's eyes.

So finally I go over to her, and I say as follows:

"What is eating you, little Miss?"

"Oh," she says, "I am waiting for Elliot. He is to come up from New

York and meet me here and take me to the game, but he is not here yet, and I am afraid something happens to him. Furthermore," she says, the tears in her eyes getting very large, indeed, "I am afraid I will miss the game because he has my ticket."

"Why," I said, "this is a very simple proposition. I will sell you a choice ducket for only a sawbuck, which is ten dollars in your language, and you are getting such a bargain only because the game is about to begin, and the market is going down."

"But," she says, "I do not have ten dollars. In fact, I have only fifty cents left in my purse, and this is worrying me very much, for what will I do if Elliot does not meet me? You see," she says, "I come from Miss Peevy's school at Worcester, and I only have enough money to pay my railroad fare here, and of course I cannot ask Miss Peevy for any money as I do not wish her to know I am going away."

Well, by this time the crowd is nearly all in the Bowl, and only a few parties such as coppers and pedlars of one kind and another are left standing outside, and there is much cheering going on inside, when Sam the Gonoph comes up looking very much disgusted, and speaks as follows:

"What do you think?" Sam says, "I am left with seven duckets on my hands, and these guys around here will not pay as much as face value for them, and they stand me better than three bucks over that. Well," Sam says, "I am certainly not going to let them go for less than they call for if I have to eat them. What do you guys say we use these duckets ourselves and go in and see the game? Personally," Sam says, "I often wish to see one of these large football games just to find out what makes suckers willing to pay so much for duckets."

Well, this seems to strike one and all, including myself, as a great idea, because none of the rest of us ever see a large football game either, so we start for the gate, and as we pass the little doll who is still crying, I say to Sam the Gonoph like this:

"Listen, Sam," I say, "you have seven duckets, and we are only six, and there is a little doll who is stood up by her guy, and has no ducket and no potatoes to buy one with, so what about taking her with us?"

Well, this is all right with Sam the Gonoph, and none of the others object, so I step up to the little doll and invite her to go with us, and right away she stops crying and begins smiling, and saying we are very kind indeed.

Anybody can see that she has very little experience in this wicked old world, and in fact is somewhat rattleheaded, because she gabs away very freely about her personal business. In fact, before we are in the Bowl she lets it out that she runs away from Miss Peevy's school to elope with this Elliot, and she says the idea is they are to be married in Hartford after the game. In fact, she says Elliot wishes to go to Hartford and be married before the game.

"But," she says, "my brother John is playing substitute with the Yales today, and I cannot think of getting married to anybody before I see him play, although I am much in love with Elliot. He is a wonderful dancer," she says, "and very romantic. I met him in Atlantic City last summer. Now we are eloping," she says, "because my father does not care for Elliot whatever. In fact, my father hates Elliot, although he only sees him once, and it is because he hates Elliot so that my father sends me to Miss Peevy's school in Worcester. She is an old pill. Do you not think my father is unreasonable?" she says.

She seems to know everything about this football business, and as soon as we sit down she tries to point out her brother playing substitute for the Yales, saying he is the fifth guy from the end among a bunch of guys sitting on a bench on the other side of the field all wrapped in blankets. But we cannot make much of him from where we sit, and anyway it does not look to me as if he has much of a job.

It seems we are right in the middle of all the Harvards and they are making an awful racket, what with yelling, and singing, and one thing and another, because it seems the game is going on when we get in, and that the Harvards are shoving the Yales around more than somewhat. So our little doll lets everybody know she is in favor of the Yales by yelling, "Hold 'em, Yale!"

Well, it seems that the idea of a lot of guys and a little doll getting right among them and yelling for the Yales to hold 'em is very repulsive to the Harvards around us, although any of them must admit it is very good advice to the Yales, at that, and some of them start making cracks of one kind and another, especially at our little doll. The chances are they are very jealous because she is out-yelling them, because I can say one thing for our little doll, she can yell about as loud as anybody I ever hear, male, or female.

A couple of Harvards sitting in front of old Liverlips are imitating our little doll's voice, and making guys around them laugh very heartily, but all of a sudden these parties leave their seats and go away in great haste, their faces very pale, pale, indeed, and I figure maybe they are both taken sick at the same moment, but afterwards I learn that Liverlips takes a big shiv out of his pocket and opens it and tells them very confidentially that he is going to carve their ears off.

Naturally, I do not blame the Harvards for going away in great haste, for Liverlips is such a looking guy as you will figure to take great delight in carving off ears. Furthermore, Nubbsy Taylor and Benny Southstreet and Gyp Louie and even Sam the Gonoph commence exchanging such glances with other Harvards around us who are making cracks at our little doll that presently there is almost a dead silence in our neighborhood, except for our little doll yelling, "Hold 'em, Yale!" You see by this time we are all very fond of our little doll because she is so cute looking, and we do not wish anybody making cracks at her or at us either, and especially at us.

Well, finally the game is over, and I do not remember much about it, although afterwards I hear that our little doll's brother, John, plays substitute for the Yales very good. But it seems that the Harvards win, and our little doll is very sad indeed about this, and is sitting there looking out over the field, which is now covered with guys dancing around as if they all suddenly go daffy, and it seems they are all Harvards, because there is really no reason for the Yales to do any dancing.

All of a sudden our little doll looks toward one end of the field, and says as follows:

"Oh, they are going to take our goal posts!"

Sure enough, a lot of Harvards are gathering around the posts at this end of the field, and are pulling and hauling at the posts, which seem to be very stout posts, indeed. Personally, I will not give you eight cents for these posts, but afterwards one of the Yales tells me that when a football team wins a game it is considered the proper caper for this team's boosters to grab the other guy's goal posts. But he is not able to tell me what good the posts are after they get them, and this is one thing that will always be a mystery to me.

Anyway, while we are watching the goings-on around the goal posts, our little doll says come on and jumps up and runs down an aisle and out onto the field, and into the crowd around the goal posts, so naturally we follow her. Somehow she manages to wiggle through the crowd of Harvards around the posts, and the next thing anybody knows she shins up one of the posts faster than you can say scat, and pretty soon is roosting out on the cross-bar between the posts like a chipmunk.

Afterwards she explains that her idea is the Harvards will not be ungentlemanly enough to pull down the goal posts with a lady roosting on them, but it seems these Harvards are no gentlemen, and keep on pulling, and the posts commence to teeter, and our little doll is teetering with them, although of course she is in no danger if she falls because she is sure to fall on the Harvards' noggins, and the way I look at it, the noggin of anybody who will be found giving any time to pulling down goal posts is apt to be soft enough to break a very long fall.

Now Sam the Gonoph and old Liverlips and Nubbsy Taylor and Benny Southstreet and Gyp Louie and I reach the crowd around the goal posts at about the same time, and our little doll sees us from her roost and yells to us:

"Do not let them take our posts!"

Of course Sam the Gonoph does not wish any trouble with these parties, and he tries to speak nicely to the guys who are pulling at the posts, saying as follows:

"Listen," Sam says, "the little doll up there does not wish you to take these posts."

Well, maybe they do not hear Sam's words in the confusion, or if they do hear them they do not wish to pay any attention to them for one of the Harvards mashes Sam's derby hat down over his eyes, and another smacks old Liverlips on the left ear, while Gyp Louie and Nubbsy Taylor and Benny Southstreet are shoved around quite some.

"All right," Sam the Gonoph says, as soon as he can pull his hat off his eyes, "all right, gentlemen, if you wish to play this way. Now, boys, let them have it!"

So Sam the Gonoph and Nubbsy Taylor and Gyp Louie and Benny Southstreet and old Liverlips begin letting them have it, and what they let them have it with is not only their dukes, but with the good old difference in their dukes, because these guys are by no means suckers when it comes to a battle, and they all carry something in their pockets to put in their dukes in case of a fight, such as a dollar's worth of nickels rolled up tight.

Well, the ground around them is soon covered with Harvards, and it seems that some Yales are also mixed up with them, being Yales who think Sam the Gonoph and his guys are other Yales defending the goal posts and wishing to help out. But of course Sam the Gonoph and his guys cannot tell the Yales from the Harvards, and do not have time to ask which is which, so they are just letting everybody have it who comes along. And while all this is going on our little doll is sitting up on the cross-bar and yelling plenty of encouragement to Sam and his guys.

Pretty soon the Harvards are knocking down Sam the Gonoph, then they start knocking down Nubbsy Taylor, and by and by they are knocking down Benny Southstreet and Gyp Louie and Liverlips, and it is so much fun that the Harvards forget all about the goal posts. Of course as fast as Sam the Gonoph and his guys are knocked down they also get up, but the Harvards are too many for them, and they are getting an awful shellacking when the nine-foot guy who flattens me, and who is knocking down Sam the Gonoph so often he is becoming a great nuisance to Sam, sings out:

"Listen," he says, "these are game guys, even if they do go to Yale. Let us cease knocking them down," he says, "and give them a cheer."

So the Harvards knock down Sam the Gonoph and Nubbsy Taylor and Gyp Louie and Benny Southstreet and old Liverlips just once more and then all the Harvards put their heads together and say rah-rah-rah, very loud, and go away, leaving the goal posts still standing, with our little doll still roosting on the cross-bar, although afterwards I hear some Harvards who are not in the fight get the posts at the other end of the field and sneak away with them. But I always claim these posts do not count.

Benny Southstreet is lying across Gyp Louie and both are still snoring from the last knockdown, and the Bowl is now pretty much deserted except for the newspaper scribes away up in the press box, who do not seem to realize that the Battle of the Century just comes off in front of them. It is coming on dark, when all of a sudden a guy pops up out of the dusk wearing white spats and an overcoat with a fur collar and he rushes up to our little doll.

"Clarice," he says, "I am looking for you high and low. My train is stalled for hours behind a wreck the other side of Bridgeport, and I get here just after the game is over. But," he says, "I figure you will be waiting somewhere for me. Let us hurry on to Hartford, darling," he says.

Well, when he hears this voice, Sam the Gonoph opens his good eye wide and takes a peek at the guy. Then all of a sudden Sam jumps up and wobbles over to the guy and hits him a smack between the eyes. Sam is wobbling because his legs are not so good from the shellacking he takes off the Harvards, and furthermore he is away off his punching as the guy only goes to his knees and comes right up standing again as our little doll lets out a screech and speaks as follows:

"Oo-oo!" she says. "Do not hit Elliot! He is not after our goal posts!"

"Elliot?" Sam the Gonoph says. "This is not Elliot. This is nobody but Gigolo Georgie. I can tell him by his white spats," Sam says, "and I am now going to get even for the pasting I take from the Harvards."

Then he nails the guy again and this time he seems to have a little more on his punch, for the guy goes down and Sam the Gonoph gives him the leather very good, although our little doll is still screeching, and begging Sam not to hurt Elliot.

Now a couple of other guys come up out of the dusk, and one of them is a tall, fine-looking guy with a white mustache, and anybody can see that he is somebody, and what happens but our little doll runs right into his arms and kisses him on the white mustache and calls him daddy and starts to cry more than somewhat, so I can see we lose our little doll then and there. And now the guy with the white mustache walks up to Sam the Gonoph and sticks out his duke and says as follows:

"Sir," he says, "permit me the honor of shaking the hand which does me the very signal service of chastising the scoundrel who just escapes from the field. And," he says, "permit me to introduce myself to you. I am J. Hildreth Van Cleve, president of the Van Cleve Trust. I am notified early today by Miss Peevy of my daughter's sudden departure from school, and we learn she purchases a ticket for New Haven. I at once suspect this fellow has something to do with it. Fortunately," he says, "I have these private detectives here keeping tab on him for some time, knowing my child's schoolgirl infatuation for him, so we easily trail him here."

"I know who you are, Mr. Van Cleve," Sam the Gonoph says. "You are the Van Cleve who is down to his last forty million. But," he says, "do not thank me for putting the slug on Gigolo Georgie. He is a bum in spades, and I am only sorry he fools your nice little kid even for a minute, although," Sam says, "I figure she must be dumber than she looks to be fooled by such a guy as Gigolo Georgie."

"I hate him," the little doll says. "I hate him because he is a coward. He does not stand up and fight when he is hit like you and Liverlips and the others. I never wish to see him again."

"Do not worry," Sam the Gonoph says. "I will be too close to Gigolo Georgie as soon as I recover from my wounds for him to stay in this part of the country."

Well, I do not see Sam the Gonoph or Nubbsy Taylor or Benny Southstreet or Gyp Louie or Liverlips for nearly a year after this, and then it comes on fall again and one day I get to thinking that here it is Friday and the next day the Harvards are playing the Yales a large football game in Boston.

I figure it is a great chance for me to join up with Sam the Gonoph again and hustle duckets for him for this game, and I know Sam will be leaving along about midnight with his crew. So I go over to the Grand Central Station at such a time, and sure enough he comes along by and by, busting through the crowd in the station with Nubbsy Taylor and Benny Southstreet and Gyp Louie and old Liverlips.

"Well, Sam," I say, as I hurry along with them, "here I am ready to hustle duckets for you again, and I hope and trust we do a nice business."

"Duckets!" Sam the Gonoph says. "We are not hustling duckets for this game, although you can go with us and welcome. We are going to Boston," he says, "to root for the Yales to kick the slats out of the Harvards and we are going as the personal guests of Miss Clarice Van Cleve and her old man."

"Hold 'em, Yale!" old Liverlips says, as he pushes me to one side and the whole bunch goes trotting through the gate to catch their train, and I then notice they are all wearing blue feathers in their hats with a little white Y on these feathers such as college guys always wear at football games, and that moreover Sam the Gonoph is carrying a Yale pennant.

In this story the Chicago Bears, who begin each year with high hopes, always seem to fall short of the Super Bowl. Then the "Monsters of the Midway" get a new coach. No, it isn't Mike Ditka, who in real life coached the Bears to a Super Bowl victory. This coach is a woman, and she has the Bears dancing their way towards the top. This delightfully comical story first appeared in Playboy. *Its author, Asa Baber, is a contributing editor to* Playboy. *He writes the enduringly popular "Men" column for the magazine, and has published many fiction and nonfiction stories there since 1969. Baber's books are* Tranquility Base and Other Stories *(1979),* The Land of a Million Elephants *(1971, 1991), and* Naked At Gender Gap *(1992). In 1984 he won the H. L. Mencken Award from the Free Press Association.*

Asa Baber

THE DANCING BEARS (1984)

THAT FIRST MORNING AT TRAINING camp was worse than Parris Island. We got no water, no salt pills, no breaks. Red Emerson stood up in the tower and yelled at us through the bullhorn like we was slaves building pyramids: "You fat bastards, nobody's in shape. I want another mile in full gear right now"—stuff like that.

You think I wasn't tired? I'd had a pony keg of beer the night before, for one thing, and I'd spent off season lying around the farm putting funny things up my nose and into my lungs. That, plus an extra 50 pounds I didn't need, made wind sprints feel like marathons, I'm here to tell you. Besides, I'd had a big fight with DeeAnn just before I drove up from Paris, Illinois, to Lakeshore College. She was on my case, and I didn't care for it. "I'm only dating you, lady," I told her. "You think just because you're a nurse you know everything. But what I do to my body is my business. I'll play myself into shape, like I always have, thank you very much."

DeeAnn just sat there and listened to my lungs wheeze. "You always do have to defeat yourself, don't you, Dewey?" she said to me. "If the rest of the Bears are treating themselves the way you are, you boys will never make the Super Bowl."

"We'll make it," I said. "Red Emerson's a hell of a coach. He'll get us there, mark my words." Well, we almost got there, but not with Red Emerson. That shows how much I knew.

" 'Bye, Dewey," DeeAnn said. She patted me on my beer belly and put on her white nurse's cap and walked out the door. "Good luck."

" 'Bye," I waved at her after she'd gone.

Was I sad about us breaking up? Not really. In those days, I thought any woman who didn't want me showed extremely poor judgment. I was the great Dewey Pinnell. The fans called me Gluey Dewey. I loved to hang all over quarterbacks after I sacked them. Yours truly, God's gift to women and the N.F.L., starting left linebacker for the Chicago Bears, number 53 in your program, cocaptain of the defense, 6'2" tall and 230 pounds by midseason, two Pro Bowl nominations, able to bench press almost twice my weight and to crank off a 4.7 40 when I had to, 11 years in the game before I hung up my jock and came back here to farm. "Me?" I laughed to myself as I heard DeeAnn drive down the road that night. "Why should I worry about a skinny little E.R. nurse from Paris when I got beauty queens and Bunnies and Honey Bears running after me in the Windy City? I've played myself into shape every year since fourth grade, damn it."

But that first morning of practice almost killed me. There were guys passing out, throwing up, quitting. We all knew Red's job was on the line, of course. The Bears started every year with good hype and a lot of hope, but the Super Bowl always seemed beyond us, and Mr. Beaupray wanted a Super Bowl ring the way a junkie wants dope. So Red was out to get to the Super Bowl or have us die trying, and it was Merciless City that first morning, as I said.

I ate what I could at lunch, but two-a-days always did spook me, and what I wanted most was to sleep. It's funny that to this day, I remember the dream I had that noon: I was back in Paris, and DeeAnn was strad-dled over me with her hair down in my face, twisting like an eel and moaning my name.

That's what I was dreaming when Marshall Chambers sneaked up be-hind me and poured a pitcher of ice water onto my crotch. Lord, that hurt. One second I was bucking like a bronco under DeeAnn's thin hips, and the next second I had a refrigerated groin. I chased Marshall out the door on that one, I can tell you.

Marshall and me was real tight. He was a fine quarterback who could throw the football 70 yards on a line off his hind leg; and when he was hot, he could pick a defense apart the way a kid scatters an anthill. We'd been with the Bears through thick and thin, Marshall and me.

I tackled him in the hall and sat on him like he was a whoopee cush-ion until he begged for mercy. Then I picked him up and dusted him off and poured him a glass of Gatorade. "You broke up my dream, Marshall," I said.

"Dewey, how can you sleep when your future's at stake?" he asked. "Don't you know what just happened? Red Emerson got fired this noon."

"They fired him on the first day of training camp?" I asked. "What's the sense in that? Give the guy a chance."

"I don't know," Marshall said. "Mr. Beaupray called down and told him he was out. Him and his staff. Said he'd had five years to prove him-self and now it was goodbye."

"Who's the new coach?"

"I don't know," Marshall said. "Mr. Beaupray said he'd found some-body new, somebody perfect for the job."

"I'm going to miss Red," I said. "He was mean, but you knew where you stood with him." I meant it, too.

"The word is we practice as usual this afternoon," Marshall said. "Sweats only. Calisthenics. No contact."

"I don't mind," I said. "I can take an easy afternoon when I get one."

"New coach comes in tomorrow," Marshall said.

"Wonderful, wonderful," I laughed. "I can hardly wait."

Lakeshore College made a good place for a training camp. It was right by Lake Michigan, and on a clear day, you could see Chicago to the south. I liked to pause at the top of the steps before I went down to the practice field and look at the lake, the clouds, the sky. I'd think about how big the world is and how small we are, even us guys that are supposed to be such tanks, and it put things in perspective. Football don't mean much to a cloud. You can bring in all the PR people in the world and hype it like Gang Busters, but the fact is that football is about as important to the universe as a grain of sand.

I liked to think about things like that before I went down to get my brains scrambled. It set things right, somehow.

I confess I wasn't ready for what I saw that afternoon, though. As I looked down at the field from the top of the steps, I thought maybe I was in the wrong place. It was maximum weird. It was like somebody was getting ready for a rock concert. There was loud-speakers up and down the side lines. And you should've seen the middle of the field. There was a whole bunch of banisters running smack down the middle of the turf from goal line to goal line right between the hash marks.

"What the hell, over," Marshall said.

"What is this shit?" I asked.

We got down to the field and the whole team stood there, blinking in the hot sun, scuffling their cleats and making those sounds guys make when they have no idea what's going on.

"Break out the footballs, Sam," Marshall yelled to the equipment manager. "Let's get something started."

"No footballs, Marshall," Sam squeaked.

"The hell you say," Marshall said. He went over and dumped open a gunny sack of balls and picked one up.

"No footballs, Marshall!" Sam yelled in that high voice.

Marshall was about to throw me a pass when there was a whistle.

It was the meanest between-your-teeth-tuck-your-fingers-in-your-mouth whistle I'd ever heard in my life. Marshall's arm froze and I stopped jogging, and I'm here to tell you that none of us was ready for what we saw.

She was tall. She wasn't young and she wasn't old. She had on a blue jump suit, and there was a red ribbon that wrapped her head tight. Her hair looked like a shining helmet. I thought she was kind of pretty, but she also looked tough.

"No footballs, Mr. Chambers," she said.

"Say what, baby?" Marshall asked.

"We're not going to use footballs this afternoon, Mr. Chambers," she said.

"Is that a fact?" Marshall said. He was doing his Rush Street walk. He was strutting like a rooster, flipping the ball from hand to hand. "Says who?"

"Says me," she smiled. Well, it was kind of a smile.

"And who are you, if you don't mind my asking?"

"Mr. Beaupray hired me to get you in shape, sir."

"Hey, I'm in shape, baby," Marshall grinned. "I'm in shape for whatever you want to do."

"Would you put the football down, please? We have a lot of work to do this afternoon."

Marshall was standing right next to her. He had his face in her face. I'd seen him do this routine a hundred times. "We sure do have work to do, hon. Where would you like to do it?" Usually, when he came out with that line, they either melted or walked away. This time, it was a little different.

It happened so fast we didn't really see it, but suddenly, the football was up in the air. The lady had kicked it right out of Marshall's hands. And to make it worse, he tried to grab her, but she flipped him over her shoulder, like a sack of grain, and he came down flat on his back.

It was as quiet as church for a second. Marshall moaned on the deck. We was waiting for the TV replay, I guess, because we didn't believe what we'd seen. Then I laughed, and everybody but Marshall laughed. Finally, he laughed. The lady didn't laugh. Marshall got up real slow, like an old man getting out of bed.

"Good shot," he said. "Where'd you learn that one?"

"Line up at the dance *barre*, please, gentlemen." She pointed at the banister on the field. "You will use that to steady yourselves as we go through the basic positions. Move it, gentlemen; we don't have all day. Sam? Music, please."

"Would you tell me what the hell is going on?" Tubby whispered to me.

"She knows judo, man," Marshall chuckled.

"Get me a coach. Just get me a coach," Buster whined.

We heard some music. Soft, summer music. There was a lot of violins and things, which made us nervous. If it had been country or rock or punk, that would've been OK, but this was fruit music.

"*Swan Lake*," Geoff Ringer said.

"First position, gentlemen," the lady called.

We stared at her. "What she say?" Buster asked.

"First position, gentlemen. Heels together, feet turned out to make a single straight line. Like this." She stood like she wanted us to.

"I've had two knee operations," I said. "I'm not getting into that." Everybody started grumbling.

The music stopped. The lady walked up and down in front of us.

"Gentlemen, I have been hired by Mr. Beaupray to condition your bodies and your minds for movement. Notice I did not say football. I said movement. Since football involves movement, I am sure you understand that by conditioning yourselves for dance, you will also condition yourselves for football." She stooped down and plucked a blade of grass and chewed on it while she talked.

"Gentlemen, we are here to build the foundation for the Chicago Bears football team. It takes years for a dancer to turn his body into an instrument that can express true grace. Years. We have only a few months. But in that time, I will do my best to mold your bodies into some sort of shape." She stopped for a minute. "I promise you this: If you will work with me, if you will do what I say, if you will follow my conditioning rules—and that includes rules for off the field as well as on—I will help you grow from a pedestrian and unimaginative football team into a troupe that is a reflection of the finest things on this earth."

"Say, lady, when do we get our real coach?" Marshall asked.

"Mr. Chambers, you will get your *real* coach when Mr. Beaupray decides, I suppose."

"OK," Marshall laughed.

"I will now show you the five fundamental positions as taught to all ballet students, gentlemen. We will do some warm-ups, some stretches, and then a little improvisation. First position, *comme ça*, do it along with me, please, gentlemen, and hold onto the *barre* if you must."

What can I tell you about that afternoon? She had us turning out our legs, stretching our hamstrings, pointing our toes, twinkling our feet. I hated fourth position *effacé* and I thought my knees would pop in fifth position. The *entrechat*, the *tour en l'air*, the *rond de jambe*—we did them all, and damned if she didn't talk us into some simple *pas de deux*. If you had come over the ridge and seen that football field while we was practicing, you'd've thought you was at a fat farm for idiots. There was guys lifting each other and prancing around and doing toework, and after a while we sort of got into it.

Marshall Chambers was probably the best dancer we had. He took to it like a duck to water. He did a great *changement de pieds*.

She had us do a final drill to close up the day. "Gentlemen," she said, "I want the entire team, one at a time, to move down the field single file. The music will be Tchaikovsky. I want to see you stretch yourselves, express yourselves, improvise. Just move as the music moves you. We'll start with you, Mr. Drombowski, and then the rest can follow. An interval of ten yards, please."

Well, it was a sight, all right. I still laugh when I think of it. There we was, supposedly tough as nails, the meanest and the greatest, the guys who everybody had made a fuss over since we was big enough to play pony ball, the studs who the cheerleaders loved to hug, the speed takers and beer drinkers and coke snorters, and what we looked like as we tried to dance to that music was something else. Lord, we was awkward.

We stumbled and jumped and tripped and fell and faked it, but the guys thought they was dancing up a storm. Junior Kirk started leaping all over the place like a castrated ape, bouncing into the dance *barre* and us and the lady, stinking up the field with his clumsiness, but believe it or not, she didn't care. She encouraged him. She ran right alongside him. "That's right, let yourself go, touch the sky, reach for it, use your body, feel it, every muscle, listen to your rhythms, let your body talk for once, don't worry, don't worry, you look fine!" Junior collapsed after about 60 yards of that shit, but he looked happy.

When the lady called us over to the bench for a final talk, she gave us a look that was laser:

"You may fancy that you are in good physical condition. Let me assure you that you are not. You may assume you understand movement. You know little of it. Flexibility? As we saw from the exercises I asked you to do, most of you could not touch the hem of Flexibility's garment. Endurance, timing, strength, perception, coordination? You show me few of those qualities. As of today, that changes. Life is a dance. Let us learn to dance." She paused. "Any questions?"

We was too tired to ask anything. We dragged ourselves off to the showers and dinner. Later that night, there was a lot of talk about the afternoon, but there was more talk about who the new coach would be. We had a betting pool on it.

"At ease, men, at ease," Mr. Beaupray smiled the next morning. He wore his usual suit and vest even in the hot weather. He was a tall man who looked like he combed his hair with money. He had steel-rimmed glasses and slicked-down hair and blue eyes and gray-blond eyebrows.

"Coldest fish in the ocean," Marshall whispered to me.

"And the richest," I whispered back.

"Men, I'm a man of few words, and as you know, I leave the coaching to the coaches. I'm proud to introduce your new coach this morning. Open the door, Sam," Mr. Beaupray said. Sam opened the door. In she walked, all gussied up in a suit, carrying a briefcase. Her nibs. The judo lady. The ballet bouncer. "Gentlemen, the new head coach of the Chicago Bears—Maria Dancing Bear."

I didn't know what to do. Neither did the rest of the team. Mr. Beaupray was clapping, and Sam was sort of clapping with him, but we was paralyzed. It was embarrassing. Mr. Beaupray made it worse by raising his hands before he spoke, as if there was something to silence.

"Coach Dancing Bear, it's an honor to welcome you aboard the Chicago Bears football team. I've watched you perform, read your fine book about dance, I've even worked out at your health spa in Arizona, and I am here to tell these men that you've changed my life, changed my perception of what constitutes exercise, diet, sportsmanship—even manhood. It is fitting that you already are our namesake. A Dancing Bear to coach the Chicago Bears." Mr. Beaupray applauded again, and we did, too, in sort of a half-assed way.

"Thank you," Maria Dancing Bear said. "Gentlemen, I'll see you on the practice field in half an hour. No pads. Any questions?"

Marshall jumped up, even though I was trying to hold him down. "Yeah, I got a question. What I want to know is, uh, what kind of offense will you put in?"

"It'll be primarily the same, Mr. Chambers, but you won't be allowed to scramble until you equalize your body," she said.

"Say what?"

"It became clear to me yesterday afternoon that you are overdeveloped on your right side and quite weak on your left. Therefore, as the films show, you're scrambling to your right ninety-three percent of the time, which gives the defense too much of an advantage. I expect you to work from the pocket until we get your body in shape, sir."

"Uh-huh," Marshall said, like he was shell-shocked.

"We're going to run the receivers a little deeper, split the zone, wear the defense out. We're going to move better than the other team and be in better shape than the other team."

"Uh-huh."

"You have a fine throwing arm, Mr. Chambers, but you're quite constricted in your neck and shoulders, and it takes you too long to see all your receivers. You're turning your entire body just to look from left to right. We'll be doing some exercises to improve that condition. Your stride has lost a foot in the past two years, if my measurements from the films are correct. You need a lot of stretching at the dance *barre* before you'll be allowed to do any more contact work. I don't think you throw to your tight ends enough; but then I don't think your tight ends are limber enough to get open when they should. It's not the choice of formation that matters, if you follow me. It's the grace with which that formation is executed."

"Uh-huh."

Marshall sat down very slowly, like he had just seen his own funeral.

"Any other questions?" Mr. Beaupray laughed. "No? Again, welcome aboard, Coach Dancing Bear." He shook her hand and left the locker room. Sam followed. Then Coach Dancing Bear.

"Coach Dancing Bear?" Marshall whooped when the doors closed.

"I can't do it!" Buster Slade yelled.

"A woman?" Tubby Reardon hit his locker. "A goddamn woman! I never let a woman tell me a goddamn thing all my life."

"How's she going to know the first thing?" Buster asked.

"Come on, boys," Marshall said, "we could do worse. Let's go out there and point our pretty little toes."

Tubby and Buster stayed inside for the morning. I guess it was a protest on their part, but Coach Dancing Bear didn't even ask about them. She just got down to the nitty-gritty.

I'll tell you something: I'd trade 16 of Red Emerson's practices to one of Coach Dancing Bear's. That's the truth. Red could make us sweat and bleed, but Maria Dancing Bear damned near made us die. I never knew how maximum hard it is to dance right. But by the end of the summer, I was in better shape than I ever was before. I could just feel it. I was slimmer but stronger, and I'd adjusted to Coach Dancing Bear's new diet: corn on corn on corn, grains and fruits and nuts and herb teas and wholewheat bread and nibbles but no gorging. "Losing weight is like losing poison for a healthy person," Coach Dancing Bear preached at us.

Pre-season went OK. We was rusty. She was just getting the hang of it. We got a lot of delay-of-game penalties and shit like that. We warmed up to *Swan Lake* before the games, and that got a lot of laughs, but we didn't care. We got to dance with the Honey Bears in the warm-ups. Most of them had taken a lot of ballet. They was good dancers, and they helped us. It's a hell of a lot more fun to warm up with a beautiful woman than to have some asshole teammate breathing snuff on you and hitting your shoulder pads.

When the season started for real, we was running the same plays as usual, nothing fancy, but we was running them better. I was hitting crisper, cleaner, faster. The defense could move like smoke in the wind. And the offense was like a perpetual-motion machine. They scored and scored. Marshall was throwing long and short, in and out, bullets and balloons.

We could run most of the other teams into the ground. We didn't have many injuries and we didn't need time outs to catch our breath. So what if the fans thought we looked like fruitcakes when we warmed up? So what if they wanted the Honey Bears out of their leotards and back in their skimpy suits? And who gave a damn that a long, tall American Indian princess was coaching us? We got the job done, didn't we?

We won our first five games. The fans in Soldier Field started to cheer us more than they booed us. That was a first. The city of Chicago began to take us for real. But we knew the acid test was just ahead. We had to beat the Dallas Cowboys to prove ourselves, and we hadn't done that for a very long time.

Now, I work on the belief that Dallas does not have football players on its team. It has replicants dressed up like football players. They run on microchips. They eat silicon for breakfast. They get produced in a secret factory near the King Ranch and they get shipped into Dallas by truck. There's a big warehouse somewhere in that city with trunkfuls of replicants waiting to get wound up and sent out to play football for the Cowboys. Just thinking about playing Dallas put me in the middle of a dark place, I can tell you. I was even thinking about eating a lot of junk food and tanking up on beer and going back to free weights and bulk. I looked at the Dallas films and I wanted to tell Coach Dancing Bear that we was going to get waltzed right out of the stadium if we didn't go back to our old ways in a hurry.

When I get depressed, I tend not to notice things, and I guess I was thinking too much about the Dallas game. That's why I didn't see the headphones in my helmet when I put it on for Monday's practice. Then Sam came up to me. "Dewey," he said, "you want to hook up, please?"

"Say what, Sam?"

"Hook up, Dewey." He handed me a cable running from the back of my pants. He fed it up under my shoulder pads and connected it to the back of my helmet.

Lord, it was gorgeous. The music poured over me. I just stood there for a minute. Sam was grinning at me. Then I took my helmet off. Sure enough, there was a set of headphones inside. And the cable led down to a cassette player that had been built into my hip pads. Sam showed me how to turn it on and off by flipping the switch.

"Goddamn, Sam," I said, "this is far out. Are all the Bears wearing these here things today?"

"You bet, Dewey."

Well, that was the week that was, if you know what I mean. Coach Dancing Bear had gone and put headphones into our helmets and cassette players into our pants, and we got choreographed more than we got coached, let me tell you. We learned to synchronize the tapes, to run plays to music, to trap and block and tackle and run and catch to Bizet and Bach and Mozart and all them fellows. It was like we had cranked the game up to another level. We ran sweeps to Strauss, off-tackle plunges to Prokofiev, pass plays to Brahms. Kickoffs were by Bartók, because Milos Nagy, our Hungarian kicker, liked him best, but I'm here to tell you that Bartók is not easy to play to. I was on the suicide squad a few times, and Bartók messed me up with all his funny rhythms. We got a lot of off-side penalties to Bartók. We worked with Copland and Stravinsky and Webern and, every once in a while, if we was way ahead, Debussy.

There were some problems, of course. On the day we first played the Cowboys and they realized what we was up to, they got their lawyers to call the commissioner of the N.F.L. and argue we was breaking the rules with our headsets. What rules? Every jogger in the world wears headphones these days. Why not football players? We weren't in radio communication with each other or nothing. The commissioner didn't bite. He let us play like we'd been practicing.

Technically, we smoothed out the kinks and didn't have too much trouble. If a cassette got busted in a collision, it was easy to replace. Same with the headphones. Once in a while, a tape would jam or speed up; but, hell, you could spot the person with that problem: He'd be out of sync.

What we had, good buddies, was a team that was coordinated down to the last eighth note. And that's why we beat the Cowboys the first time. We were precise, if you know what I mean.

After we beat the Cowboys 21-17, we went on to beat the Vikings, the Cardinals, the Giants, the 49ers, the Lions, the Eagles and the Packers and the Vikings again. We got into the play-offs for the Super Bowl, Super Bowl XX. And, yes, we found ourselves playing the Dallas Cowboys in the semifinals, and this time, it was in *their* stadium.

We flew down to the heart of Texas. I thought we had it made. I said as much when I talked to Howard Cosell on the day of the game. "We beat them once and we can do it again," I said. Howard allowed as how that was a perspicacious contention that he hoped would manifest itself in the turbulence we were about to witness. "What are you talking about, Howard?" I asked him, but they had to break for a commercial and I never did get an answer.

Then again, I forgot all about Howard Cosell right about that moment, because the Cowboys came onto the field for their first warm-ups, and I thought I was going to die. I swear my heart stopped. Because they didn't have no supercool coaches leading them. No, sir. And they didn't have no mascot, nobody dressed up like a cowboy, no cheerleader or oil baron. What they did have was the stadium-loud-speakers blaring the music from Jerome Robbins' ballet *The Four Seasons*. And standing there behind the goal post, poised and pretty, almost naked in a grape-colored tunic, was somebody we all recognized by then: Mikhail Baryshnikov.

"Oh, shit," I said. "Them copycats done stole our idea."

Yes, sir, we might have done our warm-ups to *Swan Lake,* but Baryshnikov led the Cowboys out into Texas Stadium to do a much more complicated and tough piece of work. I never saw anything like it before, and I knew then that us Chicago Bears was going to have a long afternoon. The Cowboys was fighting fire with fire.

I have the warm-up on video tape. I run it back once in a while when it's the middle of winter and I'm snowed in here and there's nothing to do but remember. Baryshnikov was dressed as Bacchus, and the Cowboys did a frenzied orgy kind of thing with the cheerleaders while he made moves that took the guts of a stunt man and the grace of a god. He did leaps and turns and grand pirouettes until I got dizzy, grand pirouettes with his knee bent at every angle and with *sautés* on his working leg. Sometimes he would stop in the middle of a pirouette, just hold it *à la seconde,* then go on spinning like a top. And the Cowboys was not doing a bad job of following him with the same goddamn moves. Tony Dorsett looked like Baryshnikov's shadow sometimes, I'll tell you.

Us Bears just stood and watched. Most of us was thinking about the Super Bowl ring we would never wear. It was just like them Cowboys to outdo and outspend us.

After warm-ups, we went back into the locker room to pout, but damned if Coach Dancing Bear wasn't smiling the biggest smile I ever saw. "Wasn't Baryshnikov terrific?" she grinned.

"Yeah," we all kind of grumbled.

"We've changed the game of football, gentlemen."

Credit to Marshall. He's the one who called her on her happiness. "So what, Coach?" Marshall stood up. "We're going to lose, probably. They got the best dancer in the world coaching them, all due respect. They got the bodies, they got the skills. They took our idea, and they'll run with it."

"Marshall, let me ask you a question: So what?"

Of course, Marshall didn't know what to do with that one, so he just sort of blinked and looked around for help. "Ma'am?" he asked.

"You say we'll probably lose this game. So what?"

"So we don't get to the Super Bowl. So we don't get the bread and the glory. You think I'm in this for the fun of it, Coach?"

"I think that's the only reason to be anywhere, Marshall." Coach Dancing Bear stared at him for a long time. It was real quiet. "I think you men saw this game of football grow to be fun again. Am I right? Well, why should that stop now? Because you're going to lose, perhaps? The score will take care of itself. You're going to be so interested in the movement of the game that you're not going to know the score." She paused. "Now get your bones out there and give us a game!"

Some people say it was the best game of football they ever saw, because both teams was in such good shape and had such coordination. And it wasn't a mean game. It is impossible to be really mean when you're surrounded by beautiful music and when you respect the human body. And the way Coach Dancing Bear had taught us, we did respect the other fellow, no matter the team he was on. There was no late hits, no spikes, no blind-side blocks, no head slaps. The game flowed like a dance, which is what it was.

I admired the way the players moved and the cheerleaders danced and the referees floated through us, and damned if I didn't start to admire the movement in the crowd—the way a mother would tuck a baby on her hip while she walked up the stadium steps, the way a father would hug a son after a good play, the way the disabled vet by the oxygen tanks could wheel himself in pirouettes of his own making.

I grew a century in understanding in those few hours, and what I'll never forget is that I felt OK even while losing. I can honestly say that it was the game that mattered, not the score.

After we lost and we was all shaking hands and things, I suddenly realized that I was through with football, that I'd had it as good as it would ever get.

"I'm hanging it up," I told Coach Dancing Bear in the locker room.

"I may do that, too, Dewey," she smiled.

"I'm going back to the farm and fit into the dance," I said.

"Sounds good to me," she said.

"Every damn N.F.L. team will have a ballet coach next year," I said.

"Probably."

"They'll be doing TV commercials for credit cards and beer. Geoff will write a book about the season and go on tour with it. Marshall will cut an album. Do I need that? I just had the best afternoon of my life, Coach, and I don't need to ruin it."

This was after all the press interviews and confusion, but it was still noisy in the locker room. The guys wasn't hanging their heads. What the hell; we'd played like champions, and to ourselves, we *was* champions. The game was something we'd be proud to tell our kids about.

I hung around after my shower, after the locker room thinned out and nobody was left but Sam. I'd shaken hands with everybody and we'd all lied about how we'd keep in touch, about how we'd have a reunion of the Bears team that *almost* went to the Super Bowl. "'Bye," I said to my gear. I confess I did take my helmet with me. I packed my ditty bag and walked out the door and came back here to Paris.

My dad and I farm 750 acres under contract. We raise corn and soybeans. DeeAnn, my wife now, has kept her job at the hospital, so we're staying alive.

Every once in a while, when nobody's looking, I climb to the top of the old windmill by the horse barn. I just hang there, listening to the wind, surveying the countryside. Sometimes I put on my old Bears helmet and crank up the cassette and listen to Mozart or Bach or Beethoven.

Life is a dance? You bet your booties it is.

While few of us have played pro or college football, nearly all have enjoyed a game of flag or touch. It's a great way to stay fit and have fun. Here's a story that celebrates "non-contact" touch football. It's lighthearted but has a serious side too. Author Gene Williams has written several stories for The New Yorker, *where this little gem is from.*

Gene Williams

STICKY MY FINGERS, FLEET MY FEET (1965)

"**W**ILL YOU EVER MATURE?" my wife asked.

"I'm a *very* mature pass receiver," I said, lacing my sneakers. "Ask anybody who's tried to cover me."

She groaned and went back to Walter Lippmann. Nobody could want more in a wife; Marian is beautiful, witty, charming, and not a graduate of Sarah Lawrence. But touch football is over her head.

"Baby, exercise is a health-must," I said patiently. "Don't you realize guys die from vegetating?"

"I do the Canadian things and yoga and isometrics, so don't call me pro-vegetation. I'm tired all the time!" She was sort of screaming. Her nerves have really gone downhill since we married. "It's your attitude that bothers me. Play football—fine. Wonderful. But to keep a record of *every* pass you catch, *every* touchdown you score, *every*—"

"Now, you know the notebook is only a joke."

"It's a farce, but it's no joke! My God, if Erich Fromm saw one page of that thing—"

I muffled the rest of her words by putting on my sweatshirt as I went out the door. Outside, it was a clear, bright morning—perfect weather for spectacular pass-snatching. Early practice is very important. Championships that bloom in December are planted in September. Turning into the Park at Seventy-second Street, I trotted through the herds of old people who are pastured on the West Side. They really knock me out, because Allie Sherman and I dig resignation. As my sneakers padded lightly on the walk, pre-game excitement got to my ulcer. (Shofner has one, too.)

We use that shabby open stretch that runs from the high to the low Sixties, and the guys were already there. They'd marked off our field with a pile of sweaters, trash baskets, and an Air France bag. Seeing me, Marv called, "There's the sticky-fingered antelope! You ready to grab a few, Norm?"

"Always ready," I said. Marv works for Port Authority and has a fine arm. We hit for six or seven bombs a week.

I traded insults with the rest of the guys. All of them were veterans of our weekly games, except for one rookie—a scrawny kid of about fifteen, wearing a green sweater. Its cuffs hid his knuckles. George Crimblings, a blocking back from J. Walter Thompson, introduced us. "This is Wesley, my nephew," he said. "I thought we might lose some dilettantes to softball, so I brought him out."

"Glad to know you, sir," Wesley said. I looked at him but he meant it. Rookies call Mike Ditka "sir," too.

George and I chose up. I took Marv, of course, and George was stuck with Wesley after all the others had been picked. Letting them receive, we all spread out as Marv put the ball on the kicking tee. My ulcer was begging for Maalox, but I didn't even wince, because Ray Berry and I dig pressure. When the going gets rough, the rough get going. Marv raised his arm, brought it down, took two steps toward the ball, stopped, and said, "Hell." A two-year-old boy had wandered onto the field.

"For God's sakes, get him out of here!" I yelled.

"Urry gurry burry," the kid answered, picking the ball off the tee. When we surrounded him, he lay, down, hugging the ball, and started to cry. The sound brought his mother.

"Did you hit him?" she demanded.

"Make him give us our ball," I said.

Holding him while we pried the ball loose, she said, "Lester, be nice, and return the children's toy."

Finally, we lined up again, and Marv got off the kick. Unfortunately, it went to Harry Gratzwald, who is fat, slow, awkward, and more feared than Jimmy Brown. I touched him, Jacob touched him, Marv touched him, *everybody* touched him, but he kept running. "We got you back here!" I called.

"No, you didn't," Harry answered and went all the way before coming back to argue. He is a lawyer. "You only got me one hand at a time and you have to get me both hands together or it's not a legal touch, and Jacob was offside and Marv was holding and . . ." We kicked again.

The show finally on the road, Marv and I dropped back in our special two-man rolling zone. I'm sensational on defense, even though my real gifts are offensive. Jacob was slapping our linemen on the tail, saying, "Big rush now! Really crash in there. Break their bones." Analysts make great line-backers. On the first play, he red-dogged and nailed them right in the middle of a triple reverse.

"Way to go, Jake baby?" I said. "Be manic."

They gained four inches on an end-around and then threw a button-hook to Harry, who was wide open. He dropped the ball and yelled, "Interference!"

"Nobody was within ten yards of you," I said.

We gave them the down over, and they tried a flare pass that Jacob intercepted. The ball was ours and glory would be mine. In the huddle, Marv said, "O.K., men. Norm, run a down-and-out to the pile of sweaters; Jack, cut to the Air France bag. On two—*break*!"

I flanked to the left and found George on me. There was fear in his ad man's eyes. I gave him the big inside move and cut to the sweaters. Marv led me nicely, and it was a thirty-yard again. On the next two plays, we ran sweeps while I lulled George with the same pattern.

"He's ripe," I said.

"Right. Long bomb to the trash basket," Marv said.

I glided out at three-quarter speed, head-faked, and broke deep. George never had a chance. Crossing the goal, I looked toward the Fifth Avenue buildings that rose above the trees. People with binoculars were probably crowding the windows. The team pounded my back. I shrugged and said, "Just lucky."

"Looks like it's your day," Marv said, and it was. Buttonhooks, slant-ins, down-and-outs—I murdered them. Finally, they really got desperate, and I flanked out to find Wesley on me. I gave him a friendly nod to show I'd go easy on him. Real pros win without shaming their opponents; always leave a guy part of his ego or he gets tougher defensively. I faked to the sideline and hooked back.

"Good fake, sir," Wesley said, after knocking the ball down.

In the huddle, Marv said, "He looks tough."

"Forget it, he's playing me much too tight. Anything deep will kill him."

This time, I gave Wesley the works—head fake, full pivot, innocent smile—and streaked downfield. I tagged him the minute he made the interception.

"My fault for not slanting in more," I lied to Marv.

"No, it was mine for not throwing sooner," he said truthfully.

As a reward for this lucky play, they shifted Wesley to tailback. He waited for the snap from center, hauling at his sleeves to make his hands visible. The play was an easy end sweep and our linemen trapped him on the sideline, but he cut back toward his own goal, and the chase was on. It lasted a long, long time. Eventually, I collapsed beside Jacob, who was kneading a stitch in his side. We watched Wesley skitter. Finally, the whole team was too tired to chase him anymore, and he jogged over the goal unpursued. His teammates pounded his back. Wesley shrugged and said, "Just lucky." If there's anything I hate, it's phony modesty.

That play took the heart (and wind) out of everybody on our team except me. Jacob stood around rationalizing, and Marv's passing became hysterical; everything he threw to me Wesley intercepted or knocked down. We fell behind. I kept my cool, though. As Vince Lombardi says, it's last-quarter teams that win championships. One big play could salvage the game. After Wesley ran back a punt for his sixth touchdown, he made his mistake—leaving me alone on two straight plays while he covered somebody else.

"He's ripe," I said.

"For what—the Hall of Fame?" Marv said. Still, he called my big tide-turner—a delayed bomb to the trash basket. Hesitating at the line, I studied my nails and faked tying my shoelace until Wesley broke toward the middle zone. Then I streaked downfield. Nobody was near me, and the pass was perfect. The pros' pro, old Stickyfingers, was in the clear! But I must have expected the flash of his green sweater in front of me, because the ball somehow ricocheted off my chest. It bounced to a stop about five yards away just as I jackknifed into the trash basket.

There was laughter from both teams. It didn't surprise me. The world is full of fair-weather hypocrites. I didn't lose my poise, though, even while peeling a Mounds wrapper from my forehead. Unfortunately it did hurt my credibility as a receiver. Marv started throwing to others and calling clown plays for me, like "O.K., Norm, go deep to the zoo and fall in the sea-lion pool." Also I'd pulled a muscle in my leg.

The game broke up a while later, and Marv, the treacherous bastard, said to the kid, "Come out next week. I'd like to have you on my squad. We'd make a great combination." He shook his head in admiration. "You must run wild on your high-school team."

"Not hardly, sir," Wesley said, "I'm the manager."

The trip home was a limping retreat from Caporetto—only with fewer laughs. I'm no fool. You don't have to draw me a picture. Football belongs to the young, and I'm only a memory, like Jim Thorpe, Mel Hein, Otto Graham, and the rest. Around me, other old people sat on benches, waiting to die a little deader. A horse galloped along the bridle path on his way into a tube of glue or can of dog food. I knew it was over. Jack Armstrong, fat and getting bald, sat behind a desk waiting for a coronary; the Mounties had retired Sergeant Preston. Britt Reid and Kato, Lamont

Cranston and the lovely Margo Lane—gone, all gone. Soon dirt would be shovelled in my face while the choir sang "Have you tried Wheaties?" in dirge tempo.

Climbing the stairs, I rested often, because of my leg and Marian. I was right. "Oh, God, this is exactly what I need—an immature cripple!" she yelled. "Is anything broken?"

"Nothing that would show on an X-ray. I'm washed up, baby." I picked up my notebook, heavy with touchdowns, yardage, and dreams, and threw it with all my elderly strength. It didn't even break anything.

"*That* was a healthy thing to do," Marian said.

She went into the bathroom, and there was the sound of water flooding into the tub. I sat and massaged my ruined thigh; they should give Purple Hearts just for living. Then she practically dragged me from the living room and stuffed me into the hot water. I complained.

"Shut up and *soak!* I've about had it with you!" For a while, she just glared at me, with her teeth pretty well gritted. Then she sighed and said, "Nobody is in your class for immaturity. There you sit with your leg and ego crippled because of football—*you*, the best tennis player in the West Seventies."

"That's not true," I said. "You're just cheering me up."

It *is* true, but you won't admit it. Your ground strokes are unbelievable." Her voice was much softer.

"That's not altogether true."

"Why do I try? You have no sense of proportion. Nobody else would waste that tennis leanness on body contact."

She left me, and I eased lower in the water. Marian was vicious but astute; football *is* immature. It belongs to kids like Wesley and would-be kids like Marv, Harry, and Jacob, who want to hide from adult responsibilities. They can't, though. A man grows up and stays grown; he can't go home again. My leg wasn't hurting quite so much, and I tried a few backhands with the soap. Rosewall uses the Continental grip, too.

This is more than a story, as John Updike's poignantly lovely word pictures take on a kind of lyrical magic. A Friday night high school football game, in an age of innocence, powerfully evokes the wonderment of youth in small-town America. There is no game action, just the feelings of being there and what they mean to the narrator. This is Updike at his best, suggestive of his rank as the nation's leading literary figure. He has written over forty books and scores of short stories, poems, and critiques. Updike's book Rabbit is Rich *(1981) won the Pulitzer Prize, and* Rabbit At Rest *(1990) won the Howells Medal. He has also been honored with the National Book Award and the American Book Award. Updike's short stories regularly appear in the* New Yorker, *where this story is from, and he has also written for* Harper's, Esquire, *and* Playboy.

John Updike

IN FOOTBALL SEASON (1962)

DO YOU REMEMBER A FRAGRANCE girls acquire in autumn? As you walk beside them after school, they tighten their arms about their books and bend their heads forward to give a more flattering attention to your words, and in the little intimate area thus formed, carved into the clear air by an implicit crescent, there is a complex fragrance woven of tobacco, powder, lipstick, rinsed hair, and that perhaps imaginary and certainly elusive scent that wool, whether in the lapels of a jacket or the nap of a sweater, seems to yield when the cloudless fall sky like the blue bell of a vacuum lifts toward itself the glad exhalations of all things. This fragrance, so faint and flirtatious on those afternoon walks through the dry leaves, would be banked a thousandfold and lie heavy as the perfume of a flower shop on the dark slope of the stadium when, Friday nights, we played football in the city.

"We"—we the school. A suburban school, we rented for some of our home games the stadium of a college in the city of Alton three miles away. My father, a teacher, was active in the Olinger High athletic department, and I, waiting for him beside half-open doors of varnished wood and frosted glass, overheard arguments and felt the wind of the worries that accompanied this bold and at that time unprecedented decision. Later, many of the other county high schools followed our lead; for the decision was vindicated. The stadium each Friday night when we played was filled. Not only students and parents came but spectators unconnected with either school, and the money left over when the stadium rent was paid supported our entire athletic program. I remember the smell of the grass crushed by footsteps behind the end zones. The smell was more vivid than that of a meadow, and in the blue electric glare the green vibrated as if excited, like a child, by being allowed up late. I remember my father taking tickets at the far corner of the wall, wedged into a tiny wooden booth that made him seem somewhat magical, like a troll. And of course I remember the way we, the students, with all of our jealousies and antipathies and deformities, would be—beauty and boob, sexpot and grind—crushed together like flowers pressed to yield to the black sky a concentrated homage, an incense, of cosmetics, cigarette smoke, warmed wool, hot dogs, and the tang, both animal and metallic, of clean hair. In a hoarse olfactory shout, these odors ascended. A dense haze gathered along the ceiling of brightness at the upper limit of the arc lights, whose glare blotted out the stars and made the sky seem romantically void and intimately near, like the death that now and then stooped and plucked one of us out of a crumpled automobile. If we went to the back row and stood on the bench there, we could look over the stone lip of the stadium down into the houses of the city, and feel the cold November air like the black presence of the ocean beyond the rail of a ship; and when we left after the game and from the hushed residential streets of this part of the city saw behind us a great vessel steaming with light, the arches of the colonnades blazing like portholes, the stadium seemed a great ship sinking and we the survivors of a celebrated disaster.

To keep our courage up, we sang songs, usually the same song, the one whose primal verse runs,

> *Oh, you can't get to Heaven*
>   *(Oh, you can't get to Heaven)*
> *In a rocking chair,*
>   *(In a rocking chair)*
> *'Cause the Lord don't want*
>   *('Cause the Lord don't want)*
> *No lazy people there!*
>   *(No lazy people there!)*

And then repeated, double time. It was a song for eternity; when we ran out of verses, I would make them up:

> *Oh, you can't get to Heaven*
>   *(Oh, you can't get to Heaven)*
> *In Smokey's Ford*
>   *(In Smokey's Ford)*
> *'Cause the cylinders*
>   *('Cause the cylinders)*
> *Have to be rebored.*
>   *(Have to be rebored.)*

Down through the nice residential section, on through the not-so-nice and the shopping district, past dark churches where stained-glass windows, facing inward, warned us with left-handed blessings, down Buchanan Street to the Running Horse Bridge, across the bridge, and two miles out the pike we walked. My invention would become reckless:

> *Oh, you can't get to Heaven*
>   *(Oh, you can't get to Heaven)*

In a motel bed
  (In a motel bed)
'Cause the sky is blue
  ('Cause the sky is blue)
And the sheets are red.
  (And the sheets are red.)

Few of us had a license to drive and fewer still had visited a motel. We were at that innocent age, on the borderline of sixteen, when damnation seems a delicious promise. There was Mary Louise Hornberger, who was tall and held herself with such upright and defiant poise that she was Mother in both our class plays, and Alma Bidding, with her hook nose and her smug smile caricatured in cerise lipstick, and Joanne Hardt, whose father was a typesetter, and Marilyn Wenrich, who had a gray front tooth and in study hall liked to have the small of her back scratched, and Nanette Seifert, with her button nose and black wet eyes and peach-down cheeks framed in the white fur frilling the blue hood of her parka. And there were boys, Henny Gring, Leo Horst, Hawley Peters, Jack Lillijedahl, myself. Sometimes these, sometimes less or more. Once there was Billy Trupp on crutches. Billy played football and, though only a sophomore, had made the varsity that year, until he broke his ankle. He was dull and dogged and liked Alma, and she with her painted smile led him on lovingly. We offered for his sake to take the trolley, but he had already refused a car ride back to Olinger, and obstinately walked with us, loping his heavy body along on the crutches, his lifted foot a boulder of plaster. His heroism infected us all; we taunted the cold stars with song, one mile, two miles, three miles. How slowly we went! With what a luxurious sense of waste did we abuse this stretch of time! For as children we had lived in a tight world of ticking clocks and punctual bells, where every minute was an admonition to thrift and where tardiness, to a child running late down a street with his panicked stomach burning, seemed the most mysterious and awful of sins. Now, turning the corner into adulthood, we found time to be instead a black immensity endlessly supplied, like the wind.

We would arrive in Olinger after the drugstores, which had kept open for the first waves of people returning from the game, were shut. Except for the street lights, the town was dark like a town in a fable. We scattered, each escorting a girl to her door; and there, perhaps, for a moment, you bowed your face into that silent crescent of fragrance, and tasted it, and let it bite into you indelibly. The other day, in a town far from Olinger, I passed on the sidewalk two girls utterly unknown to me and half my age, and sensed, very faintly, that flavor from far-off carried in their bent arms like a bouquet. And I seemed, continuing to walk, to sink into a chasm deeper than the one inverted above us on those Friday nights during football season.

For after seeing the girl home, I would stride through the hushed streets, where the rustling leaves seemed torn scraps scattered in the wake of the game, and go to Mr. Lloyd Stephens' house. There, looking in the little square window of his front storm door, I could see down a dark hall into the lit kitchen where Mr. Stephens and my father and Mr. Jesse Honneger were counting money around a worn porcelain table. Stephens, a local contractor, was the school-board treasurer, and Honneger, who taught social science, the chairman of the high-school athletic department. They were still counting; the silver stacks slipped and glinted among their fingers and the gold of beer stood in cylinders beside their hairy wrists. Their sleeves were rolled up and smoke like a fourth presence, wings spread, hung over their heads. They were still counting, so it was all right. I was not late. We lived ten miles away, and I could not go home until my father was ready. Some nights it took until midnight. I would knock and pull open the storm door and push open the real door and it would be warm in the contractor's hall. I would accept a glass of ginger ale and sit in the kitchen with the men until they were done. It was late, very late, but I was not blamed; it was permitted. Silently counting and expertly tamping the coins into little cylindrical wrappers of colored paper, the men ordered and consecrated this realm of night into which my days had never extended before. The hour or more behind me, which I had spent so wastefully, in walking when a trolley would have been swifter, and so wickedly, in blasphemy and lust, was past and forgiven me; it had been necessary; it was permitted.

Now I peek into windows and open doors and do not find that air of permission. It has fled the world. Girls walk by me carrying their invisible bouquets from fields still steeped in grace, and I look up in the manner of one who follows with his eyes the passage of a hearse, and remembers what pierces him.

Frank Deford treats the reader to a humorous spoof on the most popular live and televised event in America: the Super Bowl. The scene is the actual 1977 game between the Oakland Raiders and Minnesota Vikings (won by the Raiders), but the happy hysteria he depicts is completely fictional. The story originally appeared in Sports Illustrated. *On SI's staff for many years, Deford was widely held to be the best sportswriter in the country. During this time he also wrote books on tennis with Arthur Ashe, Billie Jean King, Jack Kramer, and Pam Shriver. Many of his stories are collected in* The World's Tallest Midget: The Best of Frank Deford *(1987).* Readers of Baseball's Best Short Stories *will remember his classic tale of "Casey at the Bat," written in 1988. Deford's versatility as a writer is reflected in his nonsports books,* There She Is: The Life and Times of Miss America *(1971), and* Love and Infamy *(1993). He is a commentator for National Public Radio, and returned to SI as a correspondent in 1998.*

Frank Deford

SOOPER DOOPER (1978)

HELLO, THIS IS CHERYL, may I help you?"

"Yeah, Cheryl, I have a message to call Operator 6 in Amarillo, Texas."

"You can dial that direct, sir."

"No, Cheryl, I don' think you unnerstan' me. I'm in a motel."

"Yes, sir. I know. Just dial eight, and then zero, the call-back area code and number, and an operator will come on the line."

"Is that a fact? I didn't know you could do that in a motel. Thank you now, Cheryl. . . ."

"Hello, this is Jessie. May I help you?"

" 'Deed you can, Jessie. I'm tryin' to git aholt of Operator 6 in Amarillo."

"This is Operator 6."

"Son of a buck. Now ain't that a coincidence? All the operators in the Lone Star State, and I get right on through to you."

"Uh, yes, sir. And who is your call-back party?"

"Mah what-all?"

"Who are you trying to reach, sir?"

"Why, Herb Wiley. Mah boss over in Mesquite Creek. You unnerstan' now—it's him tryin' to git me."

"Yes, sir."

"Mesquite Creek *Globe-Express,* good afternoon."

"This is Los Angeles, and I have a WH on the line for Mr. Wiley. And your name, sir?"

"I'm Punch Zimmer."

"Hey, Punch! Hey, how's old Ellay? It's me, Doreen."

"Hey, Doreen, is Herb around?"

"Sir, ma'am please. This call is for Mr. Herb Wiley."

"Well, operator, you tell Mr. Bigtime Punch, Mr. Super Bowl Hotshot, that Herb's in the little boys' room right now."

"Shoot, Doreen, he's rilly been tryin' to git aholt of me."

"Well, uh, ma'am, we can hold for one minute."

"Hang on, operator. I see him goin' over by Emil now. Herb! Herb! Punch is callin' from Ellay. . . . He's comin', Punch."

"Mr. Herb Wiley?"

"You bet."

"I have your call-back party from Los Angeles. Will you accept?"

"You bet."

"Hey, Punch, what's up? Here I go sendin' you off to the Super Bowl— the first reporter from the Panhandle ever to git within spittin' distance of the big time—and here it is Tuesday, two whole days later, and we ain't heard one word outta you."

"Herb, I was jes' now gonna phone in mah early prediction story to Emil."

"I ain't jes' talkin' 'bout your ole story, Punch. I mean, you could have called us—collect, o'course—jes' to let us know how-all it's a-goin'. God-*dam*, it must be some excitin', right, ole buddy?"

"Well, Herb, I, uh. . . ."

"You bet. The greatest, most thrillin' single e-vent in the whole wide world of sports. Bar none! It must rilly be sumpin'. Right, Punch?"

"Fact is, Herb, uh, it's uh. . . ."

"What-all is this. Punch? You ain't tellin' me one word 'bout how tee-riffic it all is."

"Well, now, Herb, I don't know real well how to let on to this, but the truth is, Super Bowl Week's 'bout the most borin'est, the most blowed-up, the most stupid. . . ."

"Punch, Punch! Hush up! Doreen, are you still on this here line?"

"I'm jes' now hangin' up, Herb."

"Hold on there, boy. That's all we need—ole Doreen goin' round tellin' every soul in the county that mah sports staff don' like the Super Bowl. You plumb crazy, Punch? You been drinkin' too many of them sissy California drinks, where they stick Morton's salt up alongside the rim?"

"Well, it's a damn nothin', Herb. It's all hokey, it ain't got nothin' to do with sports, let alone the gridiron, and. . . ."

"Punch, Punch Zimmer! You gone be committed, you talkin' so foolish. Why, all the nationally known fellas I'm a-watchin' on NBC, they tell me the Super Bowl's 'bout the next best thing to heaven. And CBS allows that only heaven and last year's Super Bowl beats it. Now, Punch, who am I gonna b'lieve: ole Punch Zimmer from Mesquite Creek, or NBC and CBS? Hmmm?"

"Flat-out, Herb, I'd b'lieve me. 'Cause I ain't sellin' no commercials. And I ain't no regular NFL writer, shillin' for the league callin' it a 'show-case.' I give you a little hint, Herb: anytime you hear a fella say this here is a showcase, that is one sure sign you have got yourself a shill."

"But Punch, jes' ever'body says it's a showcase. If it ain't a showcase, what is it?"

"Well, I guarantee you it ain't no football game. You and me seen football games all over the Panhandle and as far away as Waco, and this sure ain't no game. This here is one big ole commercial that runs for a week, with a football game chucked in at the end. And excitin'? I seen more interest generated in a pinball game down at Skeeter's Starlight Lounge than for what-all Ellay cares. They might as well be playin' this game on the moon."

"Punch Zimmer, you stop with that subversive talk. Why, it says right here in the wire service that, quote, interest is at an all time high, unquote, and Vikki Carr herself gonna sing *America the Beautiful.* And then you come on the phone tellin' me stories that it ain't a showcase."

"You know, Herb, maybe I ain't on no first-name basis with the players, maybe I ain't never been to no Indonesia to see Muhammad Ali fight, maybe I only got the one off-cream leisure suit to mah name, but I can spot me a phony. This ain't no Super Bowl; this is a supermarket."

"Well, damn you, Punch, you keep these anti-'Merican thoughts to yourself, you hear me? And what do you know about traditional classic American e-vents, anyhow?"

"All right, I'll tell you one thing. When I was in the service up in Fort Knox, a spec-four in armor, I seen me two Kentucky Derbies, and also one year a bunch of us went up to Indy and seen that, too. And when I got released, 'fore I came back home, I went over to see mah cousin Ralph who lives in Greater Pittsburgh, P.A., and it was when the Pirates was playin' the O-ree-oles in the World Series; so no, I ain't no virgin in these exact matters. And lemme tell you, Herb Wiley, the Derby and Indy and the World Series is altogether diffrunt from this here showcase. Them other things was fun and there was real folks. And you know whatall, Herb? They had charm. And you're sayin' to yourself, what does ole Punch Zimmer know about charm from a carburetor, and I'll jes' tell you flat-out that if sumpin' ain't got no charm, then all of a sudden you know what charm is. And that's a fact, Herb."

"Well now, Punch, don't git me wrong. It's the 'Merican way to let a man holt a diffrunt opinion."

"Shoot, Herb. Ain't nobody even talks about the game here. All you hear is how much money it's a-goin' to pump into the local e-conomy, like it was some kind of new shoe factory comin' to town.

"I was down in the press room yestiddy, pickin' up the press releases they churn out ever' few minutes, and I started talkin' to this bigshot reporter from New York City, and he says, must be your first Super Bowl, and I says, yes, it sure is, and he says, it is sure one large slice of 'Mericana. And I says, well, this sure ain't no 'Mericana I ever seen. This here is only Hollywood and Madison Avenue thrown together.

"And he says, well it sure-all beats the World Series, don't it, 'cause, he says, he has to go to places like Cincinnati to see it. And he says, they are sure takin' the World Series away from Joe Fan, 'cause they play the games at night when it is a little cool and inconvenient for his deadline. And I says, it seems to me to play the games at Cincinnati at night is just about perfect for the workin' man in Cincinnati. And he says to me, what-all are you, son, some kind of Communist?

"He says, this here is the way sports should be played: someplace in the Sunbelt where there is plenty of nice hotels and restaurants for the press. He says, don't you unnerstan' what a showcase the Super Bowl is? They would never get the corporate biggies and the movers of Madison Avenue to come to the Super Bowl unless they played it for their convenience in the right resort areas. He says to me, I'm afraid you don't unnerstan' the bottom line a-tall, and I says, I always thought the bottom line in sports is the final score, and he says that jes' goes to show you you're jes' another naive country boy when it comes to this here showcase."

"Well, Punch, how is your 'commodations?"

"We are what is called 'centrally located,' which means that the press is 40 miles from the players in one direction and 'bout another 40 from the stadium in the other. And then, all the real important folks. . . ."

"The players?"

"No, the owners and advertisers. They're out in Beverly Hills. So all us press is stuck here, talkin' to ourselves. They have got more PR men than Heinz has pickles to take care of us, so I asked one of them why are we here, plumb in the middle of nowhere. I says, if I was coverin' the President, would you put me in Baltimore? And he says, this location is for your convenience, and I says, oh, thank you. I din't 'preciate that. He says, why sure, it is real convenient to the airport. I says, that would be nice if I was a 727, but I ain't goin' nowhere for another week. I says, I b'lieve I would rather be convenient to the football game.

"So we hang around the motel here, watchin' the airplanes overhead and speculatin' on the TV ratings, and, most important, talkin' 'bout this golf toonament they're havin' for us Thursday. I was a-wonderin' where all them cardigan sweaters came from, Herb. And another PR man says to me, do you know that Warner-Lambert is puttin' out nearly $100,000 for this golf toonament, and I says, sorry, I don' know the fella, and, besides, I'm a bowler.

"Well, he says, there is always a first time for ever' thin', but, he says, the NFL does have a free gift for you, which turns out to be this fruity little briefcase the color of spit-up that looked to me like it had been picked out by one of them faggots in Green-wich Village. Herb, if I was to tote this briefcase into the pressbox at West Texas, they would laugh me clear to Albukerk."

"Don't you ever get to see the players, Punch?"

"Sure, Herb. Ever' mornin' this bus picks us up and drives us off to Mexico or wherever it is they're at. The bus has a big ole sign up front that it also goes to Lion Country Safari, to Marineland, and to the picture studios at Universal, so the Super Bowl fits in right well with this bunch.

"First it takes us to the Vikin's, till this other PR man says, 'For your convenience, the buses will roll to the Raider camp at 9:45.' The players is all sorted out. At the Raider hotel, it is like a sock hop, with each table havin' a Raider's number on it, and the important ones like Stabler and Atkinson has tables full of writers, and some of the other fellas just sit all by their lonesome, like they was an ugly-type girl at a dance.

"O' course, nobody much-all talks about football. All the talk is 'bout the media theirselves and how-all will the media affect the game, so the more ever'body talks 'bout it, the more effect it has. I 'magine. This whole thing jes' turns in on itself so.

"I am over at the Vikin's, and I see this pretty blonde who is some kind of built, and I hear somebody say, lookee there, it is Chrystie Jenner, the wife of the world's greatest athalete, and a celebrity in her own right. And so I move up close to where she is talkin' to a bunch of hotshot writers from New York City, and they are sayin', remember me from Montreal and where is Bruce at and so forth, and one says, well, what are you doin' here anyway, Chrystie, and she says, well, I am coverin' the players' wives for ABC, and what brings you here yourself? And he says to her, well, I am coverin' all the hoopla at this showcase. Are you followin' me, Herb? Here we got a football championship, and we got a wives reporter and a hoopla reporter.

"But, for our convenience, it is time to see the Raiders. And their coach, the heavy-set guy, stands up. This is Madden, who they call Pinky, which is the part I like best 'cause that means the coaches at the Super Bowl is Bud and Pinky, jes' like they was over to Skeeter's. And a writer says that Tarkenton has let on that his team is obsessed, and what do you have to say to that? And Madden says, well, we will outobsess them, a remark which gets some kind of guffaw out of me. And then he starts gettin' all these questions about rhetoric, which, b'lieve me, Herb, if I didn't know any better, I would think was some kind of a formation, or a linebacker, maybe. Ever'body is askin' Pinky, will the rhetoric hurt the Raiders, and will they get used to the rhetoric and how will they dee-fense the rhetoric and what-all.

"Half the time, Herb. I don't know what anybody is talkin' 'bout. Bud Grant, he keeps referrin' to stature-type players. At first I thought he meant they were, you know, like statues that didn't move laterally real good, but later on I caught his drift. He means they have reputations. Ever'body talks funny at the Super Bowl, Herb. It's kinda a simulated language, they way the astronauts used to carry on.

"Well, I'm goin' to hang up now, 'cause it's your nickel. But I'll phone Emil mah early prediction story soon."

"O.K., Punch, and lissen up now: I'm gonna tell ever'one you're havin' one great ole time. I don' want folks to think you're no traitor to our 'Merica, Punch. I'm gonna do that for your own damn good, you hear?"

"O.K., Herb. And you tell Mary Beth I'm still scoutin' 'round for that simulated Vikin' corsage she asked for."

"You bet, Punch. Bye now."

"Operator, this is Los Angeles. Routes for Northfield, Ohio, please."

"Two-one-six, plus seven digits."

"Thank you. . . . There's your number ringing, Miss."

"Hello."

"Hello, Karen, it's me, Dianne!"

"Ooh, Dianne! Where are you, hon?"

"I'm calling direct from Beverly Hills!"

"Ooooohhhh. I won't keep you, but. . . ."

"Don't worry about the three minutes, Karen. Sandy told me—you want to call your girl friend, take as long as you want. He says he has a WATS line on his expense account!"

"Ooohhh, Dianne!"

"I can't begin to tell you, Karen. It's so fantastic, like. I saw Bob Newhart and Lorne Greene. . . ."

"Nooooo!"

"And Joe Namath was in the Polo Lounge, and last night was the official Super Bowl party, given by the National Football League itself! Oh Karen, if only you could have been there to share it with me. Up With People entertained!"

"Ooh! I've seen them on TV."

"And there was just nothing spared on the food and beverages, Karen! The canapes would not stop! And Sandy introduced me to this exotic foreign drink that has salt on the rim!"

"Oh Dianne, I'm so happy for you. How is . . . he?"

"Karen, he's just a doll. Some women . . . his wife doesn't understand him at all. He told me that confidentially. He's so sensitive, so concerned about my feelings. I told him back in Akron, in the cafeteria, oh Sandy, how could I come with you to the Super Bowl? Why, I would feel just like a common. . . . And you know what he said, Karen?"

"What?"

"He said, Dianne, don't ever say that about yourself. He said, I am the real hustler, I am the one forced by my company to go out to the Super Bowl and go to meetings and dumb parties, to drink with network people and football people, to try and keep our products in the corporate

and video spotlight. Your going with me would give me the respectabil-
ity I can't get from my job."

"Oh, Dianne, that is beautiful."

"He's just a beautiful-type person, Karen."

"Where is he now?"

"He had to play tennis today. His company makes him do that. It's
one of his obligations, like. Sandy says if he doesn't play tennis with the
right people, his company might not be allowed to buy football commercials next year. And Sandy says that is the upwardly mobile, high-
demographics audience he seeks."

"Oh, I see."

"Sandy's so conscientious, Karen. He hates all these meetings he has
to go to around the pool, but it is his nature, like, never to miss a one.
And yesterday, he had to play golf all day. He was so tired, the poor thing,
we were late getting to the party."

"But it was good?"

"Good? Karen, I saw Julie London there."

"Ooohhh, Dianne!"

"You see, like Sandy says, you really have to know someone to get in,
Karen. Either that or you have to help make money for the NFL. They
hold the guest list down to 2,500 VIPs. Some years they have had it on
the _Queen Mary_ or in the Astrodome. It's not for any Tom, Dick or Harry,
like. This year they had it at the Pasadena Civic Center, and it was all
decked out. Sandy said it was a south-of-the-border decor. He knew that
because there was a mariachi band."

"Dianne, you said Up With People were there."

"They _both_ were, Karen, Up With People _and_ the mariachis."

"Oh, my Godddd, Dianne, two bands!"

"And two rooms, Karen! Two ballrooms! Adjacent, like."

"Oh, it's a fairyland, Dianne!"

"And not only that, but there was a special little section all fenced off
where the people who own these football teams could stay all by themselves, like, and Sandy knew one of the owners, and we got right in there,
right in the first-class section, and Sandy introduced me all around."

"What players did you meet there?"

"Who?"

"What players, Dianne?"

"No, there's none of them, Karen. I heard that the teams playing in the game are on the Coast, but nobody ever talks about them. Sandy says, maybe we should go down to Tijuana Sunday and see a bullfight instead. He says nobody cares abut the football game. He says, this is the great American corporate game. Sandy says there's a veritable who's-who of the business world here. He says, this is the way business gets done in America. It's fascinating. Everybody has private planes and limousines. Sandy says an NFL man told him that the people here for the game will spend $50 million in Ellay. Sandy says the NFL man told him: 'Sandy, this is not your Disneyland, Knott's Berry Farm-type crowd. This is your sophisticated, drinking, betting, upwardly, mobile-type all-American sports crowd.' Why, everybody, just everybody, stopped off at Vegas. Sandy says, that's why Ellay is the ideal place to have the Super Bowl, because it is convenient to Vegas."

"Dianne . . . did you?"

"Did we! Nipsey Russell was in the lounge and Wayne Newton himself was the main attraction, like."

"Oh Goddd, Dianne. I'm so happy for you, hon."

"That's why we had to leave Akron a day early. You see, Sandy's company made him go to Vegas first. They said he could make contacts there. Sandy says it is harder these days for a guy in the business to get the job done. Sandy says something called NFL Properties used to throw a special party for all the businessmen at the Super Bowl, but they found out they didn't have to anymore, because all the businessmen come anyway. So the businessmen have to find each other on their own. That's why Sandy has to spend so much time at bars, because as much as he hates the thought of it, a lot of business types hang around there."

"Oh, I see."

"But it's not all work for Sandy, Karen. He knows some TV types, too. Both NBC and CBS are putting on these terrific variety-type shows. With a football *motif*, like, Karen. Like we saw a rehearsal and the announcer says, 'Page sacks Stabler on the 19,' and Charo says, 'Who ees thees 19 in the sack?'"

"Oh, that's so comical, Dianne. Charo has such a funny accent."

"The casts are just star-studded, Karen. Besides Charo, there's Andy Williams, Don Rickles, Elliott Gould. . . ."

"And they'll be on TV?"

"Tonight. Live on tape from the Super Bowl. Oh, I just adore football so much, Karen. And you know, it's funny, but I never cared that much for it before, back in Akron. But I just adore the Super Bowl."

"I'm so jealous, Dianne."

"Well, I better hang up now. I have to get dressed. Sandy's going to try and take me to the theater."

"What are you going to see?"

"I really don't know. He just said he'd try to get away from the tennis long enough for us to get in a matinee."

"Oh, I hope you have good seats, Dianne!"

"Karen, believe me, Sandy's right. Every American should try and go to the Super Bowl, because it is so representative of Americana, like. I'll see you at work Monday, hon. Be good, now."

"Well, if I can't be good, I'll be careful."

"O.K., bye, Karen."

"Have a happy, Dianne."

"Hello, operator, would you be so kind as to get me a number in New York?"

"You can dial that direct, sir."

"Yes, I should like to very much, but I don't know the bloody number."

"Sir, dial one, plus 212, then 555-1212 and ask for the number."

"I see, yes. Thank you so much. . . ."

"Directory assistance."

"Oh, I'm so sorry, I was trying to reach information."

"Look, this is directory assistance, Mister. Do you want a number in Noo Yawk?"

"Indeed I do. I'm trying to secure the number of the Algonquin Hotel."

"Is it a new listing?"

"No, luv. I was there just the other day, and it was standing as straight as ever."

"What?"

"Madam Assistance, do you have the number?"

"All right, make a note of this: 687-4400."

"Thank you so much. . . ."

"Hello, this is Dale, may I help you?"

"I do hope so. I should like to reverse charges."

"Yeah, what's the name?"

"Just Room 407, please."

"Algonquin Hotel."

"Long distance for 407."

"Are you paid, operator?"

"No, it's collect to the room."

"Hello."

"Is this 407?"

"Yes it is."

"Ihaveacollectcallfromlosangeleswillyouacceptcharges?"

"I'm so sorry, what?"

"Darling, it's me, Michael."

"Sir, this is a station call!"

"Michael!"

"Lady, will you accept charges?"

"Yes, of course I will."

"All right, go ahead."

"Michael!"

"Sylvia, darling!"

"Where are you?"

"I'm in a bloody phone booth somewhere along Sunset Boulevard. I really don't know. I just had to get off this damned bus."

"Bus? What bus?"

"This awful chartered monstrosity that took me to the Super Bowl."

"Darling, the what?"

"The Super Bowl. Oh, Sylvia, you can't imagine. It's the American football championship, although as nearly as I could fathom, the journey to the bloody game, on this dreadful bus, was much more an attraction than the game itself."

"Darling, please back up. What in the world were you doing on this bus at this bowling alley?"

"No, no, football, Sylvia. And it's all so depressing. You remember Nick, that ghastly producer who belongs to the nude backgammon encounter group?"

"Oh, God, yes."

"Well, he called me up at a fever pitch last evening to say that an extra ticket to the Super Bowl football had come into his possession, and would I care to go. And of course I protested that it would be a terrible thing to waste the ticket on someone such as myself, who knows nothing about American football, but Nick insisted that this was the single most important cultural event in the United States, and for me to turn down such an opportunity would be—and I fear this is a direct quote, darling—the equivalent of turning down an invitation to have dinner with the Queen at Buckingham Palace."

"Oh, my God, Michael. I'm so sorry for you out there, poor thing."

"Well, if we're going to get the financing and a chance for McQueen, Nick is the fellow. Any port in a storm. So I accepted with gratitude. And then he informed me about the bus. This game, for reasons that still elude me, is between a team from Minnesota, which is somewhere amongst the Midwestern states, and Oakland, which is a rather shabby working-class suburb of San Francisco, but it is being played here in Los Angeles. Or rather, it is being played in some godforsaken place known as Pasadena, which is primarily famous for its smog. And it is, apparently, inaccessible by automobile, which is why everyone journeyed by bus. Well, I should not say everybody. The Midwest rooters all seem to have traveled in these awful conveyances known as vans—every last one of them boasting a CB radio—while the fans from San Francisco appeared to have arrived en masse on motorcycles. Most of these fellows even affected the early Brando."

"Poor Michael. Was it all so bad?"

"Worse, I'm afraid. These people who inhabit the Sunbelt take a rather perverse pride in the vulgar, you know. They absolutely lack taste in all things but the climate. They can discourse upon a partially sunny day as literate men and women once spoke of poetry or philosophy. And saddest of all, they try mightily to bring the rest of the nation down to their level. I was told that this utterly tasteless exhibition was a classic representation of America. One especially annoying buffoon on the bus, who was wearing an off-lime leisure suit and drinking another margarita. . . ."

"I'm sorry, dear, a what?"

"A margarita. It is this dreadful liquid concoction that was, alas, not stopped at the Mexican border by immigration authorities. As you know, Sylvia, Americans employ salt to excess on all foods. We should have known that before long they would find a drink they could also destroy in this way. Such is the margarita, which has become a sort of liquid French fry throughout the Sunbelt. In any event, this was the staple of our bus ride."

"Did you get to the match?"

"Oh, my God. I'm afraid we did. We had to leave at the crack of dawn to reach our assigned parking place, and to accommodate the television network, which schedules the game for the convenience of saloonkeepers in New Jersey, rather than for the poor devils, such as myself, who make the supreme effort to appear at the bloody thing in person.

"Then, when we emerged from our mobile vault, we were greeted by a scene, darling, the likes of which you would not attribute to Dante at his most vivid. A full landscape of CB vans and motorcycles, with matching people, all at their most outrageously harlequinesque, all consuming equal amounts of beer and bus exhaust and dodging Frisbees, which clattered about like hail. The lights of the stadium were already on, ready to penetrate the smog, I imagine, even though it was not yet midday. Everywhere, a profusion of vendors—of the quantity and persistence of beggars in Bombay—tried to foist upon us souvenir merchandise of such quality that it would all surely be rejected in Taiwan as beneath human standards. Here and there, as we drew closer to this antique arena, scalpers were trying desperately to sell tickets at face value."

"But Michael, I understood you to say this was the great championship that every American longed to see."

"Oh, indeed, there is a great deal of glib sociological talk about how it is the average fan who attends this spectacle, but the fact of the matter is that those present are either expense-account freeloaders, such as myself, or zealots who have traveled thousands of miles, and thus must be well-off—and further, they must also be rather asinine to do so.

"So basically, luv, what you have at a Super Bowl is not an average American at all. You don't even have an average American sports fan. Instead, you have a collection of the affluent foolish—The Affluish Americans."

"The worst of the lot."

"By and large."

"Well, I do hope that at least the game was exciting."

"No, not at all. It was perfectly dreadful. The team from San Francisco absolutely eviscerated the Midwest club."

"Oh, I'm so sorry."

"No matter. It didn't bother a soul, because they assured me that they were all quite resigned to this circumstance—that it was almost always a terrible game, and certainly always when the Minnesota club played."

"And this didn't upset the fans?"

"Oh, no. The league and the press have convinced the fans that the only important thing about the Super Bowl is that it be played in nice weather. I came to understand that the Super Bowl really was very representative of America—at least of the worst of modern America. It is all flash and no substance. A duel of transients passing by, played before transients. Of course the games are always going to be awful. Even the players must sense that they are the end result of a programmed, franchised society. The Super Bowl is the ultimate remove in this nation, luv."

"I do hope you kept these sentiments to yourself, dear."

"Oh, I was the perfect guest. Besides, we were kept busy in the stadium. Soon enough the public-address announcer advised us: 'You are sitting in the world's largest card-stunt section, and for all of us to get ready our cards."

"Michael, what in the world?"

"Well, darling, we were programmed rather like those poor Chinese in Peking on Mao Tse-tung Day, holding up these cardboard sections to form rather infantile color patterns. I did ask why we were expected to perform these maneuvers, and Nick explained to me that it was for the convenience of the TV audience. It seemed to me that this was all rather backward, inasmuch as we had paid $20 a seat—a hard seat—while the people watching on the telly were enjoying the proceedings more comfortably and *gratis,* but since I was a guest myself, I agreed to quietly go along with this dreadful mass exercise."

"Oh, I'm so sorry for you, darling."

"Well, thereafter, like any drone, I merely followed the path of least resistance and tried valiantly to develop a taste for margaritas. And, at last, we were back on the bloody bus, and when I happened to glance out the window an hour or two later and saw a street sign indicating that we had returned to civilization—or at least to that second cousin of civilization that calls itself 'Ellay'—I made very hasty apologies, claiming that I was going to meet a dear old friend at the next corner, and exited precipitously from the bus as soon is it came to a stoplight. Darling, if I ever get a taxi back to the hotel, I'll be on the nine o'clock flight tomorrow morning. Till then, Sylvia."

"Good night, Michael. Oh, you poor dear."

The story "Trojan Horse" poses and solves a crime during a game at the venerable Rose Bowl stadium in Pasadena. Its author, Ellery Queen, is universally recognized as a master of mystery and detective stories. "The Queen's Awards," an annual detective short story contest, and the Ellery Queen Mystery Magazine *attest to his reputation. He has edited several books of short stories, collecting both his own stories and those of other writers. An early favorite is* The New Adventures of Ellery Queen *(1940). A wonderful group of stories by various authors is* 101 Years' Entertainment: The Great Detective Stories, 1841–1941 *(1945). Among Queen's novels are* Cat of Many Tails *(1949),* The Glass Village *(1954), and* The Hollywood Murders *(1957).*

Ellery Queen

TROJAN HORSE (1940)

WHOM," DEMANDED MISS PAULA PARIS across the groaning board, "do you like, Mr. Queen?"

Mr. Queen instantly mumbled: "You," out of a mouthful of Vermont turkey, chestnut stuffing, and cranberry sauce.

"I didn't mean that, silly," said Miss Paris, nevertheless pleased. "However, now that you've brought the subject up—will you say such pretty things when we're married?"

Mr. Ellery Queen paled and, choking, set down his weapons. When he had first encountered the lovely Miss Paris, Hollywood's reigning goddess of gossip, Miss Paris had been suffering from homophobia, or morbid fear of man; she had been so terrified of crowds that she had not for years set foot outside her virginal white frame house in the Hollywood hills. Mr. Queen, stirred by a nameless emotion, determined to cure the lady of her psychological affliction. The therapy, he conceived, must be both shocking and compensatory; and so he made love to her.

And lo! although Miss Paris recovered, to his horror Mr. Queen found that the cure may sometimes present a worse problem than the affliction. For the patient promptly fell in love with her healer; and the healer did not himself escape certain excruciating emotional consequences.

His precious liberty faced with this alluring menace, Mr. Queen now choked over the luscious Christmas dinner which Miss Paris had cunningly cooked with her own slim hands and served *en tête-à-tête* in her cosy maple and chintz dining-room.

"Oh, relax," pouted Miss Paris. "I was joking. What makes you think I'd marry a creature who studies cut throats and chases thieves for the enjoyment of it?"

"Horrible fate for a woman," Mr. Queen hastened to agree. "Besides, I'm not good enough for you."

"Darned tootin' you're not! But you haven't answered my question. Do you think Carolina will lick USC next Sunday?"

"Oh, the Rose Bowl game," said Mr. Queen, discovering his appetite miraculously. "More turkey, please! . . . Well, if Ostermoor lives up to his reputation, the Spartans should breeze in."

"Really?" murmured Miss Paris. "Aren't you forgetting that Roddy Crockett is the whole Trojan backfield?"

"Southern California Trojans, Carolina Spartans," said Mr. Queen thoughtfully, munching. "Spartans versus Trojans . . . Sort of modern gridiron Siege of Troy."

"Ellery Queen, that's plagiarism or—or something! You read it in my column."

"Is there a Helen for the lads to battle over?" grinned Mr. Queen.

"You're *so* romantic, Queenikins. The only female involved is a very pretty, rich, and sensible co-ed named Joan Wing, and she *isn't* the kid-naped love of any of the Spartans."

"Curses," said Mr. Queen, reaching for the brandied plum pudding. "For a moment I thought I had something."

"But there's a Priam of a sort, because Roddy Crockett is engaged to Joan Wing, and Joanie's father, Pop Wing, is just about the noblest Trojan of them all."

"Maybe you know what you're talking about, beautiful," said Mr. Queen, "but *I* don't."

"You're positively the worst-informed man in California! Pop Wing is USC's most enthusiastic alumnus, isn't he?"

"Is he?"

"You mean you've never heard of Pop Wing?" asked Paula incredulously.

"Not guilty," said Mr. Queen. "More plum pudding, please."

"The Perennial Alumnus? The Boy Who Never Grew Up?"

"Thank you," said Mr. Queen. "I beg your pardon?"

"The Ghost of Exposition Park and the LA Coliseum, who holds a life seat for all USC football games? The unofficial trainer, rubber, water-boy, pep-talker, Alibi Ike, booster, and pigskin patron-in-chief to the Trojan eleven? Percy Squires 'Pop' Wing, Southern California '04, the man who sleeps, eats, and breathes only for Trojan victories and who married and, failing a son, created a daughter for the sole purpose of snaring USC's best fullback in years?"

"Peace, peace; I yield," moaned Mr. Queen, "before the crushing brutality of the characterization. I now know Percy Squires Wing as I hope never to know anyone again."

"Sorry!" said Paula, rising briskly. "Because directly after you've filled your bottomless tummy with plum pudding we're going Christmas calling on the great man."

"No!" said Mr. Queen with a shudder.

"You want to see the Rose Bowl game, don't you?"

"Who doesn't? But I haven't been able to snag a brace of tickets for love or money."

"Poor Queenie," purred Miss Paris, putting her arms about him. "You're *so* helpless. Come on watch me wheedle Pop Wing out of two seats for the game!"

The lord of the château whose towers rose from a magnificently preposterous parklike estate in Inglewood proved to be a flat-bellied youngster of middle age, almost as broad as he was tall, with a small bald head set upon small ruddy cheeks, so that at first glance Mr. Queen thought he was viewing a Catawba grape lying on a boulder.

They came upon the millionaire seated on his hams in the center of a vast lawn, arguing fiercely with a young man who by his size—which was herculean—and his shape—which was cuneiform—and his coloring—which was coppery—could only be of the order *foot-ballis,* and therefore Mr. Wing's future son-in-law and the New Year's Day hope of the Trojans.

They were manipulating wickets, mallets, and croquet balls in illustration of a complex polemic which apparently concerned the surest method of frustrating the sinister quarterback of the Carolina eleven, Ostermoor.

A young lady with red hair and a saucy nose sat cross-legged on the grass near by, her soft blue eyes fixed on the brown face of the young man with that naked worshipfulness young ladies permit themselves to exhibit in public only when their young men have formally yielded. This, concluded Mr. Queen without difficulty, must be the daughter of the great man and Mr. Roddy Crockett's fiancée, Joan Wing.

Mr. Wing hissed a warning to Roddy at the sight of Mr. Queen's unfamiliar visage, and for a moment Mr. Queen felt uncomfortably like a spy caught sneaking into the enemy's camp. But Miss Paris hastily vouched for his devotion to the cause of Troy, and for some time there were Christmas greetings and introductions, in the course of which Mr. Queen made the acquaintance of two persons whom he recognized instantly as the hybrid genus *house-guest perennialis.* One was a bearded gentleman with high cheek-bones and a Muscovite manner (pre-Soviet) entitled the Grand Duke Ostrov; the other was a thin, dark, whiplike female with inscrutable black eyes who went by the astonishing name of Madame Mephisto.

These two barely nodded to Miss Paris and Mr. Queen; they were listening to each word which dropped from the lips of Mr. Percy Squires Wing, their host, with the adoration of novitiates at the feet of their patron saint.

The noble Trojan's ruddiness of complexion, Mr. Queen pondered, came either from habitual exposure to the outdoors or from high blood-pressure; a conclusion which he discovered very soon was accurate on both counts, since Pop Wing revealed himself without urging as an Izaak Walton, a golfer, a Nimrod, a mountain-climber, a polo-player, and a racing yachtsman; and he was as squirmy and excitable as a small boy.

The small-boy analogy struck Mr. Queen with greater force when the Perennial Alumnus dragged Mr. Queen off to inspect what he alarmingly called "my trophy room." Mr. Queen's fears were vindicated; for in a huge vaulted chamber presided over by a desiccated, gloomy, and mono-syllabic old gentleman introduced fantastically as "Gabby" Huntswood, he found himself inspecting as heterogeneous and remarkable an assemblage of junk as ever existed outside a small boy's dream of Paradise.

Postage-stamp albums, American college banners, mounted wild-animal heads, a formidable collection of match-boxes, cigar bands, stuffed fish, World War trench helmets of all nations . . . all were there; and Pop Wing beamed as he exhibited these priceless treasures, scurrying from one collection to another and fondling them with such ingenuous pleasure that Mr. Queen sighed for his own lost youth.

"Aren't these objects too—er—valuable to be left lying around this way, Mr. Wing?" he inquired politely.

"Hell, no. Gabby's more jealous of their safety than I am!" shouted the great man. "Hey, Gabby?"

"Yes, sir," said Gabby; and he frowned suspiciously at Mr. Queen.

"Why, Gabby made me install a burglar-alarm system. Can't see it, but this room's as safe as a vault."

"Safer," said Gabby, glowering at Mr. Queen.

"Think I'm crazy, Queen?"

"No, no," said Mr. Queen, who meant to say "Yes, yes."

"Lots of people do," chuckled Pop Wing. "Let 'em. Between 1904 and 1924 I just about vegetated. But something drove me on. Know what?"

Mr. Queen's famous powers of deduction were unequal to the task.

"The knowledge that I was making enough money to retire a young man and kick the world in the pants. And I did! Retired at forty-two and started doing all the things I'd never had time or money to do when I was a shaver. Collecting things. Keeps me young! Come here, Queen, and look at my *prize* collection." And he pulled Mr. Queen over to a gigantic glass case and pointed gleefully, an elder Penrod gloating over a marbles haul.

From his host's proud tone Mr. Queen expected to gaze upon nothing less than a collection of the royal crowns of Europe. Instead, he saw a vast number of scuffed, streaked, and muddy footballs, each carefully laid upon an ebony rest, and on each a legend lettered in gold leaf. One that caught his eye read: ROSE BOWL, 1930. USC 47–Pitt 14 The others bore similar inscriptions.

"Wouldn't part with 'em for a million dollars," confided the great man. "Why, the balls in this case represent every Trojan victory for the past fifteen years!"

"Incredible!" exclaimed Mr. Queen.

"Yes, sir, right after every game they win the team presents old Pop Wing with the pigskin. What a collection!" And the millionaire gazed worshipfully at the unlovely oblate spheroids.

"They must think the world of you at USC."

"Well, I've sort of been of service to my Alma Mater," said Pop Wing modestly, "especially in football. Wing Athletic Scholarship, you know; Wing Dorm for Varsity athletes; and so on. I've scouted prep schools for years, personally; turned up some mighty fine Varsity material. Coach is a good friend of mine. I guess—" and he drew a happy breath—"I can have just about what I damn well ask for at the old school!"

"Including football tickets?" said Mr. Queen quickly, seizing his opportunity. "Must be marvelous to have that kind of drag. I've been trying for days to get tickets for the game."

The great man surveyed him. "What was your college?"

"Harvard," said Mr. Queen apologetically. "But I yield to no man in my ardent admiration of the Trojans. Darn it, I did want to watch Roddy Crockett mop up those Spartan upstarts."

"You did, huh?" said Pop Wing. "Say, how about you and Miss Paris being my guests at the Rose Bowl Sunday?"

"Couldn't think of it—" began Mr. Queen mendaciously, already savoring the joy of having beaten Miss Paris, so to speak, to the turnstiles.

"Won't hear another word." Mr. Wing embraced Mr. Queen. "Say, long as you'll be with us, I'll let you in on a little secret."

"Secret?" wondered Mr. Queen.

"Rod and Joan," whispered the millionaire, "are going to be married right after the Trojans win next Sunday!"

"Congratulations. He seems like a fine boy."

"None better. Hasn't got a cent, you understand—worked his way through—but he's graduating in January and . . . shucks! he's the greatest fullback the old school ever turned out. We'll find something for him to do. Yes, sir, Roddy's last game . . ." The great man sighed. Then he brightened. "Anyway, I've got a hundred thousand dollar surprise for my Joanie that ought to make her go right out and raise another triple-threat man for the Trojans!"

"A—how much of a surprise?" asked Mr. Queen feebly.

But the great man looked mysterious. "Let's go back and finish cooking that boy Ostermoor's goose!"

New Year's Day was warm and sunny; and Mr. Queen felt strange as he prepared to pick up Paula Paris and escort her to the Wing estate, from which their party was to proceed to the Pasadena stadium. In his quaint Eastern fashion, he was accustomed to don a mountain of sweater, scarf, and overcoat when he went to a football game; and here he was *en route* in a sports jacket!

"California, thy name is Iconoclast," muttered Mr. Queen, and he drove through already agitated Hollywood streets to Miss Paris's house.

"Heavens," said Paula, "you can't barge in on Pop Wing that way."

"What way?"

"Minus the Trojan colors. We've got to keep on the old darlin's good side, at least until we're safely in the stadium. Here!" And with a few deft twists of two lady's handkerchiefs Paula manufactured a breast-pocket kerchief for him in cardinal and gold.

"I see you've done yourself up pretty brown," said Mr. Queen, not unadmiringly; for Paula's figure was the secret envy of many better-advertised Hollywood ladies, and it was clad devastatingly in a cardinal-and-gold creation that was a cross between a suit and a dirndl, to Mr. Queen's inexperienced eye, and it was topped off with a perky, feathery hat perched nervously on her blue-black hair, concealing one bright eye.

"Wait till you see Joan," said Miss Paris, rewarding him with a kiss. "She's been calling me all week about *her* clothes problem. It's not every day a girl's called on to buy an outfit that goes equally well with a football game and a wedding." And as Mr. Queen drove off towards Inglewood she added thoughtfully: "I wonder what that awful creature will wear. Probably a turban and seven veils."

"What creature?"

"Madame Mephisto. Only her real name is Suzie Lucadamo, and she quit a dumpy little magic and mind-reading vaudeville act to set herself up in Seattle as a seeress—you know, we positively guarantee to pierce the veil of the Unknown? Pop met her in Seattle in November during the USC-Washington game. She wangled a Christmas-week invitation out of him for the purpose, I suppose, of looking over the rich Hollywood sucker-field without cost to herself."

"You seem to know a lot about her."

Paula smiled. "Joan Wing told me some—Joanie doesn't like the old gal nohow—and I dug out the rest . . . well, you know, darling, I know everything about *everybody*."

"Then tell me," said Mr. Queen. "Who exactly is the Grand Duke Ostrov?"

"Why?"

"Because," replied Mr. Queen grimly, "I don't like His Highness, and I do like—heaven help me!—Pop Wing and his juvenile amusements."

"Joan tells me Pop likes you, too, the fool! I guess in his adolescent way he's impressed by a real, live detective. Show him your G-man badge, darling." Mr. Queen glared, but Miss Paris's gaze was dreamy. "Pop may find it handy having you around today, at that."

"What d'ye mean?" asked Mr. Queen sharply.

"Didn't he tell you he had a surprise for Joan? He's told everyone in Los Angeles, although no one knows what it is but your humble correspondent."

"And Roddy, I'll bet. He did say something about a 'hundred thousand dollar surprise.' What's the point?"

"The point is," murmured Miss Paris, "that it's a set of perfectly matched star sapphires."

Mr. Queen was silent. Then he said: "You think Ostrov—"

"The Grand Duke," said Miss Paris, "is even phonier than Madame Suzie Lucadamo Mephisto. *His* name is Louie Batterson, and he hails from the Bronx. Everybody knows it but Pop Wing." Paula sighed. "But you know Hollywood—live and let live; you may need a sucker yourself someday. Batterson's a high-class deadbeat. He's pulled some awfully aromatic stunts in his time. I'm hoping he lays off our nostrils this sunny day."

"This," mumbled Mr. Queen, "is going to be one heck of a football game, I can see that."

Bedlam was a cloister compared with the domain of the Wings. The interior of the house was noisy with decorators, caterers, cooks, and waiters; and with a start Mr. Queen recalled that this was to be the wedding day of Joan Wing and Roddy Crockett.

They found their party assembled in one of the formal gardens—which, Mr. Queen swore to Miss Paris, outshone Fontainebleau—and apparently Miss Wing had solved her dressmaking problem, for while Mr. Queen could find no word to describe what she was wearing, Mr. Roddy Crockett could, and the word was "sockeroo."

Paula went into more technical raptures, and Miss Wing clung to her gridiron hero, who looked a little pale; and then the pride of Troy went loping off to the wars, leaping into his roadster and waving farewell with their cries of good cheer in his manly, young, and slightly mashed ears.

Pop Wing ran down the driveway after the roadster, bellowing: "Don't forget that Ostermoor defense, Roddy!"

And Roddy vanished in a trail of dusty glory; the noblest Trojan of them all came back shaking his head and muttering: "It ought to be a pipe!"; flunkies appeared bearing mounds of canapés and cocktails; the Grand Duke, regally Cossack in a long Russian coat gathered at the waist, amused the company with feats of legerdemain—his long soft hands were very fluent—and Madame Mephisto, minus the seven veils but, as predicted, wearing the turban, went into a trance and murmured that she could see a "glorious Trojan vic-to-ree"—all the while Joan Wing sat smiling dreamily into her cocktail and Pop Wing pranced up and down vowing that he had never been cooler or more confident in his life.

And then they were in one of Wing's huge seven-passenger limousines—Pop, Joan, the Grand Duke, Madame, Gabby, Miss Paris, and Mr. Queen—bound for Pasadena and the fateful game.

And Pop said suddenly: "Joanie, I've got a surprise for you."

And Joan dutifully looked surprised, her breath coming a little faster; and Pop drew out the right-hand pocket of his jacket a long leather case, and opened it, and said with a chuckle: "Wasn't going to show it to you till tonight, but Roddy told me before he left that you look so beautiful I ought to give you a preview as a reward. From me to you, Joanie. Like 'em?"

Joan gasped: "*Like* them!" and there were exclamations of "Oh!" and "Ah!," and they saw lying upon black velvet eleven superb sapphires, their stars winking royally—a football team of perfectly matched gems.

"Oh, *Pop!*" moaned Joan, and she flung her arms about him and wept on his shoulder, while he looked pleased and blustery, and puffed and closed the case and returned it to the pocket from which he had taken it.

"Formal opening tonight. Then you can decide whether you want to make a necklace out of 'em or a bracelet or what." And Pop stroked Joan's hair while she sniffled against him; and Mr. Queen, watching the Grand Duke Ostrov, *né* Batterson, and Madame Mephisto, *née* Lucadamo, thought they were very clever to have concealed so quickly those involuntary expressions of avarice.

Surrounded by his guests, Pop strode directly to the Trojans' dressing-room, waving aside officials and police and student athletic underlings as if he owned the Rose Bowl and all the multitudinous souls besieging it.

The young man at the door said: "Hi, Pop," respectfully, and admitted them under the envious stares of the less fortunate mortals outside.

"Isn't he grand?" whispered Paula, her eyes like stars; but before Mr. Queen could reply there were cries of: "Hey! Femmes!" and "Here's Pop!" and the Coach came over, wickedly straight-arming Mr. Roddy Crockett, who was lacing his doeskin pants, aside, and said with a wink: "All right, Pop. Give it to 'em."

And Pop, very pale now, shucked his coat and flung it on a rubbing table; and the boys crowded round, very quiet suddenly; and Mr. Queen found himself pinned between a mountainous tackle and a behemoth of a guard who growled down at him: "Hey, you, stop squirming. Don't you see Pop's gonna make a speech?"

And Pop said, in a very low voice: "Listen, gang. The last time I made a dressing-room spiel was in '33. It was on a January first, too, and it was the day USC played Pitt in the Rose Bowl. That day we licked 'em thirty-three to nothing."

Somebody shouted: "Yay!" but Pop held up his hand.

"I made three January first speeches before that. One was in '32, before we knocked Tulane over by a score of twenty-one to twelve. One was in 1930, the day we beat the Panthers forty-seven to fourteen. And the first in '23, when we took Penn State by fourteen to three. And that was the first time in the history of the Rose Bowl that we represented the Pacific Coast Conference in the inter-sectional classic. There's just one thing I want you men to bear in mind when you dash out there in a few minutes in front of half of California."

The room was very still.

"I want you to remember that the Trojans have played in four Rose

Bowl games. And I want you to remember that the Trojans have *won* four Rose Bowl games," said Pop.

And he stood high above them, looking down into their intent young faces; and then he jumped to the floor, breathing heavily.

Hell broke loose. Boys pounded him on the back; Roddy Crockett seized Joan and pulled her behind a locker; Mr. Queen found himself pinned to the door, hat over his eyes, by the elbow of the Trojan center, like a butterfly to a wall; and the Coach stood grinning at Pop, who grinned back, but tremulously.

"All right, men," said the Coach. "Pop?" Pop Wing grinned and shook them all off, and Roddy helped him into his coat, and after a while Mr. Queen, considerably the worse for wear, found himself seated in Pop's box directly above the fifty-yard line.

And then, as the two teams dashed into the Bowl across the brilliant turf, to the roar of massed thousands, Pop Wing uttered a faint cry.

"What's the matter?" asked Joan quickly, seizing his arms. "Aren't you feeling well, Pop?"

"The sapphires," said Pop Wing in a hoarse voice, his hand in his pocket. "They're gone."

Kick-off! Twenty-two figures raced to converge in a tumbling mass, and the stands thundered, the USC section fluttering madly with flags . . . and then there was a groan that rent the blue skies, and deadly, despairing silence.

For the Trojans' safety man caught the ball, started forward, slipped, the ball popped out of his hands, the Carolina right end fell on it—and there was the jumping, gleeful Spartan team on the Trojans' 9-yard line, Carolina's ball, first down, and four plays for a touchdown.

And Gabby, who had not heard Pop Wing's exclamation, was on his feet shrieking: "But they can't *do* that! Oh, heavens—Come *on*, USC! Hold that line!"

Pop glanced at Mr. Huntswood with bloodshot surprise, as if a three-thousand-year-old mummy had suddenly come to life; and then he muttered: "Gone. Somebody's—picked my pocket."

"*What!*" whispered Gabby; and he fell back, staring at his employer with horror.

"But thees ees fantastic," the Grand Duke exclaimed.

Mr. Queen said quietly: "Are you positive, Mr. Wing?"

Pop's eyes were on the field, automatically analyzing the play; but they were filled with pain. "Yes, I'm sure. Some pickpocket in the crowd . . ."

"No," said Mr. Queen.

"Ellery, what do you mean?" cried Paula.

"From the moment we left Mr. Wing's car until we entered the Trojan dressing-room we surrounded him completely. From the moment we left the Trojan dressing-room until we sat down in this box, we surrounded him completely. No, our pickpocket is one of this group, I'm afraid."

Madame Mephisto shrilled: "How dare you! Aren't you forgetting that it was Mr. Crockett who helped Mr. Wing on with his coat in that dressing-room?"

"You—" began Pop in a growl, starting to rise.

Joan put her hand on his arm and squeezed, smiling at him. "Never mind her, Pop."

Carolina gained two yards on a plunge through center. Pop shaded his eyes with his hand, staring at the opposing lines.

"Meester Queen," said the Grand Duke coldly, "that ees an insult. I demand we all be—how you say?—searched."

Pop waved his hand wearily. "Forget it. I came to watch a football game." But he no longer looked like a small boy.

"His Highness's suggestion," murmured Mr. Queen, "is an excellent one. The ladies may search one another; the men may do the same. Suppose we all leave here together—in a body—and retire to the rest rooms?"

"Hold 'em," muttered Pop, as if he had not heard. Carolina gained 2 yards more on an off-tackle play. Five yards to go in two downs. They could see Roddy Crockett slapping one of his linemen on the back.

The lines met, and buckled. No gain.

"D'ye see Roddy go through that hole?" muttered Pop.

Joan rose and, rather imperiously, motioned Madame and Paula to precede her. Pop did not stir. Mr. Queen motioned to the men. The Grand Duke and Gabby rose. They all went quickly away.

And still Pop did not move. Until Ostermoor rifled a flat pass into the end zone, and a Carolina end came up out of the ground and snagged the ball. And then it was Carolina 6, USC 0, the big clock indicating that barely a minute of the first quarter's playing time had elapsed.

"Block that kick!"

Roddy plunged through the Spartan line and blocked it. The Carolina boys trotted back to their own territory, grinning.

"Hmph," said Pop to the empty seats in his box; and then he sat still and simply waited, an old man.

The first quarter rolled along. The Trojans could not get out of their territory. Passes fell incomplete. The Spartan line held like iron.

"Well, we're back," said Paula Paris. The great man looked up slowly. "We didn't find them."

A moment later Mr. Queen returned, herding his two companions. Mr. Queen said nothing at all; he merely shook his head, and the Grand Duke Ostrov looked grandly contemptuous, and Madame Mephisto tossed her turbaned head angrily. Joan was very pale; her eyes crept down the field to Roddy, and Paula saw that they were filled with tears.

Mr. Queen said abruptly: "Will you excuse me, please?" and left again with swift strides.

The first quarter ended with the score still 6 to 0 against USC and the Trojans unable to extricate themselves from the menace of their goal post ... pinned back with inhuman regularity by the sharp-shooting Mr. Ostermoor. There is no defense against a deadly accurate kick.

When Mr. Queen returned, he wiped his slightly moist brow and said pleasantly: "By the way, Your Highness, it all comes back to me now. In a former incarnation—I believe in that life your name was Batterson, and you were the flower of an ancient Bronx family—weren't you mixed up in a jewel robbery?"

"Jewel robbery!" gasped Joan, and for some reason she looked relieved. Pop's eyes fixed coldly on the Grand Duke's suddenly oscillating beard.

"Yes," continued Mr. Queen, "I seem to recall that the fence tried to involve you, Your Highness, saying you were the go-between, but the jury wouldn't believe a fence's word, and so you went free. You were quite charming on the stand, I recall—had the courtroom in stitches."

"It's a damn lie," said the Grand Duke thickly, without the trace of an accent. His teeth gleamed wolfishly at Mr. Queen from their thicket.

"You thieving four-flusher—" began Pop Wing, half-rising from his seat.

"Not yet, Mr. Wing," said Mr. Queen.

"I have never been so insulted—" began Madame Mephisto.

"And you," said Mr. Queen with a little bow, "would be wise to hold your tongue, Madame Lucadamo."

Paula nudged him in fierce mute inquiry, but he shook his head. He looked perplexed.

No one said anything until, near the end of the second quarter, Roddy Crockett broke loose for a 44-yard gain, and on the next play the ball came to rest on Carolina's 26-yard line.

Then Pop Wing was on his feet, cheering lustily, and even Gabby Huntswood was yelling in his cracked, unoiled voice: "Come on, Trojans!"

"Attaboy, Gabby," said Pop with the ghost of a grin. "First time I've ever seen you excited about a football game."

Three plays netted the Trojans 11 yards more: first down on Carolina's 15-yard line! The half was nearly over. Pop was hoarse, the theft apparently forgotten. He groaned as USC lost ground, Ostermoor breaking up two plays. Then, with the ball on Carolina's 22-yard line, with time for only one more play before the whistle ending the half, the Trojan quarterback called for a kick formation and Roddy booted the ball straight and true between the uprights of the Spartans' goal.

The whistle blew. Carolina 6, USC 3.

Pop sank back, mopping his face. "Have to do better. That damn Ostermoor! What's the matter with Roddy?"

During the rest period Mr. Queen, who had scarcely watched the struggle, murmured: "By the way, Madame, I've heard a good deal about your unique gift of divination. We can't seem to find the sapphires by natural means; how about the supernatural?"

Madame Mephisto glared at him. "This is no time for jokes!"

"A true gift needs no special conditions," smiled Mr. Queen.

"The atmosphere—scarcely propitious—"

"Come, come, Madame! You wouldn't overlook an opportunity to restore your host's hundred thousand dollar loss?"

Pop began to inspect Madame with suddenly keen curiosity.

Madame closed her eyes, her long fingers at her temples. "I see," she murmured, "I see a long jewel-case . . . yes, it is closed, closed . . . but it is dark, very dark . . . it is in a, yes, a dark place . . ." She sighed and dropped her hands, her dark lids rising. "I'm sorry. I can see no more."

"It's in a dark place, all right," said Mr. Queen dryly. "It's in my pocket." And to their astonishment he took from his pocket the great man's jewel-case.

Mr. Queen snapped it open. "Only," he remarked sadly, "it's empty. I found it in a corner of the Trojan's dressing-room."

Joan shrank back, squeezing a tiny football charm so hard it collapsed. The millionaire gazed stonily at the parading bands blaring around the field.

"You see," said Mr. Queen, "the thief hid the sapphires somewhere and dropped the case in the dressing-room. And we were all there. The question is: Where did the thief cache them?"

"Pardon me," said the Grand Duke. "Eet seems to me the theft must have occurred in Meester Wing's car, after he returned the jewel-case to his pocket. So perhaps the jewels are hidden in the car."

"I have already," said Mr. Queen, "searched the car."

"Then in the Trojan dressing-room!" cried Paula.

"No, I've also searched there—floor to ceiling, lockers, cabinets, clothes, everything. The sapphires aren't there."

"The thief wouldn't have been so foolish as to drop them in an aisle on the way to this box," said Paula thoughtfully. "Perhaps he had an accomplice—"

"To have an accomplice," said Mr. Queen wearily, "you must know you are going to commit a crime. To know that you must know there will be a crime to commit. Nobody but Mr. Wing knew that he intended to take the sapphires with him today—is that correct, Mr. Wing?"

"Yes," said Pop. "Except Rod—Yes. No one."

"Wait!" cried Joan passionately. "I know what you're all thinking. You think Roddy had—had something to do with this. I can see it—yes, even you, Pop! But don't you see how silly it is" Why should Rod steal something that will belong to him anyway? I *won't* have you thinking Roddy's a thief!"

"I did not," said Pop feebly.

"Then we're agreed the crime was unpremeditated and that no accomplice could have been provided for," said Mr. Queen. "Incidentally, the sapphires are not in this box. I've looked."

"But it's ridiculous!" cried Joan. "Oh, I don't care about losing the jewels, beautiful as they are; Pop can afford the loss; it's just that it's such a mean, dirty thing to do. Its very cleverness makes it dirty."

"Criminals," drawled Mr. Queen, "are not notoriously fastidious, so long as they achieve their criminal ends. The point is that the thief has hidden those gems somewhere—the place is the very essence of his crime, for upon its simplicity and later accessibility depends the success of his theft. So it's obvious that the thief's hidden the sapphires where no one would spot them easily, where they're unlikely to be found even by accident, yet where he can safely retrieve them at his leisure."

"But heavens," said Paula, exasperated, "they're not in the car, they're not in the dressing-room, they're not on any of us, they're not in this box, there's no accomplice . . . it's impossible!"

"No," muttered Mr. Queen. "Not impossible. It was done. But how? How?"

The Trojans came out fighting. They carried the pigskin slowly but surely down the field toward the Spartans' goal line. But on the 21-yard stripe the attack stalled. The diabolical Mr. Ostermoor, all over the field, intercepted a forward pass on third down with 8 yards to go, ran the ball back 51 yards, and USC was frustrated again.

The fourth quarter began with no change in the score; a feeling that was palpable settled over the crowd, a feeling that they were viewing the first Trojan defeat in Rose Bowl history. Injuries and exhaustion had taken their toll of the Trojan team; they seemed dispirited, beaten.

"When's he going to open up?" muttered Pop. "That trick!" And his voice rose to a roar. "Roddy! Come on!"

The Trojans drove suddenly with the desperation of a last strength. Carolina gave ground, but stubbornly. Both teams tried a kicking duel, but Ostermoor and Roddy were so evenly matched that neither side gained much through the interchange.

Then the Trojans began to take chances. A long pass—successful. Another!

"Roddy's going to town!"

Pop Wing, sapphires forgotten, bellowed hoarsely; Gabby shrieked encouragement; Joan danced up and down; the Grand Duke and Madame looked politely interested; even Paula felt the mass excitement stir her blood.

But Mr. Queen sat frowning in his seat, thinking and thinking as if cerebration were a new function to him.

The Trojans clawed closer and closer to the Carolina goal line, the Spartans fighting back furiously but giving ground, unable to regain possession of the ball.

First down on Carolina's 19-yard line, with seconds to go!

"Roddy, the kick! The kick!" shouted Pop.

The Spartans held on the first plunge. They gave a yard on the second. On the third—the inexorable hand of the big clock jerked towards the hour mark—the Spartans' left tackle smashed through USC's line and smeared the play for a 6-yard loss. Fourth down, seconds to go, and the ball on Carolina's 24-yard line!

"If they don't go over next play," screamed Pop, "the game's lost. It'll be Carolina's ball and they'll freeze it . . . *Roddy!*" he thundered. "*The kick play!*"

And, as if Roddy could hear that despairing voice, the ball snapped back, the Trojan quarterback snatched it, held it ready for Roddy's toe, his right hand between the ball and the turf . . . Roddy darted up as if to kick, but as he reached the ball he scooped it from his quarterback's hands and raced for the Carolina goal line.

"It worked!" bellowed Pop. "They expected a place kick to tie—and it worked! *Make it, Roddy!*"

USC spread out, blocking like demons. The Carolina team was caught completely by surprise. Roddy wove and slithered through the bewildered Spartan line and crossed the goal just as the final whistle blew.

"We win! We win!" cackled Gabby, doing a war dance.

"Yowie!" howled Pop, kissing Joan, kissing Paula, almost kissing Madame.

Mr. Queen looked up. The frown had vanished from his brow. He seemed serene, happy.

"Who won?" asked Mr. Queen genially.

But no one answered. Struggling in a mass of worshipers, Roddy was running up the field to the 50-yard line; he dashed up to the box and thrust something into Pop Wing's hands, surrounded by almost the entire Trojan squad.

"Here it is, Pop," panted Roddy. "The old pigskin. Another one for your collection, and a honey! Joan!"

"Oh, Roddy."

"My boy," began Pop, overcome by emotion; but then he stopped and hugged the dirty ball to his breast.

Roddy grinned and, kissing Joan, yelled: "Remind me that I've got a date to marry you tonight!" and ran off towards the Trojan dressing-room followed by a howling mob.

"Ahem!" coughed Mr. Queen. "Mr. Wing, I think we're ready to settle your little difficulty."

"Huh?" said Pop, gazing with love at the filthy ball. "Oh." His shoulders sagged. "I suppose," he said wearily, "we'll have to notify the police—"

"I should think," said Mr. Queen, "that that isn't necessary, at least just yet. May I relate a parable? It seems that the ancient city of Troy was being besieged by the Greeks, and holding out very nicely, too; so nicely that the Greeks, who were very smart people, saw that only guile would get them into the city. And so somebody among the Greeks conceived a brilliant plan, based upon a very special sort of guile; and the essence of this guile was that the Trojans should be made to do the very thing the Greeks had been unable to do themselves. You will recall that in this the Greeks were successful, since the Trojans, overcome by curiosity and the fact that the Greeks had sailed away, hauled the wooden horse with their own hands into the city and, lo! that night, when all Troy slept, the Greeks hidden within the horse crept out, and you know the rest. Very clever, the Greeks. May I have that football, Mr. Wing?"

Pop said dazedly: "Huh?"

Mr. Queen, smiling, took it from him, deflated it by opening the valve, unlaced the leather thongs, shook the limp pigskin over Pop's cupped hands . . . and out plopped the eleven sapphires.

"You see," murmured Mr. Queen, as they stared speechless at the gems in Pop Wing's shaking hands, "the thief stole the jewel-case from Pop's coat pocket while Pop was haranguing his beloved team in the Trojan dressing-room before the game. The coat was lying on a rubbing table and there was such a mob that no one noticed the thief sneak over to the table, take the case out of Pop's coat, drop it in a corner after removing the sapphires, and edge his way to the table where the football to be used in the Rose Bowl game was lying, still uninflated. He loosened the laces surreptitiously, pushed the sapphires into the space between the pigskin wall and the rubber bladder, tied the laces, and left the ball apparently as he had found it.

"Think of it! All the time we were watching the game, the eleven sapphires were in this football. For one hour this spheroid has been kicked, passed, carried, fought over, sat on, smothered, grabbed, scuffed, muddied—with a king's ransom in it!"

"But how did you know they were hidden in the ball," gasped Paula, "and who's the thief, you wonderful man?"

Mr. Queen lit a cigaret modestly. "With all the obvious hiding places eliminated, you see, I said to myself: 'One of us is a thief, and the hiding place must be accessible to the thief after this game.' And I remembered a parable and a fact. The parable I've told you, and the fact was that after every winning Trojan game the ball is presented to Mr. Percy Squires Wing."

"But you can't think—" began Pop, bewildered.

"Obviously you didn't steal your own gems," smiled Mr. Queen. "So, you see, the thief had to be someone who could take equal advantage with you of the fact that the winning ball is presented to you. Someone who saw that there are two ways of stealing gems: to go to the gems, or to make the gems come to you.

"And so I knew that the thief was the man who, against all precedent and his taciturn nature, has been volubly imploring the Trojan team to win this football game; the man who knew that if the Trojans won the game the ball would immediately be presented to Pop Wing, and who gambled upon the Trojans; the man who saw that, with the ball given immediately to Pop Wing, he and he exclusively, custodian of Pop's wonderful and multifarious treasures, could retrieve the sapphires safely unobserved—grab the old coot, Your Highness!—Mr. Gabby Huntswood."

The author of this story wrote one of the nation's most acclaimed books in 1997, called Underworld. *Don DeLillo's eleventh novel begins with Bobby Thomson's dramatic home run in 1951 to win the National League pennant for the New York Giants in a playoff with the Brooklyn Dodgers. This landmark baseball event happened on the same day that the cold war began with the announcement of a Soviet nuclear test. In over eight hundred pages,* Underworld *portrays the American psyche during the cold war era, up to the fall of the Soviet empire. A movie about the book is anticipated. Elmore Leonard has said about DeLillo, "For my money, our finest current novelist." DeLillo's sports knowledge and interest show up in many of his writings, and especially in this witty football story. "Game Plan" was originally published in* The New Yorker.

Don DeLillo

GAME PLAN (1971)

OF THE GAME ITSELF, a spectacle of high-shouldered men panting in the grass, I remember little or nothing. We played well that night or didn't play well; we won or lost. What I do recall are the names of plays and of players. Our opponent was West Centrex Biotechnical Institute. They were bigger than we were, a bit faster, possibly better trained, but as far as I could tell our plays had the better names.

At the kickoff, the receiving team dropped back and found its ground, holding a moment. Under the tumbling ball, the other team charged, verbs running into mammoth nouns, small wars commencing here and there, exultation and first blood, a helmet bouncing brightly on the phosphorescent grass, the breathless impact of two destructive masses, quite pretty to watch.

We huddled at the thirty-one.

"Blue turk right," Hobbs said. "Double-slot, re-T chuck-and-go, gap-angle wide, near-in belly toss, counter-sag, middle-sift W, zero snag delay."

"You forgot the snap number," Onan Moley said.

"How about three?" Ed Jessup said.

"How about two?" I said.

"Two it is," Hobbs said.

Six plays later, we left the huddle with a sharp handclap and trotted up to the Centrex twenty, eager to move off the ball, sensing a faint anxiety on the other side of the line.

"How to hit!" George Dole shouted out to us from the bench. "Way to pop, way to go, way to move! How to sting them, big Jerry! Huh huh huh huh! How to play this game!"

We scored, and Bing Jackmin kicked the extra point. I went over to the sideline and got down on one knee, the chin strap of my helmet un-done—material for a prize-winning sports photo. Commotion every-where. Offensive Backfield Coach Oscar Veech was shouting into my left ear.

"On the 32-break I want you to catapult out of there. I want you to really bulldoze. I want to see you cascade into the secondary."

"Tremendous imagery," I said.

"But be sure you protect that ball."

"Right."

"Get fetal, get fetal."

"Fetal!" I shouted back.

Our defense rolled into a gut 4–3 with variable off-picks. Down at the end of the bench, Raymond Toon seemed to be talking into his right fist. I got up and went over there. When he saw me coming, he covered the fist with his other hand.

"What are you doing, Toonie?" I asked.

"Nothing."

"I know what you're doing."

"Broadcasting the game," he admitted.

Their quarterback, Artie Telcon, moved them on the ground past mid-field. At the sideline, I listened to one of our backfield coaches lecturing Garland Hobbs: "Employ the aerial game to implement the running game whereby you force their defense to respect the run, which is what they won't do if they can anticipate pass and read pass and if our frequency, say on second and long, indicates pass. If they send their linebackers, you've been trained and briefed and you know how to counter this. You counter this by audibilizing. You've got your screen, your flare, your quick slant-in. Audibilize. Audibilize. Audibilize."

They tried a long field goal, wide, and we went out. Hobbs hit Ron Steeples for good yardage. Steeples was knocked cold on the play, and the ref called a time-out to get him off. Chuck Deering came running in to replace him, tripping and falling as he reached the huddle. His left ankle appeared to be broken, and the ref called time again to get him off.

When we rehuddled Hobbs said, "Stem left, L and R hitch and cross, F weak switch to strong. On hut."

"What?" Flanders said.

"On hut."

"No, the other thing, F something."

"F weak switch to strong."

"What kind of pattern is that?"

"Are you kidding? Are you serious?"

"What a bunch of turf-eaters," Co-Captain Moody Kimbrough said.

"When did they put that pattern in, Hobbsie?"

"Tuesday or Wednesday. Where were you?"

"It must have been Wednesday," Flanders said. "I was at the dentist Wednesday."

"Nobody told you about the weak switch to strong?"

"I don't think so, Hobbsie."

"Look, run out ten yards, put some moves on your man, and then wait for further instructions."

"I'm co-captain to a bunch of turf-eaters," Kimbrough said.

"On hut. Break."

Centrex sent their linebackers. Hobbs left the pocket and I had Mallon, their psychotic middle linebacker, by the jersey. He tripped and I released, moving into a passing plane for Hobbs. He saw me but threw low. I didn't bother diving for it. One of the coaches, Vern Feck, screamed into our chests as we came off. "What in the hell is going on here? What are you feebs doing out there? What in the goddam goat-smelling hell is the name of the game you people are playing?"

Head Coach said nothing.

Lenny Wells came off in pain—groin damage or hamstring. Telcon spotted a man absolutely alone in the end zone and hit him easily, and I looked around for my helmet.

"Our uniforms are green and white," Bing Jackmin said as we watched them kick off. "The field itself is green and white—grass and chalk markings. We melt into our environment. We are doubled in the primitive mirror."

Centrex called time because they had only seven men on the field. We assembled near our own forty-five while they got straightened out. Ed Jessup, our tight end, was bleeding from his mouth.

"That ass-belly 62 got his fist in," he said.

"You'd better go off," I said.

"I'm gonna hang in."

"A tough area to bandage, Ed. Looks like it's just under the skin-bridge running to the upper gum."

"I get that 62. I get that meat-man" he said.

"Let's ching those nancies," Flanders said.

"Maybe if you rinsed with warm water, Eddie."

Their left tackle was an immense and very geometric piece of work, about six-seven and two-seventy—an oblong monument to intimidation. It was the responsibility of our right guard, Cecil Rector, to contain this man. Offensive Line Coach Tweego had Cecil Rector by the pads as I crossed the sideline.

"I want you to fire out, boy," Tweego said. "You're not blowing them out. You're not popping. You're not putting any hurt on those people."

I sat on the bench next to Billy Mast as Telcon riddled our secondary with seam patterns. Billy was wearing his helmet. I leaned toward him and spoke in a monotonous intonation.

"Uh, this is Maxcom, Robomat."

Billy Mast looked at me.

"Robomat, this is Maxcom. Do you read?"

"Uh, Roger, Maxcom," he said.

"You're looking real good, Robomat. Is that affirm?"

"Uh, Roger. We're looking real good."

"What is your thermal passive mode control?"

"Vector five and locking."

"Uh, what is your inertial thrust correction on fourth and long?"

"We read circularize and non-adjust."

"That is affirm, Robomat. You are looking real super on the inset retro deployment thing. We read three one niner five niner. Twelve seconds to adapter vent circuit cutoff."

"Affirmative, Maxcom. Three one niner five niner. Twelve seconds to vent cut. There is God. We have just seen God. He is all around us."

"Uh, Roger, Robomat. Suggest braking burn and mid-course tracking profile. Blue and holding."

Hobbs faked a trigger pitch to Taft Robinson and handed to me, a variation off the KC draw. I was levelled by Mallon. He came down on top of me, chuffing like a train. In the huddle, Hobbs called the same play. For some reason, it seemed a very beautiful thing to do. More than the thoughtful gesture of a teammate—a near-philosophic statement. Hobbs received the snapback, Roy Yellin pulled, and there I was with the football, the pigskin, running to daylight, to starlight, and getting hit again by Mike Mallon, by No. 55, by five five. A lyrical moment, the sum of something doubled.

Three firecrackers went off in the stands. The crowd responded with prolonged applause. I flared to the left, taking Mallon with me. Taft Robinson held for a two-count and then swung over the middle. Hobbs threw high under pressure. Third and four, or maybe fourth and three. The gun sounded and we headed for the tunnel.

Here before our cubicles we sit quietly, content to suck the sweet flesh out of quartered oranges. We are preoccupied with conserving ourselves for the second half and do not make work by gesturing to each other, or taking more than the minimum number of steps from here to there. A park bench has somehow found its way into the dressing area.

From nearby, I hear Sam Trammel's voice: "Crackback. Crackback."

I get to my feet and take six steps to the water fountain. Cecil Rector stands against the wall. Tweego has him by the shoulder pads once again.

"Contain, contain, contain that man," Tweego says. "Rape him. Rayyape that sumbitch. Do not let that sumbitch infringe."

Slowly I swing my arms over my head. I see Jerry Fallon and approach him. He is standing in front of his cubicle, hands at his sides, headgear on the floor between his feet.

"Jerry boy, big Jerry," I say.

"Huh huh huh," he mutters.

George Owen, a line coach, stands on a chair. His gaze moves slowly across the room, then back again. He holds his clenched fists against the sides of his head. Slowly his knees begin to bend. "Footbawl!" he shouts. "This is footbawl. You thow it, you ketch it, you kick it. Footbawl! Footbawl! Footbawl!"

Bing Jackmin squib-kicked down the middle. Andy Chudko hit the ball-carrier at full force and skidded on his knees over the fallen player's body. I watched Head Coach assume his stance at the mid-field stripe. Dennis Smee, our middle linebacker, shouted down at the front four: "Tango-2. Reset red. Choke off that sweep!"

Garland Hobbs opened with a burn-7 hitch to his flanker off the fake picket. I moved into my frozen-insect pose, ready to pass-block. Their big tackle shed Cecil Rector and came dog-paddling in. I jammed my helmet into his chest and brought it up fast, striking his chin. He kept coming, kept mauling me, finally driving me down and putting an elbow into my neck. I couldn't think of anything to say.

Hobbs looked toward the head coach for guidance on a tough third-down call. Head Coach said nothing. His arms remained folded, his right foot tamping the grass. This was his power, to deny us the words we needed. He was the maker of plays, the namegiver. We were his chalk-scrawls. Something like that.

Hobbs said, "Zone set, triple tex, delta-3 series, jumbo trap delay, cable blocking, double-D to right, shallow hinge reverse."

The crowd was up and screaming—a massive, sustained, but somehow vacuous roar. I slowed to a walk and watched Taft Robinson glide into the end zone. Touchdown. He executed a dainty little curl to the left and casually dropped the football. Moody Kimbrough lifted him up. Spurgeon Cole stood beneath the goalposts, repeating them, arms raised in the shape of a crossbar and uprights, his fists clenched.

Jessup to No. 62: "Suckmouth. Nipplenose. Bluefinger."

I walked down to the end of the bench. Raymond Toon was all alone, still broadcasting into his right fist.

"There it goes, end over end, a high spiral. The deep man avoids—or evades would be better. Down he goes, woof. First and ten at the twenty-six or thirty-one. Here they come and Andy Chudko, in now for Butler, goes in high, No. 61, Andy Chudko—Fumble! Fumble!—six feet even, about two-twenty-five, doubles at center on offense. Chudko, majoring in airport-commissary management, plays a guitar to relax, no other hobbies, fumbles after the whistle. College football—a pleasant and colorful way to spend an autumn afternoon."

"It's nighttime, Toonie," I said.

"There he goes—five, six, seven, eight, nine, ten, eleven yards, power sweep, *twelve* yards, from our vantage point here at the Orange Bowl in sun-drenched Miami, Florida. John Billy Small combined to bring him down. John Billy, as they break the huddle—what a story behind this boy, a message of hope and inspiration to all those likewise afflicted, and now look at him literally slicing through those big ball-carriers! Flag, flag, flag—a flag down. All the color and excitement here. Oh, he's got it with a yard to spare off a good block by 53 or 63. Three Rivers Stadium in Pittsburgh or Cincinnati. Perfect weather for football. He's a good one, that Telcon. Multi-talented. Woof! Plenty of hitting down there. I'm sure glad I'm up here. D.C. Stadium in the heart of the nation's capital. Crisp blue skies. A new wrinkle in that offense, or is it a broken play? Time-out on the field with the score all locked up at something—something. And now back to our studios for this message."

I watched Lloyd Philpot, Jr., come toward the bench. His jersey wasn't tucked into his pants. Tape was hanging from his left wrist and hand. He squatted down next to me on the sideline.

"I didn't infringe," he said sadly. "The coaches wanted optimum infringement. They insisted on that all week in practice. But I didn't do the job. I didn't infringe."

Centrex was running sweeps. I went over and sat with Garland Hobbs. Somebody in the stands behind us, way up high, was blowing into some kind of air horn. It sent a prehistoric cry across the night.

"String-in left, modified crossbow, quickside brake and swing, flow-and-go, dummy stitch, on two, on two," Hobbs said.

"You're always giving us on two, on two," Roy Yellin said. "All freaking night—'on two, on two.' What about four for a change? 'On four?'"

"Four it is," Hobbs said.

More firecrackers went off in the stands, and newspapers blew across the line of scrimmage. I ran a desultory curl pattern over the middle, putting moves on everybody I passed, including teammates. The stadium was emptying out. I returned to the huddle. We went to the line and set. The left side of our line was offside. The gun sounded, and we walked off the field and went through the tunnel into the locker room.

Onan Moley is already naked as we walk in. We sit before our cubicles and pound our cleated shoes on the stone floor ten times. One of the school's oldest traditions. The coaches gather at one end of the room. Onan's right arm is in a cast and he stands against a wall absently waving his left hand to keep a fly away from his face. There are blades of grass stuck to the dried blood on his cheekbone. Next to me, Garland Hobbs takes a long red box from the bottom of his cubicle. The label on it reads: "All-American Quarterback. A Mendelsohn-Topping Sports Motivation Concept." Hobbs opens the box and puts it on the bench between us. He arranges twenty-two figurines on a tiny gridiron and then spins a dial. His team moves smartly downfield. Before it gets to be my turn to spin, the coaches call for quiet, clapping their hands and whistling. Head Coach is standing before a blackboard at the front of the room. His arms are crossed over his chest and he holds his baseball cap in his right hand. We are all waiting. He looks at his watch and then nods to Rolf Hauptführer, his defensive backfield coach.

Hauptführer faces us, assuming a stance of sorts. "Be ready," he says.

We sit waiting, immobile in our soaked equipment, until Hauptführer begins to read our names from the team roster, pausing after each one to give us time to chant an answer.

The chief interest in this story is personal character. A down-on-his-luck father goes to see his son play a big game for Yale. The gridiron drama is first-rate but the real value is ethical, showing that one can wrest victory from defeat, and that it is necessary to go the distance and never give up. These qualities may seem corny to some, but they are just as important to contemporary success as they were in the past. An interesting aspect of football is that it can reveal as well as develop character. Ralph D. Paine (1871–1925) is best known as a scholarly writer on U.S. naval history. His books include The Fight For a Free Sea: A Chronicle of the War of 1812 *(1920),* Roads to Adventure *(1922), and* Blackbeard, Buccaneer *(1922). Paine had a longtime attachment to Yale University, which comes through lovingly in "The Freshman Full-Back." Written in the first decade of the twentieth century, it is the oldest story in the book.*

Ralph D. Paine

THE FRESHMAN FULL-BACK (1909)

THE BOYISH NIGHT CITY EDITOR glanced along the copy-readers' table and petulantly exclaimed:

"Isn't that spread head ready yet, Mr. Seeley? It goes on the front page and we are holding open for it. Whew, but you are slow. You ought to be holding down a job on a quarterly review."

A portly man of middle age dropped his pencil and turned heavily in his chair to face the source of this public humiliation. An angry flush overspread his face and he chewed at a grayish mustache as if fighting down rebellion. His comrades at the long table had looked up from their work and were eyeing the oldest copy-reader with sympathetic uneasiness while they hoped that he would be able to hold himself in hand. The night city editor felt the tension of this brief tableau and awaited the threatened outbreak with a nervous smile. But Seeley jerked his green eyeshade so low that his face was partly in eclipse, and wheeled round to resume his task with a catch of the breath and a tone of surrender in his reply.

"The head will be ready in five minutes, sir. The last pages of the story are just coming in."

A much younger man, at the farther end of the table, whispered to his neighbor:

"That's cheap and nasty, to call down old man Seeley as if he were a cub reporter. He may have lost his grip, but he deserves decent treatment for what he has been. Managing editor of this very sheet, London correspondent before that, and the crack man of the staff when most of the rest of us were in short breeches. And now Henry Harding Seeley isn't any too sure of keeping his job on the copy-desk."

"That's what the New York newspaper game can do to you if you stick at it too long," murmured the other.

"Back to the farm for mine."

It was long after midnight when these two put on their coats and bade the city editor's desk a perfunctory "Good-night."

They left Henry Harding Seeley still slumped in his chair, writing with dogged industry.

"He's dead tired, you can see that," commented one of the pair as they headed for Broadway, "but, as usual, he is grinding out stuff for the Sunday sheet after hours. He must need the extra coin mighty bad. I came back for my overcoat at four the other morning, after the poker game, and he was still pegging away just like that."

Other belated editors and reporters of the *Chronicle* staff drifted toward the elevator, until the gray-haired copy-reader was left alone in the city room as if marooned. Writing as steadily as if he were a machine warranted to turn out so many words an hour, Seeley urged his pencil until the last page was finished. Then he read and corrected the "story," slipped it through a slit in a door marked "Sunday Editor," and trudged out, while the tower clock was striking three.

Instead of seeking the chop-house, wherein the vivacious and tireless youth of the staff were wont to linger over supper, he turned into a side street and betook himself to a small café as yet unfrequented by the night owls of journalism. Seeley was a beaten man, and he preferred to nurse his wounds in a morbid isolation. His gait and aspect were those of one who was stolidly struggling on the defensive, as if hostile circumstances had driven him into a corner where he was making his last stand.

Through the years of his indomitable youth as a reporter of rare ability and resourcefulness, he had never spared himself. Burning the candle at both ends, with a vitality which had seemed inexhaustible, he had won step after step of promotion until, at forty, he was made managing editor of that huge and hard-driven organization, the *New York Chronicle*. For five years of racking responsibility Henry Harding Seeley had been able to maintain the pace demanded of his position.

Then came an error of judgment—a midnight decision demanded of a fagged mind—and his O.K. was scrawled upon the first sheet of a story of embezzlement in Wall Street. By an incredible blunder the name of the fugitive cashier was coupled with that of the wrong bank. Publication of the *Chronicle* story started a terrific run on this innocent institution, which won its libel suit against the newspaper in the amount of one hundred thousand dollars.

The managing editor, two reporters, and the copy-reader who had handled the fatal manuscript, were swept out of the building by one cyclonic order from the owner thereof. Henry Seeley accepted his indirect responsibility for the disaster in grim, manly fashion, and straightway sought another berth befitting his journalistic station. But his one costly slip was more than a nine-days' scandal along Park Row, and other canny proprietors were afraid that he might hit them in the very vital regions of their pockets. Worse than this, his confidence in himself had suffered mortal damage. The wear and tear of his earlier years had left him with little reserve power, and he went to pieces in the face of adverse fortune.

"Worked out at forty-five," was the verdict of his friends, and they began to pity him.

The will to succeed had been broken, but Seeley might have rallied had not his wife died during the ebb-tide of his affairs. She had walked hand in hand with him since his early twenties, her faith in him had been his mainstay, and his happiness in her complete and beautiful. Bereft of her when he stood most in need of her, he seemed to have no more fight in him, and, drifting from one newspaper office to another, he finally eddied into his old "shop" as a drudging copy-reader and an object of sympathy to a younger generation.

There was one son, strong, bright, eager, and by dint of driving his eternally wearied brain overtime, the father had been able to send him to Yale, his own alma mater. More or less pious deception had led young Ernest Seeley to believe that this father had regained much of his old-time prestige with the *Chronicle* and that he had a hand in guiding its editorial destinies. The lad was a Freshman, tremendously absorbed in the activities of the autumn term, and his father was content that he should be so hedged about by the interests of the campus world as to have small time or thought for the grizzled, taciturn toiler in New York.

This was the kind of man that trudged heavily into the little German café of an early morning after his long night's slavery at the copy-desk. His mind, embittered and sensitive to slights like a raw nerve, was brooding over the open taunt of the night city editor, who had been an office boy under him in the years gone by. From force of habit he seated himself at a table in the rear of the room, shunning the chance of having to face an acquaintance. Unfolding a copy of the city edition, which had been laid on his desk damp from the press-room, Seeley scanned the front page with scowling uneasiness, as if fearing to find some blunder of his own handiwork. Then he turned to the sporting page and began to read the football news.

His son Ernest had been playing as a substitute with the university eleven, an achievement which stirred the father's pride without moving his enthusiasm. And the boy, chilled by his father's indifference, had said little about it during his infrequent visits to New York. But now the elderly Seeley sat erect, and his stolid countenance was almost animated as he read, under a New Haven date line:

"The Yale confidence of winning the game with Princeton tomorrow has been shattered, and gloom enshrouds the camp of the Elis to-night. Collins, the great full-back, who has been the key-stone of Yale's offensive game, was taken to the infirmary late this afternoon. He complained of feeling ill after the signal practice yesterday; fever developed overnight, and the consulting physicians decided that he must be operated on for appendicitis without delay. His place in the Princeton game will be filled by Ernest Seeley, the Freshman, who has been playing a phenomenal game in the back-field, but who is so lacking in experience that the coaches are all at sea to-night. The loss of Collins has swung the betting around to even money instead of 5 to 3 on Yale."

The elder Seeley wiped his glasses as if not sure that he had read aright.

Ernest had seemed to him no more than a sturdy infant and here he was, on the eve of a championship football battle, picked to fight for the "old blue." The father's career at Yale had been a most honorable one. He, too, had played on the eleven and had helped to win two desperate contests against Princeton. But all this belonged to a part of his life which was dead and done for. He had not achieved in after years what Yale expected of him, and his record there was with his buried memories.

Supper was forgotten while Henry Seeley wondered whether he really wanted to go to New Haven to see his boy play. Many of his old friends and classmates would be there and he did not wish to meet them.

And it stung him to the quick as he reflected:

"I should be very happy to see him win but—but to see him whipped! I couldn't brace and comfort him. And supposing it breaks his heart to be whipped as it has broken mine! No, I won't let myself think that. I'm a poor Yale man and a worse father, but I couldn't stand going up there to-day."

Even more humiliating was the thought that he would shrink from asking leave of the city editor. Saturday was not his "day off," and he so greatly hated to ask favors at the office, that the possibility of being re-buffed was more than he was willing to face.

Into his unhappy meditations broke a boisterous hail:

"Diogenes Seeley, as I live. Why, you old rascal, I thought you were dead or something. Glad I didn't get foolish and go to bed. Here, waiter, get busy."

Seeley was startled, and he looked much more distressed than rejoiced as he lumbered from his table to grasp the outstretched hand of a class-mate. The opera hat of this Mr. Richard Giddings was cocked at a rakish angle, his blue eye twinkled good cheer and youthful hilarity, and his as-pect was utterly care-free.

"How are you, Dick?" said Seeley, with an unusual smile which singu-larly brightened his face. "You don't look a day older than when I last saw you. Still cutting coupons for a living?"

"Oh, money is the least of my worries," gayly rattled Mr. Giddings. "Been doing the heavy society act tonight, and on my way home found I needed some sauerkraut and beer to tone up my jaded system. By Jove, Henry, you're as gray as a badger. This newspaper game must be bad for the nerves. Lots of fellows have asked me about you. Never see you at the University Club, nobody sees you anywhere. Remarkable how a man can lose himself right here in New York. Still running the *Chronicle*, I sup-pose."

"I'm still in the old shop, Dick," replied Seeley, glad to be rid of this awkward question. "But I work nearly all night and sleep most of the day, and am like a cog in a big machine that never stops grinding."

"Shouldn't do it. Wears a man out," and Mr. Giddings sagely nodded his head. "Course you are going up to the game to-day. Come along with me. Special car with a big bunch of your old pals inside. They'll be tick-led to death to find I've dug you out of your hole. Hello! Is that this morning's paper? Let me look at the sporting page. Great team at New Haven, they tell me. What's the latest odds? I put up a thousand at five to three last week and am looking for some more easy money."

The alert eye of the volatile Richard Giddings swept down the New Haven dispatch like lightning.

With a grievous outcry he smote the table and shouted:

"Collins out of the game? Great Scott, Henry, that's awful news. And a green Freshman going to fill his shoes at the last minute. I feel like weeping, honest I do. Who the deuce is this Seeley? Any kin of yours? I suppose not or you would have bellowed it at me before this."

"He is my only boy, Dick," and the father held up his head with a shadow of his old manner. "I didn't know he had the ghost of a show to make the team until I saw this dispatch."

"Then, of course, you are coming up with me," roared Mr. Giddings. "I hope he's a chip of the old block. If he has your sand they can't stop him. Jumping Jupiter, they couldn't have stopped you with an axe when you were playing guard in our time, Henry. I feel better already to know that it is your kid going in at full-back to-day."

"No, I'm not going up, Dick," said Seeley slowly. "For one thing, it is too short notice for me to break away from the office, and I—I haven't the nerve to watch the boy go into the game. I'm not feeling very fit."

"Stuff and nonsense, you need a brain cure," vociferated Richard Giddings. "You, an old Yale guard, with a pup on the team, and he a Freshman at that! Throw out your chest, man; tell the office to go to the devil—where all newspapers belong—and meet me at the station at ten o'clock sharp. You talk and look like the oldest living grad with one foot in the grave."

Seeley flushed and bit his lip. His dulled realization of what Yale had been to him was quickened by this tormenting comrade of the brave days of old, but he could not be shaken from his attitude of morbid self-effacement.

"No, Dick, it's no use," he returned with a tremulous smile. "You can't budge me. But give my love to the crowd and tell them to cheer for that youngster of mine until they're blue in the face."

Mr. Richard Giddings eyed him quizzically, and surmised that something or other was gravely wrong with his grizzled classmate. But Seeley offered no more explanations and the vivacious intruder fell to his task of demolishing sauerkraut with great gusto, after which he nimbly vanished into a cruising hansom with a sense of having been rebuffed.

Seeley watched him depart at great speed and then plodded toward his up-town lodgings. His sleep was distressed with unhappy dreams, and during a wakeful interval he heard a knock at his sitting-room door.

An office boy from the *Chronicle* editorial rooms gave him a note and waited for an answer.

Seeley recognized the handwriting of the managing editor and was worried, for he was always expecting the worst to happen. He sighed with relieved surprise as he read:

"My Dear Mr. Seeley:

"Please go to New Haven as soon as possible and do a couple of columns of descriptive introduction of the Yale-Princeton game. The sporting department will cover the technical story, but a big steamboat collision has just happened in North River, two or three hundred drowned and so on, and I need every man in the shop. As an old Yale player I am sure I can depend on you for a good story, and I know you used to do this kind of stuff in fine style."

Seeley fished his watch from under a pillow. It was after ten o'clock and the game would begin at two. While he hurried into his clothes he was conscious of a distinct thrill of excited interest akin to his old-time joy in the day's work. Could he "do this kind of stuff in fine style"? Why, before his brain had begun to be always tired, when he was the star reporter of the *Chronicle,* his football introductions had been classics in Park Row. If there was a spark of the old fire left in him he would try to strike it out, and for the moment he forgot the burden of inertia which had so long crushed him.

"But I don't want to run into Dick Giddings and his crowd," he muttered as he sought his hat and overcoat. "And I'll be up in the press-box away from the mob of old grads. Perhaps my luck has turned."

When Henry Seeley reached the Yale field the eleven had gone to the dressing-rooms in the training house, and he hovered on the edge of the flooding crowds, fairly yearning for a glimpse of the Freshman full-back and a farewell grasp of his hand. The habitual dread lest the son find cause to be ashamed of his father had been shoved into the background by a stronger, more natural emotion. But he well knew that he ought not to invade the training quarters in these last crucial moments. Ernest must not be distraught by a feather's weight of any other interest than the task in hand. The coaches would be delivering their final words of instruction and the old Yale guard could picture to himself the tense absorption of the scene. Like one coming out of a dream, the past was returning to him in vivid, heart-stirring glimpses. Reluctantly he sought his place in the press-box high above the vast amphitheatre.

The preliminary spectacle was movingly familiar: the rippling banks of color which rose on all sides to frame the long carpet of chalked turf; the clamorous outbursts of cheering when an eddy of Yale or Princeton undergraduates swirled and tossed at command of the dancing dervish of a leader at the edge of the field below; the bright, buoyant aspect of the multitude as viewed en masse. Seeley leaned against the railing of his lofty perch and gazed at this pageant until a sporting editor, long in harness, nudged his elbow and said:

"Hello! I haven't seen you at a game in a dozen years. Doing the story or just working the press-badge graft? That namesake of yours will be meat for the Tigers, I'm afraid. Glad he doesn't belong to you, aren't you?"

Seeley stared at him like a man in a trance and replied evasively:

"He may be good enough. It all depends on his sand and nerve. Yes, I am doing the story for a change. Have you the final line-up?"

"Princeton is playing all her regular men," said the sporting editor, giving Seeley his note-book. "The only Yale change is at full-back—and that's a catastrophe."

Seeley copied the lists for references and his pencil was not steady when he came to "Full-back, Ernest T. Seeley." But he pulled his thoughts away from the eleven and began to jot down notes of the passing incidents which might serve to weave into the fabric of his description. The unwonted stimulus aroused his talent as if it were not dead but dormant. The scene appealed to him with almost as much freshness and color as if he were observing it for the first time.

A roar of cheering rose from a far corner of the field and ran swiftly along the Yale side of the amphitheatre, which blossomed in tossing blue. The Yale eleven scampered into view like colts at pasture, the substitutes veering toward the benches behind the side-line. Without more ado the team scattered in formation for signal practice, paying no heed to the tumult which raged around and above them. Agile, clean-limbed, splendid in their disciplined young manhood, the dark blue of their stockings and the white "Y" gleaming on their sweaters fairly trumpeted their significance to Henry Seeley. And poised behind the rush-line, wearing his hard-won university blue, was the lithe figure of the Freshman full-back, Ernest Seeley.

The youngster, whose fate it was to be called a "forlorn hope," looked fragile beside his comrades of the eleven. Although tall and wiry, he was like a greyhound in a company of mastiffs. His father, looking down at him from so great a height that he could not read his face, muttered to himself while he dug his nails into his palms:

"He is too light for this day's work. But he carries himself like a thoroughbred."

The boy and his fellows seemed singularly remote from the shouting thousands massed so near them. They had become the sole arbiters of their fate, and their impressive isolation struck Henry Seeley anew as the most dramatic feature of this magnificent picture. He must sit idly by and watch his only son battle through the most momentous hour of his young life, as if he were gazing down from another planet.

The staccato cheers of Princeton rocketed along the other side of the field, and the eleven from Old Nassau ran briskly over the turf and wheeled into line for a last rehearsal of their machine-like tactics. Henry Seeley was finding it hard to breathe, just as it had happened in other days when he was waiting for the "kick-off" and facing a straining Princeton line. The minutes were like hours while the officials consulted with the captains in the centre of the field. Then the two elevens ranged themselves across the brown turf, there was breathless silence, and a Princeton toe lifted the ball far down, toward the Yale goal. It was the young full-back who waited to receive the opening kick, while his comrades thundered toward him to form a flying screen of interference. But the twisting ball bounded from his too eager arms, and another Yale back fell on it in time to save it from the clutches of a meteoric Princeton end.

"Nervous. Hasn't steadied down yet," exclaimed a reporter behind Henry Seeley. "But he can't afford to give Princeton any more chances like that. Her ends are faster than chain lightning."

The father groaned and wiped the sweat from his eyes. If the team were afraid of this untried full-back, such a beginning would not give them confidence. Then the two lines locked and heaved in the first scrimmage, and a stocky Yale half-back was pulled down in his tracks. Again the headlong Princeton defense held firm and the Yale captain gasped, "Second down and three yards to gain." The Yale interferers sped to circle one end of the line, but they were spilled this way and that and the runner went down a yard short of the needed distance.

The Yale full-back dropped back to punt. Far and true the ball soared into the Princeton field, and the lithe Freshman had somewhat redeemed himself. But now, for their own part, the sons of Old Nassau found themselves unable to make decisive gains against the Yale defense. Greek met Greek in these early clashes, and both teams were forced to punt again and again. Trick-plays were spoiled by alert end-rushers for the blue or the orange and black, fiercely launched assaults at centre were torn asunder, and the longer the contest raged up and down the field the more clearly it was perceived that these ancient rivals were rarely well matched in point of strength and strategy.

The Yale coaches were dismayed at this turn of events. They had hoped to see the ball carried toward the Princeton goal by means of shrewdly devised teamwork, instead of which the burden of the game was shifted to one man, the weakest link in the chain, the Freshman at full-back. He was punting with splendid distance, getting the ball away when it seemed as if he must be overwhelmed by the hurtling Tigers. Once or twice, however, a hesitant nervousness almost wrought quick disaster, and the Yale partisans watched him with tormenting apprehension.

The first half of the game was fought into the last few minutes of play and neither eleven had been able to score. Then luck and skill combined to force the struggle far down into Yale territory. Only ten yards more of trampled turf to gain and Princeton would cross the last white line. The indomitable spirit which had placed upon the escutcheon of Yale football the figure of a bulldog rampant, rallied to meet this crisis, and the hard-pressed line held staunch and won possession of the ball on downs. Back to the very shadow of his own goal-posts the Yale full-back ran to punt the ball out of the danger zone. It shot fairly into his grasp from a faultless pass, but his fingers juggled the slippery leather as if it were bewitched. For a frantic, awful instant he fumbled with the ball and wildly dived after it as it caromed off to one side, bounded crazily, and rolled beyond his reach.

The Princeton quarter-back had darted through the line like a bullet. Without slackening speed or veering from his course, he scooped up the ball as he fled toward the Yale goal-line. It was done and over within a twinkling, and while the Yale team stampeded helplessly in his wake the devastating hero was circling behind the goal-posts where he flopped to earth, the precious ball apparently embedded in his stomach. It was a Princeton touchdown fairly won, but made possible by the tragic blunder of one Yale man. While ten thousand Princeton throats were barking their jubilation, as many more loyal friends of Yale sat sad-eyed and sullen and glowered their unspeakable displeasure at the slim figure of the full-back as he limped into line to face the try for goal.

The goal was not scored, however, and the fateful tally stood six to nothing when the first half ended, with the blue banners drooping disconsolate.

Henry Seeley pulled his slouch hat over his eyes and sat with hunched shoulders staring at the Yale team as it left the field for the intermission. He had forgotten about his story of the game. The old spectre of failure obsessed him. It was already haunting the pathway of his boy. Was he also to be beaten by one colossal blunder? Henry Seeley felt that Ernest's whole career hung upon his behavior in the second half. How would the lad "take his medicine"? Would it break his heart or rouse him to fight more valiantly? As if the father had been thinking aloud, the sporting editor at his side observed:

"He may win the game yet. I like the looks of that boy. But he did make a hideous mess of it, didn't he? I hope he hasn't got a streak of yellow in him."

Henry Seeley turned on his neighbor with a savage scowl and could not hold back the quivering retort:

"He belongs to me, I want you to understand, and we'll say nothing about yellow streaks until he has a chance to make good next half."

"Whew-w-w, why did you hold it out on me, old man?" gasped the sporting editor. "No wonder you kicked me black and blue without knowing it. I hope he is a chip of the old block. I saw you play here in your last game."

Seeley grunted something and resumed staring at the field. He was thinking of the present moment in the training quarters, of the muddy, weary players sprawled around the head coach, of his wise, bitter, stinging rebukes and admonitions. Perhaps he would take Ernest out of the game. But Seeley was confident that the coaches would give the boy a chance to redeem himself if they believed his heart was in the right place. Presently the two teams trotted on the field, not as nimbly as at their first appearance, but with dogged resolution in their demeanor. Henry Seeley saw his son glance up at the "cheering sections," as if wondering whether their welcome was meant to include him. One cheer, at least, was intended to greet him, for Henry Seeley stood on his chair, waved his hat, and thundered:

" 'Rah, 'rah, 'rah, for Yale, my boy. Eat 'em alive as your daddy used to do."

The men from Princeton had no intention of being devoured in this summary fashion. They resumed their tireless, whirlwind attack like giants refreshed, and so harried their Yale foemen that they were forced to their utmost to ward off another touchdown. This incessant battering dulled the edges of their offensive tactics, and they seemed unable to set in motion a consistent series of advances. But the joy of Princeton was tempered by the knowledge that this, her dearest enemy, was not beaten until the last play had been signalled.

And somehow the Yale machine of muscle, brains, and power began to find itself when the afternoon shadows were slanting athwart the arena. With the ball on Princeton's forty-yard line the chosen sons of Eli began a heroic advance down the field. It was as if some missing cog had been supplied. "Straight old-fashioned football" it was, eleven minds and bodies working as one and animated by a desperate resolve, which carried the Yale team along for down after down into the heart of Princeton's ground.

Perhaps because he was fresher than the other backs, perhaps because the captain knew his man, the ball was given to the Yale full-back for one swift and battering assault after another. His slim figure pelted at the rush-line, was overwhelmed in an avalanche of striped arms and legs, but somehow twisted, wriggled, dragged itself ahead as if there was no stopping him. The multitude comprehended that this despised and disgraced Freshman was working out his own salvation along with that of his comrades. Once, when the scrimmage was untangled, he was dragged from beneath a heap of players, unable to regain his feet. He lay on the grass a huddled heap, blood smearing his forehead. A surgeon and the trainer doused and bandaged him, and presently he staggered to his feet and hobbled to his station, rubbing his hands across his eyes as if dazed.

When, at length, the stubbornly retreating Princeton line had been driven deep down into their end of the field, they, too, showed that they could hold fast in the last extremity. The Yale attack crumpled against them as if it had struck a stone wall. Young Seeley seemed to be so crippled and exhausted that he had been given a respite from the interlocked, hammering onslaught, but at the third down the panting quarter-back croaked out his signal. His comrades managed to rip a semblance of an opening for him, he plunged through, popped clear of the line, fell to his knees, recovered his footing by a miracle of agility, and lunged onward, to be brought down within five yards of the coveted goal-posts.

He had won the right to make the last momentous charge. Swaying in his tracks, the full-back awaited the summons. Then he dived in behind the interference for a circuit of the right end. Two Princeton men broke through as if they had been shot out of mortars, but the Yale full-back had turned and was ploughing straight ahead. Pulled down, dragging the tackler who clung to his waist, he floundered to earth with most of the Princeton team piled above him. But the ball lay beyond the fateful chalk-line, the Yale touchdown was won, and the game was tied.

The captain clapped Seeley on the shoulder, nodded at the ball, and the full-back limped on to the field to kick the goal or lose a victory. There were no more signs of nervousness in his bearing. With grave deliberation he stood waiting for the ball to be placed in front of the goal-posts. The sun had dropped behind the lofty grand-stands. The field lay in a kind of wintry twilight. Thirty thousand men and women gazed in tensest silence at the mud-stained, battered youth who had become the crowning issue of this poignant moment. Up in the press-box a thick-set, grayish man dug his fists in his eyes and could not bear to look at the lonely, reliant figure down yonder on the quiet field. The father found courage to take his hands from his face only when a mighty roar of joy boomed along the Yale side of the amphitheatre, and he saw the ball drop in a long arc behind the goal-posts. The kick had won the game for Yale.

Once clear of the crowds, Henry Seeley hurried toward the training quarters. His head was up, his shoulders squared, and he walked with the free stride of an athlete. Mr. Richard Giddings danced madly across to him:

"Afraid to see him play were you, you silly old fool? He is a chip of the old block. He didn't know when he was licked. Wow, wow, wow, blood will tell! Come along with us, Henry."

"I must shake hands with the youngster, Dick. Glad I changed my mind and came to see him do it."

"All right, see you at Mory's to-night. Tell the boy we're all proud of him."

Seeley resumed his course, saying over and over again, as if he loved the sound of the words, "chip of the old block," "blood will tell."

This verdict was like the ringing call of bugles. It made him feel young, hopeful, resolute, that life were worth having for the sake of its strife. One thing at least was certain. His son could "take his punishment" and wrest victory from disaster, and he deserved something better than a coward and a quitter for a father.

The full-back was sitting on a bench when the elder Seeley entered the crowded, steaming room of the training house. The surgeon had removed the muddy, blood-stained bandage from around his tousled head and was cleansing an ugly, ragged gash. The boy scowled and winced but made no complaint, although his bruised face was very pale.

"Must have made you feel pretty foggy," said the surgeon. "I shall have to put in a few stitches. It was a deuce of a thump."

"I couldn't see very well and my legs went queer for a few minutes, but I'm all right now, thanks," replied the full-back, and then, glancing up, he espied his father standing near the door. The young hero of the game beckoned him with a grimy fist. Henry Seeley went over to him, took the fist in his two hands, and then patted the boy's cheek with awkward and unaccustomed tenderness.

"Sit still, Ernest. I won't interfere with the doctor's job. I just wanted to let you know that I saw your bully work. It made me think of—it made me think of—"

Henry Seeley's voice broke curiously and his lip quivered. He had not meant to show any emotion.

His son replied with a smile of affectionate admiration:

"It made you think of your own teams, didn't it? And I was thinking of you in that last half. It helped my nerve a whole lot to remember that my dad never knew when he was licked. Why, even the coaches told me that between the halves. It put more ginger into me than anything else. We've got to keep up the family record between us."

The father looked beyond the boy as if he were thinking of a bigger, sterner game than football. There was the light of a resurrected determination in his eyes, and a vibrant earnestness in his voice as he said:

"I'm not worrying about your keeping the family record bright, Ernest. And, however things may go with me, you will be able to hang fast to the doctrine which helped you to-day, that your father, too, doesn't know when he is whipped."

Here is another father-son piece. This time the son is a star player and the father a coach. They have to oppose each other in a game, however, which poses special difficulties. This story was written for Esquire. *Samuel W. Taylor is coauthor of* Fighters Up: The Story of American Fighter Pilots in the Battle of Europe *(1945).*

Samuel W. Taylor

THERE MUST BE A LOSING COACH (1942)

WHEN THE GIRL CAME INTO the lodge lobby, the State football squad was sitting around waiting out the hour until bedtime. They'd traveled halfway across the continent to play tomorrow's game and they were nervous but trying not to show it. According to all the dope, they'd win at a walk, but you never could tell. And the Wildcats would be pointing for them. In fact, it was known that the job of the Wildcat coach depended on winning this game. He'd shoot the wad against State.

But when the girl came into the lobby, the thirty-four State huskies for the moment forgot about the game; and even Coach Happy Hough, in the middle of telling something important to a reporter from the *Telegram,* trailed off. The reporter didn't notice it, for he'd also seen the girl. She stood just inside the doorway, oblivious of—or accustomed to— the open admiration, and slowly surveyed the faces of the squad.

Then she said, "Swede," and envious eyes turned to the tall end who got to his feet, face a dull, flushed red in contrast to straw-colored hair.

"Hello, Marta," he said, and crossed to her, automatically avoiding a foot stuck out to trip him.

They stood a moment together, and then she said, "I thought maybe you'd call."

"Been pretty busy." His eyes went to the floor. "We only got in yesterday. We had a workout, and there was a banquet last night, and then tonight Coach brought us out here to this lodge where we wouldn't be molested—I mean, where things would be quiet—"

"I know you've been busy," she said. "But I thought you might give us a ring." Her voice lowered. "Andy wants to see you."

He glanced over his shoulder, almost furtively. "It's almost bedtime," he said.

"You could be decent about it," she said, and added with a faint touch of scorn: "Or perhaps you think he'll try to bribe you?"

"Let's not go into things."

"Swede, you've hurt him terribly. He's still your father, you know. And you haven't even given him a ring."

"I'll ask Coach." Swede crossed to where Happy Hough was talking with the *Telegram* reporter.

"I'd like to go out for an hour, Coach."

Happy Hough glanced at the lobby clock. Four minutes to nine. "Be in by ten," he said. He didn't mean five after ten.

"Nothing can happen in an hour," the reporter said. He began laughing loudly, then sobered abruptly under Happy Hough's ice-blue gaze. The coach had got his nickname for the same reason fat men are called Tiny.

"Just like old times," the girl said as she drove Swede down the twisting canyon road. "A moon and a car and—us." The light touch came with an effort.

Swede said nothing. Looking backwards always hurt, and he didn't like to do it.

"How are you making out, Swede?"

"Okay."

"You're first-string end, I hear."

"Yes."

"That's nice going for a sophomore."

He said nothing, and she gave up trying to make conversation. A decrepit dine-dance spot had been wedged against the hillside where the canyon widened out briefly. Marta pulled up before it, and Swede followed her in. It was a dismal place with a low ceiling and dirty floor, and deserted but for the heavy-set man in the last of the three booths. He was a big man, florid, always a bit rumpled, hearty but with small bitter lines at his mouth corners when he wasn't smiling.

He was Andy Jones, coach of the team Swede had come half across the continent to play.

"Hello, Swede."

"Hello, Dad."

There was reserve in their smiles and handshakes, almost a caution, that each tried not to show. Swede saw that his father had changed in the year and a half since he'd last seen him. That had been in Texas, before Andy Jones got the head coaching position out here. He'd always been a big man, but now there was a certain looseness about him, as if he were beginning to sag under the pressure of twenty-odd years in the coaching grind. Twenty-odd years can be a long time—high school coach, anonymous assistant in universities here and there and everywhere hoping and waiting for the big chance while the world forgot you were once All-American. And then last spring he'd finally got his bid for head coach—on a one-year contract. After all that waiting, he had to produce a winning team in one season, or drop back out of sight again. And he hadn't come through. This season his Wildcats had won two, tied one, and lost four. It was an open secret that he'd be thrown to the wolves unless the Wildcats won tomorrow's intersectional game with State.

"You're looking fine, Swede," Andy Jones said. Swede replied that he felt all right. Marta remarked about the weather and the three of them squeezed the last word out of that subject. It was stuffy and uncomfortable, and Swede had wanted to avoid it all. There was nothing he could say any more to his girl or his father, without bringing up the past, and that was all settled long ago.

The door of the place opened and slammed shut. A voice said, "A beer." Then, rising: "Hello, Andy! What bringeth thou? Are you–?" It died away.

Swede turned to see the reporter for the *Telegram* who'd been talking with Coach Happy Hough back at the lodge. The reporter was looking from Andy Jones to Swede and trying not to appear surprised.

"Hello," Andy Jones said. He nodded at Swede. "This is my boy."

"*Your* boy?"

"My *boy*. No; I'm not buying off the State players. Swede's my son."

"Oh, your *son*. Say!–that's a story! Father against son. And if the son's team wins–You don't mind if I use it, Andy?"

"Yes, I do mind. It's just a little cheap."

"Well, after all, Andy–somebody else would pick it up if I didn't. And where'd my job be?"

Andy Jones shrugged. He might have argued a year ago, but not now.

"Say, Andy, how come your boy's not playing for us instead of for State? How come–"

"Get out of here," Swede said, rising. "You've got your story, now get out of here."

"Well, sure, Swede," the reporter said hurriedly, backing away. "Sure. I was just leaving anyhow."

"I'm sorry this happened," Andy Jones said.

Swede shrugged. "It'll sell more tickets. I've got to go, Dad. It was nice seeing you again."

Driving up the twisting canyon road, the girl said, "You see how he's changed?"

"Yeah."

"Football did it to him. Do you understand why we wanted to keep you out of the game?"

Swede shrugged. "Dad's getting old, is all."

"He's forty-four. . . . If they'd given him a three-year contract—or even a two-year contract. What can a man do in one year? And if he fails now, how long will it be before he gets another chance as head coach? It isn't that he'll be out of a job. He's a good classroom man. Did you know they offered him a full professorship, back in Texas?"

"No."

"He turned it down for the one-year coaching contract here. Swede, he's got to win against your team tomorrow. He's got to have his chance."

Swede didn't say anything.

When she pulled up before the lodge they sat a few moments, awkwardly, in silence. He'd always kissed her goodnight after they'd been out together. At first teasingly, then seriously. She'd been sixteen when his father married her mother. During the trouble that made Swede leave home, Marta had taken his father's side, and that, he'd long ago decided, was that. But now as he looked at her in the moonlight the old feeling came welling up; and he abruptly got out of the car. No use starting that all over again.

"Maybe I'll see you again before we go," he said.

As he turned to the lodge she said, "Swede," and it took all the strength he had not to turn back to her.

He didn't sleep much that night. At ten the next morning the State squad had the last meal before the game. He didn't eat much. A bus took them around the city to take their minds off the game. A barker pointed out places of interest but nobody listened. The squad's wisecracks were strained, laughter too loud. The bus took them to the field house an hour before the game and they began getting into their equipment.

"Jones," Coach Happy Hough said to Swede, and motioned towards the showers. There was a moment of inaction as the squad paused, eyes on Swede. "Break it up, boys!" the trainer bawled. "Don't forget we're playing football today!"

"You read the *Telegram* this morning?" the coach asked Swede at the shower room door.

"No; but I know what it said."

Coach Hough waited, icy-blue eyes steady. A successful coach can't be a soft man at any time.

"It makes a good story. It'll help the gate." And when Swede still didn't say anything: "I might have been told about a thing like that."

"I hoped it wouldn't come out." Swede took a deep breath. "Dad and I never got along. That's all. He didn't want me to play football. So I left home."

"He didn't want you to get hurt?"

"Not that, exactly." It was hard for Swede to put this into words. He'd never talked about it outside the family, and it seemed somehow a violation of good taste. "It's because I want to follow it up, and be a coach myself. Dad wanted me to be a doctor. He said that—well you know what the coaching game is, Coach."

Happy Hough nodded. "I know." He'd failed with his first chance, and spent sixteen years waiting for another. By the time he got the second chance, he'd learned how to be ruthless. "I know. One team always has to lose. And a coach always has to win." This was almost being garrulous for Happy Hough. "Your father's right, Jones."

"I know it; but that doesn't change anything."

Happy Hough nodded. "I know. You want to be All-American end, and then go on to coaching. You've got some ideas about the game. You've worked out some variations to my system. You don't like some of the things I do with my team. You're going to set the world on fire, when you're coach." Then as Swede's jaw clenched, Happy Hough smiled, a rare thing for him, and he put his hand on the boy's shoulder. "I'm not being sarcastic, Swede. I know."

He turned to three newspapermen coming in. One of them was the *Telegram* reporter, who asked, "Any change in the lineup, Coach?"

"Yes; Warbuck at right end."

The *Telegram* man glanced at Swede. "Instead of Jones?" He knew Swede played right end; there was no need of stating it. Happy Hough ignored the question.

As the game started, Swede sat with his chin in his big hands, watching from the bench. The Wildcat guards were charging too hard. Yes, Flint, State quarterback, called for a mousetrap play and ran the ball to first downs. Then as the guards stopped charging, Flint rifled a pass to Warbuck, playing Swede's position at right end. Warbuck got his hands on the ball and dropped it. Flint's passes had a lot of stinging pace and spin; but Swede had the knack of holding them. The Flint-to-Jones pass was already becoming famous, and Flint was also a sophomore. With two more years of competition, they'd both be All-American, if nothing happened. . . . Swede tried to pick out Marta's face in the sea of the Wildcat rooting section. She was there, but he couldn't see her. The crowd was good, thanks to the curiosity aroused by the *Telegram* article. Father *versus* son. The thing seemed cheaply melodramatic. . . . The Wildcats had the ball now, and the offense rolled. They had power. The fullback, Lincoln, was terrific, a coach's dream. But he didn't have precision blocking from the Wildcat line, and they lost the ball down in pay dirt where the going got tough.

At the end of the half, Coach Hough gave brief advice about each position. He said to the quarterback: "Flint, they can be suckered. Watch out for Lincoln; he's a natural. But open up the trick stuff. They can be suckered." This was saying they weren't well coached, and Swede felt his face hot in a flush. Happy Hough did not look at him.

Except for Lincoln, the State trick stuff would have rolled in the third quarter. The Wildcat fullback was the coach's dream—the man who plays with some sixth sense, smelling out plays by instinct, leaving his position time after time, but always being in it when State passed into his territory. Late in the quarter he intercepted a pass and broke loose. The State safety man downed him deep in State territory. Held for three downs, the Wildcats place-kicked for three points, the first score of the game. Swede saw his father dancing like a boy at the Wildcat bench.

In the fourth quarter Warbuck dropped two more of Flint's stinging passes. Either one, if completed, would have meant a State score and would have put them in the lead. Swede found himself watching Andy Jones on the bench across the field. With another year, Andy Jones could polish his team up. He had material. With a chance, he might become another Warner or Sutherland—or even a Rockne.

"Jones!" Coach Hough barked. "Warm up!"

Swede ran up and down before the bench, bringing his knees high. The loudspeaker said, "Jones warming up for State," and then, in answer to the expectant hush from the crowd, it added that Jones was the son of the Wildcat coach. The crowd knew this, but wanted to hear it said. Coach Hough stood up, lean and solid and hard and tough, and Swede paused before him.

"How are you?" The ice-blue eyes were steady.

"Okay."

"Look, Swede." It was the first time the coach had called him by his nickname. "I don't want to put you in there today, but you can hang onto Flint's passes. Do you want to go in?"

"Yes," Swede said. He had no choice.

"It's only a game—but the game's like that. You understand?"

"Yes."

The coach spatted him on the rump and Swede ran onto the field, feeling tight inside. He'd never known before that Happy Hough's ice-blue eyes could be other than hard.

State made yardage as the Wildcats anticipated a pass. Then when the defense had pulled in, Flint called the seventy-one play. That was the Flint-to-Jones play, already becoming famous.

Swede dropped into position, counting for rhythm. The shift; flanker to the left. At the count of nine the ball snapped from center. Swede put a glancing block on the Wildcat tackle and drifted diagonally three steps to his left, then spurted to his right past the Wildcat back assigned to him on pass defense, catching the man flat-footed. Running downfield, he saw that Lincoln had smelled out the play and was cutting for him. Swede put on all the steam he had for thirty steps, and then looked back over his shoulder. The pass was leading him, and still high. Lincoln was alongside now. The ball had too much lead.

And then somehow, right then, everything seemed to freeze. The ball was motionless, seams showing. In this curious frozen moment, Swede wondered if he really should call on that reserve that always came to him in a pinch. It was a mysterious surge of energy that briefly lifted him above what he was capable of doing. It was this thing that had made him sure, deep inside, that he'd become All-American. But now in this moment his father was on the Wildcat bench, and the fate of that pass was the fate of his future.

His father was praying that Swede should miss that pass. Coach Hough had put Swede in the game for the purpose of catching the pass. Swede hadn't stopped to realize fully until this moment just how hard and merciless the game of football was. He'd only known the rising fire within him that wouldn't be downed. He'd seen himself All-American, and going on to be another Warner or Sutherland—or perhaps even a Rockne. But he hadn't known there would be this moment.

He was still running; the ball was spinning; Lincoln was stride and stride with him. The ball was out of reach.

Then almost automatically he took an extra stride faster than he could possibly run, leaped higher than he possibly could leap, and when his wide-spread fingers felt the sharp sting of the ball Lincoln was a full step behind. The single step made the difference, and Lincoln's desperate tackle grazed Swede's heels as he went over the line for six points and the game.

At the final gun, Andy Jones arose from the bench and started across the turf to congratulate the winning coach, which was the formality. The crowd was pouring out of the stadium, flowing over the edge and onto the field like molten metal from a huge ladle. The flood swept over the Wildcat goalposts, bearing them down; waving autograph cards, it engulfed the State players on their way to the field house. A mob was around Coach Hough, shaking his hand and laughing at his slightest word. Coach Andy Jones came alone across the close-clipped turf, picking his way among the eddies of the human flood, unnoticed, a heavy man beginning to sag with the pressure, eyes straight before him and with the howl of the wolves in his ears. The crowd around Coach Hough jostled him as he picked a way through.

"Congratulations, Happy," he said, shaking hands. "Your boys played a great game."

"Thanks, Andy," Hough said. "I was just lucky."

Those were the formalities, and with them over Andy Jones turned away to face the wolves alone.

The shadows were long and cool as Swede came out of the field house. Marta was waiting. She'd been crying. Swede knew she was thinking: "I hope you're satisfied!" She'd been against him in the old argument with his father. She was hurt, now. It hurt her to see Andy Jones defeated.

"That was a great catch, Swede," she said.

"Thanks." There was nothing more to say. "Well, goodbye."

"I'll drive you home," she said.

He didn't know how to refuse the ride. They picked their way among the thousands of cars all trying to get out at once.

"Mother will have dinner ready. Steak for you," Marta said when they reached the car. "Let's sit here awhile until the jam smoothes out."

Swede knew he couldn't face his father. He said, "There's a banquet for the squad tonight. So if you'll drop me at the hotel."

She took his big hand, looking up at him understandingly, her fine eyes still red from crying. "It's all right, Swede. We want you home with us for dinner. We all understand."

Swede said nothing. He didn't understand.

"That professorship's still open in Texas. Andy's going to take it."

Swede swallowed. His throat was tight. It was hard to see his father beaten.

She said, "I really think he's glad, in a way. It's a weight off him. He laughed at me for crying. I think he's really happy in a way."

"If he'd had another year here to build a squad—"

"No; he doesn't feel that way, now. He had good boys, and he knows it. And the fullback—Lincoln—there's a coach's dream. I believe Andy knows it now. He knows that he just isn't cut out for a big-time coach. You either are or you aren't. Now he knows. That's something, to know. But you see he couldn't give up until he'd had his chance—until he *did* know. Now he'll be happy as a professor. If he'd taken the job last year, he'd always have known he should have been a great coach. It would have continually gnawed at him."

Swede nodded miserably. They sat there while the cars crawled slowly past like grains into a giant funnel.

"It's the toughest game of all," Marta went on. "One coach always has to lose, and every coach must always win. That's *why* it calls you, Swede. It's a challenge. You're like Andy was twenty years ago. You can't ignore the challenge. You've got to meet it. You've got to know. You'll never be satisfied until you've made the try."

That was it, Swede realized. He'd never reduced it to so many words.

"I'm running off at the mouth," Marta said. "But you see, I'm trying to reason things out for myself. There was a moment when you were after that pass, when things seemed to stand still, and I realized what I'm trying to say now. Swede, if you hadn't made that last try for that pass, I wouldn't have been waiting for you. Shall we go home?"

Yes," Swede said, "let's go." He realized he was hungry, and happy at the prospect of having dinner again at home.

This story will tug at your heartstrings. It's about a boy whose father died when he was very young, leaving him alone with his mother. Football fills a void, drawing son and mother closer, and providing some worthwhile lessons. The story originated in the Atlantic Monthly. *Its author, Jay Neugeboren, is a professor and writer-in-residence at the University of Massachusetts. His stories have appeared in leading magazines like* Gentlemen's Quarterly, Sport, *and* The American Scholar, *and have been reprinted in several anthologies, including* Best American Short Stories *and* Prize Stories: The O. Henry Awards. *Among Neugeboren's twelve books are* Sam's Legacy *(1974),* Before My Life Began *(1985), and* Don't Worry About the Kids *(1997). He is the only author to have won six consecutive Syndicated Fiction Prizes, and his screenplay for "The Hollow Boy," which premiered on American Playhouse in 1991, has won many honors.*

Jay Neugeboren

THE ST. DOMINICK'S GAME (1979)

THOUGH I MISSED MY FATHER most at school football games, when the other boys' fathers were there, I never told Mother. I didn't feel I had the right. My father died over eight years ago, and I was too young then to remember him much, so I figured the best thing was not to bother Mother about what I was feeling. It wasn't even as if I ever knew him well enough to miss him, I'd tell myself. It was more that at things such as football games, I was aware of his absence.

Mother didn't attend any of our football games and I could understand that. Ever since Father died, any kind of violence upsets her terribly. There are some days when she can't bear to look at raw meat or raw fish. Maybe if I'd been there when he died I'd feel the same. Mother has never told me what it was like, but it seems they were both sitting up in bed and reading that night, when he suddenly grabbed her arm and then blood started spilling from his mouth. She screamed and locked the door and wouldn't let me into the room until others had arrived, so I never got to see my father again until the funeral. He lived through the frozen hills of Korea, I heard her say to her sister, but he died in our bed in New Jersey. Go figure.

I used to try to picture what the scene was like, and I always imagined that his eyes must have been as wide and round as they could be—as if somebody had just surprised him—and then I'd find myself picturing Mother scrambling back and forth across the bed and the floor, trying to wipe things up, and the look I'd see in her eyes would be awful—so frantic and helpless and dazed that I'd just clench my fists and get more and more angry. Sometimes, trying to feel what she must have felt. I used to wonder if it was possible to love another person too much.

What I couldn't understand, though, was the way she acted when I told her I was trying out for the Fowler football team. Mother had been teaching French at the Fowler School since before Father died, and sometimes she worried that I was too quiet or too much of a loner, and I thought she'd be glad to hear that I wanted to participate in a team sport. But the first thing she did when I gave her my news was to threaten to get Dr. Hunter, our headmaster, to remove me from the squad. If she didn't receive satisfaction from him, she declared, she would go straight to Mr. Marcus, our coach.

I liked Mr. Marcus and I didn't want him to think I was a sissy, so what I did the next morning, despite her threat, was to talk with Dr. Hunter myself, before she could get to him. I told him about going out for the team and about how Mother was against it and about how I didn't want to disobey her, but that I was continuing to play anyway, and he sat in his big leather chair for a while, just thinking. I looked right at him, trying hard not to stare at his left arm, even though it fascinated me. It was shorter than his right one, and sort of hung from his shoulder, swinging gently to and fro whenever he walked, as if it were made of foam rubber. Most of us at school figured that, given his age, he'd maimed it in World War II, but nobody ever asked him, or knew for sure.

"You know," he said, "that your mother has not had the easiest life."

"I know," I said.

"Still, you can't be expected to sacrifice your boyhood because of the misfortunes she has endured, can you?"

I shrugged and said I didn't know. He nodded then and asked me a few more questions, all of which made me feel very uncomfortable, and then, after making some remarks about how contact sports built character, he said he would speak to her for me. The next evening he stopped by our house. Mother was upstairs grading papers, and when I told her who was there, she didn't seem to know what to do first. Finally, after starting down the stairs and coming back up two separate times, she sent me to entertain Dr. Hunter while she changed clothes.

My mother is a very attractive woman, with reddish-brown hair and very beautiful eyes. People tell me that I inherited her eyes. They're blue, but not pale blue—slate-blue, I would call them. She's tall and she makes a lot of her own clothing. When she's upstairs working at her sewing machine, which her mother used when my mother was a girl, and looking out the window, she always hums to herself in an easy way that lets me know she's feeling very peaceful. She's thirty-eight years old now, but people are never certain of her age. Sometimes she looks as if she's in her twenties, and other times, especially when she wears her hair up, she can look as if she's in her forties. It may sound strange, but one of the reasons I was sorriest that she objected to my playing football was that I'd always hoped I'd see her at a football game. She has the kind of face and coloring that's just perfect for a football game—what I would call an autumn kind of face.

When she came down the stairs that evening, she looked absolutely gorgeous. It wasn't what she was wearing—it was more the proud way she carried herself and the high color in her cheeks. Dr. Hunter must have noticed also, because he seemed a bit awkward when he stood up and shook her hand and said hello.

I went upstairs and tried to do my homework, but I couldn't. I put on the radio so they wouldn't think I was eavesdropping, and then I took out the sheets of plays that Mr. Marcus had passed out and I studied my assignments. At about ten-thirty, when I closed my door to go to bed, Dr. Hunter was still downstairs.

The next morning at breakfast Mother said that she'd decided it was all right for me to be on the football team. She warned me not to get hurt, and I said I'd be careful, and then she changed the subject. I tried not to smile too much, but I felt really good, and at practice that afternoon I nearly killed myself trying to impress Mr. Marcus. I dove for fumbles like a maniac, I was a tiger on defense, I wore myself out on wind sprints, and somehow I managed to intercept two passes. That was the day Mr. Marcus began using me as an example. At first I liked the idea. I wasn't an especially good athlete and I knew it. So did Mr. Marcus. But he kept pointing me out to the other guys and telling them that if they would only try as hard as I did, they *might* have a good team.

Mr. Marcus wasn't very tall—maybe five-foot-seven—but there was something powerful about him and, like the other guys, I used to be scared sometimes that he would get so angry at us that he would pick us up, one by one, and smash our heads against each other. He yelled and screamed and never stopped moving. "My Aunt Tillie could do better—" he'd shout. Then, when the guys laughed, he'd counter with, "What are you laughing at?—Get in there and drive. What do you guys thinks this is—a church social? Put your shoulder in there and drive. Come on, girls—let's hustle. *Hustle!* Watch Eddie—there's guts for you! Watch that little guy give it his heart—" He could keep up patter like this for the entire two-hour practice, and at first I was thrilled with the way he praised me so much. After a while, however, I saw how it made the other guys resent me. Still, even though I didn't want them to, I kept giving it everything I had. I couldn't do anything else. I'd be as calm as could be during the day, or when I was standing on the sidelines watching—but the minute I was on the field and there were players opposite me, something inside me went click and I turned into a virtual madman. I didn't care what happened to me! It wasn't because I was angry or bitter or anything like that. In fact, whenever a fight broke out during a scrimmage or a game, I'd move back a step or two, instinctively, and stay away.

When I got home for supper, at about six-fifteen, I'd be totally beat. I'd stay in a hot tub for a long time, soaking my bruises, but when I came down for supper, Mother never asked me about practice or about Mr. Marcus or about any of my scratches or black-and-blue marks. As the weeks went by, it made me feel more and more depressed to sit with her each night and talk about the weather or her classes or my homework or our vacation plans, when all the time I was wanting to share the practices with her, and how great I was feeling just to be on a team with other guys. Finally one night, after a day on which a few of the guys had really had it with the way Mr. Marcus kept praising me and damning them, and they'd gotten me during a pile-up and given me some hard knuckles to the nose and eyes, I asked her straight out if, when he was young, my father had liked football.

She seemed surprised that I should ask, but when she answered, she didn't seem at all nervous. "I don't know," she said. "I suppose he did, but he never talked to me about it. Handball was your father's sport."

"Handball?" I asked.

She laughed then. "He grew up in a city, remember? Not out here with birds and trees. That came later—with me."

"Was he good?" I asked.

She wiped her lips, and when she sighed I could see that she was making a decision, to tell me something about him. "I suppose so," she said. "He was good at most things he tried. He was a very competitive man. He took me down to Brighton Beach once—this was when we were courting—and I stood behind the fence and watched him banging this little black ball against a brick wall on one of the hottest days of the year. He wore leather gloves." She brushed her hair back from her forehead and breathed heavily, almost as if she were feeling the heat of that summer day all over again. "I couldn't believe it, if you want the truth. And, as I recall things, it made him happy that I kept suggesting to him that it was too hot to play. I think he liked the idea of resisting my suggestions." She leaned forward then, her chin on her hands, looking very young. "Oh, Eddie," she said. "Your father was very special, did you know that? There was nobody quite like him. My parents couldn't understand for the life of them how a *cultivated* young woman like their daughter could be attracted to such a rough-and-tumble young man from the streets of Brooklyn, but there it was, wasn't it?" She smiled, as if dreaming, and I told myself I'd been right about why she always had such a hard time talking about him before—that it was because they'd loved each other too much, that for her it was always as if he'd died only a few weeks ago. "I mean, there was something about the way the sweat dripped along his chest and the ferocious look he got in his eyes whenever he slammed the ball, and then—the instant the game was over—that easy smile of his. Oh, he had a smile, Eddie! Bright and white in that dark surly face. And not just for me, I can assure you. Not just—"

She stopped and her smile became a straight line. "Not just what—?" I asked.

She looked away, and then stood and went to the sink. "Nothing," she said, and she changed the subject so abruptly—asking me about our Spanish class's magazine drive—that I knew there was nothing I could do to make her tell me any more.

Although our school went up to the twelfth grade, we fielded a team that represented only the seventh through the ninth grades. The Fowler School wasn't very large—four hundred students, including girls—and the other schools that were in our league were about the same size, so we played six-man football. We wore full uniforms and the rules were basically the same as in eleven-man football, except that no direct hand-offs were allowed and you had to go fifteen yards for a first down. The second week of practice Mr. Marcus made me a defensive end; I liked the position, especially when a blitz was on: this meant that instead of "boxing," and protecting my end against a run, I just crashed through the line and tried to knock over everybody I could until I got to the ballcarrier. Except for Charlie Gildea, who was the best player on our team, I seemed to be the only player who tried hard during practices. At games, when everyone's parents and girlfriends were there, the other guys would exert themselves, but it didn't matter much. "Games are won from Monday to Friday," Mr. Marcus would say, and he was right.

At the end of every practice session we would "run the gauntlet." We'd line up in a straight line, about three yards apart from each other, and Mr. Marcus would give the first man a football and he'd have to run through the entire team, one man at a time. When he finished he'd become the last man and the second man would get the football. The guys hated him for it. By the time you came to the fifth or sixth man you were usually dead, but Mr. Marcus wouldn't let you stop to get your wind back, either, so most of the guys would just fake the rest of the run, falling to the ground before they were tackled. What I'd do, though, would be to tuck the ball into my stomach, both hands around it, put my head down, and charge ahead, ramming as hard as I could into each guy I came to. I suppose it hurt me more than it did the others, but it made me feel so good! Mr. Marcus would tease me because I never tried to fake anybody out or even to sidestep. "Here comes Deion Sanders," he'd say. "Come on, girls, are you going to let this little runt bowl you over? Or is he too fast for you? Move toward the runner—*toward* him!" His voice kept me going, I think. "Way to drive, Eddie," he'd say, as I got up after each guy had rolled me to the ground. "Way to hang in there—"

Mr. Marcus wasn't very big, but we all knew he'd played halfback at a teacher's college in Pennsylvania, and once, on a hot day at the beginning of the season, he came to practice in short pants and I'd never seen such powerful legs. They weren't hairy, either. Just broad, smooth, and muscular. When he was teaching during the day, though, all his power seemed gone. He taught social studies and he could never control a class. I didn't have him for a teacher yet because he taught ninth and tenth grade and I was only in the eighth, but the guys on the team from the ninth grade would talk in the locker room about crazy things that went on in his classrooms. They said that some of the students actually smoked or made out right in front of him.

What seemed especially strange to me, though, wasn't anything Mr.

Marcus said or did, but this look he had on his face when he walked through the halls. It was as if he were lost. The way my classes were arranged, I used to pass him in the halls three or four times a day and sometimes I'd say hello to him. He always said hello back to me, but I had the definite feeling that when I was out of my uniform, he didn't know who I was. He seemed to be thinking about something else, I thought, and when I was home remembering what his face had looked like as we passed each other, I'd start thinking that I'd been wrong: it wasn't as if he were lost, really—it was more as if he had lost something.

He was never lost at practice, though. His eyes were all fire then. Especially when he began to get us ready for the big game against St. Dominick's on Parents Day.

St. Dominick's was an orphanage about twenty miles away, run by Jesuits, and we were playing them for the first time. Mr. Marcus told us that he'd seen them play the year before and that we would have to play more than perfectly if we expected to win. By this time we'd played six games, winning four of them, and I wasn't starting but I was getting in, usually near the end—at garbage time—when either victory or defeat seemed certain. I didn't expect to get into the St. Dominick's game, however, because even though I was hitting harder and playing better than ever before, so were the other guys. Dr. Hunter showed up at two of our practices that week, and once, when we were running through our kick-off return drill, I saw him pat Mr. Marcus on the shoulder in a friendly way. Until then I'd had the feeling Dr. Hunter didn't like him. It was nothing he ever said, but what he didn't say. He'd stopped by our house twice after that first time, and both times I'd tried to entertain him while Mother got ready to come downstairs, by telling him about our team. But whenever I said something nice about Mr. Marcus, and waited for him to say something back, he either changed the subject or agreed with me. He never added anything.

"You certainly are a quiet lad," he said to me one night, when, as usual, I'd run out of things to say. I shrugged. Nobody else I knew ever used a word like "lad," I thought to myself, looking down at the rug. But then he added something that made me look up fast. "Not at all like your father was, are you?"

"I don't know," I said. "I—I don't really remember him much. . ."

"Of course," he replied, but before I could get up the courage to ask him for more information, Mother had come down.

I went upstairs to my room, so they could talk. After the first time he came by, I'd begun to think of the fact that he might eventually marry Mother. The thing was, though, that every time I began to imagine what it would be like to have a man like Dr. Hunter for a father, I'd wind up by thinking of what it would be like to have Mr. Marcus as one. I knew this was foolish, especially since Mr. Marcus was seven or eight years younger than Mother, but I thought about it anyway and I wondered a lot about what he did after he went home from practice. I kept thinking what a waste it was that a man like him wasn't married, and how sad it would be if he somehow went the rest of his life without a son or daughter of his own.

I tried hard, a few times that week, to get Mother to talk about my father again, but she wasn't very interested. She did bring down a box of photos for me to look at one night—and after going through the first few, of them before they were married, going to Coney Island and Jones Beach and to her parents' home in Connecticut together, she got up and told me to come to her if I had any questions. All the photos were marked on the back, she said. Then she went upstairs.

I looked at the photos for as long as I could, but without Mother next to me, to give me stories about what wasn't in the photos, I got depressed. I closed my eyes tight a few times, and tried to force myself to remember things I'd done with my father, but it was hard, and the only clear pictures that came into my head were one of him laughing and giving me a ring for my thumb that he'd made out of a folded dollar bill—and another of him tossing me into the air and of how scared I was until I fell back down and he caught me and rubbed his rough beard against my cheek. I went upstairs and gave my mother each of these memories—asking her if he'd ever told her how to make a ring out of a dollar bill, and if he used to toss me in the air a lot or just once in a while, and if his beard had been very thick—but even though she answered my questions, she didn't add things to her answers, and she made me feel I was intruding on a part of her life I didn't have any right to.

The day before the St. Dominick's game, Dr. Hunter made a speech in our assembly about how we should be as friendly as possible toward the boys from the other school. They were less fortunate than we were, and he hoped we would all learn something from watching them and meeting them. The speech made me squirm. Words weren't going to do any tackling for us, I said to myself. But there was something else that was making me uneasy, and that was the way Mother was acting. When I turned to look at her in the back of the assembly hall, her cheeks were flushed, and this annoyed me. A lot of things annoyed me about her during this period, I know—the way she walked down the halls, the way she stopped to look in mirrors so much at home, the way she smiled at Dr. Hunter and the other teachers, the kind of clothing she wore—and the best way I can explain is to say that during this period, for the first time in my life, I was unhappy that Mother was pretty.

I certainly felt this way when we went to Parents Day together. Very few of the mothers came up to her to ask her questions about their children, but a lot of the fathers did, and the way she smiled, and the way they tried to impress her or make her laugh, bothered me. I kept wanting to go over to her and order her to stop—or to grab her and take her far away—and at the same time I kept wishing she would just pay a little more attention to me, and that she'd ask me about the game and about what our chances were and if I thought I'd get to play.

We were going through our passing drills when the St. Dominick's team arrived. They came in a pale yellow school bus, and they already had their uniforms and cleats on when they stepped down from the bus onto the field. Mr. Marcus went over to their coach, who wore a priest's black shirt and white collar, and shook hands with him, and while they talked we kept going through our drills, trying to act indifferent to their arrival. Their uniforms were black and gold, and I think we were all surprised at how new and clean they were.

I noticed, too, how serious they were about everything they did, even their jumping jacks. The other thing I noticed, of course, was the blacks on their team. Almost half their squad was black and there were also a few Puerto Rican-looking players. Although we had seven or eight at our school, and a few of the other teams in our league had one or two black players, I felt certain we were terrified by the sheer *percentage* of blacks on their team. One of the players standing near me confirmed my suspicion by saying that he wished we had "a few of those" on our team. "Can they run!" he exclaimed. I turned to him, wanting to contradict him, but I didn't say anything because I had to admit that my reaction had been pretty much the same. I assumed that black athletes were faster than whites, and that a team full of blacks would be almost impossible to beat.

By the time the whistle blew for the kickoff, our spirits were high, though, and the guys were all patting each other on the rear end and everybody was giving everybody else encouragement. On the sidelines the students and the parents were watching and clapping for us, and the girls stood together and did cheers most of the guys pretended to be an-noyed by. I looked for my mother, but she wasn't there. We huddled around Mr. Marcus. "They look fast," he said, "but they're not very big. If you hit hard on the opening play, the game is ours. Is that clear? Hit hard and keep hitting. Drive, drive, drive! Let the man opposite you know you're the boss, okay? I think we can win this game. What do you think—?" We yelled back that we would kill them, smash them, obliter-ate them, and then Mr. Marcus put his hand into the middle of the cir-cle and we thrust our own hands in, pyramiding them until he shouted, "*Let's go!*" and then we all let out a big roar and the starting team ran out onto the field.

We kicked off and St. Dominick's ran the ball back to the twenty-five-yard line, but on the first play from scrimmage, Charlie Gildea red-dogged into their backfield and smashed this little black kid. The ball skittered out of his arms and John Weldon, our left end, fell on it. I threw my helmet into the air and raced down the sideline with the others to get closer to the play. Mr. Marcus tried not to seem excited, but I could tell he was just as thrilled as we were. Charlie Gildea went around right end on the first play after that and gained three yards. Mr. Marcus yelled at our guys to hit hard and I believe they were hitting as hard as they could, but on the next play I watched the way the St. Dominick's team dug in on defense. They dumped Guy Leonard to the ground for no gain. As I expected, Charlie Gildea went back to pass on the next play. I didn't watch him, though. I watched the line. The three St. Dominick's linemen charged through our men as if they weren't there. Charlie sidestepped one of them but the other two smashed him for a ten-yard loss.

Going back to pass again, on fourth down, Charlie was pulled down on the forty-two-yard line. It was their ball, first and fifteen to go, and it took them exactly four running plays to cover the fifty-eight yards they needed for a touchdown. The crowd was quiet. The St. Dominick's coach was yelling at his boys, and none of them were even smiling. Mr. Marcus was angry. "X-15!" he called. "And stop looking at the ground—look into their eyes. I want them to know they're in a ball game! Pick out a man on the kickoff and lay him flat!" X-15 was a reverse play, and it worked. The St. Dominick's team charged too quickly, and before they knew it, Charlie Gildea was in the clear, along the far sideline. Their safety man pulled him down on their own thirty-yard line, and we went wild. The thrill was short-lived. After the first play, when Guy Leonard gained four, our guys seemed to die again. As soon as the ball was snapped, the first thing you noticed was that our linemen seemed to move back a step, in unison. I could tell that Mr. Marcus noticed also because he started calling our guys girls, and right in front of the parents.

A few of us were still shouting encouragement to the guys on the field, but it didn't make much difference. After we gave up the ball, St. Dominick's began chewing up yardage again. "What's the matter?" Mister Marcus yelled. "Didn't you ever see a straightarm before? Christ!" He smacked his head with the palm of his hand and looked to either side of him. "Eddie," he called. "Where's Eddie?"

I ran to him, my heart pounding. "Go in for Shattuck. Show these girls something, okay? You show 'em, Eddie."

I dashed onto the field, pulling my helmet on and snapping the chin strap. "You're out, Shattuck," I said in the huddle. St. Dominick's was on our thirty-yard line. The other guys stared at me and none of them said anything, but I knew they were probably thinking that Mr. Marcus had put me in for spite. I didn't care. The first quarter wasn't even over and I was getting a chance to play. I lined up at right end, and when the ball was snapped, something went click inside my head. I took a step back, so as not to be taken in, and then I saw men moving toward me with the ballcarrier behind them. I charged forward, hand-fighting past the first man. The second man hit me with a cross-body block and laid me flat, however, and all I could do as the ballcarrier went by was to reach out with my hand, snatching for his ankle. I missed, and looking up I saw that he was laughing as he chugged by, his white teeth gleaming inside his brown face. Charlie Gildea came up from the secondary and made the tackle. He helped me up. "Good try," he said.

"I'll get him next time," I said. I heard my name and I looked sideways. Mr. Marcus was having fits. "Eddie! *Eddie!*" he was wailing. "How many times do I have to tell you? When you see men coming at you like that, don't try to fight them all—roll up the play and leave the tackle for somebody else. Is that clear? Roll it up!" I nodded and set myself for the next play. They ran the other end and made a first down. On the following play, though, they came my way again, and I did what Mr. Marcus wanted. Instead of trying to fight my way to the ballcarrier, I faked at the first blocker and then threw myself into him, low and sideways. It worked. He toppled over me and the other blocker tripped over him and the ballcarrier was slowed down long enough for Guy Leonard to bring him down for no gain.

The first half ended with the score 28 to 0, in favor of St. Dominick's. Between halves I lay under this big apple tree in back of the school, alongside the players, sucking on oranges. The St. Dominick's team stayed on the field, under the goalposts. Nobody said much. Mr. Marcus paced up and down, and it seemed to me that he had a million things he wanted to tell us and felt frustrated because he'd get to say only a few of them. In the distance I could see some of the fathers playing catch with a football. Beyond the football field I thought I spotted my mother, near where they were serving coffee and hot chocolate. I wanted her to look at me—to watch me sitting with the other guys and to be proud of me. I wanted her to know what it meant to me to have gotten into the game so early, and I wished too that I could just hear her voice—even if she was only laughing at some stupid joke one of the fathers was telling her—but, at such a distance, I couldn't be sure it was her.

"Do you know what the trouble is?" Mr. Marcus asked, his hands on his hips. "Do you?"

John Weldon shrugged. "They're too fast," he said. Some of the players covered their mouths and giggled.

"I see," Mr. Marcus said, nodding up and down. "I see. They're too fast. They're too fast. What else?"

Somebody to his left mumbled something. Mr. Marcus whirled toward him, then seemed to catch hold of himself, and when he spoke he did so firmly. "Would you mind repeating that for the other boys, Phil?"

Phil Siegel looked at the ground. "They got all those jigs on their team," he said. Everybody laughed.

"Do you know what the trouble is?" Mr. Marcus said again, ignoring Phil and the laughing. "Do you know what the trouble is?—You're not hungry ballplayers." He sighed, as if he knew how useless his words were. "Damn it, pay attention!" he snapped, and he grabbed John Weldon by his shoulder pad, yanked him from the ground, and then shoved him back down.

"In your little fingers you guys don't have—you don't have . . . Oh, what's the difference—" He looked around and his eyes flicked from one side to the other. He took a deep breath, concentrating hard, and then he spoke again. "Do you want to know what else? Do you? I'm glad you're getting beaten. How's that? This is probably the last time any of those boys will ever beat you at anything. When you're coming back here someday, watching your pansy children run around the field against the latest group of orphans or deprived kids, the boys you're playing against will be, will be . . ." He threw up his hands. "—God knows where! And while you and you and you," he said, pointing, "will be reminiscing about that time those jigs slaughtered you, none of them will even re-member what the Fowler School was." He stopped. He seemed very tired suddenly, and I wished more than anything that I could help him. "Okay," he said, blinking. "This is the way it's going to be. I'm giving every one of you a chance to play, because I want every one of you, for once in your lives, to know what it is to get hit and to get hurt. Is that clear?" Nobody said anything. I was angry, and I wondered for a second if this was really what Mr. Marcus intended—if he'd only wanted to get us angry enough to go out and play hard-nosed football during the sec-ond half.

"That was a most interesting speech, Mr. Marcus." Some of the boys started to stand up. "Sit, boys. Please. Sit—" Dr. Hunter said. "You've been playing hard and you need the rest." He smiled, and when he did I looked at Mr. Marcus and the anger in his eyes made me imagine for a split second what my father's eyes might have looked like when he was moving in for a ball on the handball court, moving in to kill it. "I just wanted to wish you luck for the second half, boys. I know you'll do your best."

Mr. Marcus muttered something under his breath.

"What was that?" Dr. Hunter asked.

"Nothing I haven't said in other words," Mr. Marcus answered.

"Fine, fine—well. I'll leave you to your discussion."

Dr. Hunter left. Mr. Marcus waited a few seconds, then started off to-ward the playing field. "Follow me, girls," he said. "Don't be scared, now—"

The guys really hated him then, and during the second half they showed it. By the fourth quarter, when almost all the parents had stopped watching, they'd called their girlfriends over and were standing with them, wisecracking and showing off. One or two of them even took drags on cigarettes and necked with their girlfriends. It hardly affected Mr. Marcus. He just kept yelling at us and mocking us and he was true to his word about putting everybody into the game. For their part, the St. Do-minick's team kept coming. At the time I would have given anything, I think, to have been one of them. And I kept hoping, all through the second half, that before the end of the game one of them would speak to me—would say something about how hard I was playing, about how I was hanging in there—would make some gesture toward me. None of them did.

When the game was over, Charlie Gildea and I were the only players who stayed on the field and shook hands with them. I shook hands with as many of them as I could, even though they hardly seemed interested. They huddled at the far end of the field, gave us a 2-4-6-8 cheer, then walked to their bus and left. The final score was 54 to 0.

After I got dressed in my regular clothes, my gray flannel slacks and blue Fowler blazer, I went back to the field to look for my mother. Most of the parents were gone by now, and I couldn't find Mother anywhere. I walked over to the school building, and went inside, but it was deserted and her homeroom was locked. I came back outside—the sky was starting to turn orange from the sun—and, scared suddenly of being left alone, I found myself wondering for a second if she'd gone off with some other guy's father, if maybe one of them was divorced or a widower and if they were already sitting together in some plush lounge, having cocktails. I kicked at the ground and then got angry with her for not having told me where she'd gone, and for making me think such stupid thoughts and see such stupid pictures in my head. Didn't it ever occur to you that I might think things like that if you went off and left me alone? I wanted to shout at her. Didn't it? *Didn't* it . . .?

Mr. Marcus saw me walking across the field, and he called to me and asked if I wanted a ride home with him. He had an old 1966 green Dodge Dart, and when I sat next to him we didn't say anything to each other. He smoked one cigarette after another, and since I'd never seen him smoke at school or practice, I was surprised. I gave him directions to our house, and when we got there I was relieved to see Mother's car in the driveway, and lights on in the kitchen. I asked Mr. Marcus if he wanted to come inside. I told him Mother could make us some coffee or hot chocolate.

"Some other time, Eddie. Okay?" He put his hand on my head and he stared at me for what seemed like ages, his mouth slightly open and a cigarette stuck to his lower lip. His eyes didn't shift or blink at all. Then he seemed to wake up. He looked at his hand as if he were puzzled to find it resting on my head. "Christ!" he said, ruffling my hair. "You're a sweet kid, Eddie. Now get inside, take a nice hot shower, and stay warm."

"Thanks for the ride home, sir," I said, when I was out of the car.

"Sure," he said. He backed the car out of the driveway and I started toward the house. Then he honked and I turned toward him. He looked out of the window and waved to me. "You played a good game, Eddie," he called.

On Monday I looked for him at school but he wasn't there. He didn't show up all week, and in assembly on Friday morning, Dr. Hunter announced that owing to illness in his immediate family, Mr. Marcus had been forced to leave the school for the remainder of the term. He said he hoped Mr. Marcus would be returning for the spring semester. When the spring semester began, Mr. Marcus didn't return. No announcements were made, and I was probably the only student in the school who even remembered what Dr. Hunter had said. I was feeling pretty upset, and when, on the evening after the first day of classes for the new term, Mother told me that Dr. Hunter was calling for her and that she'd have to leave me alone in the house for the evening, something inside me went click.

I stalked off, but while she was dressing, I walked straight into her room and asked her if she was going to marry Dr. Hunter.

"You should knock before you come in, Eddie. I might have been undressed." She looked into her mirror and fastened an earring.

"*Are* you?" I asked again. "I'm serious. I have a right to know!"

She kept working at her earring, as if I hadn't said a thing, but then I saw her mouth open slightly. I didn't give her a chance and I spoke before I even thought about what I was going to say. "How–how could you ever marry a man with a gimpy arm?" I demanded. "How could you–?"

She turned toward me and looked at me sternly for a second or two. Then her face broke into a big smile. "Oh, Eddie," she laughed. "Of course I'm not getting married." She stood and came to me and hugged me. Her perfume was strong, and I struggled to get loose. "You know you're the only man in my life."

"I'm not," I said, freeing myself. "I'm your son. You should get a husband while you're still young and pretty."

She backed off and looked at me for a long time after I said that, and I kept having these alternate feelings—that I shouldn't have said it and that I should have. I think she wanted to kiss me and hug me again, but for some reason she seemed afraid to do it now. She simply closed her eyes, nodded once, and then opened them. She turned back to her mirror. "Will you finish the dishes while I'm gone?" she asked.

"Sure," I said. And then: "How come Mr. Marcus didn't come back this term?"

"You're full of questions, aren't you?"

"Can I ask Dr. Hunter why Mr. Marcus didn't come back?"

She sighed, then smiled again, but in a much easier way than she had a few minutes before. "I don't think that would get us anywhere, do you?"

"No," I admitted.

"Well, then?"

"I guess I ask too many questions."

When Dr. Hunter called for her, I didn't go out to say hello to him. After they left, though, still feeling worried about what I'd said to Mother, I kept walking around our house, going from room to room, upstairs and downstairs. It seemed terribly large to me, and I wondered if Mother was afraid when she stayed in it by herself sometimes. I tried hard to remember what things had been like when Father was there, but I couldn't. I went into Mother's room and took out her box of photos again and looked at the pictures of him, but that didn't help either. Not even when I found a picture of him with his arms around some other guys in sweatshirts, and a football on the ground in front of them.

But looking at the pictures of him, and seeing the way he smiled, reminded me of Mother being alone with Dr. Hunter, and when I saw that picture in my head, for the first time I asked myself if she could actually *enjoy* going out with him. Then I closed the box of photos and went downstairs to watch television.

I must have fallen asleep on the living room couch, because the next thing I knew, Mother was sitting next to me, stroking my forehead with her fingertips. The television set was still on.

"Hi, Eddie," she said. She bent over and kissed me. She held me for a long time, pressing her lips against my forehead in a very gentle way. Then she sat up.

"Did you have a good time tonight?" I asked.

She seemed surprised that I should ask her, but when she answered me I saw that I'd said the right thing. "Thrilling," she whispered. "I talked about irregular French verbs, and he told me about his eating club at Princeton."

"His *what?*" I asked.

"Never mind," she said, laughing. "At any rate, there was one interesting thing that occurred tonight. I couldn't stop thinking about our conversation, and about how much, when you get angry, you remind me of your father. You made good sense, you know . . ." I looked away from her then. She stood up, turned off the television, and sat down across from me, letting her shoes drop to the rug. "All right," she said. "Let me ask you something, Eddie. What would you think of our leaving the Fowler School and moving somewhere else? Maybe back to New York City, where—"

"Do you really mean it?" I exclaimed. My face must have registered how happy I was at the idea, and when she smiled and said that she did mean it, I tried to check myself, to hold back my enthusiasm. "Well, don't do it because of me," I said.

"You?" she laughed. "If we do it—and I'm not promising anything yet— we'll do it for the two of us." She leaned forward, and bit her lower lip before she spoke again. "I think we could both benefit by giving ourselves the chance to meet new people, don't you?"

"I suppose," I said, trying not to appear too excited. I didn't fool her, of course, and soon I stopped pretending and we were both talking about what it would be like to live in a place like Manhattan and of all the things we might do there together, and all the interesting people we might meet.

When she spoke about selling our house, though, I began to feel sad, and when she began talking about my going away to college someday and beginning a life of my own, what I wanted to do was to cry out that I would *never* leave her. *Never!* I didn't say anything, though. Because I guess I knew she was right about my leaving her someday, and what I was hoping was that by the time I did she would be married again. But I knew that she might not be. I guess she knew it too, even though you never would have guessed it from the sweet way she kept smiling at me.

The dread of all professional football players is that day when, as a result of injury or diminishing skills, the game is up. The players call this "waiting for the Turk," the news that their career is over. Peter Gent, a former receiver for the Dallas Cowboys, writes about this situation as only a player can. Gent was launched to national prominence by his sensational first novel, North Dallas Forty *(1973). It is an exposé about pro football, featuring a washed-up player required to take drugs in order to stay on the team. Paramount Pictures made a successful movie out of the book in 1979. Since then, Gent has continued to write novels, including* Texas Celebrity Turkey Trot *(1978) and* The Franchise *(1983). In 1996 he published a nonfiction memoir about youth league base-ball in Michigan, called* The Last Magic Summer: A Season With My Son.

Peter Gent

WAITING FOR THE TURK (1978)

I DON'T KNOW WHAT IT is that wakes me at this time every morning, but I have been doing it since I was a rookie. That's nine years of Southern California summers, waking just before the trainer makes his rounds.

The first thing I see is the white plaster ceiling. I always sleep on my back with my legs elevated. It gives me low-back pain but keeps my knee from swelling. Down the dormitory hall I hear the squeak of Dobie's crepe-soled Riddell trainer's shoes. I always wake before the squeaks. I don't know why.

I wake up completely, instantly, my mind alert and functioning at full speed. I begin to concentrate on the day's challenge. It's a good feeling, a slight rush. It's concentration that keeps me intact, and in this business staying intact is what it's all about. I believe in the psychology of the victim. Alert is not only a good feeling, it's necessary. You have to make your breaks and never let down.

Dobie Rank, the trainer, rattled the door open.

"L.D., Mabry, get up. Breakfast at seven, the taping schedule is posted." He moved down the hall.

I stretched and listened to him continue his wake-up circuit. He would finish waking all the veterans on the first floor and then climb to the second floor and start rousing the rookies.

Today is the last of two-a-day practices. Two-a-days are tough, with the humiliation and the heat of 85° Southern California days. We train in California because Texas summers are brutal. Today is also a cut day. Some guys can't stand the anxiety of waiting out the cuts, waiting for the Turk. But anxiety is the price of living in the future, and I'll pay it.

"Aaahh." L. D. Groover, my roommate, stirred on the other bed. He's a defensive tackle; I'm a cornerback. An ice pack slid from L.D.'s knee to the floor with a muted splash. "Damn. My bones have gone soft."

Doors started slamming up and down the hall. L.D. switched on his radio. ". . . and the pollution index is a big 105 . . . that's unacceptable . . . and now the CB song of the day, *God's Got His Ears On.*"

A phone rang down the hall. L.D. leaned over and took our phone off the hook. On cut days Coach Buck Binder phones players and has them bring their playbooks to the coaches' wing. We disconnect the phone on cut days. It won't keep us from getting cut, but it will make it more difficult for Buck.

This year I am not worried about cut days. I am having my best camp ever and after today the practice schedule eases off. We begin exhibition season Saturday against the Rams. I have made it through the hard part. We still don't answer the phone. It is tradition and superstition and has worked so far.

The dining hall was across the common from the dormitory. L.D.'s tray was heaped with food and a rainbow of pills. Besides anabolic steroids to bulk up, L.D. had vitamins, protein pills for energy, salt pills for fluid retention and muscle cramps, calcium pills to prevent pulls and strains, and Papase for swelling.

"They cut Costa."

"I know," L.D. nodded, "I saw him packing." He scanned the busy room. "Anybody else?"

We all shrugged. Ezra Lyttle, the other cornerback, popped a prune into his mouth, grimaced and quickly spit it out. A clattering drone filled the dining hall with energy.

Buck Binder and the other coaches walked in from their morning meeting. "They gotta cut nine more," L.D. said, touching the running sore between his eyes where his headgear wore away the flesh during butt-blocking drills. He would have the ulcer until contact work tapered off. Until then he'd just bleed and scab up. Most linemen had years of scar tissue between their eyes.

I glanced around and tried to figure who would be gone by nightfall. As camp progresses it gets harder to pick the likely cut victims. Each cut-down day brings its own surprises. Cut days make this business lonely, but the intensity counters the loneliness. You feel and taste more on one Sunday afternoon than most people do in a lifetime and you don't have to wait years to find out if you are doing a good job. The hitting gets me off—the strange mixture of pain and power, the shock in opponents' eyes when they realize they are overmatched. I give it all I've got. I never walk off the playing field confused or uptight. Eventually all that adrenaline burns up your circuits, but. . . .

It is my ninth season, my fifth straight without missing a game. Confidence is the key. Confidence and discipline.

"Negative thinking never got nobody nothin'," Buck Binder always says.

I figure I have five more years in me. By then most guys will be into selling insurance or used cars. The average pro career covers about four years. I've already doubled that because I take care of myself. I never waste energy or emotions.

I left the dining hall and walked across campus to the field house to get taped. A rookie passed me, heading back toward the dormitory, his eyes down and his football shoes in his hand. I never did learn his name. Two down. They had to cut eight more to get down to the roster limit. The sun warmed me. It was a nice day. I like California.

In the training room Dobie Rank taped my ankles.

"Buck's going to Los Angeles." Dobie was slapping Vaseline on my heels. "He's dealing for another quarterback." Sonny Jeeter, our first-string quarterback, was out with a bad leg. The training room was a prime source of rumor. "The doctor looks at Sonny this afternoon. They'll probably cut on him. He's all through for this year."

I can't say I am surprised. After nine years you get a feel for things. You pick up little signs.

Back at the dormitory I told the news.

"That so." Ezra Lyttle was throwing darts at the target on the back of our door. He was shooting poorly and punching holes in the woodwork.

Bobby Doyle, a second-year quarterback from Tulsa, passed by the open door heading toward the coaches' wing. He was carrying his playbook. Three down.

"I wonder what we're giving up?" Smoking Jim Stewart sat back on my bed and opened a letter from his lawyer. "For a quarterback, I mean." The big running back unfolded his lawyer's letter and studied it. "Well, I see what *I'm* giving up. Jim kept his eyes on the letter. His wife was suing for divorce again. The letter informed him that his wife had taken possession of his Eldorado convertible and was demanding a look at the incorporation papers on Smoking Jim Stewart's Wig Rental. "Ain't that a shame. A damn shame." Jim shook his head and then rotated his shoulders, trying to ease his chronic neck and back pain.

I waited for L.D. to wrap his knee for the walk to the practice field. We had to go through the lobby. It was a $50 fine for using the closer north corridor exit. Buck Binder's sign on the door read:

$50. THERE ARE NO SHORTCUTS IN LIFE.

In the lobby a bunch of just-cut rookies stood awkwardly waiting for somebody to drive them to the airport. Their bags were piled by the door. They were embarrassed.

"I got a buddy with Pittsburgh," a defensive back from Grambling said to no one in particular. "I'm calling him."

"Hell, there's always Edmonton."

"The rosters are set in Canada."

"They just don't know I'm available."

"You was always available. You just didn't know it."

They all laughed. There were six of them. One more to go.

We walked across the parking lot. "I think I'm having a good camp," I said.

L.D. grunted and limped along beside me. The day was starting to get hot.

"No kidding, I feel great." I did. I turned and backpedaled up the street. I made light, tentative jabs to each side.

"You are obviously mistaking me for someone who gives a damn." L.D. winced and stopped to rub his knee. "God, I'm gonna have to get me some cortisones."

"No, really. I'm having my best camp ever."

"Famous last words." L.D. shook his head and resumed limping toward the field house. "I'm having my best camp ever. The check is in the mail."

Bobby Doyle, the just-released Tulsa quarterback, came out the field-house door. His jaw was tight and his eyes were red. He waved at us but looked down. His lips were a tight line.

Inside, on a rubbing table, Alex Hart, who had taken over for Jeeter at quarterback, was holding a cold compress to his chin. The cloth was blood-spotted. Ezra Lyttle was climbing into the whirlpool. He grinned at us and pointed over at Hart. "Bobby Doyle," he said.

"The guy sucker-punched me," Hart whined.

"They ain't no such thing as a sucker-punch," L.D. said. "Just the first punch and the last. In some fights they're the same."

"If a guy can't take getting cut, he shouldn't play the game." Hart inspected the compress and then touched his chin. The bleeding had slowed.

"Full pads . . . full pads . . . full pads. . . ." Buck Binder marched through announcing the equipment of the day. His voice faded off as he disappeared through the training-room door.

"Hell." L.D. yanked his shoulder pads off the wall hook where he had hung them to dry last night. They were still damp from sweat. He shivered. "Damn, I'll bet we got pass rush." He slammed the pads to the floor, building emotions for drill.

I felt an anxious ripple through my stomach. Early in camp I like to hit to show the rookies who is boss and to remind any of the veterans who might have forgotten in the off-season. But this late in camp there's no percentage in it. If you haven't convinced anybody by now it's too late.

L.D. filled a cup at the water cooler and washed down a pill. "Good morning, gentlemen." The deep, measured voice of Dr. Stanley Friedman filled the cement-block room. Buck hired him to administer psychological tests and to counsel us into more productive attitudes. It was like artificial respiration. Out go the bad neuroses, in go the good neuroses. Friedman was friendly, outgoing and good for a few prescriptions.

"What do you think, pal?" Friedman put his hand on my shoulder. I was trying to pull on a sock without having to bend over. "You've got a lot of energy blocked that I could free up for you. I could make you All-Pro if you pick a positive mode. I can help you control those emotions." He gave my shoulder a pat and strolled into the training room.

I was suddenly tired. I could use that energy Friedman said he could free up. I hope we don't have full-speed force drill. It always gives me a headache. I took three aspirin and went out.

L.D., Ezra and I walked to the practice field. We topped a sand hill and started down toward the field. "Oh-oh," L.D. said. Buck Binder was watching us through binoculars. We broke into a trot. Walking was a $25 fine. Buck kept the binoculars on us until we entered the practice field, ran the compulsory lap and split up. L.D. went off to hit the blocking sled. Ezra and I ran the ropes, then picked up a ball, played catch and stretched our legs.

Buck, still on the coaching tower, blew his whistle to start practice. He announced through his bullhorn that we would have a full scrimmage. Then he fined L.D., Ezra and me $25 for walking to practice and fined L.D. an additional $25 for carrying his pads halfway.

Nobody was happy about the scrimmage. Guys got hurt in scrimmages. L.D. was furious about the fine. I accepted it. I can control my own emotions.

We broke into offensive and defensive teams. The offense took the ball on the 20 and Alex Hart was at quarterback. He ran an EGO sweep right at me. Billy Carr, the flanker, cracked back on the outside linebacker and I had the force. I charged up to meet the two rookie guards, looking over their mountainous bodies into Smoking Jim's bright eyes. The running back keyed himself for the result of the collision between me and 500 pounds of crazed rookie. I took the outside away and planted to take the blow on my left shoulder. After contact I would spin to the inside and make the tackle. I took the lead guard's block on my shoulder and was making my spin when the second guard hit me just below the knee. I went down under both guards. Smoking Jim cut inside, but L.D., pursuing from the tackle, hit him at the line. The crash could be heard out to the freeway.

"Now, that's good force action." Buck was standing in the center of the huddle, a freshly lit Camel clenched between his teeth. He was grinning and had one eye closed against the smoke.

"Good force action," Buck repeated.

I rotated my arm and tried to work the soreness out of my left shoulder. Forcing end runs was dirty and dangerous. The willingness to crash was the difference between those who made it and those who didn't. Buck was the greatest force man of all time. In his 12 years as a player he had dislocated both shoulders and had arthritic spurs on his cervical vertebrae the size of marbles.

"The secret of a good force man," Buck would say, "is not minding that it hurts."

Near the end of the scrimmage Hart broke out of the pocket and I hit him at the sideline. He tried to spin free and I twisted his legs pulling him down.

"Goddamn you, Mabry," Hart yelled. "You're not supposed to tackle the quarterback."

I had wrenched his knee twisting him down. He was mad. I held tightly to his legs to keep him from kicking me. Finally he stopped moving and I released him and rolled away.

Hart threw the ball at me.

"Come on, you guys." Ezra got between me and Hart. They were roommates and friends. Ezra liked for everybody to get along.

Buck gave me a rest. I sat in the bleachers in front of Sonny Jeeter and watched the remainder of the scrimmage. Ezra, from his corner spot, piled up the onside guard and totally destroyed the running back on a power sweep.

"Damn," Sonny said, "that Ezra can hit. But not like you, Mabry . . . not like the old destroyer."

"What do you mean, 'old?' "

Sonny laughed.

That night in the auditorium we had the annual rookie show. It was a standard rookie show, with all the standard jokes. As it ended, Buck called Smoking Jim off to one side.

"Oh-oh," L.D. said, looking back at the two men talking. "The Turk."

I glanced back. Smoking Jim's eyes were on the floor. Buck put his hand on Jim's shoulder. The big back was being cut. We were down to roster limit.

L.D. lay on his bed, reading. The television was making warming-up noises. I pulled off my Levi's. My knee was swollen to about twice its normal size.

"Son of a bitch," I said. "Look at this." I worked the knee and could feel the fluid squishing through the joint. There was a dull ache.

"Better get some ice on it." L.D. peered over the top of his book. "Get me some, too."

I was in a panic. Injury is very disorienting to me. I limped into the bathroom, where we keep a Styrofoam chest filled with ice and beer and Dr Pepper. I grabbed a couple of plastic bags off the floor and filled them with ice. I tossed one bag to L.D., then lay down and put the other bag on my swollen right knee.

"Do you feel any chips?" L.D. asked, watching me massage and probe the knee with my thumb.

"I dunno, it's too swollen." I grimaced, fighting panic more than pain. "I'm not letting them cut on me again."

I lay back and tried to relax.

I first hurt my knee last season, right after we had broken camp and returned to Dallas for the Baltimore exhibition game.

It was the third quarter. Short yardage. We had a pistol force, which put me close to the line. The Colt flanker was in a short split and I could tell he was getting ready to cut-block me. At the snap I knifed inside and got to the running back just as he took the pitch. The flanker chased me and all three of us collided in the backfield. We went down in a tangle and I felt something pop in my knee. I tried to stand and couldn't straighten my leg. On the sideline, Felix Badd, our team doctor, stressed the joint for stability. It popped again and I could straighten it.

"I don't think it's too serious, not much pain." Dr. Badd was probing the knee with his thumb and forefinger. "There's no ligament damage . . . ah . . . there it is." He trapped a bean-sized chip of cartilage in the lower left front of the joint. "A joint mouse—probably broke off the articular surface. As long as it's in the front we'll just block it, make a little incision right there"—he traced a short line on the side of my knee—"and slip the little bastard out. We won't have to open up the whole joint and you'll be back in a couple of weeks."

That sounded good to me. The club had drafted a defensive back from UCLA, No. 2 that year. I couldn't afford to miss much time.

"If the chip stays in the front we can do it tomorrow." Badd started toward the tunnel. "I'll go to call now and schedule you for surgery." He usually scheduled his surgery according to his golf calendar and mortgage payments.

By the time I had showered, the game was over. We won, and Buck walked into the locker room with his arm around the No. 2 draft choice from UCLA.

I was dressing, trying to step into my pants leg, when the knee locked again. The joint ground and snapped and I felt the chip slide into the back of the joint. I told the doctor.

"Well, no sense checking into the hospital tonight. Come on in in the morning. It may slip to the front again. We can't get it out if it's in the back."

L.D. drove from the stadium to the team party at the Holiday Inn. I worked my knee viciously, trying to pop the piece to the front of the joint, but each time that I freed it the mouse slid to the back. I was totally depressed. The season, potentially my greatest, was going down the drain. I began drinking Champale. The next morning L.D. pulled me out of bed and took me to the hospital. The sun hurt my eyes. My knee throbbed and I had a terrific hangover. I could feel the chip.

On the surgical floor L.D. stayed in the nurses' station while a frowning surgical nurse escorted me into a small dressing room. I put on a gown and went to the operating theater.

"Sit up," Badd instructed. "We may need your help to locate the chip."

I was on the operating table, surrounded by people in surgical gowns and masks. The light hurt my eyes. Badd was probing my knee with his thumb and forefinger. He caught the joint mouse and pushed it to the inside of my knee.

"O.K., I've got it." He held his hand out and the nurse laid a four-inch needle in his palm. "O.K., I'll secure it now." He drove the needle through my skin and into the cartilage chip, pinning it. His forehead wrinkled with the strain of pushing the needle through the cartilage. It hurt like hell. I broke into a sweat.

Badd injected the skin around the pinned chip. The skin ballooned with Xylocaine. The Champale from the night before began to seep through my skin. I noticed the smell. A nurse laid a sheet over my leg. She wrinkled her nose and frowned as she rewashed the area with alcohol. Badd made the incision. When the nurse reached over to sponge the blood, she knocked the needle loose, and the cartilage chip slipped into the recesses of my knee.

"What the Goddamn hell are you doing?" Badd screamed. "Get out of here." The nurse broke into tears and ran from the room.

"Now what are we gonna do?" Badd stared at my bleeding knee. His face was obscured by the mask. His eyes were wild. "You'll be out all season if I open this thing all the way up."

My gown was beginning to soak with sweat. The doctor probed around inside of my knee. Looking for the elusive chip.

"Try the rakes." He nodded to a nurse who hooked each side of the incision with two instruments that looked like miniature garden rakes. She pulled and the cut stretched open. The doctor inserted one of his thick fingers. Big hands. Big scars. He wiggled the finger around inside the joint, trying to catch the chip. No luck. A nurse wiped the sweat from his brow. I was sweating more than he was. The smell off my body was overpowering. Champale does not travel well.

"I can't find it." He stuck a pair of forceps into the incision and dug around. The pain shot dully up and down my leg as he scraped around the inside of my knee. No luck.

"Can you feel where it is?"

He shook his head. "A knee like this is no damn good."

I groaned. The Xylocaine had only deadened the skin, but the swelling it caused had obscured the small chip. He was blaming my knee. My back was aching and sharp pains shot up my neck and into my head.

"Get me an anesthesiologist. We got to put him under."

"You're not not putting me under," I said. "Ether and Champale don't mix. Lemme try and find it myself."

The nurses looked at Badd. He shrugged.

They scrubbed my hands and I slapped into a pair of surgical gloves. I was faint and nauseous. I dug into the recesses of my own knee joint and after what seemed like hours I extracted the lima-bean-sized chip and dropped it into the doctor's hands. Then I leaned over and threw up. A nurse wiped off my face. I lay down and watched the spots swim across my eyeballs. My whole leg throbbed.

I worked out again in five days and started in the opener. I just didn't let down. The rookie from UCLA went in the last cut that year. I had a good season and never had another bit of trouble with the knee. Until now.

"Buck says Smoking Jim is trying to rip off the insurance company," L.D. said. "Jim says his back needs surgery. He's filing a grievance. Buck says he's gonna fight on this one."

"What does Buck care?" I asked.

"He says it's the premiums," L.D. said. "I never thought I'd be worrying about insurance premiums." L.D. was our player rep.

"Do you think Jim's hurt?"

"How do I know?" L.D. said. "I don't know if *I'm* hurt." He shuffled off.

I drank the rest of L.D.'s orange juice and limped down to the training room.

The league sure has gotten strange in the last few years. Maybe I've just begun to pay attention. Go along to get along. It was fine with me. When I sign I'll knock down $80,000 this year with a contract that pays $90,000 next year and $100,000 the year after. A couple more days bluffing on my option and I'll finally be able to put some real money away.

"Two minutes in the hot. One minute in the cold." Dobie Rank was explaining the contrast treatment to me. I had done it many times before. Soak my knee two minutes in a 115° whirlpool and then immerse the leg to the hip for one minute in 33° ice water.

"What happened to Smoking Jim?" I asked, trying to put the pain out of my mind.

"I think he ruptured a disc." Rank was rolling gauze and stacking it on his taping table, getting ready for the workout. "He's had trouble with it for several years. I put a lot of hot packs on that boy's back." Dobie sounded weary from all the hot packs.

"I'll bet you did."

I changed from cold water to hot. The skin stung, but the deep ache ceased. Sonny Jeeter limped into the training room.

"What's the matter with L.D.?" Sonny said.

"He's preoccupied." I changed from hot to cold. "Jim Stewart is suing the club for surgery and his salary." The pain washed up into my stomach. "L.D.'s gotta get involved."

Dobie was listening.

"Is Jim hurt bad?" Sonny asked.

"Dobie says it's a ruptured disc." I was bobbing up and down to distract myself from the cold ache.

"Hey," Dobie said. "I didn't tell you that for publication. You didn't tell me he was suing the club." Dobie wiped his hands in the towel he kept around his waist. "I didn't know you were collecting evidence."

"I ain't collecting evidence, for Christ's sake. I was just asking." My foot had begun to throb. I moved it around in the water. It throbbed more. "Besides, if he *is* hurt. . . ."

"Who knows if he's hurt." Dobie began rolling gauze again. He picked up speed. "The back's a funny thing. I ain't seen no X-rays." He rolled faster. "He could be trying to rip us off."

"Oughta shoot the chiseler," Sonny mocked.

"You guys can laugh,"—Dobie began stacking rolls of tape—"but it happens all the time."

Back at the room there was a message to call Buck. He invited me to his room and we discussed my contract. It was a friendly discussion. We were only $1,500 apart and just had to get the wording right on a couple of bonus clauses and deferred-payment schedules. I'm a good negotiator.

The swelling went down rapidly in my knee and by Friday I felt better and worked out with the first team during short-pass skeleton. I wasn't 100%, but I was close. Discipline and confidence. I would be ready Saturday. I ran 10 extra wind sprints.

While getting taped before the Ram game I noticed Ezra pop a couple of dexedrine hearts. That was his business. I had my own problems. The knee. My shoulder.

"That collarbone is loose." Dobie Rank grabbed my clavicle and jerked. Pain shot through my shoulder and neck. "See. You oughta think about getting it fixed in the off-season."

I nodded. Nobody was cutting on me.

I went out with the kickers and practiced catching punts. I liked pregame warm-up in the Coliseum. Between punts I could scan the stands for movie stars and knockout chicks. No wonder the Rams don't play well at home. Who can pay attention?

We lost the toss and kicked off. I was second man on the right and was closing in on the L.A. return man when a yellow-and-blue flash knocked me out of bounds and into the photographers. Ezra helped me to my feet. He had a distant, angry look. He was up. His eyes were bright as we walked to the defensive huddle.

The Rams had the ball on their 28. We were in a flex 4–3 man-to-man. The Rams tried a draw-delay trap. L.D. slipped his block, filled the seam and hit the ballcarrier a yard deep in the backfield.

Second and 11. We were in a 4–3 roll strong. The tight end and flanker set to my side. I inched up to cover the short side. At the snap I tried to bump the flanker. The pain in my knee made me stagger and I lost recovery. I left too big a zone and the Ram quarterback dropped the ball behind me to the flanker, who had hooked up. I was a step too slow. I dragged the flanker down from behind, but they had their first down.

Buck shook his fist at me. I can imagine what he was whispering. My knee ached as I leaned into the huddle.

The next play they swept right at me, leading with the onside guard. I tried to protect my knee, but the guard ducked under my outstretched hands and his helmet smashed into my kneecap. I went down like I had been shot. The runner cut inside, but L.D. closed fast along the line and cut him down. The L.A. guard lay next to me as I writhed on the ground. "Sorry, man," he said. "Didn't mean to hurt you."

As Dobie helped me off the field, Buck sent a rookie from Arizona State in at my corner spot.

I sat on the bench with my knee packed in ice. A couple of plays later I got up and jogged. The pain was minimal and I was ready to return. Buck told me to take a rest. Sonny came and sat with me and we watched the Ram defense totally intimidate Hart. But our defense played well, particularly Ezra, who played with a vengeance, making several unassisted tackles and a key interception in the end zone, and it was only 7–0 Rams at the half.

"I'm going to rest you," Buck told me in the locker room. "No sense getting really hurt this early in exhibition season."

I didn't mind. My knee was beginning to stiffen.

Hart couldn't generate much offense in the second half, but neither could the Rams. Our defense held them scoreless, we scored once to tie it. Ezra was all over the field, making tackles and knocking down passes. The job was doubly tough because they had to call the zones to the rookie at my corner, leaving Ezra man-to-man most of the night.

In the last two minutes, with the score 7–7, Ezra fielded a punt on the six and took it back 94 yards for the winning touchdown.

In the locker room after the game Buck awarded Ezra the game ball and fined him $100 for fielding a punt inside the 10-yard line.

I was getting my knee wrapped when Ezra walked up, his face streaked with dirt. He was smiling and wired.

"You'da won this if you hadn't gotten hurt." He tossed me the ball. "They did everything we were expecting."

"I sure didn't think you'd field that one on the six." I tossed back the ball.

"No guts, no glory." Ezra's eyes flashed.

L.D., still wet from the shower, stopped by.

"How is he, Dobie?" he asked the trainer.

"It ain't bad—a couple of days," Dobie said.

I immediately began to plan my rehabilitation and comeback. The rookie hadn't looked too good, but then he hadn't looked too bad. The films on Monday would tell.

"How's it feel?" Buck slid into the bus seat next to me and grabbed my thigh. "I'm sorry you got hurt."

"Thanks." I was embarrassed. He *was* sorry. I liked old beat-up Buck Binder.

"I just want you to know you're still No. 1 with me. We need older guys like you."

"What do you mean by that?" I asked.

"My God, Mabry." His Scotch breath reminded me that Buck was a sentimental drinker. "I was just trying to cheer you up. What's gonna happen in this world when everybody's as paranoid as you?" He got up and staggered back to the front of the bus. The lights glared off the freeway.

Monday afternoon Buck was nailing the posterboard performance charts on the lobby wall. A player was graded on every play: a zero if he did his job, a plus if he did more than his job, a minus if he failed.

"Damn," someone growled. "How can they give me a minus? I pushed him all over the field." Other players were making similar claims. Ezra had gotten a plus 42, an unheard-of score. I looked for my name. It was followed with a red-inked minus 2 and the small notation "injured due to bad basic position." Because I was injured I had figured on getting a pass, not blame.

Buck walked up. "Say, can I talk to you?" He clapped me on my shoulder.

I followed him to his room. I figured he wanted to discuss some of the final details of my new contract. I wanted to get it signed this week. I needed the $15,000 front money.

"Listen, Mabry, we hate to do this . . ." Buck said as soon as I entered his room. ". . . it's just the way things worked out . . . I mean we have some real problems setting the roster, what with Sonny's injury and now your knee"—Buck dug in his pocket for his Camels—"and today Bobbyday Burke was available. We traded for him." Bobbyday Burke was the Ram cornerback.

"You traded me?" I was shocked.

"No." Buck frowned.

That was a relief. I could beat out Bobbyday Burke.

"We couldn't make a deal for you. Nobody was interested." Buck put his hand on my shoulder. "We're putting you on waivers. I'm sorry, you're a hell of a guy."

I lost my breath, and my heart started pounding. Confusion and fear and embarrassment crashed together in the back of my head. I shifted my eyes to stare at a spot on the wall behind Buck's head. I concentrated hard to keep from coming apart. Discipline. Discipline. What the hell was happening here?

"What do you mean nobody was interested?" I was suddenly mad.

"Nobody was interested," he repeated calmly, lighting up a Camel.

I was afraid that was what he meant.

"Not even Tampa Bay?"

He shook his head. "Still, somebody might pick you up on waivers. . . ." He tried to sound hopeful.

"Not even Goddamn Tampa Bay?" I couldn't believe this was happening. It's not the kind of thing you think about a lot. "I'm better than anybody in that whole damned secondary."

"I know you are, Mabry." Buck patted my shoulder. "Listen, I was wondering. We gotta make this move today." He looked at his watch. Smoke wafted off the cigarette in his hand. My mind raced, looking for a place to rest. I knew this would happen sometime, but not now. I was having my best camp ever. "Mabry, why don't you retire? You're 30 years old. It'll save the embarrassment of having to put you on waivers. You've had a great career. Go out with your head up."

I had my head down, staring at the gray asphalt tile. One of the squares had been placed wrong and the pattern ran opposite to the rest of the tiles.

A long time passed.

"C'mon, buddy," Buck urged, checking his watch. "Make a decision."

"Me? Retire? I'm only 30 years old. I feel great. I'm having my best camp ever." My brain searched for some explanation, some calming circumstance.

Buck shrugged. "It's up to you."

I needed to rest my mind; it was racing too fast. "O.K.," I said suddenly. "You make the announcement." I turned and walked away. It was like a dream—a nightmare.

"O.K., Mabry," Buck yelled after me. "I'll tell them you retired to spend more time with your business interests."

My business interests?

I had my bags packed when L.D. returned to the room.

"Traded? Cut?" He saw my luggage.

"Cut." I nodded; embarrassed to the point of tears. My mind still searched for someone to blame, some kind of soothing thought. This had to be a mistake. "Officially I'm retired."

"What about the knee?"

"The doc's looking at it in a little while—it ain't that bad." My voice creaked.

"Why today? I thought we were down to the limit."

"They just traded for Bobbyday Burke, they had to make room." I walked into the bathroom and rinsed my face.

"Bobbyday Burke," L.D. said. "He's one hittin' son of a bitch."

"Dammit," I yelled from the bathroom, "*I'm* one hittin' son of a bitch."

"Yeah, but you ain't gonna be around."

I limped over to my bed. "Jesus, am I embarrassed. I don't know if I can stand this."

"Hell, Mabry," L.D. stared at the floor. "It's just football."

I lay back and stared at the ceiling. "I was going to have a great season. I was having my best camp ever."

"Famous last words."

I knew he was going to say that.

Ezra came into the room and saw my packed bags. "Those dirty bastards." His voice turned to a whine. "I told you not to go on your option. I told you."

He was right. He told me.

"C'mon, Ezra," L.D. said. "Everybody told him. He don't wanna hear that."

"Nobody picked you up?"

"Not yet. Buck says nobody was interested."

"Not even Tampa Bay?" Ezra couldn't believe it. "Not even Goddamn Tampa Bay?"

"That's what I said."

"I'm getting out of here." L.D. opened the door. "This might be catching. I'll see you back in Dallas in a few weeks." He was gone down the hall.

"You just can't stand to see Mabry cry," Ezra yelled.

"Mabry who?" L.D. yelled back.

Ezra tossed some darts while I lay on the bed. My life flashed by. All that work come to this. All those miserable hours, the lumps, the scars, the hours spent feeling bad. All that work and it's over so quick it's like it never happened. I began to feel old. I never thought I'd feel old at 30. Jesus, was I sad.

"I'll shoot you to 50 for that $10 you already owe me." Ezra retrieved the darts from the target. "I'll shoot first." Ezra's first five darts all hit in the eight-point zone. He dropped his last dart in the bull. I still hadn't gotten off the bed.

"That's $20. I'd like it before you leave. Damn," he said, looking at the dart board, "no wonder they cut you."

I walked over to the campus medical clinic to have my release physical. First they X-rayed my knee and shoulder. Then I sat on a brown leather table in the small examining room and played with the stainless-steel stirrups.

Badd came into the room holding my still-wet X rays. He clipped them against the light box. His upper lip was sweating. He nodded and grunted at the X rays of my knee and then nodded and grunted at the X rays of my shoulder. He wrote something on his clipboard.

"O.K., up on your feet."

I stood. I was in my shorts.

"Bend over and touch your toes." He checked the alignment of my spine. "O.K., up." He grabbed my clavicles and pulled. I flinched at the pain.

"That doesn't hurt," he said.

"It doesn't hurt *you*."

"O.K., up on the table." He began probing my knee with his thumb and forefinger. I flinched again at the pain. Badd frowned.

"Boy, you sure are tender." He wrote something on his clipboard.

"Dobie said it could be torn."

"Dobie isn't the doctor," he responded, "and it isn't torn. Maybe a little hyperextension." He looked at me wryly. "But not enough to get your contract, so don't you go trying to rip off the club like Smoking Jim."

"Hey, I just want to get well. I want to play again."

The doctor looked puzzled. "They already cut you, boy. You aren't playing anymore and it isn't because of that knee."

"I'll play again."

"You've got fluid in there." He pointed at the knee. "You want me to drain it?"

I shrugged.

"Make up your mind. It won't be as stiff."

I frowned and nodded. It hurt to have a knee drained.

He got out his syringes and needles and went to work, placing the point of the needle at the top of my knee, pushing and twisting simultaneously, trying to screw the needle in under my kneecap. The needle was large to allow the passage of the bloody, thick joint fluid, and it took pressure to punch through my skin.

"I know this was your only chance at being something." The doctor talked while he struggled with the needles. "I wanted you to make it."

Finally, with a sharp sting, the needle popped through and slid in behind my kneecap. Drawing the plunger back, he filled the syringe with bloody pink fluid. Then, leaving the needle imbedded in my knee, he unscrewed the syringe and emptied it into a stainless-steel pan.

"You'll suffer with arthritis, but you'd suffer later anyway. Getting old is a crime, but at least you've got your memories."

He filled and emptied the syringe four times before he injected cortisone into the joint and withdrew the needle. He was tense and sweating heavily when he finished. He slapped a Band-Aid on the hole, then ran his thumb over the old scar on the inside of the knee.

"You remember the time we took that out?"

"What do you mean, we?" I said. "*I* took it out. All you did was cuss and sweat."

The doctor laughed. "That was some surgery." He wrote something on his clipboard. "O.K., Mabry, that's it. It was nice knowing you." He clapped me on the shoulder. I pulled on my clothes and started out the door.

"You have to recognize the real trauma here, deal with it and get it behind you." Dr. Friedman had dropped by the room after I returned from my physical.

"I'll be back." I limped into the bathroom.

"Is your knee that bad?" He sounded like he didn't think it was.

I didn't answer.

"You know," Friedman continued, "setting your goals too high can be worse than setting them too low. You're being too hard on yourself. Now, Smoking Jim, for instance. . . ."

"To hell with Smoking Jim." I jerked open the closet door.

Friedman went on, "Smoking Jim won't accept it that his career is over so he's created this bad back to compensate for the failure. It's going to be tough, but I'll get him straightened out."

I looked through the desk drawer, then sat on my bed. "How about some pills instead of this advice?"

"Don't you see?" Friedman held out his hands. "You don't have to do that anymore. You're free to work out other solutions to your life."

"I'll be back." I smiled and glared into his eyes. "I'll be back and you'll still be here passing out free advice."

"Look at you, just spitting and snarling. You'll haul this around with you like so much excess baggage until you learn you can just set it down and walk off that much lighter." Friedman shook his head. "I know it's tough, man. Hell, I remember when they cut me off the seventh-grade basketball team in Indianapolis. Do you know what it's like *not* to play basketball in Indiana? It isn't fun, but I didn't let it ruin my life. I picked up and went on. You can do that. Whatever you do I'll still love you as a human being." Friedman loved everybody as human beings.

"You know what you are?" I said. "You're just another groupie. We had sex groupies and press groupies and now we got a psychology groupie."

Friedman rubbed his chin and squinted at me.

"What do you mean, we?" he said.

This is the second story in the book by the exemplar of football wit, Damon Runyon. Here we meet some typical Runyonesque characters who wander up to Boston for the Harvard-Yale game. That these street-smart tricksters seem out of place with the Ivy League blue bloods is part of the fun. Runyon was a master of character invention, providing colorful monickers like Big Butch, Harry the Horse, Cutie Singleton, and Nosey Gillespie. This story features the estimable rake Meyer Marmalade. A typical Runyon tale, it is laden with humor in the American outlaw mode. Despite his shady subjects, Runyon himself is described by his sportswriting disciple, Jimmy Cannon, as a "very cultured man." His stories, books, and poems—wildly popular in the U.S.—received international acclaim, with a particularly devoted following in England and France. The great Broadway play and Hollywood movie "Guys and Dolls" is based on Runyon's stories. Frank Sinatra plays Nathan Detroit to perfection in the movie version.

Damon Runyon

UNDERTAKER SONG (1934)

NOW THIS STORY I AM going to tell you is about the game of football, a very healthy pastime for the young, and a great character builder from all I hear, but to get around to this game of football I am compelled to bring in some most obnoxious characters, beginning with a guy by the name of Joey Perhaps, and all I can conscientiously say about Joey is you can have him.

It is a matter of maybe four years since I see this Joey Perhaps until I notice him on a train going to Boston, Mass., one Friday afternoon. He is sitting across from me in the dining-car, where I am enjoying a small portion of baked beans and brown bread, and he looks over to me once, but he does not rap to me.

There is no doubt but what Joey Perhaps is bad company, because the last I hear of him he is hollering copper on a guy by the name of Jack Ortega, and as a consequence of Joey Perhaps hollering copper, this Jack Ortega is taken to the city of Ossining, N. Y., and placed in an electric chair, and given a very, very, very severe shock in the seat of his pants.

It is something about plugging a most legitimate business guy in the city of Rochester, N. Y., when Joey Perhaps and Jack Ortega are engaged together in a little enterprise to shake the guy down, but the details of this transaction are dull, and sordid, and quite uninteresting, except that Joey Perhaps turns state's evidence and announces that Jack Ortega fires the shot which cools the legitimate guy off, for which service he is rewarded with only a small stretch.

I must say for Joey Perhaps that he looks good, and he is very well dressed, but then Joey is always particular about clothes, and he is quite a handy guy with the dolls in his day and, to tell the truth, many citizens along Broadway are by no means displeased when Joey is placed in the state institution, because they are generally pretty uneasy about their dolls when he is around.

Naturally, I am wondering why Joey Perhaps is on this train going to Boston, Mass., but for all I know maybe he is wondering the same thing about me, although personally I am making no secret about it. The idea is I am en route to Boston, Mass., to see a contest of skill and science that is to take place there this very Friday night between a party by the name of Lefty Ledoux and another party by the name of Mickey McCoy, who are very prominent middleweights.

Now ordinarily I will not go around the corner to see a contest of skill and science between Lefty Ledoux and Mickey McCoy, or anybody else, as far as that is concerned, unless they are using blackjacks and promise to hurt each other, but I am the guest on this trip of a party by the name of Meyer Marmalade, and I will go anywhere to see anything if I am a guest.

This Meyer Marmalade is really a most superior character, who is called Meyer Marmalade because nobody can ever think of his last name, which is something like Marmalodowski, and he is known far and wide for the way he likes to make bets on any sporting proposition, such as baseball, or horse races, or ice hockey, or contests of skill and science, and especially contests of skill and science.

So he wishes to be present at this contest in Boston, Mass., between Lefty Ledoux and Mickey McCoy to have a nice wager on McCoy, as he has reliable information that McCoy's manager, a party by the name of Koons, has both judges and the referee in the satchel.

If there is one thing Meyer Marmalade dearly loves, it is to have a bet on a contest of skill and science of this nature, and so he is going to Boston, Mass. But Meyer Marmalade is such a guy as loathes and despises traveling all alone, so when he offers to pay my expenses if I will go along to keep him company, naturally I am pleased to accept, as I have nothing on of importance at the moment and, in fact, I do not have anything on of importance for the past ten years.

I warn Meyer Marmalade in advance that if he is looking to take anything off of anybody in Boston, Mass., he may as well remain at home, because everybody knows that statistics show that the percentage of anything being taken off of the citizens of Boston, Mass., is less per capita than anywhere else in the United States, especially when it comes to contests of skill and science, but Meyer Marmalade says this is the first time they ever had two judges and a referee running against the statistics, and he is very confident.

Well, by and by I go from dining-car back to my seat in another car, where Meyer Marmalade is sitting reading a detective magazine, and I speak of seeing Joey Perhaps to him. But Meyer Marmalade does not seem greatly interested, although he says to me like this:

"Joey Perhaps, eh?" he says. "A wrong gee. A dead wrong gee. He must just get out. I run into the late Jack Ortega's brother, young Ollie, in Mindy's restaurant last week," Meyer Marmalade says, "and when we happen to get to talking of wrong gees, naturally Joey Perhaps' name comes up, and Ollie remarks he understands Joey Perhaps is about due out, and that he will be pleased to see him some day. Personally," Meyer Marmalade says, "I do not care for any part of Joey Perhaps at any price."

Now our car is loaded with guys and dolls who are going to Boston, Mass., to witness a large football game between the Harvards and the Yales at Cambridge, Mass., the next day, and the reason I know this is because they are talking of nothing else.

So this is where the football starts getting into this story.

One old guy that I figure must be a Harvard from the way he talks seems to have a party all his own, and he is getting so much attention from one and all in the party that I figure he must be a guy of some importance, because they laugh heartily at his remarks, and although I listen very carefully to everything he says he does not sound so very humorous to me.

He is a heavy-set guy with a bald head and a deep voice, and anybody can see that he is such a guy as is accustomed to plenty of authority. I am wondering out loud to Meyer Marmalade who the guy can be, and Meyer Marmalade states as follows:

"Why," he says, "he is nobody but Mr. Phillips Randolph, who makes the automobiles. He is the sixth richest guy in this country," Meyer says, "or maybe it is the seventh. Anyway, he is pretty well up with the front runners. I spot his monicker on his suitcase, and then I ask the porter, to make sure. It is a great honor for us to be traveling with Mr. Phillips Randolph," Meyer says, "because of him being such a public benefactor and having so much dough, especially having so much dough."

Well, naturally everybody knows who Mr. Phillips Randolph is, and I am surprised that I do not recognize his face myself from seeing it so often in the newspapers alongside the latest model automobile his factory turns out, and I am as much pleasured up as Meyer Marmalade over being in the same car with Mr. Phillips Randolph.

He seems to be a good-natured old guy, at that, and he is having a grand time, what with talking, and laughing, and taking a dram now and then out of a bottle, and when old Crip McGonnigle comes gimping through the car selling his football souvenirs, such as red and blue feathers, and little badges, and pennants, and one thing and another, as Crip is doing around the large football games since Hickory Slim is a two-year-old, Mr. Phillips Randolph stops him and buys all of Crip's red feathers, which have a little white H on them to show they are for the Harvards.

Then Mr. Phillips Randolph distributes the feathers around among his party, and the guys and dolls stick them in their hats, or pin them on their coats, but he has quite a number of feathers left over, and about this time who comes through the car but Joey Perhaps, and Mr. Phillips Randolph steps out in the aisle and stops Joey and politely offers him a red feather, and speaks as follows:

"Will you honor us by wearing our colors?"

Well, of course Mr. Phillips Randolph is only full of good spirits, and means no harm whatever, and the guys and dolls in his party laugh heartily as if they consider his action very funny, but maybe because they laugh, and maybe because he is just naturally a hostile guy, Joey Perhaps knocks Mr. Phillips Randolph's hand down, and says like this:

"Get out of my way," Joey says. "Are you trying to make a sucker out of somebody?"

Personally, I always claim that Joey Perhaps has a right to reject the red feather, because for all I know he may prefer a blue feather, which means the Yales, but what I say is he does not need to be so impolite to an old guy such as Mr. Phillips Randolph, although of course Joey has no way of knowing at this time about Mr. Phillips Randolph having so much dough.

Anyway, Mr. Phillips Randolph stands staring at Joey as if he is greatly startled, and the chances are he is, at that, for the chances are nobody ever speaks to him in such a manner in all his life, and Joey Perhaps also stands there a minute staring back at Mr. Phillips Randolph, and finally Joey speaks as follows:

"Take a good peek," Joey Perhaps says. "Maybe you will remember me if you ever see me again."

"Yes," Mr. Phillips Randolph says, very quiet. "Maybe I will. They say I have a good memory for faces. I beg your pardon for stopping you, sir. It is all in fun, but I am sorry," he says.

Then Joey Perhaps goes on, and he does not seem to notice Meyer Marmalade and me sitting there in the car, and Mr. Phillips Randolph sits down, and his face is redder than somewhat, and all the joy is gone out of him, and out of his party, too. Personally, I am very sorry Joey Perhaps comes along, because I figure Mr. Phillips Randolph will give me one of his spare feathers, and I will consider it a wonderful keepsake.

But now there is not much more talking, and no laughing whatever in Mr. Phillips Randolph's party, and he just sits there as if he is thinking, and for all I know he may be thinking that there ought to be a law against a guy speaking so disrespectfully to a guy with all his dough as Joey Perhaps speaks to him.

Well, the contest of skill and science between Lefty Ledoux and Mickey McCoy turns out to be something of a disappointment, and, in fact, it is a stinkeroo, because there is little skill and no science whatever in it, and by the fourth round the customers are scuffling their feet, and saying throw these bums out, and making other derogatory remarks, and furthermore it seems that this Koons does not have either one of the judges, or even as much as the referee, in the satchel, and Ledoux gets the duke by unanimous vote of the officials.

So Meyer Marmalade is out a couple of C's, which is all he can wager at the ringside, because it seems that nobody in Boston, Mass., cares a cuss about who wins the contest, and Meyer is much disgusted with life, and so am I, and we go back to the Copley Plaza Hotel, where we are stopping, and sit down in the lobby to meditate on the injustice of everything.

Well, the lobby is a scene of gayety, as it seems there are a number of football dinners and dances going on in the hotel, and guys and dolls in evening clothes are all around and about, and the dolls are so young and beautiful that I get to thinking that this is not such a bad old world, after all, and even Meyer Marmalade begins taking notice.

All of a sudden, a very, very beautiful young doll who is about 40 per cent in and 60 per cent out of an evening gown walks right up to us sitting there, and holds out her hand to me, and speaks as follows:

"Do you remember me?"

Naturally, I do not remember her, but naturally I am not going to admit it, because it is never my policy to discourage any doll who wishes to strike up an acquaintance with me, which is what I figure this doll is trying to do; then I see that she is nobody but Doria Logan, one of the prettiest dolls that ever hits Broadway, and about the same time Meyer Marmalade also recognizes her.

Doria changes no little since last I see her, which is quite some time back, but there is no doubt the change is for the better, because she is once a very rattle-headed young doll, and now she seems older, and quieter, and even prettier than ever. Naturally, Meyer Marmalade and I are glad to see her looking so well, and we ask her how are tricks, and what is the good word, and all this and that, and finally Doria Logan states to us as follows:

"I am in great trouble," Doria says. "I am in terrible trouble, and you are the first ones I see that I can talk to about it."

Well, at this, Meyer Marmalade begins to tuck in somewhat, because he figures it is the old lug coming up, and Meyer Marmalade is not such a guy as will go for the lug from a doll unless he gets something more than a story. But I can see Doria Logan is in great earnest.

"Do you remember Joey Perhaps?" she says.

"A wrong gee," Meyer Marmalade says. "A dead wrong gee."

"I not only remember Joey Perhaps," I say, "but I see him on the train today."

"Yes," Doria says, "he is here in town. He hunts me up only a few hours ago. He is here to do me great harm. He is here to finish ruining my life."

"A wrong gee," Meyer Marmalade puts in again. "Always a 100 per cent wrong gee."

Then Doria Logan gets us to go with her to a quiet corner of the lobby, and she tells us a strange story, as follows, and also to wit:

It seems that she is once tangled up with Joey Perhaps, which is something I never know before, and neither does Meyer Marmalade, and, in fact, the news shocks us quite some. It is back in the days when she is just about sixteen and is in the chorus of Earl Carroll's Vanities, and I remember well what a standout she is for looks, to be sure.

Naturally, at sixteen, Doria is quite a chump doll, and does not know which way is south, or what time it is, which is the way all dolls at sixteen are bound to be, and she has no idea what a wrong gee Joey Perhaps is, as he is good-looking, and young, and seems very romantic, and is always speaking of love and one thing and another.

Well, the upshot of it all is the upshot of thousands of other cases since chump dolls commence coming to Broadway, and the first thing she knows, Doria Logan finds herself mixed up with a very bad character, and does not know what to do about it.

By and by, Joey Perhaps commences mistreating her no little, and finally he tries to use her in some nefarious schemes of his, and of course everybody along Broadway knows that most of Joey's schemes are especially nefarious, because Joey is on the shake almost since infancy.

Well, one day Doria says to herself that if this is love, she has all she can stand, and she hauls off and runs away from Joey Perhaps. She goes back to her people, who live in the city of Cambridge, Mass., which is the same place where the Harvards have their college, and she goes there because she does not know of any other place to go.

It seems that Doria's people are poor, and Doria goes to a business school and learns to be a stenographer, and she is working for a guy in the real estate dodge by the name of Poopnoodle, and doing all right for herself, and in the meantime she hears that Joey Perhaps gets sent away, so she figures her troubles are all over as far as he is concerned.

Now Doria Logan goes along quietly through life, working for Mr. Poopnoodle, and never thinking of love, or anything of a similar nature, when she meets up with a young guy who is one of the Harvards, and who is maybe twenty-one years old, and is quite a football player, and where Doria meets up with this guy is in a drug store over a banana split.

Well, the young Harvard takes quite a fancy to Doria and, in fact, he is practically on fire about her, but by this time Doria is going on twenty, and is no longer a chump doll, and she has no wish to get tangled up in love again.

In fact, whenever she thinks of Joey Perhaps, Doria takes to hating guys in general, but somehow she cannot seem to get up a real good hate on the young Harvard, because, to hear her tell it, he is handsome, and noble, and has wonderful ideals.

Now as time goes on, Doria finds she is growing pale, and is losing her appetite, and cannot sleep, and this worries her no little, as she is always a first-class feeder, and finally she comes to the conclusion that what ails her is that she is in love with the young Harvard, and can scarcely live without him, so she admits as much to him one night when the moon is shining on the Charles River, and everything is a dead cold setup for love.

Well, naturally, after a little offhand guzzling, which is quite permissible under the circumstances, the young guy wishes her to name the happy day, and Doria has half a notion to make it the following Monday, this being a Sunday night, but then she gets to thinking about her past with Joey Perhaps, and all, and she figures it will be bilking the young Harvard to marry him unless she has a small talk with him first about Joey, because she is well aware that many young guys may have some objection to wedding a doll with a skeleton in her closet, and especially a skeleton such as Joey Perhaps.

But she is so happy she does not wish to run the chance of spoiling everything by these narrations right away, so she keeps her trap closed about Joey, although she promises to marry the young Harvard when he gets out of college, which will be the following year, if he still insists, because Doria figures that by then she will be able to break the news to him about Joey very gradually, and gently, and especially gently.

Anyway, Doria says she is bound and determined to tell him before the wedding, even if he takes the wind on her as a consequence, and personally I claim this is very considerate of Doria, because many dolls never tell before the wedding, or even after. So Doria and the young Harvard are engaged, and great happiness prevails, when, all of a sudden, in pops Joey Perhaps.

It seems that Joey learns of Doria's engagement as soon as he gets out of the state institution, and he hastens to Boston, Mass., with an inside coat pocket packed with letters that Doria writes him long ago, and also a lot of pictures they have taken together, as young guys and dolls are bound to do, and while there is nothing much out of line about these letters and pictures, put them all together they spell a terrible pain in the neck to Doria at this particular time.

"A wrong gee," Meyer Marmalade says. "But," he says, "he is only going back to his old shake-down dodge, so all you have to do is to buy him off."

Well, at this, Doria Logan laughs one of these little short dry laughs that go "hah," and says like this:

"Of course he is looking to get bought off, but," she says, "where will I get any money to buy him off? I do not have a dime of my own, and Joey is talking large figures, because he knows my fiancé's papa has plenty. He wishes me to go to my fiancé and make him get the money off his papa, or he threatens to personally deliver the letters and pictures to my fiancé's papa.

"You can see the predicament I am in," Doria says, "and you can see what my fiancé's papa will think of me if he learns I am once mixed up with a blackmailer such as Joey Perhaps.

"Besides," Doria says, "it is something besides money with Joey Perhaps, and I am not so sure he will not double-cross me even if I can pay him his price. Joey Perhaps is very angry at me. I think," she says, "if he can spoil my happiness, it will mean more to him than money."

Well, Doria states that all she can think of when she is talking to Joey Perhaps is to stall for time, and she tells Joey that, no matter what, she cannot see her fiancé until after the large football game between the Harvards and the Yales as he has to do a little football playing for the Harvards, and Joey asks her if she is going to see the game, and naturally she is.

And then Joey says he thinks he will look up a ticket speculator, and buy a ticket and attend the game himself, as he is very fond of football, and where will she be sitting, as he hopes and trusts he will be able to see something of her during the game, and this statement alarms Doria Logan no little, for who is she going with but her fiancé's papa, and a party of his friends, and she feels that there is no telling what Joey Perhaps may be up to.

She explains to Joey that she does not know exactly where she will be sitting, except that it will be on the Harvard's side of the field, but Joey is anxious for more details than this.

"In fact," Doria says, "he is most insistent, and he stands at my elbow while I call up Mr. Randolph at this very hotel, and he tells me the exact locations of our seats. Then Joey says he will endeavor to get a seat as close to me as possible, and he goes away."

"What Mr. Randolph?" Meyer says. "Which Mr. Randolph?" he says. "You do not mean Mr. Phillips Randolph, by any chance, do you?"

"Why, to be sure," Doria says. "Do you know him?"

Naturally, from now on Meyer Marmalade gazes at Doria Logan with deep respect, and so do I, although by now she is crying a little, and I am by no means in favor of crying dolls. But while she is crying, Meyer Marmalade seems to be doing some more thinking, and finally he speaks as follows:

"Kindly see if you can recall these locations you speak of."

So here is where the football game comes in once more.

Only I regret to state that personally I do not witness this game, and the reason I do not witness it is because nobody wakes me up the next day in time for me to witness it, and the way I look at it, this is all for the best, as I am scarcely a football enthusiast.

So from now on the story belongs to Meyer Marmalade, and I will tell it to you as Meyer tells it to me.

It is a most exciting game (Meyer says). The place is full of people, and there are bands playing, and much cheering, and more lovely dolls than you can shake a stick at, although I do not believe there are any lovelier present than Doria Logan.

It is a good thing she remembers the seat locations, otherwise I will never find her, but there she is surrounded by some very nice-looking people, including Mr. Phillips Randolph, and there I am two rows back of Mr. Phillips Randolph, and the ticket spec I get my seat off of says he cannot understand why everybody wishes to sit near Mr. Phillips Randolph today when there are other seats just as good, and maybe better, on the Harvard's side.

So I judge he has other calls similar to mine for this location, and a sweet price he gets for it, too, and I judge that maybe at least one call is from Joey Perhaps, as I see Joey a couple of rows on back up of where I am sitting, but off to my left on an aisle, while I am almost in a direct line with Mr. Phillips Randolph.

To show you that Joey is such a guy as attracts attention, Mr. Phillips Randolph stands up a few minutes before the game starts, peering around and about to see who is present that he knows, and all of a sudden his eyes fall on Joey Perhaps, and then Mr. Phillips Randolph proves he had a good memory for faces, to be sure, for he states as follows:

"Why," he says, "there is the chap who rebuffs me so churlishly on the train when I offer him our colors. Yes," he says, "I am sure it is the same chap."

Well, what happens in the football game is much pulling and hauling this way and that, and to and fro, between the Harvards and the Yales without a tally right down to the last five minutes of play, and then all of a sudden the Yales shove the football down to within about three eights of an inch of the Harvards' goal line.

At this moment quite some excitement prevails. Then the next thing anybody knows, the Yales outshove the Harvards, and now the game is over, and Mr. Phillips Randolph gets up out of his seat, and I hear Mr. Phillips Randolph say like this:

"Well," he says, "the score is not so bad as it might be, and it is a wonderful game, and," he says, "we seem to make one convert to our cause, anyway, for see who is wearing our colors."

And with this he points to Joey Perhaps, who is still sitting down, with people stepping around him and over him and he is still smiling a little smile, and Mr. Phillips Randolph seems greatly pleased to see that Joey Perhaps has a big, broad crimson ribbon where he once wears his white silk muffler.

But the chances are Mr. Phillips Randolph will be greatly surprised if he knows that the crimson ribbon across Joey's bosom comes of Ollie Ortega planting a short knife in Joey's throat, or do I forget to mention before that Ollie Ortega is among those present?

I send for Ollie after I leave you last night, figuring he may love to see a nice football game. He arrives by plane this morning, and I am not wrong in my figuring. Ollie thinks the game is swell.

Well, personally, I will never forget this game, it is so exciting. Just after the tally comes off, all of a sudden, from the Yales in the stand across the field from the Harvards, comes a long-drawn-out wail that sounds so mournful it makes me feel very sad, to be sure. It starts off something like Oh-oh-oh-oh-oh, with all the Yales Oh-oh-oh-oh-oh-ing at once, and I ask a guy next to me what it is all about.

"Why," the guy says, "it is the Yales' 'Undertaker Song.' They always sing it when they have the other guy licked. I am an old Yale myself, and I will now personally sing this song for you."

And with this the guy throws back his head, and opens his mouth wide and lets out a yowl like a wolf calling to its mate.

Well, I stop the guy, and tell him it is a very lovely song, to be sure, and quite appropriate all the way around, and then I hasten away from the football game without getting a chance to say goodby to Doria, although afterwards I mail her the package of letters and pictures that Ollie gets out of Joey Perhaps' inside coat pocket during the confusion that prevails when the Yales make their tally, and I hope and trust that she will think the crimson streaks across the package are just a little touch of color in honor of the Harvards.

But the greatest thing about the football game (Meyer Marmalade says) is I win two C's off of one of the Harvards sitting near me, so I am now practically even on my trip.

The story below is excerpted from a book called The Homecoming Game, *which was later adapted into a play. It contains some fine ideas on why folks migrate to football stadiums on weekend afternoons. Its author, Howard Nemerov, was born in New York City and educated at Harvard. He has the distinction of serving as a pilot for both the Canadian and American air forces during World War II. With three dozen works of fiction, poetry, and criticism, Nemerov is one of America's most distinguished men of letters. Among his books are* The Blue Swallows *(1967),* The Collected Poems of Howard Nemerov *(1977), and* Inside the Onion *(1984). Nemerov taught English for many years at Bennington College in Vermont and Washington University in St. Louis. He is a member of the American Academy of Arts and Sciences. Nemerov won the National Book Award in 1978 and the Pulitzer Prize for Poetry in 1981. He was the nation's third Poet Laureate, 1988–1990.*

Howard Nemerov

THE HOMECOMING GAME (1957)

OF THOUSANDS OF PEOPLE SITTING around the stadium on this brilliant November afternoon, Charles Osman was certainly the only one who believed himself to have personally guaranteed, so far as any man could, the honesty of the game. This belief, of which he was, to be sure, only intermittently conscious, had raised to a new power the nervous intensity of his feelings about football generally, so that, just as in his undergraduate days, he was unable to eat his lunch or, indeed, pay attention to much of anything else. He had walked past the stadium a number of times, telling himself it was ridiculous to be so before-handed, and suddenly, three-quarters of an hour before game time, as early as the gates were opened, in fact, he had gone in, bought an inordinately expensive and glossy souvenir program—something he generally did not do—and taken his place in the mediocre seat to which as a faculty member he was entitled: about halfway up on the home team's side, between the 25- and the 30-yard lines.

His purpose in buying the program had been to assure himself that Raymond Blent was indeed in the starting lineup; and so he was, bearing the number 7, standing 6 feet and 1 inch, weighing 183 pounds. Of course Charles realized at once that the sort of assurance the program gave, since it must have been printed a fortnight before, was purely formal, official, and so to say historical; yet such was his nervousness that he would not readily have done without this paper. Also, by coming early, he was enabled to watch the practice sessions of both teams and there, since the players appeared without helmets, identify Raymond Blent for himself and make sure (as though suspecting up to the last minute some trick) that he was wearing the number 7 as certified in the program. It remained to see that he would play, but of this Charles now felt reasonably certain, since there would otherwise be no point whatever in the boy's appearing at all.

The sky was a pure blue; the sun already halfway down the sky, concentrated its royal golden light in the circle of the stadium whose intervals were marked in white. The field itself had a kind of totemic or sacrificial appearance, a ground to be kept inviolate on all profane occasions, then to be torn up by one fury only; even the players seemed aware of this quality, when they came out walking delicately as Agag; they sniffed the cold, bright air, tested the spring of the ground with a toe, danced a few tentative, mincing steps before first digging their cleats into the new green space which belonged to them and finally throwing themselves down, rolling around, turning somersaults—actions which no doubt had a rational purpose of warming-up and reducing tension but which reflected also some new, delightedly innocent relation with the earth itself. Their uniforms, the red and white on one side, black and white on the other, made the same effect

of brilliant purity, of cleanliness carefully preserved for the one ceremonial destruction.

For his part, Charles, accustomed to taking long views, felt already
something of the melancholy which was the inevitable outcome of all
this excitement; that this game, which seemed to stand brilliant and secure in the very path of time, an occasion, an event, a something of magnificent solidity devised by the wit of man to make the sun and the moon
stand still, was doomed to be itself merely a part of time; that for its two
hours' impression of timeless vigor, immortal and anonymous youthful-
ness, time exacted its usual price; which only the historian, perhaps, was
condemned to be gloomy about in advance.

He had not slept well the night before, and still suffered from a little,
wandering headache, scarcely so much a physical pain as a feeling of
mental remoteness, a tendency of the eyes to blur out of focus as though
simply refusing their attention to mere spectacle and showing an unde-
fined wish to see something else. Charles now and then was confusedly
reminded of having dreamt very numerous and very fatiguing dreams
during his broken sleep, and felt (though he could remember little or
nothing of all that) as though he had come here from a long, futile, miserable life spent elsewhere.

Well before game time the stadium was nearly full. The players retired
to their dressing rooms; the band, in red jackets and white trousers and
caps, paraded up and down the field, going sturdily from tonic to dom-
inant and back with a fine resonance of thumps and blares and booms
and a fine reflection of the light from their golden horns; six drum ma-
jorettes, high stepping with naked knees and black boots, went before,
twirling, twisting, tossing and catching their batons. It seemed as though
everyone began to roar, and yet as though no individual had any part in
the sound produced. Charles made no noise, the people around him
seemed not to be making any particular noise, yet the sound continued
to roll out in waves; one felt that *something,* not necessarily human, had
begun to roar. The band formed itself up before the visiting team's side
and played *their* "Alma Mater"; then came back to the home side and
played *their* "Alma Mater": two solemn, mournful airs which, harmoni-

cally at any rate, were hardly to be distinguished one from the other; yet when so addressed the graduates and undergraduates of each institution stood solemnly up, held felt hats against their chests, and sorrowfully sang. Many an eye was wet.

What in the world could it all be for? Charles glanced impatiently at the clock on the scoreboard, which told him nothing since it was designed to measure the game alone, and therefore had not begun to move. What a heroic view of time! That clock would move, during the afternoon, only during the instants of (allowing for a nicety of legal definition) actual play; when either side felt that things were going wrong, or had gone far enough for the moment, the clock would be stopped: *time* would be *out*. That clock, in fact, since it measured at no time any space of time greater than fifteen minutes, did not need (and did not have) a hand to tell the hour; that hour of which one might paradoxically say, considering it from a certain point of view, that it was eternal while it lasted. It was hard to say, about football as about games in general, which was more impressive, the violence or the rationality; whether the most important element was the keen demonstration of hostility and aggressiveness (with consequent arguments, developed by Plato and Aristotle, as to whether such demonstrations intensified or harmlessly liberated those passions) or, quite the contrary, the demonstration of control, of order, plan, and human meaning in the universe. Orderly violence! Did that oxymoron define civilization? Surely, to begin with, order and violence had been, or been considered to be, opposites, and order was imposed as a means of doing away with violence, on the famed model, in the individual, of reason quelling the passions. But was there in nature any violence so violent, so furious-cruel, as the violence of reason? Was any creature not gifted with reason capable of producing such orderly explosions of force as, say, the symphonies of Mozart or the advance of human armies to the assault? The avowed ideals of society were measure and reason; measure and reason had made society in the image of an armed camp, until the model of its life, the city with its squared and numbered streets, betrayed itself as based however inefficiently (for history and tradition had moved blindly in this matter at many times) upon logistical considerations, to the end that an absolute force might be instantaneously (and in an orderly manner) mobilized.

It was this, then, that thousands of apparently good-natured citizens were here in the stadium to celebrate, the ideal maximum of violence short of death or (it was hoped) serious injury, combined with the ideal maximum of the most pharisaical rationality and control. It would not do to say that people came to be entertained, for one had to ask at that point what it was that entertained people, and why of all things they were entertained by, particularly, this. Perhaps war itself, in its beginning, had been no more than such a ceremony as a football game, and scarcely more heroic or more dangerous than that village game of football anciently played in England, on Shrovetide Tuesday, where the unmarried women were always, by law, defeated by the married women. It might be—again the odd joke of history!—that the earliest form of war was predetermined as to its outcome, having a magical purpose and a ceremonial arrangement which, entering history as garbled traditions, were misinterpreted as both real and necessary: a nasty joke, if true. But civilization at present, and historically, depended on one decision and one decision alone: that it was better to sacrifice, at need, thousands and millions of men by accident—that is, in reality—than to sacrifice one man by pre-election—that is, ceremonially. Better? No, it was absolute, there was no choice allowed. And this same civilization paradoxically preserved at its very root a supreme instance of the other sort: better that one man should die for the people. . . .

The reappearance of the teams on the playing field caused Charles to break off at this place the thread of these somewhat elevated considerations. The captains advanced from either side to the center and there conferred with the referee. After this, both sides lined up for the kickoff and stood to attention, along with the entire audience, while the national anthem was played by the band and metallically sung by a tenor voice.

The game should have begun forthwith but there was a further delay. A devout voice, on the same public address system, began to intone some species of prayer mixed with explanations, from all of which Charles obscurely was able to gather that someone, a student, had somehow managed to fall into that bonfire last night at one stage or another of the proceedings, that this person had been terribly burned and taken to hospital that he—or she, Charles did not catch the name—was on the critical list and might not live. The voice ended by suggesting a minute of silent prayer, and since no one in the stadium controverted the suggestion, that minute then followed, while the football players stood uneasily with bowed heads and held their helmets like extra heads in their hands. At the end of one minute exactly, the voice coughed and said "Amen." The Homecoming Game then began.

When it was over, when in the cold shadows of the coming dark small mobs of people tore down the goal posts, while others seemed to stray aimlessly over the torn battleground as though seeking something they had lost, when the great crowd migrated slowly through many gates and dispersed, moving with the sheepish, bewildered resignation of men and women wakened from a dream in which some sad and terrible truth has been revealed, which they are unable to interpret although they will soon reduce it to the practical commonplaces of their daily lives, Charles remained for a long time where he was. . . .

It, whatever it was, at any rate was over. Charles stopped outside the gate and looked at the black implacable bulk of the wall, at the stars, at the remaining band of pure, red-gold light in the west, outlining the hills. Autumn, football, the pale, clear, fictitious glory. Adolescent glory. But what would you put in its place? Football is unreal, if you care to say so; but as you grow older many things become unreal, and football stands out somehow as an image. And there under the shadow of the stone, empty stadium after the captain and the kings depart, after all the others too depart, in that last lonely and cold air, you may, if you care for games, experience something of what is meant by vanished glory. Symbolical—perhaps. But it is commonly allowed that you may more easily call the things of this world symbolical than say what they are symbolical of.

This is an exceptionally graphic piece on deteriorating health and the woes it can bring. The illness of the retired pro quarterback in the story is described in gut-wrenching terms. Providing the story with a special irony is that author Herbert Wilner was himself a former quarterback, at Brooklyn College. And, like the protagonist in the story, he went through a devastating illness, from a malignant growth on his chest. Wilner died at a relatively young age as a result, and this story is based on his own illness. Wilner was a professor and director of the creative writing program at San Francisco State University. That school had more than its share of student rebellion in the late 1960s and early 1970s, which is chronicled in Wilner's memoir, College Days in Earthquake Country: Ordeal at San Francisco State *(1971). Wilner's main literary accomplishments are found in his novel* All the Little Heroes *(1966), and the collection of short stories called* Dovisch in the Wilderness *1968). This story first appeared in* Esquire, *and was included in* The Best American Short Stories 1979.

Herbert Wilner

A QUARTERBACK SPEAKS TO HIS GOD (1978)

BOBBY KRAFT, THE HEROIC OLD pro, lies in his bed in the grip of medicines relieving his ailing heart. Sometimes he tells his doctor your pills beat my ass, and the doctor says it's still Kraft's choice: medicine or open heart surgery. Kraft shuts up.

He wasn't five years out of pro football, retired at thirty-six after fourteen years, when he got the rare viral blood infection. Whatever they were, the damn things ate through his heart like termites, leaving him with pericarditis, valve dysfunction, murmurs, arrhythmia, and finally, congestive failure. The physiology has been explained to him, but he prefers not to understand it. Fascinated in the past by his strained ligaments, sprained ankles, torn cartilage, tendinitis, he now feels betrayed by his heart's disease.

"You want to hear it?" Dr. Felton once asked, offering the earpieces of the stethoscope.

Kraft recoiled.

"You don't want to hear the sound of your own heart?"

Sitting on the examining table, Kraft was as tall as the short doctor, whose mustache hid a crooked mouth.

"Why should I?" Kraft said. "Would you smile in the mirror after your teeth got knocked out?"

This morning in bed, as with almost every third morning of the past two years, Kraft begins to endure the therapeutic power of his drugs. He takes diuretics: Edecrin, or Lasix, or Dyazide, or combinations. They make him piss and piss, relieving for a day or two the worst effects of the congesting fluids that swamp his lungs and gut. He's been told the washout dumps potassium, an unfortunate consequence. The depletions cramp his muscles, give him headaches, sometimes trigger arrhythmias. They always drive him into depressions as deep as comas. He blames himself.

"It has nothing to do with will power," Dr. Felton explained. "If you ran five miles in Death Valley in August, you'd get about the same results as you do from a very successful diuresis."

To replenish some of his losses, Kraft stuffs himself with bananas, drinks orange juice by the pint, and takes two tablespoons a day of potassium chloride solution. To prevent and arrest the arrhythmia, he takes quinidine, eight pills a day, 200 mg per pill. To strengthen the enlarged and weakened muscle of his heart wall, he takes digoxin. Together they make him nauseous, gassy, and distressed. He takes anti-nausea pills and chews antacids as though they were Life Savers. Some nights he takes Valium to fall asleep. If one doesn't work, he takes two.

"I can't believe it's me," he protests to his wife, Elfi. "I never took pills, I wouldn't even touch aspirins. There were guys on coke, amphetamines,

Novocaine. I wouldn't touch anything. Now look at me, I'm living in a drugstore."

His blurred eyes sweep the squads of large and small dark labeled bottles massed on his chest of drawers. His wife offers little sympathy.

"Again and again the same thing with you," she'll answer in her German accent. "So go have the surgery already, you coward ox."

Coward? Him? Bobby Kraft?

"I have to keep recommending against surgery," said Dr. Felton, named by the team physician as the best cardiologist in the city for Kraft's problems. "I'm not certain it can provide the help worth the risk. Meanwhile, we buy time. Every month these hotshot surgeons get better at their work. Our equipment for telling us precisely what's wrong with your heart gets better. In the meantime, since you don't need to work for a living, wait it out. Sit in the sun. Read. Watch television. Talk about the old games. Wait."

What does coward have to do with it?

This morning, in his bed, three hours after the double dose of Lasix with a Dyazide thrown in, Kraft has been to the toilet bowl fourteen times. His breathing is easier, his gut is relieved; and now he has to survive the payments of his good results.

He's dry as a stone, exhausted, and has a headache. The base of his skull feels kicked. The muscles of his neck are wrenched and pulled, as if they'd been wound on a spindle. His hips ache. So do his shoulder joints. His calves are heavy. They're tightening into cramps. His ankles feel as though tissue is dissolving in them, flaking off into small crystals, eroding gradually by bumping each other in slight, swirling collisions before they dissolve altogether in a bath of serum. His ankles feel absent.

He's cold. Under the turned up electric blanket, he has chills. His heart feels soaked.

He wants to stay awake, but he can't help sleeping. By the sixth of his returns from the bowl, he was collapsing into the bed. Falling asleep was more like fainting, like going under, like his knee surgery—some imperfect form of death. He needs to stay awake. His will is all that's left him for proving himself, but his will is shot by the depression he can't control.

By tomorrow he'll be mostly out of bed. He'll have reduced the Lasix to one pill, no Dyazide, piss just a little, and by the day after, with luck guarding against salt in his food, he'll have balanced out. He'll sit on the deck in his shorts when the sun starts to burn a little at noon. He'll squeeze the rubber ball in his right hand. He'll take a shower afterwards and oil himself down to rub the flaking off. He'll look at himself in the full-length mirror and stare at the part of his chest where the injured heart is supposed to be. He'll see little difference from what he saw five years ago when he was still playing. The shoulders sloping and wide, a little less full but not bony, the chest a little less deep but still broad and tapered, the right arm still flat-muscled and whip-hanging, same as it was ten years ago when he could throw a football sixty yards with better than fair accuracy. What he'll see in the mirror can infuriate him.

He once got angry enough to put on his sweat suit, go through the gate at the back fence and start to run in the foot-wide level dirt beside the creek bed in the shade of the laurels. After five cautious strides, he lengthened into ten hard ones. Then he was on his knees gasping for air, his heart arrhythmic, his throat congested. He couldn't move for five minutes. By the next day he'd gained six pounds. He told Elfi what he'd done.

"Imbecile!" She called the doctor. Kraft, his ankles swollen, was into heart failure. It was touch and go about sending him to the hospital for intravenous diuretics and relief oxygen.

It took a month to recover, he never made another effort to run, but he knew even today, that after all this pissing and depression, exhaustion and failure, when he balanced out the day after tomorrow and he was on the deck and the sun hit, nothing could keep the impulse out of his legs. He'd want to run. He'd feel the running in his legs. And he'd settle for a few belittling house chores, then all day imagine he'd have a go at screwing Elfi. But at night he didn't dare try.

When she gets home from her day with the retards, she fixes her Campari on ice, throws the dinner together, at which, as always, she pecks like a bird and he shovels what he can, making faces to advertise his nausea, rubbing his abdomen to soothe his distress and belching to release the gas. After dinner he'll report his day, shooting her combative looks to challenge the boredom glazing her face. They move to the living room. Standing, he towers over her. He's six foot two inches and she's tiny. His hand, large even for his size, would cover the top of her skull the way an ordinary man's might encapsulate an egg. She stretches full length on the couch; he slouches in the club chair. She wears a tweed skirt and buttoned blouse, he's in his pajamas and terry cloth robe. He still has a headache. His voice drones monotonously in his own ears, but he's obsessed with accounting for his symptoms as though they were football statistics. When he at last finishes, she sits up and nods.

"So all in all today is a little better. Nothing with the bad rhythm."

He gets sullen, then angry. No one has ever annoyed him as effectively as she. He'd married her six years ago, just before his retirement, as he'd always planned. He knew the stewardesses, models, second-rate actresses, and just plain hotel whores, would no longer do. He'd need children, a son. And this tiny woman's German accent and malicious tongue had knocked him out. And sometimes he caught her reciting prayers in French (she said for religion it was the perfect language), which seemed to him—a man without religion—unexplainably peculiar and right.

Now, offended by her flint heart (calling *this* a better day!), he goes to the den for TV. He has another den with shelves full of his history—plaques, cups, trophies, photos (one with the President of the United States), footballs, medals, albums, video tapes—but he no longer enters this room. After an hour, she comes in after him. She wants to purr. He wants to be left alone. His headache is worse, his chest tingles. She recounts events of her day, one of the two during the week when she drives to the city and consults at a school for what she calls learning-problem children. He doesn't even pretend to listen. She sulks.

Words go back and forth. He didn't think he could do it, but he tells her.

In roundabout fashion, the TV jabbering, he finally makes her understand his latest attack of anxiety: the feel of his not feeling it. His prick.

She looks amazed, as if she were still not understanding him, then her eyes widen and she taps herself on the temple.

"You I don't understand," she sputters. "To me your head is something for doctors. Every day I worry sick about your heart, and you give me this big soap opera about your prick. Coward. You should go for the surgery. Every week you get worse, whatever that Dr. Felton says. You let all those oxes fall on you and knock you black and blue, then a little cutting with a knife, and you shiver. When they took away your football, they broke your baby's heart. So now, sew it up again. Let a surgeon do it. You don't know how. You think your heart can get better by itself? In you, Bobby, never."

When it suits her, she exaggerates her mispronunciation of his name. "*Beaubee. Beaubee.* What kind of name is this for a grown man your size, Beaubee?"

He heads to the bedroom to slam the door behind him. After ten minutes, the door opens cautiously. She sits at the edge of the bed near his feet. She strokes the part of the blanket covering his feet, puts her cheek to it, then straightens, stands, says it to him.

"I love you better than my own life. I swear it. How else could I stay with you?"

He hardly hears her. His attention concentrates on the first signs of his arrhythmia. He tells her, "It's beginning." She says she'll fetch the quinidine. She carries his low sodium milk for him to drink it with. He glances at her woefully through what used to be ice-blue eyes fixed in his head like crystals. He stares at the pills before he swallows them. He can identify any of them by color, shape and size. He doesn't trust her. She can't nurse, she always panics.

His heart is fluttering, subsiding, fluttering. Finally it levels off at the irregularity of the slightly felt extra beat which Felton has told him is an auricular fibrillation. Elfi finds an excuse to leave the room. He sits up in bed, his eyes closed, his thick back rammed against the sliding pillows, his head arched over them, the crown drilling into the headboard.

The flurries have advanced to a continuously altering input of extra beats. They are light and rapid, like the scurryings under his breastbone of a tiny creature with scrawny limbs. After ten minutes, the superfluous beats intensify and ride over the regular heartbeats.

There's chaos in his heart. Following a wild will of its own, it has nothing to do with him, nor can he do anything with it. Moderate pain begins in his upper left arm, and though the doctor has assured him it's nothing significant, and he knows it will last only through the arrhythmia, Kraft begins to sweat.

The heart goes wilder. He rubs his chest, runs his hands across the protruding bones of his cheeks and jaw. Ten minutes later the heart begins to yank as well as thump. It feels as if the heart's apex is stitched into tissues near the bottom of his chest, and the yanking of the bulk of the heart will tear the threads loose. Again and again he tries to will himself into the cool accommodation he can't command. Then at last it seems that for a few minutes the force of the intrusive beats is diminishing. He dares to hope it's now the beginning of the end of the episode.

Immediately a new sequence of light and differently irregular flurries resumes. The thumpings are now also on his back. He turns to his right side, flicks the control for the television, tries to lose himself with it, hears Elfi come in. She whispers, "Still?" and leaves again.

The thumpings deepen. They are really pounding. The headache is drilled in his forehead. It throbs. He thinks the heart is making sounds that can be heard in the room. He claws his long fingers into the tough flesh over the heart. It goes on for another hour. He waits, and waits. Then, indeed, in moments, they fade into the flutter with which they began. After a while the flutter is hard to pick out, slips under the regular beating of his heart, and gives way at last to an occasional extra beat which pokes at his chest with the feel of a mild bubbling of thick pudding at a slow boil. Then that's gone.

His heart has had its day's event.

Kraft tells himself: nothing's worth this. He's told it to himself often. He tells himself he'll see Felton tomorrow. He'll insist on the surgery.

Afraid of surgery? Coward? She wasn't even in his life when he had his knee done after being blindsided in Chicago. He came out of the anesthesia on a cloud. The bandage on his leg went from thigh to ankle, but the girl who came to visit him—stewardess, model; the cocktail waitress—he couldn't remember now, she was the one whose eyes changed colors—she had to fight him off because he kept rubbing his hand under her skirt up the soft inside of her thigh. She ended on his bed on top of him. He was almost instantaneous. He had to throw her off, remembering his leg, his career. But was it really that Felton runt who was keeping him from surgery?

In despair now, could he really arrange for the surgery tomorrow? Not on a knee, but on his opened heart?

Bobby Kraft's heart?

That's crap," he once said to a young reporter. "Any quarterback can throw. We all start from there. Some of us do it a little better. That's not what it's all about. Throwing aint passing, sonny, and passing aint all of quarterbacking anyway."

"You mean picking your plays. Using your head. Reading defenses?"

"That's important. It's not all of it."

"What's the mystique?" the youth asked shyly, fearful of ignorance. "Not in your arm; not in your head. I know you all have guts or wouldn't play in such a violent game. If it's a special gift, where do you keep it?"

"In your goddamn chest, sonny. Where the blood comes." He smiled and stared icily at the reporter until the young man turned away.

Actually, Kraft worked hard mastering the technical side of his skills. If he needed to, for instance, if the wind wasn't strong against him, he could hang the ball out fifty yards without putting too much arc in it. It should've been a heavy ball to catch for a receiver running better than ten yards to the second. But Kraft, in any practice, could get it out there inches ahead of the outstretched arms and have the forward end of the ball, as it was coming down, begin to point up slightly over its spiralling axis. That way it fell with almost no weight at all. The streaking receiver could palm it in one hand, as if he were snatching a fruit from a tree he ran by. It took Kraft years to get it right and do it in games.

There were ways of taking the ball from the center, places on it for each of his fingers, ways of wrist-cradling the ball before he threw if he had to break his pocket, and there was the rhythm set up between his right arm and the planting of his feet before he released the ball through the picket of huge, upraised arms.

He watched the films. He studied the game book. He worked with the coaches and his receivers for any coming Sunday. What the other team did every other time they played you, and what they did all season was something you had to remember. You also had to be free of it. You had to yield to the life of the particular game, build it, master it, improvise. And always you not only had to stand up to their cries of "Kill Kraft," you had to make them eat it. The sonsabitches!

That's what Kraft did most of the week waiting for his Sunday game. He worked the "sonsabitches" into a heat. Then he slid outside himself and watched it. It was like looking at a fire he'd taken out of his chest to hold before eyes. Tense all week, his eyes grew colder and colder as they gazed at the flame. By game time he was thoroughly impersonal.

Sunday on the field in the game, though he weighed 203, he looked between plays somewhat on the slender side, like someone who could get busted like a stick by most of those he played among. He stood out of the huddle a long time before he entered it through the horseshoe's slot to call the play. Outside the huddle, except in the last minutes when they might be fighting the clock, his pose was invariable. His right foot was anchored with the toe toward the opening for him in his huddle about nine feet away, the left angled toward where the referee had placed the ball. It threw his torso on a rakish slant toward the enormous opposing linemen, as though he'd tight-rigged himself against a headland. He kept the knuckles of his right hand high on his right ass, the fingers limp. His left hand hung motionless on his left side. Under his helmet, his head turned slowly and his eyes darted. He wasn't seeing anything that would matter. They'd change it all around when he got behind the center. He was emptying himself for his concentration. It was on the three strides back to the huddle that he picked his play and barked it to them in a toneless, commanding fierceness just short of rage.

Then the glory began for Kraft. What happened, what he lived for never got into the papers; it wasn't seen on television. What he saw was only part of what he knew. He would watch the free safety or the outside linebackers for giveaway cues on the blitz. He might detect from jumping linemen some of the signs of looping. The split second before he had the ball he might spot assignment against his receivers and automatically register the little habits and capacities of the defending sonsabitches. He could "feel" the defenses.

But none of it really began until, after barking the cadence of his signals, he actually did have the ball in his hand. Then, for the fraction of a second before he gave it away to a runner, or for the maximum three seconds in the pocket before he passed, there was nothing but grunting and roaring and cursing, the crashing of helmets and pads, the oofs of air going out of brutish men and the whisk of legs in tight pants cutting air like a scythe in tall grass and the soft suck of cleats in the grassy sod, and the actual vibration of the earth itself stampeded by that tonnage of sometimes gigantic, always fast, cruel, lethal bodies. And if Kraft kept the ball, if he dropped his three paces back into his protective pocket, he'd inch forward before he released it and turn his shoulders or his hips to slip past the bodies clashing at his sides. He would always sense and sometimes never see the spot to which he had to throw the ball through the nests of the raised arms of men two to five inches taller than himself and twice as broad and sixty, eighty pounds heavier. One of their swinging arms could, if he didn't see it coming, knock him off his feet as though he were a matchstick. He was often on his back or side, a pile of the sonsabitches taking every gouge and kick and swipe at him they could get away with. That was the sweetness for him.

To have his ass beaten and not even know it. To have that rush inside him mounting all through the game, and getting himself more and more under control as he heated up, regarding himself without awareness of it, his heart given to the fury, and his mind to a sly and joyous watching of his heart, storing up images that went beyond the choral roaring of any huge crowd and that he would feed on through the week waiting for the next game, aching through the week but never knowing in the game any particular blow that would make him hurt. Not after the first time he got belted. They said he had rubber in his joints, springs in his ass, and a whip for an arm.

The combination of his fierce combativeness and laid back detachment infuriated the sonsabitches he played against. They hated him; it made them lose their heads. It was all the advantage Kraft ever needed. His own teammates, of course, went crazy with the game. They wound themselves up for it in the hours before it, and some of them didn't come down until the day after, regardless of who won.

Kraft depended on their lunacy. He loved them for needing it. And he loved them most during the game because no one ever thought of him as being like them. He was too distant. Too cunning. Too cold. But on the sideline, among them, waiting for his defensive team to get him back into the game, he might run his tongue over his lips, taste the salty blood he didn't know was there, and swallow. Then he'd rub his tongue across his gums and over the inside of a cheek, and an expression of wonder might flicker across his face, as if he were a boy with his first lick at the new candy, tasting the sweetness of his gratified desires, not on his tongue but in his own heart.

Three more months passed with Kraft delivered up to the cycles of his illness and medicines and waiting and brooding. Then he was sitting in his sweat socks and trunks at the side of the pool one late afternoon. He gazed vacantly at the water. His chest had caved a little; and his long head seemed larger, his wide neck thicker. Elfi had been reading on a mat near the fence under the shade of a laurel.

"So how long are you going to live like this?" she asked. Immediately he thought she was talking sex. "Two more years? Five? Ten?" She crossed her arms over her slender, fragile chest. "Maybe even fifteen, hah? But sooner or later you'll beg them for the surgery. On your knees. So why do you wait? Look how you lose all the time you could be better in."

His answer was pat.

"I told you. They can cut up my gut. They can monkey with my head. They can cut off my right arm even, how's that? But they're not going to cut up my heart. That's all. They're not putting plastic valves in my heart."

"Again with this plastic. Listen, I am reading a lot about it. There are times they can put in a valve from a sheep, or a pig."

He looked at her in amazement. He stood up. She came to his collarbone; he cast a shade over all of her.

"Sheep and pig!"

He looked like he might slam her, then he turned away and headed for the glass door to the bedroom.

"Your heart," she said. "You have such a special heart?"

When he turned she looked up at him and backed off a step.

"Yeah, it's special. My heart's me." He stabbed his chest with the long thumb of his right hand.

"You think I don't understand that? With my own heart I understand that. But this is the country where surgeons make miracles. You are lucky. It happens to you here, where you are such a famous ox. And here they have the surgeon who's also so famous. For him, what you have is a—is a—a blister."

He glared. She backed off another step. He turned and dove suddenly into the pool, touched bottom, came up slowly and thought he could live a long time in a chilly, blue, chlorinated water in which he would, suspended, always hold his breath. He rose slowly, broke the water at the nearer wall, hoisted himself at the coping and emerged from the water, with his back and shoulders glistening. He was breathless, but he moved on to the bedroom. He didn't double over until he had closed the glass door behind him. While he waited for his throat to empty and his chest to fill, he hurt. He got dizzy. Bent, he moved to the bed and fell on it. He stretched out.

He napped, or thought he did. When he woke, or his mind cleared, words filled him. He clasped his hands behind his neck, closed his eyes and tried to shut the words out. He got off the bed and stood before the full-length mirror. He put his hands to his thighs, bent his weight forward, clamped the heels of his hands together, dropped his left palm to make a nest for the ball the center would snap. Numbers barked in his head. When he heard the hup-hup he moved back the two swift steps, planted his feet, brought his right arm high behind his head, the elbow at his ear, then released the shoulder and snapped the wrist. He did it twice more. He was grinning. When he started it the fourth time, he was into arrhythmia.

Kraft consults Dr. Felton. Felton examines him, sits, glances at him, gazes at the ceiling, puts the tips of his index fingers to a pyramid point on his mustache, and says, "I'm still opposed, but I'll call him." He means the heart surgeon, Dr. Gottfried. They arrange for Kraft to take preliminary tests. He has already had some of them, but the heart catheterization will be new. A week later Kraft enters the hospital.

An hour after he's in his room, a parade of doctors begin the listening and thumping on Kraft's chest and back. A bearded doctor in his early thirties who will assist in the morning's catheterization briefs him on what to expect. He speaks rapidly.

"You'll be awake of course. You'll find it a painless procedure. We'll use a local on your arm where we insert the catheter. When it touches a wall of the heart, you might have a little flurry of heartbeats. Don't worry about it. Somewhere in the process we'll ask you to exercise a little. We need some measurements of the heart under physical stress. You won't have to do more than you can. Toward the end we'll inject a purple dye. We get very precise films that way. You'll probably get some burning sensations while the dye circulates. A couple of minutes or so. Otherwise you'll be quite comfortable. Do you have any questions?"

Kraft has a hundred and asks none.

The doctor starts out of the room, stops, comes back a little haltingly. He has his pen in his hand and his prescription pad out.

"Mr. Kraft, I have a nephew. He'd get a big kick out of . . ."

Kraft takes the extended pad and pen. "What's his name?"

"Oh, just sign yours."

He writes: "For the doc and his nephew for good luck from Bobby Kraft." He returns the items. He feels dead.

In the morning they move him on a gurney to a thick walled room in the basement. He's asked to slide onto an X-ray table. They cover him with a sheet. He raises himself on his elbows to see people busy at tasks he can't understand. There are two women and two men. All of them wear white. One of the women sits before a console full of knobs and meters on a table near his feet. Above and behind his head is a machine he'll know later is a fluoroscope. In a corner of the room there's a concrete alcove, the kind X-ray technicians hide behind. One of the men keeps popping in and out of its opening on his way to and from the fluoroscope. The ceiling is full of beams and grids on which X-ray equipment slides back and forth and is lowered and raised. The other man plays with it, and with film plates he slides under the table. A nurse attaches EKG bands to his ankles.

The two doctors come in. They are already masked, rubber-gloved, and dressed in green. The bearded one introduces the other, who has graying hair and brown eyes. A nurse fits Kraft's right arm into a metal rest draped with towels. "I'm going to tie your wrist," she says. She ties it and tucks the towels over his hand and wrist and over his shoulder and biceps. She washes the inside of his shaved arm with alcohol, rubbing hard at the crook of his elbow. The bearded doctor ties his arm tightly with a rubber strap, just above the elbow, then feels with his fingers in the crook of the elbow for the raised vessels. He swabs the skin with the yellow Xylocaine and waits. The other doctor asks the nurse at the console if she is ready. She says, "Not yet." He looks at Kraft, and Kraft looks up at the rails and grids.

In a few minutes the bearded doctor injects the anesthetic into several spots high on the inside of Kraft's forearm. It takes ten more minutes before the woman at the console is ready. She gets up twice to check with the man in the alcove. The older doctor goes there once. When the woman finally signals she's ready, Dr. Kahl says, "OK." Kraft looks. The older doctor stands alongside Kahl. The scalpel goes quickly into Kraft's flesh in a short cut. He doesn't feel it. Kahl removes the scalpel, and a little blood seeps. The doctor switches instruments and goes quickly into the small wound. Blood spurts. It comes in a few pumps about six inches over Kraft's arm, a thick, rich red blood. Kraft is astonished. Then the blood stops. The towels are soaked with it.

"I'm putting the cath in."

The older doctor nods. He turns toward the fluoroscope. Kraft watches again. The catheter is black and silky and no thicker than a cocktail straw. Still Kraft feels nothing. Kahl's brow creases. He's manipulating the black, slender thing with his rubbered fingers. He rolls his thumb along it as he moves it. Kraft waits to feel something. There is no feeling. He can't see where the loose end of the catheter is coming from. He turns his head away and takes a deep breath. He takes another deep one. He wants to relax. He wants to know how the hell he got into all this. What really happened to him? When? What for?

"You're in," the older doctor says.

The thing is in his heart.

It couldn't have taken more than ten seconds. They are in his heart with a black silky tube and he can't feel it.

"Hold it," the nurse at the console says. She begins calling out numbers.

"How are you feeling?" Dr. Kahl asks. Kraft nods.

"You feeling all right?" the older doctor repeats, walking toward the fluoroscope.

"Yeah."

They go on and on. He feels nothing. He hears the older doctor instructing the younger one: "Try the ventricle . . . Hold it . . . What's your reading now . . . There's the flutter . . . Don't worry about that, Mr. Kraft . . . Watch the pulmonary artery . . . He's irritable in there . . . Withdraw! . . . Fine, you're through the cusps . . . Try the mitral . . . You're on the wall again . . . How are you feeling, Mr. Kraft?"

Kraft nods. He licks his lips. He tries not to listen to them. When the flutter goes off in his chest, he thinks it will start an arrhythmia. It doesn't. It feels like a hummingbird hovering in his chest for a second. Something catches it. Occasionally the other doctor comes beside Kahl and plays for a moment with the catheter while he watches the fluoroscope. The bearded doctor chats sometimes, saying he's sorry Kraft has to lie so flat for so long, it must be uncomfortable. Does he use many pillows at home? Would he like to raise up for a while?

The arm hurts where the catheter enters it. Kraft feels a firm growing lump under the flesh, as if a golf ball is being forced into the wound. Kraft concentrates on the pain. He thinks of grass.

"How much longer?" he asks.

"We're more than half way."

In a while the nurse tells him they are going to have him do the exercises now. Something presses against his feet. The brown-eyed doctor talks.

"We have an apparatus here with bicycle pedals. Just push on them as you would on a bike. We'll adjust the pedals to keep making you push with more force. If it gets to be too much work, tell us. We want you to exert yourself, but not tire yourself."

What's he talking about, Kraft asks himself. He begins to pump. There's no resistance. He pumps faster, harder.

"That's fine. Keep it going. You're doing real fine."

He gets a rhythm to it quickly, thrusting his legs as rapidly as he can. He expects to get winded, but he doesn't. He's doing fine. He almost enjoys it. He concentrates. He feels the pain in his arm and pumps harder, faster. He imagines he's racing. For a moment it get more difficult to pump. He presses harder, feels his calves stretch and harden. He gets his rhythm back. They encourage him. He licks his lips and clasps the edge of the table with his left hand and drives his legs. He forgets about any race. He knows he's doing well with this exercise. It will show on their computation. They'll tell him his heart is getting better. The resistance to his pumping gets stronger. He pumps harder.

"That was very good. We're taking the apparatus away now. You feel all right?"

"Fine."

Kraft closes his eyes. There's the pain in his arm again. His forearm is going to pop. It's too strong a pain now. They are moving in the room. He grinds his teeth.

"We're going to inject the dye now," the older doctor says.

Kraft turns his head and sees the metal cylinder of the syringe catch glinting light for a moment in Kahl's raised hand. He sees the rubbered thumb move; a blackish fluid spurts from the needle's tip. The needle goes toward his arm—into the wound or the catheter, he can't tell. He turns away.

"You'll feel some heat in your head very soon. That's just the effect of the dye. It'll wear off. You'll feel heat at the sphincter too. Are you all right?"

Kraft nods. He turns away. Why do they keep asking him? He sees the man from the alcove hurrying with X-ray plates that he slides into the slot under the table just below Kraft's shoulder blades. He hurries back to the alcove. The doctors call instructions. The voice from the alcove calls some words back and numbers. Kraft closes his eyes and tries to think of something to think of. He thinks if Elfi could—then Kraft feels the rush. It comes in way over the pain in his arm. It raises him off the table. He feels the heat racing through him. A terrific pounding at his forehead. It doesn't go away. He tries to think of the pain in his arm, but he feels the heat rushing through him in a rising fever. Then it hits his asshole and he rises off the table again. It burns tremendously. They have lit a candle in his asshole and the burned flesh is going to drop through.

"Wow!"

"That's all right. It'll go away soon."

It does, but not the headache. It burns and throbs in his forehead. He hears metal dropping under the table. The man runs out and removes film plates. Someone else inserts others. They call numbers. The plates fall again. They repeat the process. He closes his eyes. The rush is fading, but the headache remains, throbbing.

"How you doing?"

"All right. My head aches."

"It'll pass."

"How was the exercise part?"

"You did fine. We'll be through soon. How's the arm?"

"Hurts."

"No problem. More Novocaine."

"No. Leave it."

They hurry again. Words are exchanged about the films. Someone leaves the room. Someone enters it later. Kraft keeps his eyes closed. The ache is still in his forehead, but he thinks he might sleep.

"Well, that's it," the bearded Kahl says. Kraft looks toward him, then down at his arm. The wound is stitched. He hasn't felt it. The doctor covers it with a gauze pad and two strips of tape. The catheter's gone. Kraft sees no sign of it. They wash his arm of blood and get him onto the gurney. He hears someone say "I think we got good results." The older doctor tells Kraft they'll know some things tomorrow. "It looks good."

Back in his room Elfi is waiting for him. He gets into bed, and they leave. She throws herself on him. She's breathless. Her cheeks are streaked, her eyes are red. She's been crying. She's almost crying now.

"I don't want to talk about it now," he says when she begins to speak.

"I don't want to hear it. That's the truth. Listen, I'm going home. Beaubee, I'm not good here."

She rushes from the room. He contemplates the increasing pain in his arm. It reaches into his biceps now. He keeps thinking about his heart. They had their black tube in *his* heart. The sonsabitches.

On the next day, just before lunch, reading a magazine in the chair in his room, he sees Dr. Gottfried for the first time. With him, in his white coat, is the gray-haired doctor from the catheterization. Dr. Gottfried is in the short-sleeved green shirt and the green baggy cotton trousers of the operating room. He has scuffed sneakers, and the stethoscope—like a metal and rubber noose, hangs from his neck. He looks tired. He has the sad eyes of a spaniel. And yet the man—in build neither here nor there, just a man—introduced by his colleague, stares and stares at Kraft before he moves or speaks, like a man before a fight. He keeps looking into Kraft's eyes, as if through his patient's eyes he could find the as yet untested condition of his true heart. He keeps on staring; Kraft stares back. Then the great famous doctor nods; a corner of his mouth flickers. He has apparently seen what he has needed to—and judged. He leans over Kraft and listens with the stethoscope to Kraft's chest. He could not have heard more than three heartbeats when he removes the earpieces, steps back, and speaks.

"Under it all, you've got a strong heart. I can tell by the snap."

Kraft, the heroic old pro, begins to smile. He beams. The doctor speaks in a slow, subdued voice; Kraft's smile fades.

"There's no real rush with your situation. However, the sooner the better, and there's a cancelled procedure two weeks from today. We can do you then. I'll operate. Right now I want to study more of the material in your folder. "We've got several base lines. I'll be back soon. Dr. Pritchett will fill you in and answer any questions you have. He knows more than anyone in the world about pulmonary valve disease."

Leaving, Dr. Gottfried moves without a sound, his head tilted and the shoulder on that side sagging. When he closes the door, Kraft turns on Dr. Pritchett.

"What operation? He said my heart's good. You said you got good results on that catheter. The fat one yesterday said he got good results on his machine."

The doctor explains. The "good" results meant they were finding what they needed to know. They are all agreed now the linings of the heart should be removed. A simple procedure for Dr. Gottfried—"he's the best you could find"—even if the endocardium is scarred enough to be adhesive. They are also agreed about the pulmonary valve. It will be removed and replaced by an artificial device made of a flexible steel alloy. "Dr. Gottfried will just pop it right in. We're not, however, certain of the aortic valve. Dr. Gottfried will make that decision during surgery." Positive results are expected. There's the strong probability of the heart restored to ninety percent efficiency and a good possibility of total cure. Of course, you'll be on daily anticoagulant medicines for the rest of your life. No big affair. The important point, as Dr. Gottfried said, is the heart is essentially strong. Surgery, done now, while Kraft is young and before the heart is irrepairably weakened, is the determining factor. Of course, as in any surgery, there's risk.

"Have I made it clear? Can I answer any questions, Mr. Kraft? I know we get too technical at times."

"I'm not stupid."

"No one implied you were."

Emptying with dread, Kraft slips his hands under the blanket to hide their trembling. "Will I still need pissing pills after the operation?"

"Diuretics? No. I wouldn't think so."

"No more arrhythmia?"

"We can't be sure of that. Sometimes the—"

"Then what kind of total cure, man?"

"I can't explain all the physics and chemistry of the heart rhythm, Mr. Kraft. If you'd continue to have the arrhythmia, it would be benign. A mechanical thing. We have medicine to control it."

"You said I did great with the exercises."

"Yes. We got the results we needed."

Dr. Gottfried returns, still in his operating clothes, holding the manila folder, looking now a little bored as well as fatigued, his voice slow, quiet.

"Any questions for me?"

"The risk? Dr. What'shisname here said . . ."

"There's ten percent mortality risk. That covers all open heart surgery. A lot of it relates to heart disease more advanced than yours, where general health isn't as good as yours. There's risk however, for you too. You know that."

Kraft nods. He suddenly detests this man he needs, who'll have the power of life over him. He closes his eyes.

"As I said, there's no emergency. But I can fit you in two weeks from now. You could have it over with. Decide in a day or two. I'd appreciate that. Talk it over with your wife. With Dr. Felton. Let us know through him."

Home again, Kraft, on his medicines, pissed, grew depressed, endured his headaches and lassitude, the arrhythmias, the miscellaneous pains, his sense of dissolution, the nausea; and, as before, continued to blame himself as well as feel betrayed. He submitted, and he waited. He never looked in the mirror anymore. While he shaved, he never saw himself. Sometimes he felt tearful. On the few days that he came around, he no longer went out to the sun and the pool but stayed indoors. He called no one, but answered the phone on his better days and kept up his end of the bullshit with old buddies and some writers who still remembered. No one but Elfi knew his despair.

When he passed the closed door to the den of his heroic history, his trophy room, he wasn't even aware that he kept himself from going in. The door might as well have been the wall. What he kept seeing now was behind his eyes: The face of Dr. Gottfried. It flashed like a blurred, tired, boneless, powerful shape, producing a quality before which Kraft felt weak. He began to exalt the quality and despise the man and groped for a way by which he could begin to tell Elfi.

One night, in bed with her, a week after he'd made the decision to go for the surgery, which was now less than a week away, with the lights out and her figure illumined only by a small glow of clouded moonlight entering through the cracked drapes, he thought her asleep and ventured to loop his hand over her head where he could easily reach her outside shoulder. He touched it gently. It was the first time since his discovery of his impotence that he'd touched her in bed.

Immediately she moved across the space, nestled her head in his armpit, and pressed against his side. He resisted his desire to pull away. He was truly pleased by the way she fit.

"Every day now I pray," she said. "Oh, not for you, don't worry. You are going to be fine. I swear it, how much I believe that. You don't need me to pray for you. I need it. I do it for myself. Selfishly. Entirely."

He spoke of what was on his mind. "That surgeon's freaking me."

"You couldn't find anyone better. I have the utmost confidence. To me that is what you call a man. You should see in his clinic. What the patients say about him. The eyes they have when they look at him. He walks through like a god. And I tell you something else. He has a vast understanding."

He moved his hand from her arm. "It's *my* heart, not yours." His voice fell to despair. "It's a man thing. You can't understand. A sonofabitch puts his hand in Bobby Kraft's heart. He pops in some goddamned metal valve. He's flaky. He freaks me."

"I tell you, I feel sorry for you. Too bad. For any man I feel sorry who doesn't know who are his real enemies. Not to know that, that's your freak. That's the terrible thing can happen to a man in his life. Not to know who his enemies are."

"That's what *he* is," Kraft declaimed in the darkness. "He's my enemy. If there's one thing I've always known, that's it. The sonsabitches. Now Gottfried is. And there aint no game. I don't even get to play."

"You baby. Play. Play. It's because all your life you played a game for a boy. That's why you can't know. Precisely. I always knew that."

He pulled away from her. He got out of bed and loomed over her threateningly.

"Go on back home, Kraut. I don't need you for the operation. To hell with the operation. I'll call it off. How's that?"

"Here is home, with you. Try and make me leave. I am not a man. I don't need enemies."

He got out of bed to get away. The bitch. She'd caught him at a time when there was nothing left of him.

Kraft enters the hospital trying to imagine it's a stadium. The act lasts as long as his first smell of the antiseptics and the rubbery sound of a wheeled gurney. He tastes old metal in his mouth. He refuses the tranquilizers they keep pushing at him. He wants wakefulness. Elfi keeps visiting and fleeing.

He has nothing to say to her. She wants his buddies to come, she says he needs them. He says if one of them comes, that's it. He clears out of the hospital, period. He wants to talk, but he can't imagine a proper listener. For two years he endured what he never could have believed would've befallen him. There was no way to understand it, and this has left him now with loose ends. He can't think of any arrangement of his mind that could gather them. They simply fall out.

It occurs to him he doesn't know enough people who are dead.

It occurs to him he isn't sick enough.

He thinks he will be all right. He thinks he will be able to brag about it afterwards. Then he sees his heart and Gottfried's hand, and he wants the man there at once to ask him what right he thinks he has.

It occurs to him he never really liked football. It was just an excuse for something else.

It occurs to him he just made that up. It can't be so.

He wonders if he has ever really slept *with* Elfi. With any woman.

He laments his development of a double chin.

Sleep is a measure of defeat. Before games he never slept well.

Here, even at night, he keeps trying not to sleep. Most of the time he doesn't. He asks one of the doctors if it will matter in the outcome that he isn't sleeping now. The doctor says, Nope.

On the morning of the surgery, a nurse comes in. She sneaks up on him: She jabs a needle in his arm before he can say: What are you doing? She leaves before he can say: What the hell'd you do? I told you I aint taking anything will make me sleep. He begins to fight the fuzzy flaking in his head. He thinks he will talk to himself to keep awake and get it said. Say what?

Say it's only me here to go alone if there's no one going with me when he comes down like that from my apple to my gut to open where my heart is with a band of blood just before the saw goes off and rips from the apple to the gut down the middle of the bone while they pull the ribs wide the way mine under the center's balls when I made the signals to my blood and was from the time it ever was until they saw the goddamned Bobby Kraft slip a shoulder and fake it once and fade back and let it go uncorked up there the way it spirals against the blue of it, the point of it, leather brown spiralling on the jolted blue to the banging on me that was no use to them. You sonsabitches. Cause the ball's gone and hearing the roar of them with Jeffer getting it on his tips on the zig and in and streak that was going all the way cause I read the free safe blitz and called it on the line and faded against his looping where Copper picked him up and I let it go before the rest caved me with their hands pulling my ribs now and cranking on some ratchet bar to keep me spread and oh my God his rubbered hand on. Gottfried down with his knife in my heart's like a jelly sack the way he cuts through it with my blood in a plastic tube with the flow of it into some machine that cleans it for going back into me with blades like wipers on cars in the rain when I played in mud to my ankles and in the snows and over ninety in the Coliseum like in hell before the roar my God. Keep this my heart or let me die you sonsabitches. Pray for me again Elfi that I didn't love you the way such a little thing you are, and it was to do and I couldn't, but what could you know of me and what I had to and what it was for me, born to be a thing in the lot and the park, and in the school too with all of them calling me cold as ice bastard, and I wasn't any of that or how would I come to them in the pros out of a dink pussey college and be as good as any of them and better than most of all those that run the show on the field that are Quarterbacks. Godbacks goddammit. The way he's supposed to, this Gottfried with that stare and not any loser. Me? A loser? Because I cry in the dread I feel now of the what?

E. A. Durand's "The Football Story" originally appeared in Esquire. *This is a tongue-in-cheek yarn about a fictional character who would like to have been an All-American player, except that his "author" had something else in mind. A parody on authorship, it is also a delightful tale of a schoolboy star who'll do anything to help his downtrodden mother. There is some intricate plotting, great writing, and a snappy conclusion—just what readers like in a short story.*

E. A. Durand

THE FOOTBALL STORY (1938)

A FINE END I'VE COME to. And through no fault of my own, either. But that doesn't help matters any. If I had had anything to say about it I would have ridden on in a blaze of glory to a happy ending. But did I have anything to say about it? Did I have anything to say about anything? I should say not. My author had the whole say right from the beginning. And that was all right with me. But what did he have to go and let me down for? And so suddenly, too. Right at the peak of my career. I suppose he thinks, in his superior way, that I don't mind it here in the wastebasket! Well, it may be all right for tailor bills and essays on new thought, but not for Jack Weston, All-American quarter! That is, I would have made All-American if my author hadn't given up.

We had gotten to be such good friends, Fred and I, and I had such faith in him. Fred—that's what I called my author—gave me everything: a wonderful physique, a logical and quick-thinking mind, a zest for life, and no inhibitions or complexes except the hero one. His own words—the words with which he started the story of my life—may better describe me.

"Jack Weston, one hundred and ninety pounds of bone and muscle, the crack quarterback of Lincoln Prep, stood on the thirty-nine-yard line, his alert brain quickly analyzing the situation."

There. Could anyone wish for a better start than that? My own reaction was that the thirty-nine-yard line was a swell place to start one's life, taking into consideration the one hundred and ninety pounds and the alert brain. But what to do? Suppose you suddenly came into being standing on the thirty-nine-yard line, quickly analyzing a situation? What would you do? Well, I'll tell you what I did. Or rather, I'll let Fred tell you.

"The score was six to nothing against Lincoln with one minute to play. Jack hesitated only an instant and then started barking out his signals in his confident staccato. 'Kick formation! 37–42–59.' The coach sat on the bench, aghast. What was Weston thinking of! Why, that play was suicide! It hadn't a chance in the world!"

But the coach figured without Fred. Fred knew what to do. "The ball came rifling back from center. Jack deftly gathered in the pigskin and started out wide around his left end. He gathered momentum quickly, his powerful legs working like pistons. The opposing team was caught flatfooted. Who but a madman would try such a play on fourth down with ten to go? When they snapped out of it, Jack was already around the end, the effortless motion of his lithe body belying the speed with which his cleats were eating up the distance to the goal line. There were only two men who had a chance to stop him!"

Well, Fred, what do I do now? I suppose it depends on the appetite of my cleats.

"He changed direction in a flash. A right-angle pivot top speed! What co-ordination!"

There, you see, Fred didn't desert me. It was things like this that built up my confidence in Fred. That's why I feel so forsaken here in the waste-basket.

"There was one man left in Weston's way—Brandt Bilkes, Jack's arch rival through four years of prep school. Could he stop him?"

Good old Brandt. Always in there trying to stop me and never doing it. Must have been discouraging. He made some nice tries, though. Like this next.

"He set himself for the tackle. Jack was bearing down on him like one of those new, streamline, Diesel engine, railroad trains. Brandt lunged forward, but his arms closed on empty air. Jack stepped over the goal line, once more the hero of Lincoln Prep."

Then I kicked a beautiful drop-kick for the extra, and winning point. Oh, yes, Fred made me versatile. I could punt and pass, too. In short, the ideal football star. A coach's dream. And modest? Why, in one part of the story when someone asks me if I play football, Fred has me say, "Yes, a little." A little, eh? Damn near a one man team!

During the next few months, or paragraphs, Fred did a lot for me. He gave me a background. I was the only son of a fine, American family. My father had died during my early childhood, but I had the sweetest mother in the world whose whole life was lived for her wonderful son. She sent me to Lincoln Prep for my education where I studied diligently and stood highest in my class. I was upright and square, had a fine disposition, and was champion of the underdog. So, you see, it was pretty hard for me to go wrong with Fred arranging matters.

But I did go wrong. And it was O.K. with me. It was Fred's idea anyway. Had to have a plot, he said. And I always let Fred have his way. Couldn't do much else.

It seems that while I was cavorting between the football field and the class room, my poor mother was, unbeknownst to me, having difficulties in a financial way. You know, the old story. Tuition to be paid, graduation expenses, and, of course, the interest on the mortgage due. About this time, Fred started having difficulties, as was evidenced by the parts he X-ed out and the parts he penciled in. There was one little scene between my mother and Old Skrunck, who held the mortgage.

"Oh, Mr. Skrunck," said my mother, "have mercy on an old lady with a fine upstanding son in Lincoln Prep where he stands highest in his class, and, I understand, plays football, if one can believe the papers."

But Old Skrunck was "adamant"—a nice word, Fred—and left my mother in tears, "knowing not which way to turn."

Now, I thought that was a fine, dramatic touch, that scene. It would give the *reader* a few tears. But Fred X-ed it out. Said it was overdrawn. All I could think of was a crack like, so was my mother's bank account, so I let it go.

Well, to get on with the story, there comes a day in June.

"Jack sat in his study, looking out over the greensward that was the Lincoln Campus. He was writing the Valedictory Address which, as highest in his class, he was to deliver at the graduation exercises. To look at his placid countenance one would not guess the emotional turmoil that was going on within him. The thought of leaving those hallowed halls brought mental tears, though his eyes were dry. Then the realization would surge over him that next year would find him at Yale, and leave him in mental ecstasy. Would anyone think that fate was about to deal this fine young man a dreadful blow?"

"Listen, Fred, don't blame fate. You did all the dealing. And with a stacked deck, too.

"But such was the case. There was a knock at the door. It seemed to jerk Weston back to the present from both the past and the future."

At any rate, Fred had fate deal me a bobtail flush in the form of a letter from a friend of mine at home. This letter told me of my "poor old mother's plight." So I sat there waiting for Fred to figure a way out of this difficulty, which, presently, he did. It seems I had received several offers from different colleges of cold cash to enter their respective institutions.

"As nearly as Jack could figure it, his mother would need at least two thousand dollars. And the best offer he had received was for fifteen hundred, which was very flattering but not adequate. There was another offer of one thousand. If he could only accept both of these! He *must* help his mother. To Jack she was more important than God, his country, or Yale.

"He looked at the two letters idly. What was this? Coach Snodgrass of Wantoona U. who had offered the one thousand dollars, had included in his letter the football schedule for the next fall. And, Jack noted, they played all their games on Friday evenings, under floodlights. Weston quickly turned to the other letter. It was from Spagoda Tech. Their schedule was also included, and they played all their games on the traditional Saturday afternoons. The solution to his problem was at once evident to Jack. (Just a quick thinker, that's me.) He would accept both offers. Could a man do less for his mother?"

Could Fred do more for me? It seems he could. He gave me phony names, phony records, (those good marks I got in prep school all went for nothing) and enrolled me in both Wantoona U. and Spagoda Tech. He situated these colleges in the Middle West, about thirty miles apart. There were, of course, a number of difficulties, and the whole story seemed like a figurative steeplechase with Fred, Jack Weston up, taking the jumps in stride. Or maybe it was Jack Weston, Fred up. Anyway, Fred was the brains, which, I guess, is reiteration.

But let me tell you, in Fred's words, the event leading up to the travesty.

"Jack was duly matriculated at both colleges. Being a football player he never had to go to classes, and he split his afternoons between the two institutions. He practiced with Spagoda on Mondays, Wednesdays, and Fridays; with Wantoona on Tuesdays and Thursdays. Every Friday night he would play with Wantoona in their scheduled game and on Saturday with Spagoda. For Spagoda he used the name Dick Whipple, and for Wantoona, Tom Stubble.

"As the season wore on, the football world was, each succeeding week, set on fire by these two great quarterbacks, Whipple and Stubble, who were leading their respective teams to decisive victories. Controversy raged throughout the country as to which was the better. Committees which had been chosen to choose the All-American team were hoping that one of these two stars would show some weakness and make their task easier.

"But neither man weakened, and week after week Wantoona and Spagoda triumphed, due solely to the physical and mental genius of Stubble and Whipple."

Well, you can see what was going to happen. The game was scheduled, the receipts to go to charity. A new stadium was built to accommodate the vast throng who would storm the gates. Scalpers would be getting as high as forty dollars a ticket for the fifty-yard line. All stuff like that.

"It was New Year's Eve. Jack Weston, alias Dick Whipple, alias Tom Stubble, was in a quandary."

Well, Fred wasn't in any big, blue limousine himself. He'd put me on the spot and couldn't get me off except by the wastebasket route. It wasn't without a struggle, though, I'll say that for him. He thought and thought, but couldn't figure out a logical conclusion. And so there I was on the eve of the big game, forsaken.

It would have been very easy just to forget the whole thing. But I couldn't. Think of those thousands of people waiting to see me. I couldn't disappoint them. And anyway, I wanted to go on living and being a hero. "God damn it," I thought, "I will, Fred or no Fred."

So, having decided to continue on my own hook, what was I to do? Well, whatever it was it had to be done quickly for tomorrow was the big game.

"The first thing to do," I said to myself, "is to see what the other 'characters' in the story think about continuing without Fred, and find out if they have any ideas."

I found my mother back on the third page, so I said, "Hello, Mom, what do you think of Fred dumping us all into the wastebasket?"

"Who, me?" said Mom. "Why I think it's fine. It's the only *good* idea Fred ever had. I was getting pretty well fed up with his having me slave away my life, taking in washing and being a martyr so a big, healthy good-for-nothing like you could waste your time being upright and square and playing football. When I think back—"

Her voice trailed off, and so did I, in search of Old Skrunck. After the way my mother talked I didn't expect much help from Skrunck.

Fred had painted him pretty mean. But I decided to try him anyway. I found him on page six.

"Mr. Skrunck," I said, hopefully, "what do you think of Fred dumping us all in the wastebasket?"

"Oh, Hello, Jack," he replied, dreamily. "Isn't it lovely here? I'm so glad Frederick gave up. Goodness knows I didn't like being mean. I like peace, and quiet, and good-will, and happiness. Can you imagine a man of my temperament putting penniless widows out in the street! Ugh! Now, be a good boy and go away. I'm going to sleep."

And to sleep he went, leaving me alone with my problem.

Well, let's see. There were Whipple and Stubble. I could count on their co-operation. But that still left just one of us. Brandt Bilkes. He was left. I found him on the first page.

I said, "Hello Brandt, old pal, how do you like being thrown in the wastebasket?"

"Oh, it's you again," he said, with a sneer. "I thought I had gotten rid of you. You and your high and mighty airs. Pal, eh! Thought you were pretty smart throwing me for losses all over the football field, didn't you? And now that you've been thrown for a loss yourself, you can't take it. Too bad you can't go on playing hero. As for me, I've had enough. I'm glad it's all over. And I'm glad you've been reduced to scrap paper, too. Well, so long, Hero, see you in the trash heap."

Trash heap, eh! Not if I knew it. Maybe if I went a little farther afield than my own story. I took a look around the basket. Here was some stuff. *Can a Man Have a Family and Also a Career?* No, that wouldn't help any. *Fun in the Himalayas.* No good, either. *Nudism at a Glance.* Not yet. What was this? *John Masters: Pioneer.* That sounded better, so I read what followed.

"John Masters, one hundred and ninety pounds of bone and muscle, crouched behind a big oak, his alert brain quickly analyzing the situation."

That sounded vaguely familiar. I read on.

"Though he could not hear a sound he knew that Indians, treacherous Iroquois, were closing in on him. He hesitated only an instant."

And there it ended. I guess Fred gave up right at the beginning on that one. Well, that was all right with me. And maybe John Masters could help me with my problem.

He seemed like a fellow with the right angle. Say, why couldn't he play on one of those teams for me tomorrow? He certainly answered my description. It was an idea anyway.

I took a chance and spoke to him.

"Oh, pardon me, Mr. Masters," I said, "but if you can leave those Indians a moment, I'd like to make your acquaintance."

"Just call me John," he said. "I'm glad you come along. I been crouching behind this here oak, where Fred left me, long enough. The Indians is tired, too. So if you'll tell me your moniker and what's on your mind, I reckon we can git acquainted."

"My name's Jack, Jack Weston," I replied, "and I'd like to know what you think of being thrown in the wastebasket?"

"Well, I don't mind saying, in fact I even like saying, that I don't think a hell of a lot of it. But look here, who are you? I mean besides being Jack Weston? You seem to have me pretty well labeled, but I don't seem to recall you, that I remember."

"That's because I came after your time," I replied. "I read your story, what there was of it. That's why I know you. And I think you can help me."

So I told him my story.

"Well," he said, when I had finished, "it's all mighty int'restin', I reckon, to anyone who could understand it. As for me, I'll just have to take your word for it that you're in a predicament. All the same, it seems to me that to be surrounded by Indians is a hell of a lot worse than to be in one of them quandaries you was speakin' of. Nevertheless, you seem like a honest gent and, leastways, more fun than crouching here, so I'll go along with you and maybe we can git you out of this here mess. But don't think I'm goin' to understand that game you were talking about. It seems kinda silly and complicated to a Indian fighter."

"Now listen," I said, "don't despair. You can learn football. After all, you have one hundred and ninety pounds of bone and muscle, and an alert brain. That's all I had to start with and I became the greatest player in the country. You certainly haven't done so much Indian fighting that you can't turn to something else. As a matter of fact, you've really done nothing but crouch. So get up and stretch, and I'll tell you what you're to do tomorrow. Why, man alive, don't you realize I'm giving you a chance for life!"

"I reckon you're right," he said, giving in, "and it's in your hands, Pard. Here's my hand on it."

I grasped his hand eagerly, and was pleased to note that the same look of determination lighted both our eyes.

"Now," I said, "we must go into a huddle and figure this thing out. The first thing to do is to change your name. You are now Dick Whipple, football star of Spagoda Tech. You must try and forget that you were ever anyone else. And so, Dick, here is the plan I have worked out."

I really hadn't worked it out very well, but I knew I had to keep him interested in my problem and confident in me.

"First," I began, "we'll have a rainy day tomorrow. This is easy to do in fiction. Just write it in. That will make it possible for us to get ourselves so muddy before we start that neither the spectators nor the players can tell us apart."

"But look here, Jack," interrupted John, "I should think that the first thing to do would be to give me a better idear about this here game, tomorrow. What kind of weapons do we use?"

I suppose the task of explaining twentieth century football to an eighteenth century Indian fighter and making it seem important, would daunt a less dauntless fellow. But am I not Jack Weston? I am! So I started to explain just what would happen on the morrow.

I told him only those things essential to his part in the play. His job would be to play defensive quarterback, or safety man, as he is called, for both teams. At this position he wouldn't have to know any signals. His main job would be to catch punts. I, of course, would make this easy for him by kicking right into his hands. Thus he would have nothing to do except play about forty yards back of whichever team was on the defensive. Whenever I kicked to him he was to catch the ball and run as far as he could in a straight line towards me. I, myself, would play offensive quarterback for both teams, changing sides with the ball.

I was certainly thankful that John had an alert brain. With anyone less smart I would have had an impossible task. Even as it was, it took considerable time and patience to explain his duties to him, simple as they might seem to you and me. There were a few details like when to change goals and what to do between periods. You can imagine for yourself my difficulties. If I were Fred I could put all this down so much more clearly. Anyway, it's just fiction so let tomorrow come.

Day dawned! Night faded into day! Say it anyway you like. At any rate, it was the next day. The day of the big game.

I went over John's duties with him once more. Then I set about completing some preparations which did not concern him. I started the rain, wrote some headlines for the papers (*Whipple or Stubble—Which?—Never before in the history of football—All-American post at stake—*), and, finally, filled the stands to overflowing with wet fans who could not be kept away even by rain. I stopped the rain about two o'clock, giving the fans a break, and had the opening whistle blown at two-thirty.

Everything went fine during the first half. I made three touchdowns for each team, amid thunderous applause. What a game I played! And what a game John played. Of course, he didn't have to do anything but catch punts and run them back a few yards, but he did this so well no one even suspected what was going on.

Along about midway in the third quarter I decided it was time for another touchdown. I started out wide around the end for one of my spectacular runs. Just as I had got clear, bango! I went down with a thud and there was John hugging my knees. I hadn't told him anything about tackling. He certainly caught on quickly. And was he enjoying himself!

Thereafter, I couldn't seem to go anywhere without that dumb cluck of an Indian fighter barging into me. Here the game was, all tied up, 21 to 21, and if he kept up getting in my way that's how it would end. If I was going to be a hero I'd have to make another score. It didn't matter for which side.

The last quarter started. I used all the deceptive plays in the bag. But, no go. John didn't even know I was trying to deceive him.

The game dragged on. I was becoming more and more discouraged. And tired. With less than a minute to play I punted on fourth down. With a terrifying war-whoop John caught the ball. He was entering into the spirit of the thing a little too well. He knocked off about five would-be tacklers and romped right over the rest of them, leaving a clear field, except for me, to the goal. And could that boy war-whoop! No wonder Indians scared the early settlers to death.

I set myself for the tackle. John never swerved from his path. He hit me and rode over me like an avalanche.

From my position on the ground I saw him cross the goal line as the final gun sounded. I just lay there, watching him being carried off the field, a hero. I guess I should have quit when Fred did.

Ben Ames Williams (1889–1953) was a regular contributor of short stories to the Saturday Evening Post, where this one was first published. It's about a star player who is asked by his coach to hold back on his play and even to sit out the big game, in order to instill motivation to the rest of the team. Williams was an accomplished novelist and short story writer. His special interest was fictional accounts of Civil War history, particularly from the Confederate side. Among the many books that Williams wrote are Come Spring (1940), House Divided (1947), and The Unconquered (1953).

Ben Ames Williams

SCAPEGOAT (1925)

HE SAW PERRINE GET POSSESSION of the puck behind his own cage and swing to the right around the boards to begin another dash down the rink, and he glided a little toward that side, preparing to meet Perrine and stop him. His muscles were tired, and his head was heavy and aching from the long, incessant clamor of the cries echoing across the ice, ringing with a hollow booming sound beneath the vaulted roof, pounding upon his ear-drums. He was bruised from head to foot; there was a swollen lump on his right shin and a cut just above the ankle on the same leg, hurriedly caught together with plaster, bleeding in a little oozing stream. Only his courage was unwearied; it drove him as fiercely as in the first heat of the game.

Perrine was coming; his incredibly long, lean legs in their dull red tights swung tirelessly, his skates flashed and dug as he swerved to avoid the first defenders. Owens waited for him, knowing the advantage held by the man who is standing still, intent on forcing Perrine to pass between him and the boards. Time after time during the long game he had stopped Perrine thus; stopped him with a fierce body check which left them both entangled, the puck free for one of his fellows to recover. That was his function—to stop Perrine. Others would look after the puck; he had been coached to pay no heed to it, to take care only to stop Perrine. Only once tonight Perrine had passed him, and then the other man scored. He should not, Owens told himself fiercely, get by again. His unwearied courage drove him to the encounter even while his bruised body cringed before the coming crash of the blow.

Behind him he heard Al Shorter shout a warning. Al, an immense figure in shin guards and mask and great gauntlets, crouching in the mouth of the cage.

"Get him, Evan!" Al boomed.

Al, his roommate, was the only one who ever called him Evan. He was Buck Owens to the college at large; Evan only to Al. In this moment he drew a sudden surge of strength from Al, who was so indomitably strong. And at exactly the right instant his skates dug, he swung and sprang, his movements perfectly timed.

He caught Perrine fairly; caught Perrine against the boards as he had planned. His left hip locked with Perrine's; his body struck Perrine in the side. Perrine's own momentum carried them forward and down; and as they fell, Owens heard, with a curious distinctness, a sharp and disconcerting crack. A curious sound, not at all ominous in itself; yet not like any sound he had ever heard before, so that, even while he freed himself and struggled to his feet, he wondered what it was. He saw that Perrine was slow in rising, looked swiftly for the puck; and then a whistle blew at his ear and the others were coming toward him, gliding smoothly on their skates, their movements slowed and easy; and the tremendous clamor of sound which filled the rink died to a murmur and was still. Perrine lay on his back on the ice and he breathed in a distressing way; and his heels clattered a little, kicking spasmodically.

Perrine was hurt, and Owens drew back. His heart was sick, but there is an etiquette in such matters. He loved Perrine. For two years now they had been meeting in fierce encounters, on the gridiron, on the ice; flesh to flesh, buffeting, clinging, bruising, thrusting, always in the white heat of desperate endeavor. And sometimes Perrine had the better of it, and sometimes Owens. Owens had a flattened nose Perrine had given him one day with a particularly efficient stiff arm; Perrine would wear all his life the scar from a cut he had received when he missed his tackle and caught Owen's shoe against his cheek. Their meetings had been battles; they spoke to each other—when they spoke at all—in terms truculent and bitter. But Perrine loved him, and he loved Perrine; and Perrine was hurt now, and Owens was sick at heart. Nevertheless, he drew away. It was no part of the game to show, at such moments, sympathy or compunction. Now they were carrying Perrine off the ice, carefully. Owens seemed to hear slow music playing; he knew Perrine was badly hurt and he felt a desperate desire to help, to lift his opponent in his arms, to cry out his sorrow. Al clapped him on the shoulder.

"That's the old game, Evan," he approved. "That's stopping them."

One of the opposing team swung up to Owens with a swirl and a grind of his skates, and his lips were drawn.

"You big yegg," he snarled, "I'll get you for that!"

"I'll be right here," Owens told him coldly. "Come and do it."

"I'm coming," the other promised.

"They'll carry you out on a stretcher," Owens told him.

"They'll have to dig you out of the ice," the other retorted, and he swung away again.

Al gripped Owens by the shoulder.

"That's telling him, Evan," he approved.

But the words of youth must be read with a glossary. What the opponent meant was merely "He's badly hurt, but you can't scare us." And what Owens meant was "I'm terribly sorry, but I've got to play the game."

And what Al meant was "It wasn't your fault, Evan. Don't let it worry you."

A moment later the ice rang again beneath their runners. But without Perrine the other team was crippled. As it happened, Owens himself scored the winning goal.

Perrine was badly hurt. A concussion, perhaps a compound fracture. For forty-eight hours he lay in the college hospital, his life in the balance. His team mates went home; but his father and mother came, and Owens saw them once or twice, at the hospital or about the college inn. Also doctors came from the city and labored with Perrine. And Owens, furtively, as though he were ashamed of the weakness, haunted the hospital corridors, appearing secretly and unexpectedly at all hours to ask shy questions, his eyes pleading for a hopeful word.

A good many people saw him there, and some of them talked about it. This was not altogether surprising, for Owens, though he never guessed the fact himself, was in the college world a great man. In the fall the football team had elected him captain, after that crushing defeat in which he had borne himself so splendidly, doing such deeds that his personal triumph had almost compensated for the wreckage of the team. He had had the better of Perrine that day. Perrine, up till then acclaimed as the greatest fullback of the year, had been displaced by Owens on the basis of that day's showing, so that the after-season comment made Owens all-American fullback in Perrine's place. The team elected him captain without dissent. A great man, thus, in the college world, and a man whose movements could not go unremarked.

Dave Glade, the football coach, remarked them; and he talked to Owens one evening about the matter.

"You don't want to let Perrine get on your mind," he suggested. He had made it his business to meet Owens outside the hospital. "It wasn't your fault, Buck."

"It's not worrying me," Owens said harshly.

"Don't kid yourself," Glade retorted. "But what I mean is, don't brood over it, Buck. It was an accident."

"I don't want him to die," Owens confessed; and his voice, to his own shame, broke a little. Glade flung an arm across his shoulder.

"He'll come out of it," he predicted. "Wait and see."

The event proved that Glade was right. Perrine returned to consciousness at last, made slow recovery and began to gain. They took him from the hospital to his home—Owens had no chance to see him, for Perrine was still very weak—and the incident began to be forgotten. But it seemed to some people that there was a difference in Owens; that he still had the accident upon his mind. Al Shorter spoke of it to his friend. The words that passed between these two were often oblique, and to the outsider meaningless; but in this matter Al spoke openly.

"It's getting your goat, Evan," he said accusingly.

"You're crazy," Owens retorted. Al shook his head.

"Don't forget you've got a job to do this fall."

"I'm not forgetting anything," Owens assured him.

"Well, you want to forget Perrine," Al insisted. "He's on your mind. Cut it out."

"You tell 'em," the other jeered; and Al said grimly, "If you throw us down next fall I'll knock you dead."

"You and what regiment of Marines?" Owens challenged derisively, and Al grinned.

"All right," he rejoined. "Only you mind what I say."

It is doubtful whether Al had any real misgivings. He did not attach too much importance to the new gentleness apparent in his friend. But there is always someone to notice these matters. A curious speculation began to run through the undergraduate conversation. No one knew where it had started, but it gained some currency. The question was a philosophic one. The strength of Owens had always been his fearlessness, his ruthlessness, his driving power.

"But he half killed Perrine," the word went. "Maybe that'll slow him down next fall. Maybe he'll pull his punches. Maybe he won't play the game so hard."

Those who knew Owens best, Al and some others, fought back against this whisper; but whispers are hard to kill. This one came, inevitably, to the ears of Dave Glade, for it was his business to hear such whispers as this one was, and to deal with them.

Glade was an alumnus of ten years' standing who had been in his day an all-American quarterback, attaining to that position much more by mental than by physical abilities. He conceived the game not as a battle between weight and power and speed, but fundamentally as a struggle between mind and mind, soul and soul. Such men are not bound by conventions or habit. Glade was not so bound.

He had been brought back to college, two years before, on a five-year contract—a contract which he dictated. Upon the matter of salary he did not insist at all, but he demanded absolute authority and noninterference, and he got them. The team, during half a dozen years preceding, had been in the doldrums, neither one thing nor the other. His first year showed little improvement; his second was outwardly as disappointing. The team lost two games; an early season contest in which, still raw, they met a prepared opponent; and the final and climactic game, when, encountering the greatest team of the year, they were overwhelmed by half a dozen touchdowns, routed and demoralized.

After the game, Glade had a word or two to say to his men.

"I don't mind your getting licked," he had told them. "Everybody gets licked now and then. But here's one thing, and those of you who come back next fall want to remember it: God hates a quitter. After they scored the second touchdown, you weren't a team any longer. Three of you, Owens and Al Shorter and McCay, kept on fighting. The rest of you just went through the motions. Captain McCay is graduating. Owens and Shorter will be here next year, and four others of you regulars. You four men have got to earn your places next fall, and you might as well make up your mind to that now." He added, in a softer tone, "I'm not worried about Owens and Shorter."

He was less confident of Owens when that whisper began to spread, and it stayed in his thoughts during the summer vacation. When, in September, a fortnight before college opened, the regulars reported for practice, Owens was the first to come; and for three days he and Glade were much together, weighing the abilities of the individuals upon whom the team must rely, considering the places yet to be filled. The coach watched Owens, speculating, wondering. During the summer that ugly whisper had grown; and Glade, half across the continent, had heard it again and again.

Alumni asked him, "How about Owens? Has he lost his nerve?" So he studied the captain now with an acute eye, and what he saw seemed to reassure him.

He said to Owens one day, "We'll be better this year."

"We've got to be," Owens agreed.

"We've got the men," Glade explained. "You and Al to start with, and Jay and Lecker and Burke. I'm not sure about Morris. He quit cold in the last game."

"He was sick," Owens told him. "Upset stomach. He told me afterward."

"And Carroll and Lewstader from the freshman team," Glade pursued. "That leaves only three holes to fill. We can make out."

"Morris is all right," Owens said again.

"We've got a chance to lick that bunch this year," Glade repeated. Owens did not need to be told the team he meant. "They won't be so good without Perrine." And the coach looked sidewise at the young man.

"They'll miss him," Owens agreed.

"Great player," Glade commented. He was reassured by what he saw. "I hear he's coming around all right. But he won't play."

"I wrote to him," Owens confessed.

"You did?"

"He's going to be all right," the captain explained. "But he can't play football."

"Well, if we get a fighting team we can lick them," Glade concluded, and they went on to more detailed discussion.

In the first game of the season, an encounter that was little more than a practice scrimmage, the coach again gave all his attention to Owens' play. Owens had never been better. Glade allowed him a scant ten minutes in each half before replacing him with a substitute, but in these minutes Owens tore the opposing line or battered the ends as fiercely as in the past. Yet Glade, during the following week, discovered that the whispers were revived again. Some professed to have seen Owens falter at critical moments, hold back, spare his driving charges.

"He's pulling his punches," one of Glade's assistants declared.

"Get in front of one of them and see," Glade advised. But the matter stayed in his mind.

He had other reasons for concern. The game had been won easily enough, but Glade was not satisfied. The team, he thought, moved half-heartedly, without heat, too smoothly for so early in the season. They had precision but not zest; and Glade would have preferred to see them ragged but ferocious. A second game failed to reassure him. He began to seek out individual players, to talk with them, to weigh the temper of the men. They were, he discovered to his consternation, already overconfident. The fault, he recognized, was his; their training had gone smoothly; their technique was good; they had won without effort and without committing glaring faults. There had been only one fumble in two games, and the ball in that case was recovered. The interference had worked like a machine, effectively but coldly. Before the third game he had a talk with Morris, the quarterback; and after a safe lead had been acquired Morris began to make mistakes, confuse the signals, so that when the ball was passed men made false starts and the play was thrown into confusion. Glade wished to see the team made angry by these mishaps; instead, they took them with a confident good humor which he found depressing and discouraging.

During the following week, for the first time in his work with them, he abused the men in merciless terms, deriding and insulting them. They took his words, to his dismay, like lambs.

The night after that game he had gone to the room shared by Owens and Al Shorter; and when he knocked it was Al who called to him to enter, who got to his feet when he recognized the coach.

Glade nodded to him, said, "Where's Owens?"

"Out," Al retorted, so bitterly that Glade, who knew the close friendship between the two men, was surprised. He sat down, settled himself in a chair.

"Bother you if I sit here a while?" he asked. Al shook his head.

"Help yourself," he assented.

"Come through the game all right?" Glade inquired.

"Got a kick in the leg," Al confessed. "Be all right by Monday."

"How's Buck?"

"Oh, he's all right."

"Not worrying, is he?" the coach asked, groping in the dark.

"Not worrying enough," Al retorted.

"What is there to worry about?"

"We ought to have had two more touchdowns today," Al reminded him.

"We got enough," Glade replied. "I was satisfied."

"The team's satisfied," Shorter exclaimed rebelliously. "Evan's satisfied. That's the trouble."

"He hasn't slowed down any," Glade protested. "I heard some talk. They said he would. I've been watching him."

"He can slow down a lot and still be good," Al conceded. "But he ought to be better. He's been different since Perrine got hurt."

"Different?"

Al hesitated.

"Not so hard-boiled as he used to be," he confessed awkwardly.

Glade nodded, but he did not push the matter. He stayed half an hour longer, and left at last with something to think about. The alliance between Shorter and the captain was of old standing, was already almost a tradition; and the discovery that there was ill feeling between these two seemed to Glade a matter worth considering. Before the next game, in line with this thought, he spoke a word aside to Owens.

"Take it easy today, Buck," he said quietly. "Save yourself."

Owens looked at him in quick surprise, suspiciously. He had a momentary thought that Glade's tone was sardonic, wondered whether the coach had heard and credited those whispers. The effect of this suspicion showed in his early play; it was fierce and irresistible. But in the middle of the first quarter Glade called him out, kept him idle; and at the beginning of the second half, when he permitted Owens to go in again, he said more severely:

"I told you to save yourself, Buck. Do as I say. Take it easy. Play it safe. I don't want you banged up."

"I'm all right," Owens protested. "They can't hurt me."

"You don't have to break your neck against his bunch," Glade insisted. "Mind, Buck!"

The captain was bewildered but obedient, and the team caught the infection. In the last few minutes of play the opponents, taking heart and strength, scored a goal from the field. Newspaper comment next day remarked upon the change in the team in the second half.

"Captain Owens showed a disposition to stop when he was tackled," one man wrote. "There were times when he might have gained another five yards."

Now a lesser word than this has damned good men before and will again; and the whispers which had been dying rose a tone or two, became words, outspoken and forthright. Overnight the college was divided in two camps; and Al Shorter was driven by his own loyalty to Owens to fight and soundly whip two men who clung to their assertion that Captain Owens' nerve was gone.

But though Al might fight for his friend, yet he was heartsick, and between the two that week there was none but the most formal word of football. This in spite of the fact that it was the breath of life to both of them; that it filled their waking hours and pursued their dreams.

Owens felt all around him the murmuring of the whisperers, and it goaded him to a sullen and increasing irritation. Al, not so sensitive, yet understood the other's mood, and kept his tongue to himself.

Only on Saturday morning before the game, while they were dressing, he said with an attempt at heartiness, "Well, Evan, plaster them today." Owens looked at him angrily.

"What do you think I'm going to do?" he challenged. "Powder their noses?"

"That's all right," Al protested, ill at ease. "Can't I open my head?"

"Anybody'd think you were wet-nursing me," Owens told him bitterly, and Al's temper flared.

"You need somebody," he retorted. "You act like a sick kid."

Owens made no reply save silence. Each would have been happier for the healing unction of an interchange of blows, but they were forced to nurse their ill humors. And again in the game that afternoon, when the issue was no longer in doubt, Glade told Owens to slow down, to save himself, to spare his energies.

To Owens' fierce protest, the coach said sharply, "I know what I'm doing, Buck. This is vital. Do as I say."

The boy, bewildered and unhappy, nevertheless tried to obey; and after the game his fellows on the team spoke to him with a studied politeness more maddening than insults. If it had not been for that matter of Perrine in the past, they would have raged at him. That and the whispered prophecies which had since then been current had prepared them to look upon Owens with sympathy, but also with a faint contempt. So a little circle of courtesy ringed him round.

Only Al was not courteous; but Al held his fire till these two were in their room alone that night. Then opened with heavy guns.

"What's the matter with you, Evan?" he demanded. "Getting soft, are you? I told you to lay into those babies today."

Owens hesitated for a moment, wishing pitifully that he might tell Al that he had acted under orders. But also he was wounded that Al should doubt him; felt bitterly that his friend should have been loyal.

So stubbornly he held his tongue, kept the matter hidden, answered only, "Who the devil gave you a license to talk?"

"That's all right," Al replied. "I played the game, and you know I did. But you laid back like a balky horse. What's the matter? Afraid of hurting some of those babies?"

"Your job is in the line," Owens told him curtly. "You 'tend to your business and I'll look out for mine."

"My job's playing football, in the line or anywhere else," Al insisted angrily. "If I see a back laying down, I'm going to give him a boot!"

Owens' teeth set hard and his smile was icy.

"You are?" he asked politely. "Well, try it on." Al laughed.

"Say, Evan, don't try to scare me. I tell you, if you lay down on us I'll break you in two, and I can do it."

Owens was goaded to his feet; he strode toward the other man, leaned over him.

"This is a good time," he told him steadily. "We can start right away."

Al swung upward, grappling, thrusting him back. In another moment the blow would have been struck; but they were checked by Glade's rap on the door, fell back from each other as the coach came into the room.

Glade knew his men, and he knew to what an edge nerves may be whetted by the rigors of training. He looked from one to the other, and when he spoke it was to Al.

"Shorter," he said, "take a walk. I want to talk to Owens."

Shorter hesitated, then moved toward the door.

"He needs it," he commented.

"Go on," Glade directed. "Get out. Stay away an hour." And he crossed to shut the door behind the big guard. When he turned again, Owens had dropped into a chair at his desk and his fingers drummed moodily upon the chair arm. Glade came to his side and touched the captain on the shoulder. Owens, looking up, was astonished to discover that the coach was smiling, his eyes full of satisfaction.

He asked bitterly, "What's the joke?"

Glade sat down facing him.

"What do you think of the team, Buck?" he asked. Owens considered.

"Pretty smooth," he replied.

"We'll win next week," Glade predicted. "That leaves only the big game."

"They're good this year," said Owens. The coach nodded.

"As good as last year," he agreed. "But we're better than we were; know more football—if we can play it. What's the matter with the team, Buck?"

"Sir?"

"What's the matter with the team?"

Owens thought about this for a long time; he looked back through the games already played, through the contest of the afternoon just done; and he began to see, as Glade already saw.

"They don't get mad," he said. Glade nodded.

"Here's the case, Owens: Between you and me, the other fellows are a great team. They're going to lick us."

"No!" Owens cried.

"Yes!" Glade retorted coolly. "Oh, I know what you're thinking; but you're wrong, Buck. They're good. If we played them today they'd have us demoralized—the way they did last year." He hesitated, considering. "They'd beat us five or six touchdowns," he predicted.

"No, sir," Owens said hotly.

"There's only one way to hold them," Glade said steadily. "If I can get our men mad enough or scared enough, they'll fight; and if they'll fight, they can hold them—maybe win."

"They'll fight," Owens promised sternly. "They've got to."

Glade nodded. "They've got to," he agreed. "It's up to you and me, Buck, to make 'em—principally up to you."

For a moment the room was very still, while Owens weighed the other's words, his thoughts racing.

"What do you mean?" he asked at last.

The coach leaned toward him and his voice was very gentle.

"Here," he said—"here's what I want you to do."

An hour later, when Shorter came back, he found Owens alone, Glade gone. Owens, busy at his desk, did not turn his head when Al came in; and Al moved restlessly around the room, wishing to find some way to make amends to this old friend of his, helpless for lack of words. To attempt to placate Evan would be to confess weakness, and he was not strong enough for such a confession.

He said at last, provocatively, "Well, Glade lay you cold, did he?"

He expected anger, but not such a raging bitterness of fury as he saw blazing in the other's eyes. Owens came out of his chair with a leap; he crossed the room with a bound; he crouched above his friend.

"Blast you," he whispered, "will you shut your fat head?"

So Al morosely shut his fat head.

Youth is a time of high emprise; and nowhere is this more true than in the world of college, where the affairs of the moment seem incredibly important, fit to inspire any audacity or any sacrifice. But though youth has the valor for great deeds, it lacks the philosophy of age. An older man than Evan might have comforted himself with the knowledge that what he did was a fine thing; but for Owens the succeeding fortnight was a long pillory and shame. Save on formal and impersonal affairs, Al did not speak to him at all; and outside their room he met polite indifference or impersonal courtesy. Little groups which he approached fell silent at his coming, so that he knew they had been speaking of him; companies which he joined insensibly fled away, departing by ones or twos, with lame excuses, till he was left alone again. Twice in the first week he went to Glade, resentful and rebellious, refusing to carry on the plan the coach had proposed; but Glade was insistent and persuasive; he bullied and he pleaded, and he held Owens to the line.

In the anticlimactic game of the season, against an opponent usually strong, Owens started the game; and in the heat of the conflict he forgot Glade's instructions, bore through the opposing tacklers with a ferocity so great that Glade abruptly called him out, warning him to remember the part he was expected to play.

"We'll win this game anyway," Glade assured him. "I'll guarantee that, Buck. It's next week we've got to think about, and that's all up to you."

"Damn it, Dave, I can't," Owens protested. "I can go in there and win for you next week; but I can't do what you want me to."

"You'll do what I say," Glade told him. "You know I'm right, Buck. Don't be a kid. It's the only way, isn't it? Anybody can use their beef. I want you to use your heart, old man."

"What do you want me to do?" Owens cried; and Glade said implacably, "Just what I told you. When a man tackles you, fall."

He sent Owens in again to start the second half. The game was by that time, barring a miracle, won. And Owens drove himself under a curb, held his bounding strength in leash, welcomed release at last when Glade called him once more to the sidelines. The coach bade him watch what followed; and Owens saw for himself that the team seemed to take on new ferocity; show at last that fighting soul which thus far it had lacked. It drove no longer with precision, but irresistibly; and tired as it was, scored again and conclusively in the latter end of the game.

Owens had that to remember when he needed strength to live through the week ensuing—a week more bitter than the last had been. The memory upheld him when on Thursday the team left for New York for the final game. It supported him in the semi-solitude in which he moved, surrounded and walled in by politeness when he longed for harsh abuse. Even from Glade he had to accept, in public, averted glances and indifferent regard; but the coach found opportunities to be alone with Owens, to hearten him and strengthen him. And when the final moment came, in the dressing rooms waiting for the signal to run out upon the field, he sank his finger nails in his palms to hold himself under control.

Glade was saying a last word to the team. Owens, sitting on a bench across the room, seemed not to listen.

"We're going out there in a minute, men," Glade said, and his voice was cold and harsh. "I've just this to say: You're going up against a great team. You can't beat them. You haven't got the bowels. You know as much football as they do, but they're got something you haven't got.

"I'm about sick of you. And I've made up my mind to one thing. Any man that stays in the game today has got to fight. When a man slows down, I'm going to pull him out. I'm going to get eleven men in there that will fight if I have to use the whole squad. And if that won't do it, I'm going to call men out of the stands and put them in uniform. I'd rather have one man in there fighting than eleven just going through the motions. Get licked if you want to; but go down fighting."

He hesitated for a moment, looked across the room to where Sanborn stood—Sanborn, the sophomore, a fullback.

"Sanborn," he said stridently, "you'll start in place of Captain Owens. Shorter's acting captain. That's all. Get out of here."

He waved a compelling arm; and the players, momentarily paralyzed, obeyed him automatically. Only Al Shorter stood for a moment motionless, and his broad face was purple with dismay and with rage. He took a quick stride toward Glade, hesitated, looked toward where Owens sat inertly.

"Coach!" he cried.

"Go on, Al," Glade told him. "Get your men out there."

For a moment their eyes met; and Al looked at Owens again, but Owens did not raise his head. Al laughed harshly, and he swung around.

"Give me the ball," he said bitterly; and a moment later he thrust through the mass of players and led the first team, at that swift sprint which is so thrilling a spectacle, out across the chalk-lined sod.

Owens was the last man to leave the locker room, and he walked. He walked with head hanging, the picture of shamed dejection.

Three teams had run onto the field to trot through signals; the other members of the squad, those substitutes whose chances of inheriting a place were most remote, moved along the sidelines to their places on the benches at midfield. Owens went with them; and when they settled themselves under their gray blankets he was at the end of the line, a little space between him and the nearest man. He looked neither to the right nor to the left; his eyes were on the ground between his feet, nor did he raise his head during that interval when the second and third teams came to find places on the benches, while the first team adjusted head guards and grouped together for their final word. Then Al Shorter jogged to midfield to meet the opposing captain; and Owens raised his head at that and watched, while his eyes burned. Al won the toss, he saw.

When the teams spread for the kick-off, his heart pounded against the roof of his mouth; he felt intolerably that throbbing agony of waiting for the whistle; and his hands twitched and his knees trembled and his lip bled beneath his teeth. Then the tremendous thump of toe on ball; the oval sailing end over end high through the air; the rushing pack; the crash of bodies and thudding feet along the sod; and the whistle again when the ball was downed.

He watched thereafter, watched with a strained attention, a bitter hunger in his eyes. And at each charge his muscles leaped, and at each tackle his body twisted to this side or that. Once he caught himself mumbling words between his teeth; and he was afraid someone had heard, and looked at his neighbor. Young Bailey, a sophomore, a guard; a hard worker, but no football player. He would strive for three long years and get an honorary letter at the end. Owens grinned bitterly at the thought that he and Bailey sat here side by side; but also he was relieved that Bailey had not heard him muttering.

He followed the play in detail, but not as a whole; his concern was not so much with the movements of the ball as with the men on the team. He saw Shorter, bareheaded already, moving like a behemoth among the ruck of players. Shorter always lost his head guard in the first scrimmages, never bothered to replace it. His flaxen head was continually in motion; was usually to be seen emerging from beneath the thickest heap of men. Owens could hear Al's exhortations, bitter and furious and profane; his words had a scorching whip in them; and he buffeted the crouching men at either side of him resoundingly.

They were fighting, Owens saw; fighting as they had never fought before. He felt hopelessly that they could not maintain such a pace. The enemy, he perceived, met their fury with a cool confidence. They were used to opposition, but also they were used to victory. Such spasmodic effort as this never lasted against steady pressure; they had only to keep up the pressure, and they kept it up with methodical and unemotional persistence.

It was their confidence, Owens thought, which made them so invincible. Where other teams reserved the forward pass for midfield or beyond, they tried it anywhere; where other teams played a punt safely, they caught it at any hazard; where other teams punted on third down, they waited till fourth. He wondered, abstractedly, what the effect would be if this confidence could be shaken. Merely scoring against them would not shake the other team, he knew; they had been scored on before; had overcome a lead of one touchdown, or of two, with the same dispassionate persistency. Yet they must be somehow vulnerable, must have their weakness if it could be bared.

He found himself abruptly on his feet, with the thousands all about him and in the stands behind. Al Shorter had broken through to block a punt, one of those punts on fourth down; blocked the punt and fallen on the ball, within striking distance of the enemy goal. Owens had a sudden inspired thought. If he were quarterback, he told himself, he would not seriously try to score. The enemy was still fresh; they would be sure to prevent success, and failure might dishearten the team, make them doubtful of their own powers. He shook his head as he watched; for they had tried, with a quick forward pass. Batted down. A drive at tackle got two yards. Another pass failed. A run from kick formation almost made the distance. While the linesmen measured, Owens found himself trembling with exhilaration at the valor of that play; the sheer effrontery of it, trying to run the ball for an eight-yard gain when a field goal had been a better gamble. That was not the demeanor of a team accepting defeat, but rather of a team expecting victory. The fact that the play had failed, that the ball was the enemy's, did not mar his exultation at the moral strategy involved.

That was Morris, he reminded himself; Morris, the quarterback. A great player and a daring one.

On his feet again. An enemy run had gained three yards, but Lecker's tackle was so fierce that the runner dropped the ball and Burke had it, was downed. Another chance.

Jay took it into the line; Sanborn took his turn. Two yards for each of them. A pass to the side gained almost the full distance; there was left half a yard for first down. Another plunge by Sanborn would do that. Owens gripped his hands, watching. But Morris chose to try another pass, and it was batted down in turn. The chance was lost again. The roaring stands behind Owens faded into silence as the enemy, as confident and sure as ever, once more took the ball. Owens felt his hope slackening; such rebuffs shook the morale of any team. Yet this team, his team out there, was fighting still; raging against the dull red line, sifting through. One runner down for a loss, another in his tracks. The enemy would punt this time, play it safe. He sprang up screaming—the back had taken the ball for a wide run, and Burke was forcing him further and further out, dropped him at last on the sidelines for a loss. A great man, Burke, playing like one inspired. He checked himself, looked around in astonishment. Someone was sprinting out across the field, and Owens recognized the man. Jasper, replacing Burke. Replacing Burke! He saw Burke come slowly toward the sidelines—heard Glade's rasping voice.

"Get down here, Burke. I want a man in there that will fight."

Owens could see Burke's color rise, and he had a momentary impulse to seek out the man, comfort him. Held himself rigidly in check, turning his eyes again to the field.

A moment later his throat ached with pain at the fierce and rasping cry he raised—another punt blocked. Bullman, this time, and he had the ball safely under his great body. A third chance for a score and the game not ten minutes old.

He found himself shouting "Get them! Get them! Get them!" Became conscious of his own voice and in the confusion fell silent. Hall around the end, a yard. Morris himself taking the ball now. Two yards, down, crawling, smothered under a mass of red jerseys. Hall again, at tackle. A yard to go and fourth down. Hall at tackle. Held!

He cursed under his breath, snarling with rage. He could see Hall's chest heave with his sobbing breath. And—Hall was coming out. Wallmer going in for him.

Glade shouting after Wallmer, "If you want to stay in there, fight!" To Hall, "Sit down with Burke. You're a pair."

And the indomitable enemy, cool and sure, rushing the ball again, standing in the very shadow of their goal. Held once, held twice, held thrice. But this time, through Bullman's very fingers, the punt got away, far down the field. Morris was in midfield, could not get under it. The ball struck, bounded backward into enemy territory, and a red jersey infolded it where it lay. Owens grimaced. Bullman had touched it, then. He cursed Morris. They were on the defensive now.

To his amazement the whistle blew; the period had ended. Two minutes' respite. He saw the enemy team dabbling with water, rinsing their mouths. Glade sent no water to his men, nor did they seek it out. Instead they moved sullenly across the field to where play would be resumed, lined up there behind the ball, in position, waiting. After a moment the enemy came on.

Owens heard the quarterback call cheerfully, "Well, let's start, boys!"

Shorter bellowed his truculent retort, "Come my way, you red legs!"

The quarterback grinned, and nodded.

"Whatever you say," he replied. Shorter enfolded the plunging back and spurned him to earth. He did the same again. On the third play, Jasper hurried the back who would have tried a pass. The punt that followed went over the goal line, and they came out twenty yards and formed for battle once more.

A moment later Jay had made first down and the stands were screaming. Then Morris flung a pass to Carroll and the ball was at midfield. Owens found himself sprawling on the ground. He had slid off the end of the bench in his blind concentration, and he picked himself up with a sheepish grin, eyes never leaving the play. The game degenerated into a series of fruitless plunges, successful punts. To and fro, to and fro, and Owens felt in his own muscles the long weariness that must be descending on those men out in the field. It was this endless, fruitless striving which wore a man down; this desperate endeavor without reward.

Abruptly there came one of those plays when every man finds his allotted place exactly; when the confusion on the field becomes order, as the pieces of a puzzle fall into their places. The enemy had punted to midfield, and Jay took out his end, dropped him, sprawled across the other man's body. Shorter, following the punt back, got the opposing tackle, and Morris was free with the ball, running at a long slanting diagonal across the field and down. The sidelines forced him to straighten out his course. Tacklers gathered before him, and he reversed the field and came this time toward the side where Owens sat. Owens was on his feet; his heart stopped. For Morris was clear. An even sprint, one man coming to cut him off, one man with a chance. Morris reached the sideline and swerved, and his foot slipped a little so that he staggered. Owens, looking along the line, saw that Morris had kept within the field, saw him a moment later meet the tackler, the momentum of his own run carrying them both across the goal. And knew madness for an instant till he saw one of the officials calling for the ball.

The man ruled that Morris had stepped outside; the score was lost. Owens, beside himself, would have run that way, but Glade called to him, stopped him with a word. The teams were already lining up, and he heard Morris calling signals.

"Let's get it again!" Morris screamed at his men. "Let's get it again!"

They had better than a dozen yards to go. They made one, then five, then lost a yard, then, by a hair, first down. Two or three yards to go, and four downs to make it in. This time, Owens swore to himself, this time they would do it.

But the half ended before the the next scrimmage could be begun. Ended, and the men went trooping, jaded, toward the locker rooms. Owens, as much exhausted as though he himself had played that bitter thirty minutes, followed them with the others; followed them this time with a lifted head. This, for all the fact that he sat inert and useless—this was his team.

Glade did not talk to the men during that intermission, save for a single word at the end. Ominous his tone.

"Mind what I said," he warned them. "I want fighters in there. You can't lick them. I know that. But you'll fight, if you want to stay in the game!"

The team went back unchanged, but immediately disaster befell them. By one of those currents occasionally perceptible but beyond explanation, the right and left wings of the charging line of tacklers parted and the enemy runner came through. This on the kick-off. Through and on to midfield and beyond before Morris got him. Then upon the heels of one catastrophe, another; for Morris tackled with such bitter vehemence that the ball left the runner's hands, and one of his own men scooped it up and was away again and scored. Such a bitter turn of luck as happens once in years; sufficient to dishearten the stoutest fighters. Instantly Glade struck. Put Burke in for Jasper, Gray for Sanborn, Ruth for Jay. No comment this time, only scorn for the three men who came drooping to the sidelines. His eyes turned keenly on the fray beyond them in the field.

Jay came to Owens' side, willing to find any companion in his misery. But Owens offered him no word; his attention was all upon the game. Yet there was not now much for them to see. Simply the spectacle of a confident team with a comfortable lead, content to hold that lead, to hold some strength in reserve, to fling back the desperate charge of desperate men. The long quarter dragged through and only weariness came of it. The last began, and the minutes fled, and the ball clung to midfield stubbornly. Lassitude descended upon Owens. He was exhausted by his own futile prayers and entreaties. Glade was replacing the tired men now, meeting them as they came out with brief and bitter words.

The long pass from Luther to Carroll that scored their touchdown came at a moment when he was scarce watching the play at all. The game had reached that stage when the beaten team resorts to desperate measures. The ball was in enemy territory; the pass was marked before it was begun. But somehow Carroll found an open space toward which to take his way, and somehow Luther, fighting off those who sought to hurry him, held his hand till the appointed moment, and somehow at last the pass went true into Carroll's very arms and was held and borne on, and downed securely at last behind the enemy's line. Owens was almost too jaded to exult, and when the goal was missed, leaving the enemy still in the lead, his head drooped. He looked toward Glade, a prayer in his eyes, beseeching his chance, begging for even these last brief minutes of play—but Glade seemed not to see.

They had the ball again, flinging hurried passes, time pressing on their heels. And abruptly Owens, watching, saw an astonishing thing. He saw that the enemy was no longer confident, and this perception brought him to his feet, his tongue clinging to this teeth. They were beaten—those red jerseys were beaten. Not on the score, little chance of that perhaps. But beaten just the same. Their knees sagged. Fresh men were coming in. They moved slackly to their places. The resistless pressure of this fighting team had pushed them back. Another pass succeeded, brought the ball to midfield. The enemy held there, desperately enough. And at last Owens saw Lecker coming back. He knew what that meant—a last stab— a try for a field goal. Morris to hold the ball.

Owens looked at the markers on the lines—too far. Fifty yards at least, and Lecker had never done that distance even in practice. Also they were hurried; the time must be very short. Incredibly soon he saw the ball coming back into Morris' hands, saw it poised, saw it rise slowly and slowly, terribly high; saw it hover there and begin to descend. From where he sat it seemed to him for a moment that it would carry the crossbar. He thought for an instant it had done so, till by the confusion of rushing players he knew the kick had failed.

The ball landed three yards within the field, and the enemy waited for it to bound across the goal line. But the perverse thing bounced the other way, bobbed to and fro, rolled slowly toward the chalk mark. Owens, watching, saw it roll so slowly, saw the enemy waiting, saw his own men charging down. It was Lewstader who got there, who fell and gripped the ball, a matter of inches from the line.

The stands lifted their cry, "Block this punt! Block this punt!" It boomed down the field.

Owens could not utter a sound; he watched breathlessly, moving with little nervous, twitching jerks of his feet. He saw, abruptly, that they would not punt; they meant to run the ball. The backs were clustering close behind the center, the quarter exhorting them. He nodded, recognizing the strategy of delay. It continued interminably, this exhortation, but at last the men snapped into position. The ball moved. Owens could not see what happened. He did not know till afterward that it was Bullman who broke through and dropped the runner in his tracks, behind the line, for a safety that won the game.

Back in college, Owens found himself forgiven; but forgivingly. The condescension of his fellows, the joy which embraced even him seemed to him intolerable. Al Shorter, exuberant with delight, flung an arm about him, cuffed him between the shoulders, but Owens brushed him aside. Youth finds at times a certain happiness in pain.

He would not, he told himself, go to the mass meeting of celebration on Monday night. He thought of leaving college—thought with moody relish that after he was gone they might find out the truth. Al went to the meeting, angry at Owens' sullen refusal to join him. Left Evan in their room.

But after Al was gone, Owens could not bear to stay where he was alone. He went out on the campus and walked about, meeting no one, lonely and miserably content with his loneliness. From the Hall he could hear the booming of cheers that greeted speaker upon speaker. Imperceptibly his steps drifted that way, and so he came at last to a spot beneath one of the windows—a spot from which he could hear. His lips twisted grimly at what he heard.

"The usual bunk," he told himself. "A great team, a great victory, a wonderful year; the old ascendancy restored." Owens was full of bitter scorn. He heard Dave Glade called to the platform, and he hated Glade–Glade who had shamed him.

Glade was speaking. Owens listened angrily.

"You've got that game under your belts," Glade was saying. "A right to be proud of it. Know what won it, do you?"

There was a momentary silence, and then someone roared. "The old fight!" A thousand voices took up the cry, it swelled and bellowed and then abruptly was stilled again. Glade's voice once more.

"Right," he agreed. "The old fight. But there's something you don't know."

He had their attention now, and even Owens listened without scorn.

"One man won that game," Glade said.

Somebody called "Don't be so modest, Dave," and the roar of laughter drowned him out and stilled again.

"Nobody ever called me modest," Glade retorted. "But–I didn't win that game." He hesitated again. "The man that won it isn't here," he said. Owens could hear them stirring uneasily. "You know who I mean," the coach continued. "Buck Owens won that game!"

Owens cringed with shame; cringed again when someone uttered a jeering cry.

Then other voices rose, "Shut up! What do you mean, Dave?"

"The team wouldn't fight," Glade said crisply. "I had to make them fight–scare them into fighting. Buck played my game; he let me make a goat of him–to scare the rest of you. You've been saying he'd lost his nerve. Boys, he's got more backbone than I have, and I'm proud to say it."

Owens moved back, poising for flight.

Someone inside shouted, "Where is he? Where's Buck?"

"Go find him," Glade retorted. "That's up to you."

Owens heard their feet moving, gathering speed. He ran away then; ran cravenly. But of course they found him in the end.

Hours later, he and Al were alone at last in their room, and upon these two sat a great embarrassment. They spoke briefly, of unimportant things, each trying to find words for what was in his mind. Big Al Shorter at last had a try at it.

"Well, you big slob, you think you're a hero, don't you?" he challenged.

Owens grinned. "Oh, shut your fat head," he retorted.

But the words of youth must be read with a glossary.

Father-son relationships can be complex, as illustrated by the humorous saga of the Fetkos. After years of estrangement, a coach father tries to reach out to his quarterback son by inviting him to attend the traditional Jewish circumcision ceremony for his newborn son, named Sidney Luckman Fetko, after the real-life quarterback of yesteryear. Development of this zany plot reveals Michael Chabon's talents as one of America's finest young writers. His short stories have appeared in Esquire *(where this one is from) and* The New Yorker. *A collection of his short fiction is found in* A Model World and Other Stories *(1991). Chabon's two novels are* The Mysteries of Pittsburgh *(1988) and* Wonder Boy *(1995). His baseball story, "Smoke," is considered one of the best.*

Michael Chabon

THE HARRIS FETKO STORY (1997)

THE HOTEL IN TACOMA WAS a Luxington Parc. There was one in Spokane, one in Great Falls, and another in downtown Saskatoon. It was half motor lodge, half state-of-the-art correctional institution, antacid-pink with gun-slit windows. There was a stink of chlorine from the waterfall in the atrium where the chimes of the elevators echoed all night with a sound like a dental instrument hitting a cold tile floor. A message from Norm Fetko, Harris's father, was waiting at the desk on Friday night when the team got in. It said that on the previous Friday Fetko's wife had given birth to a son and that the next afternoon, at three o'clock, they were going to remove his little foreskin, of all things, in a Jewish religious ceremony to be held, of all places, at Fetko's car dealership up in Northgate. Whether by design or hotel policy, the message was terse, and Harris's invitation to his half brother's bris was only implied.

When Harris got upstairs to his room, he sat with his hand on the telephone. The passage of four years since his last contact with Fetko had done little to incline him to forgiveness. He tended, as did most commentators on the Harris Fetko story, to blame his father for his own poor character and the bad things that had happened to him. He decided it would be not only best for everyone but also highly satisfying not to acknowledge in any way his father's attempt at renewing contact, an attempt whose motives, with an uncharitableness born of long experience, Harris suspected at once.

He picked up the receiver and dialed Bob Badham. There was no answer. Harris set the receiver down on the floor of his room—it was in his contract that he got a room to himself—lay down alongside it, and squeezed out the one thousand abdominal crunches he had been squeezing out every night since he was eleven years old. When he had finished, he got up, went into the bathroom, and looked at himself in the mirror with approval and dispassion. He was used from long habit to thinking of his body as having a certain monetary value or as capable of being translated, mysteriously, into money, and if it were somehow possible, he would have paid a handsome sum to purchase himself. He turned away from the mirror and sat down on the lid of the toilet to trim the nails of his right hand. When his nails were clipped and filed square, he went back out to pick up the telephone. It was still ringing. He hung up and dialed Bob's work number.

"Screw you, Bob," Harris said cheerfully to Bob Badham's voicemail box. "I mean, hello." He then left a detailed account of his current whereabouts and telephone number, the clean result of his most recent urine test, and the next destination on the team's schedule, which was Boise, a Holiday Inn, on July 5. Harris possessed the sort of wild, formless gift that attracted the gaze of harsh men and disciplinarians, and the whole of his twenty-six years had been lived under the regimens of hard-asses. Bob Badham was merely the latest of these.

There was a knock at the door. Harris went to answer it in his pinstripe bikini briefs, hoping, not quite unconsciously, that he would find an attractive female member of the Western Washington Association of Mortgage Brokers (here for their annual convention) come to see if it was really true that the briefly seminotorious Harris Fetko was in the hotel.

"Why aren't you in bed?" said Lou Sammartino.

The coach of the Regina Kings club of the North American Professional Indoor Football League was not, as it happened, a hard-ass. He indulged his players far more than most of them deserved—housing them with his family when things went badly for them; remembering their birthdays; nudging them to save receipts, phone their wives, pay their child support. He was an intelligent man of long experience who, like many coaches Harris had played for, believed, at this point in his career rather desperately, in the myth of the football genius, a myth in which Harris himself, having been raised by a football genius, had learned by the age of seventeen to put no stock whatever. Lou Sammartino believed that the problem of winning at football was surely one susceptible to the systematic application of an inspired and unbiased mind. His lifetime record as a coach, including a stint in the short-lived Mexican Football League of 1982, was 102–563. He pushed past Harris and barked at his quarterback to close the door. He was hunched and rotund, with a jowly, pocked face and immense black-rimmed spectacles. The smell of his cologne was exactly like that of the tiny red cardboard pine trees that dangle from the rearview mirrors of taxicabs.

"What's the matter?" said Harris. He looked out into the hallway, in both directions, then closed the door against the stiff artificial breeze that came howling down the deserted corridor.

"We need to talk." Lou sat down on the bed and studied Harris. His watery brown eyes behind the lenses of his glasses were beautiful in a way that suited his losing record. "You called your PO?"

"I left a message."

"Aren't you supposed to see him in person when you're home?"

"I'm *not* home," said Harris. "Technically. My *home* is Seattle. We're in *Tacoma*."

"Technically," said Lou. "A word much beloved of screwups."

"Something to drink?" Harris went to the minibar. There was nothing in it except for a rattling ice tray and a ghostly smell of caulk. The minibars were always empty in Luxington Parcs and in most of the other hotels the Regina Kings patronized. Often they were not even plugged in. "I'm supposed to have six bottles of mineral water," Harris said. He tried not to sound petulant, but it was difficult, because he was feeling petulant.

"Aw," said Lou.

"I'm sick of this!" Harris slammed the refrigerator door shut. "Every time I walk into my room and open the minibar door, there's supposed to be six bottles of mineral water in there." The slammed door rebounded and bashed into the wall beside the minibar. Its handle gouged a deep hole in the wallboard. Crumbs of plaster spattered the floor. Harris ran his fingers along the edges of the hole he had made in the wall. A feeling of remorse took wing in his chest but with an old, sure instinct, he caught it and neatly twisted its neck. He turned to Lou, trying to look certain of himself and his position. The truth was that Harris didn't even like mineral water; he thought it tasted like saliva. But it was in his contract. "So, okay, talk. It's past my bedtime."

"Harris, in a minute or two there's someone coming up here with a proposition for you." Just as he said this, there was another knock at the door. Harris jumped. "He wants to offer you a job."

"I already have a job."

Lou turned up the corners of his mouth but somehow failed to produce a viable smile.

"Lou," said Harris, and his heart started to pound. "Please tell me the league isn't folding."

There had been rumors to this effect since before the season even began; attendance at games in all but a few sports-starved cities was declining by a thousand or more every weekend, the owner of the Portland team had been murdered by Las Vegas wiseguys, and the Vancouver bank on whose line of credit the NAPIFL depended for its operating costs was under investigation by the government of Canada.

Lou stroked the bedspread, smoothing it, watching the back of his hand.

"I just want to play out the schedule," he said sadly. "I could be happy with that."

"Harris?" said a man on the other side of the door. "You there?"

Harris put on his jeans and went to the door.

"Oly," he said. He took a step back into the room. The man at the door was enormous, six feet eight inches tall, just shy of three hundred pounds. Like Norm Fetko a member of the 1955 national champions and—unlike Fetko—a successful businessman, purveyor of a popular topical analgesic, Oly Olafsen had always been the biggest man Harris knew, a chunk of the northern ice cap, a piece of masonry, fifteen tons of stone, oak, and gristle supporting eight cubic inches of grinning blond head. He wore silver aviator eyeglasses and a custom-tailored suit, metallic gray, so large and oddly proportioned that it was nearly unrecognizable as an article of human clothing and appeared rather to have been designed to straiten an obstreperous circus elephant or to keep the dust off some big, delicate piece of medical imaging technology.

"How's my boy?" said Oly.

It had been Oly Olafsen's money, more or less, that Harris had used, more or less without Oly's knowing about it, to purchase the pound of cocaine the police had found under the rear bench of Harris's 300 ZX when they pulled him over that night on Ravenna Avenue. He gave Harris's hand a squeeze that compressed the very bones.

"So," he went on, "the coach has got himself another son after all these years. That's a thought, isn't it? Wonder what he's got cooked up for this one."

This remark angered Harris, whom the sporting world for two hectic and disappointing collegiate seasons had known as Frankenback. Among the failings of his character exposed during that time was a total inability to stand up to teasing about any aspect of his life, his father's experimentation least of all. With a great effort and out of an old habit of deference to his father's cronies, he got himself to smile, then realized that Oly wasn't teasing him at all. On the contrary, there had been in Oly's soft voice a disloyal wrinkle of concern for the fate, at his great idol's hands, of the latest little Fetko to enter the world.

"Yeah, he asked me out to the showroom tomorrow," Harris said. "To the thing where they, what's that, circumcise the kid."

"Are you people Jewish?" said Lou, surprised. "I didn't know."

"We're not. Fetko isn't. I guess his new wife must be."

"I'll be there. Ah!" Gingerly—his knees were an ancient ruin of cartilage and wire—Oly lowered himself into the desk chair, which creaked in apparent horror at the slow approach of his massive behind. "As a matter of fact, I'm paying for the darn thing." Oly smiled, then took off his glasses and pinched the bridge of his nose. When he put the glasses back on, he wasn't smiling anymore. "The coach has got himself into a little bit of a tight spot out there in Northgate," he said, pressing his palms together as if they represented the terrific forces that were putting the squeeze on Fetko. "I know things haven't been, well, the greatest between you two since . . . everything that happened, but the coach—Harris, he's really putting his life back together. He's not—"

"Get to the point," said Harris.

An odd expression came over Oly's generally peaceful and immobile face. His eyebrows reached out to each other over the bridge of his nose, and his tiny, pale lips compressed into a pout. He was unhappy, possibly even actively sad. Harris had never imagined that Oly might ever be feeling anything but hunger and gravitation.

"Harris, I'm not going to lie to you, the old man could really use a little help," said Oly. "That's what I want to talk to you about. I don't know if Lou has mentioned it, but the coach and I—"

"I told him," said Lou. "Harris isn't interested."

"Isn't he?" Oly looked at Lou, his face once again a region of blankness, his eyes polite and twinkling. He had pleasant, vacant little eyes that, along with his bulk and a recipe purchased in 1963 from a long-dead

Chinese herbalist in the International District for $250, had enabled him to do what was necessary to make Power Rub the number-three topical analgesic in the western U.S. "Somebody might think he would be very interested in finding another job, seeing as how this outfit of yours is about to go bellyup." He turned his flashbulb eyes toward Harris now. "Seeing as how what they call gainful employment is a condition of his parole."

"If that happens, and I don't personally feel that it will, Harris can find another job. He doesn't need any help from you."

"What is he going to do? He doesn't know how to do anything but be a quarterback! It's in his genes, it's in his blood particles. It's wired into his darn brain. No, I figure he has to be very interested in hearing about an opportunity like this. A chance to actually *redefine the position*, at twice his present salary, in front of a guaranteed national cable audience of *forty-four million homes*."

Harris was accustomed to having his disposition discussed and his fate decided, in his presence, by other people; it was part of that same mysterious alchemy that could transmute his body into cash and of the somewhat less obscure process that had sent him to Ellensburg for nineteen months. But at the mention of cable television, he could not restrain himself.

"What is it?" he said. "What opportunity?"

Oly reached into the breast pocket of his jacket and withdrew a manila envelope, folded in half. He took a color brochure from the envelope and handed it to Harris. Harris sat down on the bed to read. It was a prospectus designed to attract investors to a league that would feature a sport that the brochure called Powerball, "the first new major American sport in a hundred years," to be played in every major city in the U.S., apparently by men in garish uniforms that were part samurai armor and part *costume de ballet*, one of whom was depicted, on the airbrushed cover of the brochure, swinging across the playing arena from a striped rappelling cable. The description was vague, but, as far as Harris could tell, Powerball appeared to be an amalgam of rugby, professional wrestling, and old pirate movies. It was not football or anything close to football. Once Harris realized this, he skimmed through such phrases as "speed, drama, and intense physical action . . . the best elements of today's most popular sports . . . our proposed partnership with the Wrestling Channel . . . all the elements are in place . . . revolutionary, popular, and, above all, profitable . . ." until he turned to the last page and found a photograph of his father beside a caption that identified him as "coaching great Norm Fetko, inventor of Powerball, part owner and coach of the Seattle franchise."

"Fetko invented this crap?" said Harris, tossing the brochure onto the floor.

"It came to him in a dream," said Oly, looking solemn. He raised his hands to his eyes and spread his thick fingers, watching the air between them as it shimmered with another one of Norm Fetko's lunatic visions. "A guy . . . with a football under his arm . . . swinging from a rope." Oly shook his head as if awestruck by the glimpse Harris's father had vouchsafed him into the mystic origins of the future of American sport. "This will be big, Harris. We already have a line on investors in nine cities. Our lawyers are working out the last few kinks in the TV contract. This could be a very, very big thing."

"Big," said Harris. "Yeah, I get it now." For he saw with admiration and to his horror, that at this late stage of his career Fetko had managed to come up with yet another way to ruin the lives and fortunes of hapless elevens of men. None of Fetko's other failures—his golf resort out in the Banana Belt of Washington, his "revolutionary" orange football, his brief (pioneering, in retrospect) foray into politics as a candidate with no political convictions, his attempt to breed and raise the greatest quarterback the world would ever see—had operated in isolation. They had all roped in, ridden on the backs of, and ultimately broken a large number of other people. And around all of Fetko's dealings and misdealings, Oly Olafsen had hovered, loving sidekick, pouring his money down Fetko's throat like liquor. "That's why he called. He wants me to play for him again."

"Imagine the media, Harris, my gosh," said Oly. "Norm and Harris Fetko reunited, that would sell a few tickets."

Lou winced and sat down on the bed next to Harris. He put his hand on Harris's shoulder. "Harris, you don't want to do this."

"No kidding," said Harris. "Oly," he said to Oly. "I hate my father. I don't want to have anything to do with him. Or you. You guys all screwed me over once."

"Hey, now, kid." Another crack of grief opened in the glacial expanse of his face. "Look, you hate me, that's one thing, but I know you don't—"

"I hate him!"

Inside Harris Fetko the frontier between petulance and rage was generally left unguarded, and he crossed it now without slowing down. He stood up and went for Oly, wondering if somewhere in the tiny interval between the big man's jaw and shoulders he might find a larynx to get his thumbs around. Oly started to rise, but his shattered knees slowed him, and before he could regain his feet, Harris had kicked the tiny chair out from under him. A sharp pain went whistling up Harris's shin, and then his foot began to throb like a trumpet. The right foreleg of the wooden chair splintered from the frame, the chair tipped, and Oly Olafsen hit the flecked aquamarine carpet. His impact was at once loud and muffled, like the collision of a baseball bat and a suitcase filled with water.

"I'm sorry," Harris said.

Oly looked up at him. His meaty fingers wrapped around the broken chair leg and clenched it. His breath blew through his nostrils as loud as a horse's. Then he let go of the chair leg and shrugged. When Harris offered a hand, Oly took it.

"I just want to tell you something, Harris," he said, smoothing down his sleeves. He winched up his trousers by the belt, then attended to the tectonic slippage of the shoulder pads in his jacket. "Everything the coach has, okay, is tied up in this thing. Not money. The coach doesn't have any money. So far the money is mostly coming from me." With a groan he stooped to retrieve the fallen brochure, then slipped it back into its envelope. "What the coach has tied up in this thing, it can't be paid back or defaulted on or covered by a bridge loan." He tapped the rolled manila envelope against the center of his chest. "I'll see you tomorrow."

"No, you will not," said Harris as Oly went out. He tried to sound as though he were not in terrible pain. "I'm not going."

Lou lifted Harris's foot and bent the big toe experimentally. Harris groaned. A tear rolled down his cheek.

"You broke it," said Lou. "Aw, Harris."

"I'm sorry, Coach," said Harris, falling backward on the bed. "Damn Fetko, man. It's all his fault."

"Everything else, maybe it was Fetko's fault," said Lou, though he sounded doubtful. He picked up the telephone and asked room service to bring up a bucket of ice. "This was your fault."

When the ice came, he filled a towel with it and held it against Harris's toe for an hour until the swelling had gone down. Then he taped the big toe to its neighbor, patted Harris on the head, and went back to his room to revise the playbook for tomorrow. Before he went out, he turned.

"Harris," he said, "you've never confided in me. And you've never particularly followed any of the copious advice I've been so generous as to offer you over the last few months."

"Coach—"

"But regardless of that, I'm foolishly going to make one last little try." He took off his glasses and wiped them on a rumpled shirttail. "I think you ought to go to that thing tomorrow." He put his glasses back on again and blinked his eyes. "It's your brother that'll be lying there with his little legs spread."

"Screw the little bastard," said Harris, with the easy and good-natured callousness that, like so much about the game of football, had always come so naturally to him. "I hope they slice the damn thing clean off."

Lou went out, shaking his big, sorrowful head. Ten minutes later there was another knock at the door. This time it was not a lady mortgage broker but a reporter for the *Morning News Tribune* come to poke around in the embers of the Harris Fetko conflagration. Harris lay on the bed with his foot in an ice pack and told, once again, the sorry tale of how his father had ruined his life and made him into all the sad things he was today. When the reporter asked him what had happened to his foot and the chair, Harris said that he had tripped while running to answer the phone.

They beat Tacoma 10–9, on a field goal in the last eight seconds of the game. Harris scrambled for the touchdown, kicked the extra point with his off foot, and then, when in the last minute of the game it became clear that none of the aging farm implements and large pieces of antique cabinetry who made up his backfield and receiving corps were going to manage to get the ball into the end zone, he himself, again with his left foot, nailed the last three points needed to keep them happy for one more day back in Regina.

When the team came off the field, they found the Kings' owner, Irwin Selwyn, waiting in the locker room, holding an unlit cigar in one hand and a pale-blue envelope in the other, looking at his two-tone loafers. The men from the front office stood around him, working their Adam's apples up and down over the knots of their neckties. Selwyn had on blue jeans and a big yellow sweater with the word KINGS knit across it in blue. He stuck the cigar between his teeth, opened the blue envelope, and unfolded the letter from the league office, which with terse, unintentional elegance regretfully informed the teams and players of the NAPIFL that the standings at the end of that day's schedule of games would be duly entered into the record books as final. Lou Sammartino, having coached his team to first place in its division and the best record in the league, wandered off into the showers and sat down. Irwin Selwyn shook everyone's hand and had his secretary give each player a set of fancy wrenches (he owned a hardware chain) and a check for what the player would have been owed had Lou Sammartino been granted his only remaining desire. Shortly thereafter, twenty-five broken giants trudged out to the parking lot with their socket wrenches and caught the bus to the rest of their lives.

Harris went back to his room at the Luxington Parc, turned on the television, and watched a half-hour commercial for a handheld vacuum device that sheared the bellies of beds and sofas of their eternal wool of dust. He washed his underpants in the sink. He drank two cans of diet root beer and ate seven Slim Jims. Then he switched off the television, pulled a pillow over his head, and cried. The serene, arctic blankness with which he was rumored, and in fact did struggle, to invest all his conscious processes of thought was only a hollow illusion. He was racked by that particular dread of the future that plagues superseded deities and washed-up backs. He saw himself carrying an evening six-pack up to his rented room, wearing slacks and a name tag at some job, standing with the rest of the failures of the world at the back of a very long line, waiting to claim something that in the end would turn out to be an empty tin bowl with his own grinning skull reflected in its bottom. He went into the bathroom and threw up.

When he reemerged from the bathroom, the queasiness was gone but the dread of his future remained. He picked up the phone and called around town until he found himself a car. His tight end, a Tacoma native, agreed, for a price they finally fixed at seventeen dollars—seventeen having been the number on the tight end's 1979 Washington State Prep Championship jersey—to bring his brother's car around to the hotel in half an hour. Harris showered, changed into a tan poplin suit, seersucker shirt, and madras tie, and checked out of his room. When he walked out of the Luxington Parc, he found a 1979 Chevrolet Impala, eggplant with a white vinyl top, waiting for him under the porte cochere.

"Don't turn the wipers on," said Deloyd White. "It blows the fuse on the radio. Be honest, it blows a lot of fuses. Most of them."

"What if it rains?"

Deloyd looked out at the afternoon, damp and not quite warm, the blue sky wan and smeary. He scratched at the thin, briery tangle of beard on his chin.

"If it rains you just got to drive really fast," he said.

As Harris drove north on I-5, he watched nervously as the cloak of blue sky grew threadbare and began to show, in places, its eternal gray interfacing of clouds. But the rain held off, and Harris was able to make it all the way out to Northgate without breaking the speed laws. The Chevy made a grand total of seven cars parked on the lot of Norm Fetko's New and Used Buick-Isuzu, an establishment that had changed hands and product lines a dozen times since Pierce Arrow days. It sat, a showroom of peeling white stucco, vaguely art deco, next to a low cinder-block garage on one of the saddest miles of Aurora Avenue, between a gun shop and a place that sold grow lights. Fetko had bought the place from a dealer in Pacers and Gremlins, banking on his local celebrity to win him customers at the very instant in history when Americans ceased to care who it was that sold them their cars. Harris pulled in between two Le Sabres with big white digits soaped onto their windshields, straightened his tie, and started for the open door of the dealership.

A tall, fair-haired salesman, one of the constantly shifting roster of former third-stringers and practice dummies Fetko could always call upon to man the oars of his argosies as they coursed ever nearer to the maelstrom, was propped against the doorway, smoking a cigarette, as Harris walked up. He was stuffed imperfectly into his cheap suit, and his face looked puffy. He lounged with a coiled air of impatience, tipping and rocking on the balls of his feet. His hair was like gold floss.

"Hey, Junior," he said. He gestured with a thumb. "They're all in the back room."

"Did they do it already?"

"I don't think so. I think they were waiting for you."

"But I said I *wasn't* going to come," said Harris, irritated to find that his change of heart had come as a surprise only to him.

He walked across the showroom, past three metal desks, three filing cabinets, and three wastebaskets, all enameled in a cheery shade of surgical glove; three beige telephones with rotary dials; a dismantled mimeograph; and an oak hat rack that was missing all of its hooks but one, from which there hung an empty plastic grocery sack. There was no stock on the floor, a bare beige linoleum expanse layered with a composite detritus of old cigarette ash and the lost limbs of insects. The desk chairs were tucked neatly under the desks, and the desktops themselves were bare of everything but dust. Aside from a bookshelf filled with the binders and thick manuals of the automobile trade and a few posters of last season's new models tacked up amid black-and-white photographs of the owner, in his glory days, fading back to pass, there was little to suggest that Norm Fetko's New and Used was not a defunct concern and had not been so for a very long time.

"I knew you'd come," said Fetko's wife, hurrying across the back room to greet him. She was not at all what he had imagined—an ample, youngish bottle blond with an unlikely suntan and the soft, wide-eyed look, implying a certain preparedness to accept necessary pain, that Fetko had favored in all the women he had gotten involved with after Harris's mother. She was small, with thin arms and a skinny neck, her hair like black excelsior. Her eyes were deep set. She was certainly no younger than forty. Her name was Marilyn Levine.

"I almost didn't," he insisted. "I'm, uh, not too wild about . . . these things."

"Have you been to a bris before?"

Harris shook his head.

"I'm not even going to be in the room," Marilyn said. "That's what a lightweight I am." She was wearing a loose burgundy velvet dress and ballet shoes. This was another surprise. Over time, most of the women in Fetko's life allowed themselves to become, as it were, themed, favoring grass-green muumuus patterned with stiff-arming running backs, goalposts, and footballs turning end over end. Marilyn touched a hand to Harris's arm. "Did you know the coach stopped drinking?"

"When did he do that?"

"Almost a year ago," she said. "Not quite."

"That's good news," said Harris.

"He isn't the same man, Harris," she told him. "You'll see that."

"Okay," said Harris doubtfully.

"Come say hi."

She led him past the buffet, three card tables pushed together and spread with food enough for ten times as many guests as there were in attendance. Aside from one or two of Fetko's employees and a dozen or so members of Marilyn's family, among them an authentic-looking Jew, with the little hat and the abolitionist beard, whom Marilyn introduced as her brother, the room was empty. A few women were huddled at the back of the room around a cerulean football that Harris supposed must be the blanketed new Fetko.

In the old days, at a function like this, there would have been a great ring of standing stones around Fetko, dolmens and menhirs in pistachio pants, with nicknames like Big Mack and One-Eye. Some of the members of the '55 national champions, Harris knew, had died or moved to faraway places; the rest had long since been burned, used up, worn out, or, in one case, sent to prison by one or another of Fetko's schemes. Now there remained only Oly Olafsen, Red Johnnie Green, and Hugh Eggert with his big cigar. Red Johnnie had on a black suit with a funereal tie, Oly was wearing another of his sharkskin tarpaulins, and Hugh had solved the troublesome problem of dressing for the dark ritual of an alien people by coming in his very best golf clothes. When they saw Harris, they pounded him on the back and shook his hand. They squeezed his biceps, assessed his grip, massaged his shoulders, jammed their stubbly chins into the crook of his neck, and, in the case of Hugh Eggert, gave his left buttock a farmerly slap. Harris had been in awe of them most of his life. Now he regarded them with envy and dismay. They had grown old without ever maturing: quarrelsome, salacious boys zipped into enormous rubber mansuits. Harris, on the other hand, had bid farewell to his childhood eons ago, without ever having managed to grow up.

"Harris," said Fetko. "How about that." The tip of his tongue poked out from the corner of his mouth, and he hitched up the waist of his pants, as if he were about to attempt something difficult. He was shorter than Harris remembered—fatter, grayer, older, sadder, more tired, more bald, with more broken blood vessels in his cheeks. He was, Harris quickly calculated, sixty-one, having already been most of the way through his thirties, a head coach in Denver with a master's in sports physiology, before he selected Harris's mother from a long list of available candidates and began his grand experiment in breeding. As usual he was dressed today in black high-tops, baggy black ripstop pants, and a black polo shirt. The muscles of his arms stretched the ribbed armbands of his shirtsleeves. With his black clothes, his close-cropped hair, and his eyes that were saved from utter coldness by a faint blue glint of lunacy, he looked like a man who had been trained in his youth to drop out of airplanes in the dead of night and strangle enemy dictators in their sleep.

"Son," he said.

"Hey there, Coach," said Harris.

The moment during which they might have shaken hands, or even—in an alternate-historical universe where the Chinese discovered America and a ten-year-old Adolf Hitler was trampled to death by a passing milk wagon—embraced, passed, as it always did. Fetko nodded.

"I heard you played good today," he said.

Harris lowered his head to hide the fact that he was blushing.

"I was all right," he said. "Congratulations on the kid. What's his name?"

"Sid Luckman," said Fetko, and the men around him, except for Harris, laughed. Their laughter was nervous and insincere, as if Fetko had said something dirty. "Being as how he's a Jewish boy." Fetko nodded with tolerant, Einsteinian pity toward his old buddies. "These bastards here think it's a joke."

No, no, they reassured him. Sid Luckman was an excellent choice. Still, you had to admit—

"Luckman's the middle name," said Harris.

"That's right."

"I like it."

Fetko nodded again. He didn't care if Harris liked it or not. Harris was simply—had always been—there to know when Fetko wasn't joking.

"He's very glad to see you," said Marilyn Levine, with a hard edge in her voice, prodding Fetko. "He's been worrying about it all week."

"Don't talk nonsense," said Fetko.

Marilyn gave Harris a furtive nod to let him know that she had been telling the truth. She was standing with her arm still laced through Harris's, smelling pleasantly of talcum. Harris gave her hand a squeeze. He had spent the better part of his childhood waiting for Fetko to bring someone like Marilyn Levine home to raise him. Now he had a brief fantasy of yanking her out of the room by this warm hand, of hustling her and young Sid Luckman into the aubergine Chevy Impala and driving them thousands of miles through the night to a safe location. His own mother had fled Fetko when Harris was six, promising to send for him as soon as she landed on her feet. The summons never came. She had married again, and then again after that, and had moved two dozen times over the last fifteen years. Harris let go of his stepmother's hand. Probably there was no such safe place to hide her and the baby. Everywhere they went, she would find men like Fetko. For all Harris knew, he was a man like Fetko, too.

"Hello?"

Everyone turned. There was a wizened man standing behind Harris, three feet tall, a thousand years old, carrying a black leather pouch under his arm.

"I am Dr. Halbenzoller," he said regretfully. He had a large welt on his forehead and wore a bewildered, fearful expression, as if he had misplaced his eyeglasses and were feeling his way through the world. "Where are the parents?"

"I'm the boy's father," said Fetko, taking the old man's hand. "This is the mother—Marilyn. She's the observant one, here."

Dr. Halbenzoller turned his face toward Marilyn. He looked alarmed. "The father is not Jewish?"

Marilyn shook her head. "No, but we spoke about it over the phone, Dr. Halbenzoller, don't you remember?"

"I don't remember anything," said Dr. Halbenzoller. He looked around the room, as if trying to remember how he had got to the outlandish place in which he now found himself. His gaze lingered a moment on Harris, wonderingly and with evident disapproval, as if he were looking at a Great Dane someone had dressed up in a madras jacket and taught to smile.

"I'm an existential humanist," Fetko told him. "That's always been my great asset as a coach. Over the long series, an atheistic coach will always beat a coach who believes in God." Fetko, whose own lifetime record was an existential 163–162, had been out of coaching for quite a while now, and Harris could see that he missed being interviewed. "Anyway, I don't feel I could really give the Jewish faith a fair shake—"

Dr. Halbenzoller turned to Marilyn.

"Tell them I'd like to begin," he said, as if she were his interpreter. He took the pouch from under his arm. "Where is the child?"

Marilyn led him over to the back of the room, where, beside the huddle of women, a card table had been set up and draped in a piece of purple velvet. Dr. Halbenzoller undid the buckles on his pouch and opened it, revealing a gleaming set of enigmatic tools.

"And the sandek," he said to Marilyn. "You have one?"

Marilyn looked at Fetko.

"Norm?"

Fetko looked down at his hands.

"Norm."

Fetko shrugged and looked up. He studied Harris's face and took a step toward him. Involuntarily, Harris took a step back. "It's like a godfather," Fetko said. "To the kid. Marilyn and I were wondering."

Harris was honored, and wildly touched, but he didn't want to let on. "If you want," he said. "What do I have to do?"

"Come stand next to me," said Dr. Halbenzoller slowly, as you would speak to a well-dressed and intelligent dog.

Harris went over to the velvet-covered table and stood beside it, close enough to Dr. Halbenzoller to smell the steam in his ironed suit.

"Do you have to be a doctor to do this?" he asked.

"I'm a dentist," said Dr. Halbenzoller. "Fifty years. This is just a hobby of mine." He reached into the pocket of his suit coat and took out a slim volume of cracked black leather. "Bring the child."

Sidney Luckman Fetko was brought forward and placed into Harris's arms. He was wide awake, motionless, his lumpy little pinch-pot face peering out from the blue swaddling cloth. He weighed nothing at all. Fetko's wife left the room. Dr. Halbenzoller opened the little book and began to chant. The language—Hebrew, Harris supposed—sounded harsh and angular and complaining. Sid Luckman's eyes widened, as if he were listening. His head hadn't popped entirely back into place yet after his passage through Marilyn Levine, and his features were twisted up a little on one side, giving him a sardonic expression. This is my brother, thought Harris. This is Fetko's other son.

He was so lost in the meaning of this that he didn't notice when several seconds had gone by in silence. Harris looked up. Dr. Halbenzoller was reaching out to Harris. Harris just looked at his hands, calloused and yellow but unwrinkled, like a pair of old feet.

"It's all right, Harris," said Fetko. "Give him the baby."

"Excuse me," Harris said. He tucked Sid Luckman under his arm and headed for the fire door.

He sprinted across the back lot, past a long, rusting, red-and-white trailer home with striped aluminum awnings in which Harris's mother had once direly predicted that Fetko would end his days, toward a swath of open land that stretched away behind the dealership, a vast tangle of blackberry brambles, dispirited fir trees, and renegade pachysandra escaped from some distant garden. In his late adolescence, Harris had often picked his way to a large clearing at the center of the tangle, a circular sea of dead grass where for decades the mechanics who worked in the service bays had tossed their extinguished car batteries and pans of broken-down motor oil. At the center of this cursed spot, Harris would lie on his back, looking at the pigeon-colored Seattle sky, and expend his brain's marvelous capacity for speculation on topics such as women's breasts, the big money, and Italian two-seaters.

These days there was no need to pick one's way—a regular path had been cleared through the brush—and as they approached the clearing, Harris slowed. The woods were birdless, and the only sounds were the hum of traffic from Aurora Avenue, the snapping of twigs under his feet, and a low, hostile grunting from the baby. It had turned into a cold summer afternoon. The wind blew in from the north, smelling of brine and rust. As Harris approached the clearing, he found himself awash in regret, not for the thing he had just done nor for shanked kicks or lost yardage nor for the trust he had placed, so mistakenly, in others during his short, trusting, mistaken life, but for something more tenuous and faint, tied up in the memory of those endless afternoons spent lying on his back in that magical circle of poison, wasting his thoughts on things that now meant so little to him. Then he and Sid fell into the clearing.

Most of the trees around it, he saw, had been brought down, while those that remained had been stripped of their lower branches and painted, red or blue, with a white letter, wobbly and thin, running ten feet up the trunk. Exactly enough trees had been left, going around, to spell out the word POWERBALL. Harris had never seen a painted tree before, and the effect was startling. From a very tall pole at the center of the circle, each of nine striped rappelling cables extended, like the ribs of an umbrella, toward a wooden platform at the top of each of the painted trees. The ground had been patiently tilled and turned over, cleared of grass and rubbish, then patted down again, swept smooth and speckless as an infield. At the northern and southern poles of the arena stood a soccer-goal net, spray-painted gold. Someone had also painted a number of imitation billboards advertising Power Rub and the cigarettes, soft drinks, spark plugs, and malt liquors of fantasy sponsors, and nailed them up at key locations around the perimeter. The lettering was crude but the colors were right and if you squinted a little you might almost be persuaded. The care, the hard work, the childish attention to detail, and, above all, the years of misapplied love and erroneous hopefulness that had gone into its planning and construction seemed to Harris to guarantee the arena's inevitable destruction by wind, weather, and the creeping pachysandra of failure that ultimately entangled all his father's endeavors and overwhelmed the very people they were most intended to avail. Fetko was asking for it.

"Look what Coach did," Harris said to Sid, tilting the baby a little so that he might see. "Isn't that neat?"

Sid Luckman's face never lost its dour, sardonic air, but Harris found himself troubled by an unexpected spasm of forgiveness. The disaster of Powerball, when finally it unfolded, as small-scale disappointment or as massive financial collapse, would not really be Fetko's fault. Harris's entire life had been spent, for better or worse, in the struggling company of men, and he had seen enough by now to know that evergreen ruin wound its leaves and long tendrils around the habitations and plans of all fathers, everywhere, binding them by the ankles and wrists to their sons, whether the fathers asked for it or not.

"Get your ass back in there," said Fetko, coming up behind them, out of breath. "Asses."

Harris didn't say anything. He could feel his father's eyes on him, but he didn't turn to look. The baby snuffled and grunted in Harris's arms.

"I, uh, I did all this myself," Fetko said after a moment.

"I figured."

"Maybe later, if you wanted to, we could go over some of the fine points of the game."

"Maybe we could."

Fetko shook himself and slapped his palms together. "Fine, but now come on, goddammit. Before that little Jewish gentleman in there seizes up on us."

Harris nodded. "Okay," he said.

As he carried Sid past their father, Harris felt his guts contract in an ancient reflex, and he awaited the cuff, jab, karate chop, rabbit punch, head slap, or boot to the seat of his pants that in his youth he had interpreted as a strengthening exercise designed to prepare him for his career as an absorber of terrible impacts but that now, as Fetko popped him on the upper arm hard enough to make him wince, touching him for the first time in five years, he saw as the expression of a sentiment at once so complicated and inarticulate, neither love nor hatred but as elemental as either, that it could only be expressed by contusing the skin. Harris shifted Sid Luckman to his left arm and, for the first time ever, raised a fist to pop Fetko a good one in return. Then he changed his mind and lowered his hand and carried the baby through the woods to the dealership with Fetko following behind them, whistling a tuneless and impatient song through his teeth.

When they got back, Harris handed over Sid Luckman. Dr. Halbenzoller set the baby down on the velvet cloth. He reached into his pouch and took out a rectangular stainless-steel device that looked a little like a cigar trimmer. The baby shook his tiny fists. His legs, unswaddled, beat the air like butterfly wings. Dr. Halbenzoller brought the cigar trimmer closer to his tiny panatela. Then he glanced up at Harris.

"Please," he said, nodding to the fitful legs, and Harris understood that somebody was going to have to hold his brother down.

PERMISSIONS ACKNOWLEDGMENTS

Grateful acknowledgment is extended to the following authors, publications, and agents.

Grantland Rice, "Alumnus Football," from *The Sportlights of 1923*, published by G. P. Putnam's Sons.

T. Coraghessan Boyle, "56-0," from *Without A Hero*. © 1994 by T. Coraghessan Boyle. Used by permission of Viking Penguin, a division of Penguin Putnam Inc.

Bill McGrane, "Rookies," from *Insight*, © 1985 by William McGrane. Used by permission of the author.

Mary Robison, "Coach," from *An Amateur's Guide to the Night*. © 1981, 1982, 1983 by Mary Robison. Reprinted by permission of Alfred A. Knopf Inc. Originally appeared in *The New Yorker*.

Irwin Shaw, "The Eighty-Yard Run." Reprinted with permission © Irwin Shaw. Originally published in *Esquire* magazine.

Damon Runyon, "Hold 'Em Yale," from *Blue Plate Special*, 1931. Reprinted with permission of American Play Company, Inc.

Asa Baber, "The Dancing Bears," reprinted by permission of the author. Originally appeared in *Playboy* magazine.

Gene Williams, "Sticky My Fingers Fleet My Feet." Reprinted by permission; © 1965 The New Yorker Magazine, Inc. All rights reserved.

John Updike, "In Football Season," from *The Music School* by John Updike. © 1966 by John Updike. Reprinted by permission of Alfred A. Knopf, Inc.